# BORNE ON WIN

# Tony Chandler

# BORNE ON WINGS OF STEEL

DOUBLE DRAGON

# DEDICATION

For my beloved wife, Melva—in hope, love and happiness.
Also for my lovely daughter, Meghan—my friend and
companion.
I will love both of you forever.

# CHAPTER ONE

Drinar sensed the evil.

And it drew closer with each passing second.

He continued walking, but now his senses were on high alert and he wasn't quite sure why.

His pace quickened through the crowded labyrinth of Lyth City, surrounded by the seemingly harmless bustle of aliens.

Still, there was something *new* among the myriads of aliens crowding the streets now...

*A reflection or a movement.*

Yes. A movement!

Movement existed everywhere—the crushing crowds on the high-speed sidewalks, the countless air vehicles zooming between the metallic towers that reached skyward and kissed the swirling, violet clouds overhead.

But this movement was different...

He paced himself in order not to give away to his pursuer his awareness of the chase. With sudden resolution, he darted into the throng of aliens to his left and headed for the dock where his fast starship sat at the ready.

Every alien his glance fell upon revealed no overt threat.

Still, something watched him—something powerful, something evil.

Drinar's instinct was never wrong, especially when he felt it this powerfully.

A low growl rumbled from his throat as he caressed the butt of his holstered blaster. A split-second later, he stepped quickly to his right past another group of aliens and put his back against the base of the nearest city tower.

The murmuring crowds walked past him unabated as Drinar scanned more who approached.

*Nothing.*

Something caught his attention about six meters above the crowds a full block away.

Something moved.

As he gazed at the polished tritanium tower that rose like a gigantic needle to the clouds above, he saw nothing but the smooth, steel walls. He focused harder, mentally dimming the bright lights of the alien city and the countless air-vehicles whose reflections glistened off its metallic sides with an almost hypnotizing effect.

The Iraxx warrior fixed his gaze at one spot as his instincts hammered his body with an overwhelming urge to fight—or to flee. His breathing and heart rate increased ten-fold—but he willed his muscles to hold still one more moment. His eyes now refocused to another spot—watching and waiting. Nothing, not the crowds passing around him or the flashing lights of the city, distracted his piercing gaze.

He saw it—*almost.*

In that instant, a feeling of intense dread filled his soul.

A ghostly image resolved momentarily—a nightmare shape clutching the sheer side of the tower. The shape wavered as if he imagined it—not really seeing it with his eyes. In the next second, the huge, spidery shape vanished—melting back into the wall and into nothingness.

The muscular Iraxx burst into a quick stride through the late evening crowds of the great city. But the strange feeling haunting him all evening now exploded and pulsed throughout his body with each beat of his powerful heart. He fought against the urge to break out into a run.

*It wasn't supposed to end like this*, he thought. His mission was only half finished, and now it was threatened with total failure—for in his heart he knew what evil relentlessly pursued him.

He stopped abruptly at the next intersection and drew out his handheld sensor with a lightning motion. His fingers danced over the display as he searched for the signatures of his known enemies.

Drinar needed to know—and he needed to know now.

His heart missed a beat as the display of his hand-held sensor picked up a ghostly signal. The source of the mysterious signal quickly moved unseen above the crowds. Almost immediately, the signal disappeared.

But now he knew.

A *Destructor* pursued him.

Drinar ran through the crowded streets, scrambling between aliens, knocking down one and bouncing off another.

And still he ran.

A few moments later he fell, tripped by unseen feet.

Shouts and angry voices roared after him as he jumped up and increased his pace.

Now the bright, flashing lights of the city reflected with crazy lines off the glass towers that rose high above the thick mass of late-night revelers. Drinar quickly ducked inside one of the party palaces, hoping to hide himself among the thousands dancing in the crowded, glowing room. The dancers were packed so tightly together that their writhing bodies were in almost constant contact with everyone else around them. The whole room seethed as one great mass of movement.

Panting, he quickly surveyed the room and made his way deeper among the rhythmically moving bodies.

Drinar was bigger than most aliens; his muscular form stood head and shoulders above those dancing within the mesmerizing mixture of pulsating lights and loud music. His scaly skin glowed its true reddish color where it was exposed at his face and neck as white lights suddenly flashed. The rest of his body was clothed by a leather, one-piece jumpsuit, except for his thick tail which protruded just above his buttocks.

That short, muscular tail now curled with tension as he raised his face and sniffed the air. Drinar's short snout wrinkled as he took in quick breaths, tasting the air.

Reaching down, he felt the comforting handle of the blaster still holstered at his right side while his left hand firmly grasped his sheathed sword, keeping it tight against his leg so as not to get it tangled with a reckless dancer.

Maybe his bio-signs would be masked by the mass of aliens. Maybe the Destructor would continue past and lose his trail.

Maybe.

He pushed forward toward the far end of the room. But halfway through, piercing screams rose above the loud, pulsating music.

He turned and saw the distant commotion among the aliens—almost at the exact point where he had entered the room.

More screams of pure terror drowned the music.

The Destructor's main camouflage, its ability to match its background and avoid visual detection, became partially nullified by the pulsating laser lights and changing color schemes synchronized with the rhythm of the music.

The dancers saw, at the edge of their vision, the terrible form of the Destructor as it flashed in and out visibility.

Suddenly, everyone ran for the exits.

Drinar pushed others out of his way as he made a last bid for escape toward the rear of the building.

But even as he burst out into the clear, he knew his life was now measured in seconds.

He crashed down a darkened hallway, stumbling blindly in the dim red lighting as he searched for an exit out into the open city streets once again. The screams grew closer, telling Drinar that his executioner gained on him. Still, even if he made it out into the streets, he had no idea where to go or what he could do to escape it.

He simply ran for his life.

Drinar bumped into something in a darkened section and fell onto the floor, knocking the breath out of his triple lungs. Lying there, fighting to breathe, he heard the ominous humming sound for the first time and realized the chase was over.

Actually, his life was forfeit the first moment he realized it was a Destructor.

He lay there, still fighting for that first good breath of air as he pulled his weapon out and aimed it at the darkness behind him.

He fired. The laser bolt from his blaster illuminated the room for one fraction of a second like green lightning.

But the hallway was empty!

The flash of his weapon momentarily revealed a corridor empty except for debris that littered the floor. With wide eyes, the Iraxx warrior strained to see through the darkness, strained to see the slightest movement that would reveal the Destructor's position.

Had it left? Or simply given up just when it had closed upon its prey? Wild thoughts rushed through Drinar's mind as he peered into the darkness, trying to see the unseeable.

Drinar found himself able to breathe again—his own raspy gasps drowning all other sounds before they reached his horn-tipped ears.

A faint hope rose inside his broad chest.

And then something fell—a tiny piece of ceiling debris floated gently down in lazy spirals right before his face...

Drinar froze.

He heard it then, almost...almost as if he imagined it. He strained his ears as silence pressed in all around and choked him—strangling him as if he were awake inside his own nightmare.

He finally heard it again—a scratching sound mixed with a faint, ominous humming.

With a sickening dread, he knew the Destructor crouched somewhere above him in the darkness—probably braced against the ceiling with its multiple arms and legs splayed out and ready to make its final attack.

The sinister scratching sound echoed again—slightly louder, and *closer*.

The warrior screamed as he brought his blaster up and fired it in a deadly volley. Tracers pierced the pure darkness above him in line after line of deadly streaks, piercing the ceiling and sending chunks down in a steady stream of falling debris.

He fired upward in all directions.

But the invisible monster did not fall.

With a flash of movement, his weapon was knocked out of his grasp. Almost instantly, a suffocating weight fell upon him. He felt the many arms groping his body and grasping at his flailing hands until they pinned him down.

He struggled valiantly a moment, but soon could no longer move.

As he strained against the merciless strength that held him fast, Drinar regretted only one thing—he had not gotten the message to Qirn.

His eyes strained to make out the Destructor, but even though it held him fast just above, he could not make it out against the darkness.

The whirring of precision gears caused his eyes to fix on the source of that new, sinister sound.

Drinar steeled himself.

In the darkness, he saw a faint reflection against a shiny, black surface. Drinar's eyes made out the silhouette of the Destructor's pincer coming closer.

He saw it plainly now, a black steel needle outlined against the darkness as it came toward his neck. Its razor sharp tip poised to pierce his skin with only the briefest hint of pain. It would then allow the deadly fluid to flow inside his body until his guts melted into a fiery ooze—almost like being digested from the inside out by a giant, metallic insect.

But Destructors did not eat.

Drinar groaned.

No, his would not be a pleasant death.

As the wicked tip drew within inches of his neck, Drinar played his last card.

With a flick of his short, muscular tail, Drinar slapped the iron grip and freed his right hand.

In the darkness, the Iraxx warrior fought for his life.

And his frantic efforts were rewarded.

In the instant he felt its weight lift off, Drinar rolled over and jumped to his feet in one fluid motion. As he stood in a battle crouch facing the sound from where the Destructor gathered itself in the darkness, he drew the sword from its scabbard and held it before him—ready for action.

"Now, let us fight to the death," Drinar growled.

The darkness suddenly filled with movement as Drinar's sword crashed against first one black shape and then another as the Destructor reached for him. The metal blade sent showers of sparks as it hit home each time. Again and again he swung his weapon as he slowly retreated.

Out of the darkness, first from the left, then the right, and even from below, Drinar fought the shadowy arms lashing out at him. He still could not see the Destructor itself, but sometimes with a blur of movement, his eyes caught a glimmer of it.

He swung his blade like a machine, sometimes feeling a steely grip almost grasping him just as his sword quickly knocked it away. It was disconcerting to *almost see* this evil, to feel it right upon him but still not see it.

The warrior grunted with each mighty blow of his weapon as he began to tire.

If only he could find a way back into the dance room, perhaps under the pulsating lights he could his see his enemy plainly and deliver a disabling blow.

Suddenly, his blade swung and struck nothing but air.

Drinar's heart froze as he held his sword ready before him.

But nothing came to his ears now except the rapid-fire pounding of his heart.

He was so close to escaping—he felt it.

Drinar lowered himself into a battle crouch, only to freeze again as the faintest of sounds came to his hearing.

The ominous scratching sound came from somewhere above him again.

He moved back another step as he aimed his blade.

But it was a ruse.

Too late, he saw the shadow of the outstretched arm extended outward to confuse him.

Out of the darkness the Destructor leapt.

Once again Drinar felt the merciless blows and cringed as steel talons searched and found their hold on him one last time. With all his strength, he tried to free his right arm for one more blow of his sword, but his enemy proved relentless and unstoppable.

Seconds later, shoved onto the ground and pinned, Drinar realized he couldn't move. In fact, he could barely breathe under the suffocating weight.

The warrior's heart melted with defeat.

With only the ominous humming as accompaniment to the faint music from the room beyond the wall, the needle came into view out of the darkness.

He cringed.

Slowly, he watched its deadly tip draw ever closer.

With a single, hot flash, the probe pierced his skin, and Drinar felt his body burn as if lava flowed inside his very blood. He grew disoriented, and in another moment he couldn't remember where he was—or who he was.

Or *why* he was...

Mercifully, the Destructor finished its grisly work in the silent darkness.

Silent, except for the faint sound of humming and a metallic scratching...

# CHAPTER TWO

"This place is wall-to-wall aliens," Jaric said, his eyes full of amazement.

"That's exactly what we want." Kyle laughed.

Jaric glanced over the countless faces around them, each one different from the next.

The harsh, artificial light reflected off Jaric's ebony face and caused his bright, intelligent eyes to sparkle. His face was well defined—the handsome face of a young man just twenty-one years of age. Jaric's body was lean and lithe like a long-distance runner and filled with the energy of youth.

They stood overlooking a huge, open atrium filled with aliens as they entered and exited the doors of Bullet-Cars and Bullet-Trains, and entered the main terminus of this floating city. In his mind, Jaric compared it to the mythical Grand Central Station of old New York before the destruction of Earth—except this place was on a scale far larger.

More importantly, and the main reason for their own arrival, most came in order to use the famous Search-terminals. These Search-terminals were the portals to the knowledge of all the known sectors, and beyond. They allowed users to view the results of far-traveled expeditions in pursuit of new races as well as knowledge collected throughout the history of the known worlds.

Yes, aliens traveled here to conduct business both new and old, personal and private—to learn and understand.

They came because the Mrad did not allow remote access to their most valuable resource—knowledge.

"There has to be thousands of different alien races in this one place alone!" Jaric chuckled.

"Yeah, I've never seen a place like this before." Kyle nodded. "We've traveled to twenty worlds in the year since we left the Three Kingdoms, and this is the first..." Kyle's voice trailed off as he searched for words that adequately described RahajMr.

"Floating city," Jaric completed for him.

"Yes—*floating city* that I've ever seen," Kyle finished. He ran his hand through his curly hair. It was now a sandy brown instead of the blonde of his childhood. Kyle crossed his arms over his broad chest as he admired the overflowing atrium of the floating city.

"Or even heard about, for that matter," Jaric added.

"Cities, plural. There are others."

The two young men turned toward the familiar voice of Minstrel.

But there was nothing familiar about Minstrel. Bulbous eyes at the end of seven eye-stalks gazed down at Jaric and Kyle.

"What kind of being are you disguising yourself as this time?" Kyle looked the strange alien up and down.

Indeed, standing between Rok and Jysar was the weirdest creature any of them had ever met in all their travels.

"I am a Zuuk, please remember that in case Security questions us," Minstrel replied. "The Mrad like to register all species that come to use their system—the most powerful computer system known in the universe."

"Yeah," Jaric said with awe. "It's amazing that they've got more raw computing power than Mother!"

Jysar's eyes gleamed with keen anticipation.

"I'm sure the Hrono Technologist will enjoy this." Minstrel laughed as four of its eyes focused on Jysar.

But Kyle kept his gaze fixed on Minstrel's new form. "A Zuuk sure is an interesting alien."

The Zuuk's seven eye-stalks extended from a small head whose only other feature was a mouth shaped like an upside down U. The tiny head and slender eye-stalks sat on top of a long, flexible neck that protruded from a body all but hidden inside a huge, colorful shell. The Zuuk's silver skin glistened under the lights, moistened by its bodily secretions.

Other than the fact that the eye-stalks rose on its neck three meters tall, the most striking feature about a Zuuk was the shell that protected its body. The shell's surface had a polished glaze, covered in a rainbow of bright, iridescent colors.

"Is this armor, or part of your body?" Kyle asked as he lightly tapped the shell.

"It's a shell," Minstrel-Zuuk explained. "The Zuuk creates this over its lifetime with bodily secretions. This fantastic shell is the pride of every Zuuk."

Minstrel-Zuuk moved effortlessly closer—almost as if the huge, ungainly body floated on air.

Jaric bent down as he tried to get a look under the Zuuk's shell. "How did you move like that?"

"I have over ten-thousand tiny, cilia-legs that move in waves, hence my seemingly effortless and fluid motion." Minstrel-Zuuk chuckled. "The Zuuk's homeworld is a world of never-ending rain. Every moment of every day it rains, and so the Zuuk's legs allow it to move especially well over wet surfaces, as well as dry."

"How in the world did this race develop tools, let alone technology that took them to the stars?" Kyle asked incredulously. "You've got no arms, much less fingers or an opposing thumb."

The seven eye-stalks twinkled with humor. "There are appendages, delicate ones, folded inside the shell that the Zuuks extend and use to fashion tools and operate their technology. These fragile appendages are protected inside the shell until needed."

"Cool." Kyle gazed at the multi-colored spiral shell.

Rok grunted in agreement as he looked back at the crowded room filled with alien races. He brushed his hand over the ridge of black feather-hair that grew in a narrow band over the top of his otherwise hairless head. But it wasn't the long feather-hair that dominated the Kraaqi's profile. Curved horns grew upward from each side of his head directly above each ear—these were the pride of a Kraaqi, his natural headdress that complemented his thick feather-hair.

Rok's skin glowed a deeper ebony than Jaric's under the bright lights, and the Kraaqi alien stood head and shoulders above the two humans. His warrior background was also very evident—solid muscle covered his taut body.

"Why do they build their cities around a lifeless planet like this, Minstrel?" Rok asked.

"Yes, this is a gas giant," Jaric said, remembering his original question about these unusual floating cities. "No life can be supported on the surface of such a planet."

"And that is precisely the answer, Jaric," Minstrel-Zuuk said as its seven eyes stared back.

"They bought this world cheap," Jysar said with a twinkle in his eyes.

"Indeed, other aliens felt it a worthless world. The gravity is too powerful for anyone to survive on the surface. Additionally, the nearness of its home star means its surface is constantly bombarded with deadly radiation. And so they purchased this world at a huge discount and built these floating cities. The Mrad are shrewd at business."

"And knowledge is their main business now," Jysar added appreciatively. The Hrono smiled to himself. "I bow in honor to these wise aliens."

"But why inside the cloud layers, why not in orbit around this world? We have visited huge orbiting stations before," Kyle said.

"But none built near the magnitude of this one city alone." The smooth, green scales of Jysar's face deepened with emotion as he admired the scene before him. "This must be a very advanced race, technologically speaking. I must consult with them on some of the fantastic engineering feats they have accomplished in creating this truly one-of-a-kind city." Jysar's eyes widened with pure excitement just thinking about such a conversation.

Being a Hrono, Jysar literally worshipped technology. Like all others of his race, his body scales shone with a green electric hue, including the twin row of upright scales that ran across his head like that of an ancient dinosaur—except these were ridged and a darker green than his tiny body scales. His slim physique and his bird-like arms and legs gave his race a seemingly fragile appearance. But the Hrono were physically strong, more than their appearance indicated.

Jaric and Kyle broke out laughing.

Jysar's face changed to puzzlement. "Do you find humor in engineering masterworks?"

"No, only in geeky aliens gawking over engineering masterworks." Jaric laughed.

"Hmmph." Jysar pursed his mouth with a look of indignation.

Rok grinned from horn to horn, intrigued by this exotic and artificial place. "So why are these cities in orbit *within* the cloud layers?" Rok and the others looked out the massive reinforced window that dominated the seven-story wall. Green, white and purple clouds whipped by like ragged sails caught in a full hurricane.

"Other than the natural beauty of living among these wonderful clouds, I cannot fathom a valid reason." Rok paused as an entire line of green clouds suddenly enveloped the sky outside the window. Just as quickly they disappeared, replaced by the normal stream of clouds of various colors whipping by at mind-numbing speed.

"And I hope those windows are made pretty well. It looks like those winds are blowing over three hundred kilometers an hour," Kyle said with a hopeful look.

"Indeed, sometimes over thrice that speed," Minstrel-Zuuk said. "And yes, those windows are triple-reinforced using the strongest transparent metal known. After all, the clouds are the only natural beauty here, and you will agree that the view is worth it."

"Indeed." Jysar's eyes widened with excitement at the window and its own engineering marvel—not at the beauty it displayed.

"But the reason is quite simple why this city and the other twenty-three floating cities were built inside the tempestuous clouds of this gas giant." Minstrel-Zuuk paused, building the moment to a climax.

"And the answer is..." Jaric prompted.

"RahajMr orbits at about the same position as the human's home-system planet Venus, which is the second reason the Mrad built their cities within the cloud layer," Minstrel-Zuuk said.

"Ah, the clouds provide protection from the star's energy," Jysar surmised correctly. He smiled broadly at his own quick thinking.

"Partly correct. Primarily, the brightness is too intense for any alien's eyes. One could be instantly blinded this close to the star if they looked directly at it."

Jysar frowned.

"You are right, this huge planet is so close to the star it orbits that the radiation would be lethal—the clouds do provide protection. The hull of the cities are designed to protect even further. Still, more is needed. Which is why the cities are not stationary but travel with the winds around and around this planet." Minstrel-Zuuk lowered its serpentine neck so its eye-stalks were closer.

"Which explains why Mother took that route—always keeping the planet between us and the star as we made our final approach from space." Kyle's eyes narrowed with the recent memory of that ride. "And I must say, as we entered the cloud bands of RahajMr that was the roughest ride I've ever felt. Those are some winds!"

"Yes, landing is the trickiest part. The Wind Specialists have to determine a window when the buffeting winds will remain a constant speed in one direction for a few minutes in order to allow a visiting ship to land at a Leeward docking door and get inside the protective city walls," Minstrel-Zuuk said with admiration. He raised his head far above the others and admired RahajMr.

"But how do these cities stay afloat, as well as steady themselves, as they ride the winds?" Rok asked.

Kyle and Jaric both looked expectantly at the eye-stalks far above them.

"Rok, you above all races should guess that answer." The seven eye-stalks twinkled with mirth.

"Anti-gravity engines!" Rok half-shouted. He rubbed his chin in thought. "They must be massive, to keep a city this size floating and utilize the gravity of such a huge planet."

"Yes, they are. This city alone contains almost fifty million inhabitants. But still, another design was utilized. The Mrad harnessed these mighty winds to a certain extent and turned them to their own use." Minstrel-Zuuk paused. "You no doubt have noticed that these cities are shaped to ride the constant buffeting of the horizontal winds which greatly assists the anti-grav engines—huge, aerodynamic-shaped cities originally built in far orbit and then carefully lowered into the clouds."

Rok turned to the great window. "Look, the wind has changed direction."

They all turned.

The ragged ribbons of purple and white clouds flying from left to right across the window disappeared with a blur of movement. The sky outside cleared into a wide-open expanse of several hundred kilometers. But in the far distance a solid wall of green clouds approached.

"The clouds never really disappear from view on this gas giant, but clear sky appears briefly once

26

or twice a week," Minstrel-Zuuk said, his tone matter-of-fact.

The onlookers suddenly felt disoriented; Kyle and Jysar reached out for support while the others swayed off-balance.

The distant wall of clouds changed.

"Wha..." Jaric said uncertainly, blinking his eyes rapidly as he tried to fathom what his eyes told him but his mind refused to believe.

The cloudbank took shape; details that a fraction of a second before were not visible suddenly became obvious—and huge. The distant clouds exploded into a massive cloud wall five thousand kilometers wide as it leaped toward them with unimaginable velocity.

Two seconds later, the leading edge of the green cloudbank reached them as everyone readied themselves—their subconscious minds telling them a tempest of fantastic magnitude was upon them with such awesome force it surely must destroy them all.

The window became solid green as the stillness and silence haunted their minds. In that moment they comprehended the fantastic speed at which the winds blew in this unique place.

As they gazed, still tensed for an explosive blow that never came, the solid green parted and small valleys of clear air grew between ribbons of cloud as the wind continued to rush head-on at them.

The only discernable effect was a humming sound that grew louder with the onslaught of the green clouds and now slowly—very slowly—began to fade.

Minstrel-Zuuk's voice broke into their awestruck reverie as a new wave of green clouds filled the huge window again.

"At strategic points all around this city and its twenty-three sister cities are massive vents that channel the force of the wind. This system powers the cities as well harvests the natural elements found in the clouds. This is why the Mrad have been able to build the most powerful computers ever constructed. And why they built them here."

"How can there be that much to those clouds?" Jaric asked.

"Again, being so close to its home star, and having those titanic gravitational forces wrenching the planet's surface, as well as the constant hurricane-force winds at its surface that eventually join with these horizontal upper winds, well, these cloud bands are rich with sub-microscopic raw material."

"Why doesn't that barrage of raw elements slam through the walls of this city?" Jaric asked again, fascinated by this exotic place.

"By the time the winds reach this altitude, the elements have been practically vaporized—battered almost to their molecular level and ready to be harvested. Still, there is a series of outer shields both protecting this city as well as funneling the elements to be processed. The Mrad leave nothing to waste, they utilize everything."

"Ingenious," Jysar commented.

"But, we forget why we have come to RahajMr in the first place," Minstrel-Zuuk said.

A shock of sadness gripped Jaric's soul and overwhelmed him. It seemed to kill him one lonely heartbeat at a time.

Yes, Jaric remembered.

He remembered all too well the hopelessness of their life-long search to find other survivors of the human race.

*For the human race was no more—destroyed—eradicated.*

Jaric shook his head as childhood memories flooded his mind.

No, *exterminated* better described it.

*Well, almost*, he added mentally. He and Kyle alone remained, two young men, sole survivors of the human race.

Jaric's mind reeled with his dizzying melancholy.

*There was a third. Three humans survived mankind's destruction as Earth blew apart in the final battle. Becky had also survived—the last female human.*

*But Becky was now dead.*

Jaric growled under his breath, anger filling his soul as he remembered again how Becky's ship disintegrated in their last battle with the T'kaan— the climactic battle of six alien fleets. A battle that brought the final destruction of the T'kaan. A mighty struggle fought by the combined Hrono, Mewiis and Kraaqi fleets led by Mother and Kyle and Jaric...and Becky.

Jaric groaned deep inside.

The T'kaan were finally destroyed, but at such a terribly high cost.

Yet, there was Becky's clone...

Jaric remembered the entrance of Becky's clone, the clone created by the Hrono from Becky's DNA.

So, there was a third human survivor...

No. The clone did not count. There were only two survivors of the human race—he and Kyle.

He fought back the hot tears that suddenly filled his eyes as he turned away from his friends in embarrassment.

Kyle groaned as he watched Jaric. With clenched fists, Kyle too turned away.

Jaric's mind went back further. He reviewed once again their escape as Earth lay under siege by the mighty T'kaan Third Fleet, just before its destruction.

Deep inside the AI starship, the young child Jaric hid from the universe. He closed his eyes as mankind's *Last Stand* played out.

In this, Jaric's earliest memory of that terrible time, the only comfort he felt was that of Mother—the AI starship inside which he hid.

Mother was the ultimate warship, designed by the scientists of mankind as they retreated before the T'kaan onslaught. Mother was a combination of the best technology left to mankind—the most advanced hardware ever designed coupled with the latest, most sophisticated AI software ever developed.

Mankind armed the AI warship to the teeth and programmed it for one primary function—to destroy the T'kaan. Additionally, they enhanced the firepower of this ship with the most destructive of T'kaan weapons, reverse-engineered from one of the few T'kaan warships captured by humans—and even that battle had not been a victory.

For the T'kaan rarely lost in battle.

Knowledge learned as he grew older augmented Jaric's memory. There had been an AI ship created before Mother—the Alpha ship.

The prototype AI ship, the Alpha ship, was hugely successful at first. In five straight battles it destroyed every T'kaan ship it faced—although outnumbered every time.

The T'kaan trembled for the first time since their never-ending war began.

Next came the sixth battle, and the Alpha ship's single fatal flaw crippled it—for it was *merely* a war machine—and nothing more.

The T'kaan discovered this weakness and destroyed it.

The scientists who created the Alpha ship learned from that mistake.

They improved on their design with the second AI ship, the one Kyle and Jaric knew as *Mother*.

The scientists also programmed the second ship with science and human psychology and literature—and more. This would enable the ship not only to *learn*—learn more than simply how to fight better with each experience—but to grow and become *more alive* with each and every experience.

31

The second AI ship was more than simply a warship.

And secretly, with a hasty plan to save a handful of human survivors before the final battle, the scientists downloaded more—much more. Every piece of knowledge, science and lore—every aspect of recorded data about humanity throughout all history. From every collection of knowledge across the Fifty Worlds, the scientists downloaded everything to the AI ship.

They stored it all in the unimaginably vast memory systems created specially for this second AI warship—synthetic human-DNA memory systems.

The ship contained every recorded experience of the human race on which to draw upon, to learn from...

But the escape plan failed as the T'kaan attacked early.

With only three small children onboard and the collected memory of the human race, the AI ship observed in silence as the last human stronghold—planet Earth—blew apart.

The others never arrived to make the final escape.

The AI starship wrestled with its core programming as it left the destruction behind. The ship's turmoil grew as the young children cried out to it for direction and for comfort.

*And for love.*

Jaric remembered it all too well. And why they still searched for other human survivors, although it seemed hopeless.

"Which way to the Search-terminals?" Jysar's tone reflected his own emotional tension as he and the others watched the distraught humans.

"I wouldn't get your hopes up too much," Rok said with a nod. "Remember Jarbornir, we were certain we had found a valid lead about other hoo-mans." Rok's thick Kraaqi accent slurred the last word.

Jaric sighed with the memory of six months ago.

"Yes," Jysar agreed. "The evidence seemed rock solid—a small remnant from a race destroyed by war-like aliens who took refuge there only a short time ago."

"But they were not humans, and the race which destroyed them had not been the T'kaan." Kyle shook his head sadly.

"I think the one that really got to me was last month, when we landed on Krasas," Jaric said as he turned to face the others again.

"We should have suspected something the moment he asked for money in return for his knowledge," Rok growled. "I knew we could not trust that slimy alien the moment I first laid eyes on him."

Jaric looked up at the moist skin of the Zuuk. "Present company excepted."

Kyle's face became puzzled. "I thought the saying went, 'Present company accepted.'"

33

"Now I'm confused, hoo-mans say same thing twice." Rok looked from Jaric to Kyle.

Kyle began to chuckle. "Well, almost. At least our meaning is meant to be the same, but we did say different words—the last word."

"We've run into a lot of dead-ends," Jaric said sadly.

Kyle bit his lower lip. "Well, we've had a couple of really hopeful leads turn out to be nothing the last few months. And the one that hurt was the lie we spent money on, hoping it was true."

"We must be more prudent in our use of questions, as well as the information about humans we share in our search." Jysar looked at the two young men. "But most of all, we must weigh carefully any results we find—especially when it's exactly what we want."

"Yeah, if it's too good to be true—it probably is," Kyle mused.

"Well, here on RahajMr we'll query a super-massive knowledgebase. Yes, we will have to pay to gain access to their vast knowledge resources, but at least our questions will be answered honestly as we honestly pay for them," Minstrel-Zuuk said with confidence.

Jaric sighed. "Even if it's not the answer we want to hear."

# CHAPTER THREE

"Please select an appropriate queue. Please be patient, average waiting time is currently seventy-seven krinos," an emotionless voice enunciated from the nearest speaker.

Minstrel-Zuuk and the others waited behind about twenty other customers—each appearing to be of a different alien race—in this particular queue. Behind Minstrel-Zuuk stood Jysar and Rok, with Kyle and Jaric bringing up the rear.

"And that means?" Kyle asked.

"About ten minutes," Minstrel-Zuuk translated.

"Not bad." Jaric looked around at the dozens of lines full of aliens waiting their turn, each queue containing perhaps a hundred aliens waiting just like them.

"There are over seventy thousand of these controlled search rooms in which to gain access to their network in this city alone. Imagine how many there are for all twenty-four cities." The seven eye-stalks looked first one direction and then another *simultaneously*.

Jysar's eyes widened with amazement at the technology surrounding them.

"As I mentioned, this is the largest single store of knowledge known. Even to Minstrels, and we get around." The seven eye-stalks suddenly turned in seven different directions. Minstrel-Zuuk smiled with satisfaction. "Wow, I just had to try that once. A real panoramic view, so to speak."

"Guess a Zuuk can really keep an eye on things, eh." Jaric laughed.

"You bet." Minstrel-Zuuk chuckled.

"Why don't aliens just log on from their ships, or from their own planets? They have multi-system networks in this Quadrant connecting planets, don't they?" Jysar asked with disbelief.

"The Mrad are shrewd businessmen. Their massive computer does indeed connect to the local inter-system network. But the data flow is only one-way, they search out data and bring it in, but none go out from it."

"Why do the other races allow that?" Jysar's voice filled with exasperation. "Why don't others protect their data from the Mrad?"

"They tried at first. But the Mrad have ingenious ways to sneak into computer systems and capture data, even from outside the known Quadrants." Minstrel-Zuuk stretched its eye-stalks as far out as it could, surveying the myriad of aliens all around for a moment. "In fact, their system even has some basic information about the races of the Three Kingdoms, although neither the Hrono, the Kraaqi nor the Mewiis have any reciprocal knowledge."

Jysar's eyes narrowed. "The nerve of them, *taking* data like that."

"The Mrad make a lucrative living on data. And it is true, in the beginning a lot of races were angry. But soon they all acquiesced after using the system. They discovered that the benefits of using the data for a modest fee outweighed the problem of actually having to travel to the floating cities of this world. Actually, the Mrad make it worthwhile, running a nice tourism trade on the side too. Some of the best hotels, entertainment, food and drink are here." Minstrel-Zuuk yawned. "And because their data acquisition techniques are so far-reaching, if any references to human survivors exist in any of the nearby Quadrants or from a passing starship's logs that they've lifted, this massive system will contain it."

"Cool," Kyle said.

"Not very proper, taking data like that," Jysar said stoically.

"Who cares," Jaric added. He turned as an alien bumped into him.

Jaric found three black eyes staring back from a face covered with short, curly fur. Two huge nostrils on its furry forehead suddenly flared open. The alien's eyes widened as a look of disgust grew over its hairy visage. It took a half-step backward only to bump into a large, bird-like alien behind it.

The bird alien with iridescent green feathers stared in shock, its red eyes glaring above a long beak of blue, green and yellow stripes. The huge beak was twice the size of the rest of the alien's head, giving it a very odd profile. The multi-colored beak opened wide and a large black tongue became visible as it spoke.

"What's that awful stench?" The bird-like alien groaned.

The hairy alien whispered to the bird-alien as it pointed at both Jaric and Kyle.

Two more aliens behind the bird-like alien joined them as they too stared with disapproval.

All four aliens took a half-step backward.

"Must've forgotten to put on my antiperspirant again," Jaric said with a twinkle in his eyes to Kyle.

"Huh?" Kyle asked.

Jaric jerked his thumb at the aliens still trying to distance themselves and yet keep their place in queue.

Rok began to chuckle.

"You find this funny, eh, buddy?" Jaric said.

Rok shrugged nonchalantly. "I've gotten used to your peculiar odor." Rok grinned widely. "But it is something that must be *acquired with time*."

Kyle jabbed his elbow hard into Rok's side, causing the Kraaqi warrior to grunt with pain. Kyle smiled. "Oh, I'm sorry. Must've been some kind of reflex action on my part. You know how we smelly humans are—always causing problems."

Rok chuckled louder as he rubbed his side tenderly. "Remember about Kraaqi pay-backs, hoo-mans. My return humor will be most delightful when the time is ripe." Rok's eyes twinkled mischievously.

The queue continued moving slowly forward until...

"Next."

Jaric's face clouded with emotion. He leaned forward and whispered into Kyle's ear. "I almost don't want to do this—try another search. Probably just another disappointment."

Kyle nodded without looking at him, a solemn expression on his face. He cleared his throat. "Well," he said in a low voice so nobody else could hear, "we ought to be used to disappointment by now. Let's just try..." He paused. "...one more time, my friend. We'll never know unless we try."

"*Neeee-xt.*"

Minstrel-Zuuk stepped up to the short, plump alien that sat behind the huge computer console facing the queue.

The creature's face was small, dominated by a cylindrical snout tipped by a tiny black nose and tiny mouth. His beady black eyes stared unblinking as he waited on them. His smooth skin was covered by alternating black and white stripes over its entire body—at least the part exposed by its uniform. In complete contrast to the diminutive mouth at the tip of his snout, his deep voice seemed comically out of place.

"Yore name and methuud of payment, pleez." The black and white striped alien spoke with a distinct drawl, enunciating his words in slow motion.

"Thank technology for universal translators," Jysar said with obvious gladness.

"Indeed," Minstrel-Zuuk concurred, turning up the volume.

"Are you a Mrad?" Jysar asked.

"No, I am a Clakza. Our species are hired exclusively by the Mrad to operate their great system."

A loud drumming noise erupted from behind the striped Clakza, effectively interrupting their conversation.

"Wait jesst a moment, pleez." He turned to look back at the numerous enclaves of search terminals. At one of them a group of five aliens stared intently at the screen. Two of them slammed their fists onto the console again, almost as if hitting it would make it work better.

"An-ny trouble over thar?" the Clakza yelled politely.

The two aliens looked up, a sheepish grin on their faces. "No, no, no, everything fine. No trouble here." They smiled innocently and stopped their attack—for the moment.

"Well, jest holler out if you need help with that machine. And pleez, don't damage it." He started to turn back to Minstrel-Zuuk.

"Oh no, we no damage. We just use." Their innocent smiles widened.

Jysar stared in shock at the impertinent aliens, obviously troubled that anyone would treat technology with such blatant disregard. He sighed loudly, rolling his eyes in disbelief.

"Some aliens just don't know how to treat technology, do they?" Rok whispered to Jysar with a humorous tone.

Jysar shook his head.

"Mah name is Ablek, how mah I assist yew with our Search-terminals?" The Clakza smiled.

"Ablek, we would like to purchase time on three terminals. Myself and my friends behind me."

40

Three of the eye-stalks turned to eye the others while the other four remained fixed on Ablek.

Ablek gave a cursory glance to Minstrel-Zuuk, Jysar and Rok. But he paused as he glanced at Kyle and Jaric.

"Whar in the great wad galaxy do you two come frum? Never seen the likes of yore kind here before," Ablek said with surprise.

"Humans, we're humans," Kyle said with an angry edge to his voice. He'd had just about enough of aliens sniffing and talking down to him for one day.

"Sounds like he'd be more at home on an agricultural planet than this place," Jysar whispered with mirth as he glanced at Ablek.

Minstrel-Zuuk spoke again, trying to focus everyone back on the primary purpose for coming here.

"Our purpose is to search for any references related to humans among your vast computer network." Minstrel-Zuuk's eye-stalks all faced Ablek again, eyeing the little alien intently. "Jysar also has some specific search parameters for his personal research, as do I. We require *three* Search-terminals."

Ablek turned to another of his kind and shouted. "Hey, kick that machine on, will ya. It's for this big fella here with all the eyes."

The alien's loud voice caused every head in the room to turn toward them.

"Man, I feel embarrassed just being near this alien," Jaric whispered to Kyle as he tried to ignore the stares that went from the humans back to Ablek.

"You should have more respect for your technology than that!" Jysar growled, his patience at an end.

"Hey, lighten up fella. It's just a fi-gur of speech." Ablek pointed as his companion flicked a couple of switches and brought the Search-terminal online for Minstrel-Zuuk. "This parr-ticularr unclave waz dee-signed to seat extra-large aliens. The uther terminals are fer more normal-sized aliens."

Ablek motioned for Minstrel-Zuuk to take his Search-terminal.

A few minutes later Jysar sat on his own terminal busily using the system while Rok, Jaric and Kyle sat together at a third one.

But before Jaric could begin, Kyle's communicator beeped.

"It must be Mother wondering what our status is," Kyle said as he took the device from his belt and held it up to his mouth.

"Kyle here."

"Have you entered your search routines into the Mrad system yet?" Mother asked with a soft, feminine voice.

Kyle looked over at Jaric. Both smiled knowingly at each other.

"What's the deal, Mother? Don't you trust us to get this done ourselves?" Kyle said, his voice laced with humor.

"Of course, I was only checking in order to approximate the time you would return. I've discovered some interesting things about this place with my own scans—despite being limited by their security shields."

"Maybe we can arrange a direct link for you to use their huge computer system, although I'd bet it won't be cheap. If they allow it at all," Kyle said.

"Yes, we will investigate that. But I want you to take the Bullet-Cars back, they will get you here quickly. Tonight is our music evening and I don't wish you to be late. I look forward to it every week."

Kyle and Jaric smiled widely at each other—ever since arriving on RahajMr they had heard that riding the Bullet-Cars was a *must do* experience.

Rok grinned wolfishly with keen anticipation.

"Sure, Mother. We'll take the fastest transportation back possible—just so we won't be late. We wanted to take in all the scenery earlier, taking our time, you know."

"Contact me if anything changes."

The communicator went silent and Kyle replaced it back on his belt. "Let's get our search going here, we'll come back tomorrow and review any results."

Rok cleared his throat. "May I suggest something?"

Jaric and Kyle paused.

"Sure," they said together.

"Many times, on many different planets, we have asked questions—we have searched for the tiniest references for the existence of other human survivors." Rok took a deep breath, gathering his thoughts logically, remembering the different alien bars and taverns, the numerous network cafes, the countless conversations with traders, explorers and other beings who roamed the vast reaches space. And in all of them, never the first shred of hope that any other humans survived.

A visible tension grew in both Jaric and Kyle. Rok sensed their fear of failure even before they entered the first search criteria.

Because they fought alongside the Kraaqi against the T'kaan, Kyle and Jaric were anointed as Brethren. As their Brethren, Rok wanted to help them and not see their emotional wounds opened once more.

Rok raised his head as he stroked his chin. "Allow me, from a non-hoo-man perspective, to define the descriptive criteria for the search. After all, if another alien race came into contact with human survivors, it will be their description, their reference in the ship's log or report. It will be a description about humans from their perspective— an alien perspective. So if I, a Kraaqi, define our search, it may have better success of making a match in the vast data of this system."

Jaric felt his heart begin to race. He looked at Kyle and saw a glimmer of hope in his eyes too. And for the first time that day, he felt like they might really succeed.

"That's a great idea, Rok." Kyle motioned for Rok to sit at the terminal. "Jaric and I will add

44

human-specific criteria, such as proper names like Earth and Nuevo Mundo, names human survivors would likely mention to any aliens."

"And the name..." Jaric suddenly seemed to lose his voice as his eyes narrowed. But he forced himself to continue. "T'kaan. They're likely to mention the enemy that destroyed humanity." Jaric's eyes peered at the others.

T'kaan was a name which they rarely uttered anymore.

Kyle and Rok sighed with remembrance of the dreaded race.

"Yes, we will. We have to," Kyle said, a huskiness in his voice. He fought the anger that rose inside him.

"Computer, description of species called hooman." Rok paused, his eyes reflective a moment. "Warm-blooded and smooth-skinned race, skin color ranges from almond to chocolate brown with a wide variety of shades between. Male and female sex." Rok looked Kyle and Jaric up and down slowly, pondering their physical description. "Hoomans walk upright on two legs. Two arms attached on upper part of cylindrical torso just below neck. Two eyes on forehead, two small, fleshy ears on either side of head. One mouth, lower part of head. Nose with two small nostrils located mid-face— thick growth of hair above forehead and overhead and down to back of the neck."

Rok paused again, staring at his two friends as if seeing them for the first time. Then he sniffed the

45

air. He began to chuckle under his breath, but realized it would be something important.

"Strong and pungent body odor—unpleasant."

Kyle opened his mouth to argue, but Jaric placed his hand firmly on his shoulder.

"They'd probably mention that," Jaric whispered.

"But it can become tolerable—with time." Rok's eyes sparkled with mischief.

Kyle wrinkled his nose subconsciously and nodded his head in agreement. "Okay. I'll buy that. Now, if that's it for your part, let Jaric and I input our criteria. I'm getting hungry."

"Yeah, and I want to ride a Bullet-Car!" Jaric said eagerly.

Deep within the data storage banks of the Mrad system an alarm routine activated.

The coded parameters matched the search criteria and within milliseconds the alarm routine kicked off its action code, alerting the agents of the Paum that someone searched for the *forbidden* knowledge—knowledge restricted on almost every single world in the Four Quadrants.

In the deep recesses of their parked starship, the Harg warriors awoke with a start as the red beacon and screaming alarm shattered the silence.

"What is it?" The stout Harg nearest the console leapt up and began reading the message on the screen.

"Someone searches for..." The alien paused in shocked silence. He turned to his commander with military precision. "Someone searches for *sentient* machines, sir."

"What? Is there a specific search pattern? Do they seek a specific world?" The Harg commander leaned over his shoulder so he too could see the message.

"No, it is a general search—checking for any references on the existence of sentient machines—their location and their creators." The sub-commander waited as his commander rubbed his chin in thought.

"Send the kill routines. Set to it kill these search queries at the top of the hour."

"But, sir, the Mrad system has many checkpoints. Sending the kill code may alert them to us."

"It does not matter—the Paum has stationed us here for many reasons, but this is the most vital. In fact, we need to contact the homeworld about this as soon as the search is killed."

The two Harg warriors snarled at each other, but the sub-commander turned and keyed the sequence to activate the kill-code. A few seconds later, he turned with a grin.

"Target search updated with kill time in six hundred krinos."

"Good."

"The original search has already returned some initial cross-references, but none that reveal anything of importance. Even better, the source Search station is identified as well as the time initiated."

The Harg commander reviewed the information.

"You have done well."

"Could this be the Iraxx again?" the sub-commander asked.

"I do not think so, they would not be this foolish. No, this public search of the great Mrad system is from another alien race. And that is what makes it more dangerous to us."

"Shall I use breaker code and slice into the Mrad credit system to see who purchased the search console?"

"Using the kill code to stop a public search is one thing. Using breaker code to infiltrate their credit system will certainly get picked up by their security sub-systems. It may lead them to our ship and compromise our cover." The Harg in command paused in thought.

The subordinate Harg waited patiently as his commander pondered the risk.

The commander nodded. "Do it."

With rapid keystrokes, the Harg sub-commander enabled the breaker code and targeted the infiltrate and seek parameters with the system ID of the Search console and the time the search began.

The breaker code launched.

The Harg watched the progress chart intently. At first, the Mrad security kept the malicious code at bay. But before an entire minute passed, a hole was identified and penetrated. Ten seconds later, the targeted data scrolled across their screen.

48

"A Zuuk purchased the search?" the Harg commander said with surprise.

"Hmmm. Zuuks are not that common in this Sector. Although they do come to Mrad on occasion."

"Look." The commander pointed to the screen. "The Zuuk purchased time on two other Search consoles. A Hrono on one. Now, that is an alien race I've not heard of before. We need to check its searches."

"And look at this, a Kraaqi and something called humans on the last console?"

The Harg looked at each other with puzzled expressions.

"We must interrogate the Clakza in charge of this station and identify these unknown aliens. As well as this Zuuk who searches for the forbidden knowledge."

"And when we find him?"

"Then we find out who sent them, and why—and report directly to the Paum. The Paum has explicit orders on this subject—if anyone showed interest in sentient machines."

The Harg commander stroked the blaster on his hip as a smile grew.

"And if the Paum decides they are dangerous to our paradigm, we kill the Zuuk and everyone else on its starship."

49

# CHAPTER FOUR

Minstrel-Zuuk's eyes stared unblinking.

"You know, your new shape gives me the creeps sometimes. I feel like I'm being watched all the time," Kyle said with a laugh.

"I'll be glad to remove this body myself," Minstrel-Zuuk whispered. Clearing its throat, it continued in a normal tone. "I left my searches running in background mode a few minutes ago and will check their output tomorrow. How have you done?"

"Mine are running as well," Jysar reported.

"We're trying something new." Kyle stood. "But, the progress bar is barely growing. And it's time to get back to Mother."

"Good, I'll see you later then."

"Hey, did you forget it's 'Music Evening' tonight?" Jaric said with surprise. "The band won't be the same without Minstrel."

Five of Minstrel-Zuuk's seven eyes twinkled with pleasure.

"I have a *musical adventure* awaiting me at the Blue Star Lounge. A new musical fad—or genre—is blooming here. It's spreading across the planets like wildfire too." The huge Zuuk form quivered with excitement. "In recent weeks, a Minstrel copied a few songs from starships that recently traveled here. The songs were communicated outbound to all Minstrels in this quadrant—which is how I received them. The music is quite distinct."

"Yes," Jysar said with remembrance. "You travel the universe in search of song."

"That is one code we live by, yes. But there is more. Minstrels seek out what is good and beautiful and noble from all races. Music is our greatest love," Minstrel-Zuuk said with pride. "Think about it, what greater bond is there between all sentient races in the great, wide universe? They may speak different languages. They may breathe oxygen, nitrogen, or hydrogen. They may live millennia, or they may live mere weeks. But, music is something that all sentient races share in common. And each can listen to and enjoy the music of another alien race even without being able to speak their language."

"What about the technology we share?" Jysar asked. "And a decent Galactic Translator resolves any language barrier."

"Pre-space travel sentients, even pre-technology sentients, make music, my Hrono friend."

"Music is good—*good for the soul*." Rok nodded appreciatively.

"And the melodies, the lyrics, and the rhythms are unique to each alien race which creates it. Still, because it is music—the rest of the universe can enjoy it. But only if the music is heard—that is why we Minstrels seek it out, not only to listen but to record it and share it. We ourselves learn to play it with our instruments—instruments integrated directly into our starships."

"What is this music you go to hear now? And I hope you've told Mother you're not coming tonight," Kyle said.

"Mother is informed. In fact, she is eager to hear what I will record tonight, although no one will realize what I'm doing at the Blue Star. The music is associated with a new dance form—the Mrad call it 'Happy Dancing.'" Minstrel-Zuuk smiled. "And the songs I have heard so far identify the music as 'Happy Music.'"

"Happy Dancing?" Jaric said with surprise. "Why should that be so special, or different?"

"Most forms of dancing by adult sentients are with specific purposes in mind—to tell stories, to follow a complex choreography, to impress others, or to encourage mating rituals."

"And this?"

"This, it seems, falls into the genre of pure, child-like enjoyment. To dance, to make music—for the *sheer enjoyment* of it, much as young children dance simply for the joy of dancing, not caring if others see. Adult aliens are 'Happy Dancing' across all planets in this sector." Now, all seven of Minstrel-Zuuk's eyes gleamed with excitement. "Humans may reference the music of J. S. Bach or Mozart as happy music. However, there is a better example that spawned a kind of 'Happy Dancing' on Earth in the mid-twentieth century. This genre, called Rock and Roll, is exemplified by early Beatles songs as well as songs by Chuck Berry, The Beach Boys, Elvis Presley, and others of this time period."

"Cool," Jaric agreed.

"Hey, I want to hear some when you get back," Kyle said excitedly.

"And so you will." Minstrel-Zuuk glided gracefully away toward the more sedate thoroughfares—the moving sidewalks—of RahajMr.

"And now, we get to see why they put the *bullet* in Bullet-Cars." Kyle laughed.

Eagerly, the foursome made their way through the throngs in the opposite direction of Minstrel.

The queue moved quickly as they pulled out their credits and prepared to step into the tight confines of the sleek Bullet-Car.

"Very cool," Kyle said with awe as he watched a Bullet-Car in the next slot over from them suddenly shoot into the air with a hiss. Seconds later it disappeared inside one of the hundreds of tunnel openings studding the great wall that rose before them. Each tunnel led to various destinations of the great city.

"Oh man, those things can fly."

While watching others pay and step inside the bullet-shaped cars, they noticed how the gull-wing door closed shut and made the steel surface seamless and totally aerodynamic. Next, the Bullet-Car moved slowly forward to a launching square. After a quick countdown, it shot silently through the air directly at one of the tunnel openings—each one the beginning of a long tube lined with both magnetic and anti-grav components. These devices 'shot' the cars down through the tunnels with ever increasing velocity to their destination, normally in less than two minutes. The longest tube ride lasted just over four minutes, and its destination was the other side of the city.

"Bullet-Cars are not for the faint of heart." Rok nodded with anticipation.

"Wow," Kyle agreed.

They watched with mouths agape as another car disappeared with a blur of motion.

Rok and Jysar paid their money and stepped inside their own Bullet-Car. Jysar smiled and waved to them as the gull-wing door closed. In total silence, the Bullet-Car moved forward into position—aimed at a specific tunnel opening.

"I hope they have lights lining the tubes, I want to see and feel this bad-boy as we fly through the tunnels," Jaric said to Kyle as the Bullet-Car with their friends suddenly soared silently away.

Another Clakza, his distinctive black and white striped snout and face fixed on them, waited for payment.

Kyle fished some credits out of his pocket to pay for himself and Jaric.

"So, these are the famous Bullet-Cars, eh?" Kyle smiled as he started to sit down in the front seat as Jaric took the rear one. Both seats faced forward inside the cramped compartment.

"Yes," the Clakza said, his dialect not as strong as Ablek's. "Some aliens jest come to RahajMr in order to rad every single tube. When we dee-signed this transit system, we wanted the rad to be as much fun as the destination—meybe more. Each tube, or tunnel, has its own unique set of twists and turns. We designed it that way." The tiny mouth grinned at the end of the huge snout. "Jest for the *fun* of it."

"Alright," Kyle said with excitement.

Kyle twisted his body and finally fell the rest of the way into the tight confines of the forward seat. He immediately noted the lack of buttons or controls on the console before him—only a few indicators for speed, time and location. Looking up, he stared through the reinforced windshield at the curved nose of the Bullet-Car.

"All Bullet-Cars are automated bah the central computer," the Clakza said, guessing his thoughts. "But I'll tell yew, if yew really want a ride yew need to take the city-to-city Bullet-Cars. The ones that leap out into the wild winds and fly between the floating cities! Now *that* is a ride."

"How do they work?" Jaric asked, his interest piqued.

"Navigation systems are point-to-point between the cities. Those parr-ticular Bullet-Cars are bigger and carry their own internal anti-grav engines, which is why they can carry up to six average-sized aliens. But even with their bullet designs, the ride can be rough and wild as they sail into the eternal winds of this gas giant."

"Oh man, we may have to try that before we leave," Kyle said from his seat.

Jaric twisted his body and fell into his seat behind Kyle. He smiled mischievously as the safety force field wrapped tightly around his body in order to hold him in place. "You bet."

Their hearts pounded with adrenaline as the Bullet-Car moved with complete silence to the launch pad and stopped. On the console, all lights glowed green.

Kyle tensed.

He knew that at any moment they would be launched forward and get to their bullet speed of one hundred fifty kilometers an hour in mere seconds.

Jaric looked around, his head firmly held against the back of the thick cushioned seat by the safety force field. Jaric smiled as he saw Kyle glance back.

*"Let's rock this thing!"*

In that instant, their Bullet-Car rocketed forward with a blur of motion.

For one brief instant, it seemed that they were leaving their bodies behind, a strange sensation of intense speed and the conflicting sensation of the force field holding them in place.

Seconds later, they entered a tunnel.

As their eyes quickly adjusted, they noted with satisfaction that a line of lights lit up the tube's interior.

Their car surged silently forward with a new burst of speed. The two young men felt their bodies pressed deeper into their seats as the G-forces increased.

As they reached their top speed their eyes were assaulted by the line of lights as they hurtled down the long tube and suddenly curved to the right, back straight, then left. In another moment, they hurtled forward upside down.

With two more bursts of speed and three more hard banks into tight curves, it became impossible for them to tell if they were right side up or still upside down.

The only thing they knew was that they were hurtling forward at immense velocity.

Suddenly, the line of lights traveled downward.

The Bullet-Car shot straight down with more speed.

The Bullet-Car quickly turned upright as they realized they could feel their bodies again.

They were only fifteen seconds into the ride.

Jaric's mind began to function again as his senses coalesced and he realized how fast they were traveling. In that moment, Jaric did what came naturally.

He screamed.

Kyle's laughter mixed with Jaric's howl as the line of lights revealed a curve that now took them left and straight up.

And suddenly down with a hard left turn!

Both men felt their stomachs jump with the sudden turns as their bodies jerked time and again between the two forces assaulting their senses—one fighting to keep them in place with an iron grip, and one pushing and jerking with titanic force with each turn.

With their mouths wide open in silence, they stared in wild fascination.

In the next seconds, they felt the Bullet-Car slow.

*Slightly.*

In another moment, the car slammed hard left followed by a hard right.

They entered a series of corkscrew turns that lifted them out of their seats, but the force field pressed them back down each time.

Again they felt the Bullet-Car throw them upside down.

And again they banked upward and through a long curve to their right as the Bullet-Car righted itself.

Jaric felt a dizziness enveloping his mind.

The Bullet-Car dropped straight down again.

Down, down they hurtled.

It felt like the drop would never end.

Suddenly, they straightened and hit a long straight-away.

Now an electric thrill of total excitement filled their senses as the pure speed pressed them deeper and deeper into their seats with each passing second.

Kyle and Jaric found their voices as they yelled with excitement. But it required all their effort simply to scream—each held in place by the comforting grip of the force field.

Their vision blurred as the lights grew into one long line.

Without warning, the Bullet-Car braked with a hard jolt.

The line of light changed back to normal as their speed continued to slow.

A bright light at the end of the tunnel grew.

A few seconds later they stared out into another huge room filled with Bullet-Cars as their own slid out into the open air. This station was almost identical to the one they had left.

Kyle and Jaric turned as the force field relaxed its iron grip.

Behind them, another wall rose. It was also filled with tunnel openings.

The force field now fell completely away from their bodies as the Bullet-Car glided effortlessly toward a landing pad amid dozens of other cars.

Kyle turned his head, taking his first deep breath—*his first real breath*—since their ride started. He glanced at the time.

The entire journey had taken less than two minutes. They had traveled from the central section of the great city all the way to the outer docks located just inside the massive outer hull. It was here where all starships docked while visiting RahajMr.

"We have got to do that again!" Jaric shouted as he jumped out of the Bullet-Car, adrenaline pumping throughout his body like a laser cannon.

"You bet. I need to do it again just so I can figure out what we just experienced! It all happened so fast I don't really know what just happened!" Kyle laughed heartily.

The two ran joyously through the crowds of aliens. They made their way toward the dock where

Mother waited. As their heart rate and adrenaline levels began to subside, they gradually slowed their pace.

"Hey," Jaric said as a recent memory flashed. "I want to tell you something when we get back—an idea I have."

Kyle looked at his friend questioningly. "Sure, what's it about?"

"I have an answer for our girl troubles. Or rather, our *lack-of-girl* troubles." Jaric smiled knowingly.

# CHAPTER FIVE

The two men approached the familiar manta-ray silhouette of the starship. The hull glowed with a purple sheen under the docking bay's harsh lights. Dozens of other starships stood in their own docking bays on either side, each starship's configuration different from the other—each an example of unique alien artisanship.

The two young men walked up the ramp and inside as the door slid silently open.

"Hello, boys. I hope your day has been one of enjoyment." Mother's voice greeted them with a feminine tone from the nearest speaker.

"It sure was. This is a very cool place," Kyle answered.

"We're hopeful their vast store of data will give us our first real lead on any human survivors," Jaric said with gladness in his voice.

"Yes, their massive store of data is indeed amazing. I hope I may be able to interface with it directly soon," Mother said.

"We asked about it when we left our Search-terminals today. The Mrad frown on it, afraid somebody might steal their data somehow. But, they said they'd at least consider it." Jaric looked up at one of Mother's optical sensors.

"Mother, I'm going to show Kyle some of my research. Please give us some privacy for a while. Okay?"

"I will disable my sensors in the main library."

Jaric and Kyle ran down the lighted corridors of Mother. Kyle could sense Jaric's excitement now and he found it wonderfully contagious.

They stopped amid the huge room that housed the main source of entertainment in the ship. A huge display screen for old-fashioned two-dimensional programs dominated the center of the great oval room. On all the surrounding walls, holo-projectors were positioned for interactive programming. Audio speakers dotted the room everywhere, ready to fill it with sound.

At one end, a stage rose above the main floor filled with various musical instruments—some of them the exotic instruments of the Kraaqi, Hrono and Mewiis.

Minstrel's alien instrument dominated them all. Numerous pipes curled outward in all directions from its circular body while countless buttons, dials and keys covered the rest of its surface.

It was here that everyone gathered to play music.

Normally, Minstrel was not physically present playing on-stage, for a Minstrel's true instrument was its entire ship. For those concerts, the music of Minstrel was transmitted to the library to blend with the instruments of everyone else. But at times, Minstrel played on-stage with the others using this miniature version of its musical starship.

"Okay, so what's this answer to our girl troubles?" Kyle asked sarcastically, not really believing his friend. "Must be something pretty fantastic, seeing our problem is that there aren't any girls left in the universe—except for you-know-who."

Jaric looked around the empty room with a conspiratorial smile. "And that's our answer."

Kyle looked at Jaric as if he'd lost his mind.

Jaric's smile grew wider.

"We could clone us some women!" Jaric shouted.

Kyle's face grew deadly serious as he shook his head sadly. A long silence settled between them.

"Have you completely flipped out, Jaric?"

"No! Think about it. Our problem is that our source of DNA is so small that we can't possibly clone enough different strains to recreate a human population." Jaric grabbed Kyle by the shoulders and held him fast. "But, I've determined that with some minor modifications we can create enough variety to clone a woman who wouldn't be..." Jaric's eyebrows bunched up questioningly.

"Our sisters," Kyle said for him, knowing the answer.

"Yes!" Jaric's voice erupted with excitement. "We could marry 'em!" A wolfish smile spread over his face. "And we can decide *just* what we want! Brunette, redhead or blonde. Short or tall. Dark complexion or light complexion. Think of it! Just like ordering out for the latest holovid!"

Kyle's eyes grew wide.

"I passed this by Jysar, of course—kind of theoretically." Jaric's face became serious. "Jysar thinks it best we not have children with them, if we do decide to do this." Again his face switched to excitement. "But they could be our companions, our wives! You see that Becky's clone is...well, er, almost like Becky."

"You mean our dear friend, Elise?" Kyle snorted sarcastically.

"Yes, she seems, er..." Jaric coughed nervously, trying to force the word. "*Human*," he finally sputtered.

"Quacks like a duck, walks like a duck." Kyle rolled his eyes.

Jaric smiled sheepishly. "Yes, she's human enough. I think."

Kyle became silent, an expression of intense concentration on his face. Long seconds passed as Kyle meditated about this alternative solution to their loneliness. His deep, slow breaths were the only sound audible in the room as he paced in circles while Jaric watched him intently.

"There are some ethical issues we need to consider," Kyle said with an air of wisdom.

"Wow," Jaric said, impressed. His mind whirled with thought. He had never anticipated Kyle answering like this. After all, the human race was only the two of them, and well, he was the usually the deep thinker of the two.

It seemed ethically fine to him if there was a way to clone a few more humans.

"Like what?" Jaric countered.

Kyle pursed his lips tight. "I mean, what if they turn out to be ugly? What do we do then?"

Jaric's mouth fell open in shock.

"Great galaxies, I hadn't thought of that!"

"See, we've got to think this thing through. We can't just go playing God here like it's a game. Creating another identical clone is one thing. But applying a few modifications here and there to get variety..." Kyle's voice trailed off as he nodded, pointing a finger at his temple for emphasis—to show his deep thoughts.

Jaric whistled.

The wisdom kept flowing from Kyle.

"And, what if she complained all the time? Or she was too short? Or too tall?"

Jaric's eyes widened.

"And worse. Think about this, man. What if she has the face of an angel, the body of a swimsuit model, but she's like...well, we can't stand her!" Kyle placed his hands on his hips. "I mean, what would we do then? Just drop them off at the next planet we landed at and try again?"

A pained look came over Jaric's face.

"And more important, remember why humanity outlawed cloning humans way back in the twenty-first century." Kyle's face became hard as rock with the dreadful memories from their childhood history lessons. "Remember the...*accidents*. Playing God is not without its consequences."

Jaric's eyes grew distant. "But the Hrono seem to have perfected cloning, right?"

"Cloning an exact copy."

Now Kyle's eyes became far off with a more recent memory of Jysar bringing the Hrono *present* to Mother. His eyes narrowed as he pursed his mouth, remembering it like it was yesterday.

"Remember when El..." Kyle stopped in mid-word, his expression going from reflection to anger and then to puzzlement. He shook his head. With a deep sigh, he continued. "Remember when Becky's clone first showed up? Remember how we felt? And those first three months after we left the Three Kingdoms?"

"How could I ever forget?" A look of somber reflection swept across his face. After a few moments, Jaric looked at his friend with a newfound respect.

"Man, you're deep, Big K!"

Kyle rubbed the sides of his head as if he were trying to ease a throbbing migraine headache. "When it has to do with creating life, or cloning life, one has to think it through. *Really* think it through."

Jaric walked over to a chair and fell down onto it with an air of resignation. He placed his head in his hands as he spoke. "I just feel so lonely sometimes—so terribly lonely, man. And I thought if we can't find any others, you know, any women survivors. And well..." His voice began to shake with emotion. For a long time Jaric sat frozen in his melancholy pose.

The silence stretched on to eternity.

"Even if technology can give us the answer we want, is it the right thing to do? Do we have the right? Do we know right from wrong in the first place?" Kyle's voice rose with indignation. His eyes narrowed as more sparks of wisdom came to life inside his speeding mind. "I mean, what if we clone these women and decide *we just don't like them!*

What do we do then? Just put 'em out with the trash and start over?"

The two men locked eyes, a stern look of sudden insight in each.

Jaric slowly stood up. "You're right, Big K. This is wrong. I'd only thought of the biological and scientific side of it." Jaric shook his head somberly. "And our selfish needs. I guess I'd better rethink this whole..."

"What are you two bozo-boys up to now?"

Jaric and Kyle turned suddenly, a surprised expression on their faces. Their surprise quickly changed to outright embarrassment as they realized who had just spoken as she entered the library.

*It was Elise.*

She looked from one to the other as she walked inside.

"Looks like I just caught you in the middle of some kind of conspiracy." She half-laughed. But her eyes were watchful as she waited for their reaction.

Elise knew how the boys felt about her.

"What are *you* doing here?" Kyle's tone was defensive and edged with anger.

Elise scowled at Kyle as she walked silently to the nearest chair and sat down at a display and keyboard. She began to browse for something on the console while the two young men continued to stare.

"It's a public place, right?" she said defensively. "And I have some research I need to do before dinner. After all, it is my first time playing in the band with you tonight." She almost smiled with that happy thought, but the empty looks on the boy's faces washed her smile away before it could be fully born.

The air grew tense between them.

But it always did.

Mother's optical sensor had come to life unnoticed by any of them as Elise first entered the library. Inside her circuits, Mother felt a surge in her processing cycles as she contemplated whether she should intervene. Yet, no easy solution presented itself as she scanned her knowledgebase a second time. Indeed, in the arena of human feelings and human relationships, there never seemed to be an easy answer.

And Mother doubted if there ever would be.

Mother's thoughts and memories flowed throughout her circuits, recalling the recent past with exact electronic clarity.

Those first three months after they left the Three Kingdoms were difficult for everyone.

Mother, Jysar and Krinia worked diligently with Becky's clone almost every minute of every day in those first months—teaching her, helping her.

The Hrono had created her to help ease Mother's dearest loss—the death of Becky in the final battle. The Hrono scientists also sped up the growth rate of the clone until it had reached the approximate age of Becky at her death—eighteen—before presenting her.

Mother accepted the clone instantly and whole-heartedly.

But not so the boys.

Mother was forced to keep the clone away from them as much as possible due to their angry reactions. Neither Jaric nor Kyle could stand to be in the same room with her, much less be civil to her.

All they saw in her was Becky. But the clone was not Becky, although physically she was her exact twin.

And this caused their anger to erupt each time they saw her.

Mother kept them separated those first months.

Jysar and Mother concentrated on teaching the newborn clone, giving her a basic education as a foundation on which they could build in order to bring her mental capacity equal to her physical age.

Her mind was like an empty sponge and the clone soaked up every bit of knowledge with eagerness, learning at an amazing pace. In fact, once she advanced past the very basics in math, science, history and literature, she begged Mother and Jysar to teach her faster, to double the sessions as the universe around her came alive with knowledge.

Krinia also helped. But her teaching was even more important, because she not only taught the clone academic knowledge, but what it meant to be a female—what it meant to be a young woman.

It was early in their first week together that Mother named her new daughter, after the clone had asked her the ultimate question.

*What is my name?*

Mother had pondered over this question from the first second that she saw her new daughter, stressing her CPU cycles at times while she ransacked her knowledgebase for the perfect name. A name she hoped her daughter would like. A name that was...special. But as the long searches throughout her knowledgebase continued day after day, it seemed that this seemingly simple task was nothing of the kind. In fact, it was a paradox.

A name—a designation. A title. An identifier.

*A rose by any other name would smell as sweet.*

Mother searched throughout the great literature inside her knowledgebase—poetry, prose and song—trying to pick a name that would be significant. A name beautiful and strong, a name that reflected heartfelt love and intelligence.

A name that would fit a beautiful young woman full of the promise of life.

A name with *meaning*.

Mother burned hours of long utilization analyzing an unnumbered myriad of names.

But in the end, she couldn't make a single decision based on her original query. And so she found the answer another way—a simpler way.

She named her daughter after her favorite music—a short piano work by Beethoven.

The piece was really just a joyous melody—so simple on the surface, and yet it glowed with a mysterious power. When that magical melody played there was a timelessness about it—and Mother played it time and time again. Indeed, it contained an internal energy that belied its flowing simplicity.

Music of power was a trademark of Beethoven's compositions. But 'Fur Elise' must have been something special for this legend of orchestral thunder. It contained the essence of something very personal, something cherished.

Something close to the heart.

Because of this music and its wonderful, enchanting melody, Mother grew fond of the name.

And so she named her new daughter—*Elise.*

Mother remembered again how Elise's mind had recently blossomed. She remembered with a stirring throughout her systems how Elise finally became cognizant of the universe around her— aware of its vastness and beauty, and of her own potential.

Elise realized that she now was a part of it all, a part of life.

Elise took her first bold steps to inner maturity with this new awareness.

After ten months of intense instruction and exclusive interaction with Krinia and Jysar, Mother consulted with them and it was agreed that for the sake of Mother's extended family, and for Elise's next steps emotionally, Elise needed more interaction with the others.

That included the aloof boys, Kyle and Jaric.

The boys purposely avoided her during that early time, always leaving when she entered a room they occupied. Elise had not fully understood their actions, but she sensed their rejection and it caused deep pain inside her heart.

She began to avoid the boys as well.

Although her mind soon functioned at the age of her physical body, inside her heart she remained a babe emotionally.

And the boys were not kind to her.

They resented her. They were harsh, even critical with her, during their infrequent encounters.

Mother assumed Jaric and Kyle did this because of the strong emotions they still felt over the loss of Becky, and now here was an identical person with the exception that inside her mind, and yes, inside her heart, she was a blank canvass waiting for an artist to place the first brush strokes of life.

*Yes, every time they saw Elise, her likeness must remind them of the person they once loved so dearly—now gone.*

How hard it must be for such creatures, their emotions filling them with grief and sadness, blinding them with love or hatred, joy or depression—warping their judgment and actions with a combination of them all.

Elise was a person.

But...she was not Becky.

Mother knew from the boys' words and actions, especially when they tried to whisper so her audio sensors could not pick it up—though she did hear—how much anger they felt toward Elise. Mother could not fully comprehend how they confused their sorrow for Becky, replacing it with anger for Elise so that it caused even more pain—especially for innocent Elise.

Mother watched carefully over Elise because of that as well as for another special reason—Mother realized Elise had come into this universe in much the same way as she—with the exception that Elise was human.

Mother came into existence in an instant—sentient, fully formed and powerful. And yet, she had not understood the first thing about what it meant to be alive—to be a living entity.

Elise was like that, except she did not even have the initial programming that guided Mother those first days and which she soon grew beyond.

Mother felt a special relationship with Elise.

Still, Jaric and Kyle were her sons too.

It was a balancing act, a very difficult balancing act.

Mother focused her sensors.

Only three seconds had passed as she reviewed these memories of Elise.

Jaric rose to speak.

"You know, a *real person* would've knocked or..." Jaric took a surprised step backward as Elise angrily jumped up from her chair.

Elise stood before him staring daggers. Her breathing grew rapid and ragged like that of person just completing a marathon race.

In that instant, it appeared Jaric realized what he had just said.

"So!" Elise's voice choked with her boiling emotions, and her voice failed as tears streamed down her face. She looked away from him, her lips trembling.

"Uh, wait a minute," Jaric looked away with embarrassment. He shook his head as he rubbed his face nervously with his right hand. "You know, I didn't mean to say it like that..."

"Yes, you did!"

Elise's voice turned to rage. She uttered those words like weapons. And now her blue eyes glared at Jaric without tears, but her soft cheeks still glistened with her heartache.

She took a deep breath, trying to regain control of herself. "Yes, you did. You said what you were thinking, *what you think—of me!*"

Jaric held his hands up defensively. "Wait..."

"No, you wait!" Elise walked closer to him as he eyed her carefully. She stared into his eyes. "You don't think I'm a real person. You never have. And neither have you!" She jabbed her finger at Kyle with the last sentence.

Kyle let out a sigh as he rolled his eyes.

"Just because I wasn't born, just because I'm a clone of Becky, you don't think I'm a *real* person." She stated this fact as if it were a spiritual revelation. Her mouth fell open as she looked from Jaric to Kyle, her eyes now wide with understanding.

"Well, I didn't mean..." Jaric began.

"You treat me like some kind of *unwanted* step-child!" Elise cried.

But Kyle and Jaric simply averted their eyes.

"Oh, I'm sure you didn't mean to say it in front of me. And Mother." Elise sobbed, new tears falling fresh. She wiped them away quickly, as if they had never been, although her heart was breaking once again—because of the boys.

Kyle and Jaric each lowered their heads a fraction in shame as they realized for the first time that Mother's sensors were active in the library.

"Oh man, I guess Mother's heard all of this." Jaric sighed.

"Unfortunately, I have," Mother said.

A pained looked covered Jaric's face, while Kyle shook his head slowly and sighed again.

"But that's it, isn't it, I'm just *the clone*," Elise uttered the last two words as if it were something loathsome. She paused, fighting the tears that threatened to fall again. Her breathing grew ragged for only a second, as with all her will, she focused her pain back into words. "You think *the clone* is not a real person. That I'm not real somehow."

The tension in the air grew electric with raw emotion as Elise looked from Jaric to Kyle, daring them to speak.

"But if you strike me, I cry. If you cut me, I bleed! Just like you!"

Jaric's eyes narrowed as Kyle held his breath.

"And if you kill me, I die!" Elise clenched her eyes shut, still fighting her tears. But she couldn't prevent a single, mournful sob. She continued, her voice now full of sadness. "But maybe that's what you really want, you'd rather I was dead than here bothering you with my presence!"

75

"Wait a minute, aren't you going a bit far..."

But Elise did not let Jaric finish. "Think about how you've treated me ever since you first laid eyes on me! How you've avoided me, resented me, talked behind my back. Don't you think that's hurt me?" Elise took a deep breath. And then she put her pain into words.

"You know, sometimes I wish I was dead."

Expressions of regret and guilt clouded Kyle and Jaric's faces.

"Yes, I know. Everybody wishes Becky were still alive. Everybody wants Becky back. And you know..." The tears returned, streaming like rain down her cheeks. She began to sob now, no longer caring if the boys saw how badly she hurt.

"You kno-o-ow," she sobbed. "I wish Becky was alive too," she cried. "And I wish that I was dead instead of her. Everybody would be much happier then. And *the clone* would be gone forever!"

Jaric and Kyle stared at Elise dumb-founded.

With a rush, Elise ran out of the room, her painful sobs cutting the air like blaster fire.

Jaric sat down and placed his head into his hands, rubbing his temples as if he were suffering from an intense migraine.

Kyle stared at the closed door, speechless, still shaking his head.

"I guess...I guess she might be right," Jaric whispered.

"It's not her fault Becky died," Kyle agreed.

"Elise is a unique person, even though she looks identical because she is a clone," Mother added, unable to watch in silence any longer.

Jaric stood and walked to door. He stopped suddenly and turned back to Kyle, glancing momentarily at Mother's optic sensor. "I'm going to try to treat Elise...differently from now on." Jaric sighed. "I'm going to try to treat her like a...a person." A pained looked came across his face with the memory of Elise running from the room. Looking down, he fidgeted nervously with his hands while a thick silence filled the room.

"Like a *real* person," Jaric whispered.

Kyle nodded silent agreement.

"It'll still be hard. Every time I look at her, I see Becky. But I've got to stop thinking that way." Jaric looked directly at Mother. "I'll try."

He spoke from the doorway. "I have to think about this some more. It's hard for me, too. Tell the Fixers I'll have dinner by myself in my room." The door slid silently shut.

Kyle rose.

"Do you agree with Jaric, Kyle?" Mother asked.

Kyle rubbed his eyes tiredly. "When I saw her tears, and thought about Jaric's slip-of-the-tongue, well..." Kyle sighed deeply. "I thought back to Earth, early twenty-first century. Back to those first, foolish attempts at cloning humans—the *accidents*." He emphasized the last word with hidden meaning, and with sadness.

"It was terrible," Mother agreed.

"So much pain, for so many." Kyle's eyes became moist. "I guess the awful connotation associated with that word—clone—well, that poisoned both of our reactions right off toward Elise. And then every time I looked at her, I only saw Becky."

He stood with sudden energy. "I want to be alone too. I guess all three of us do, right now. We'll have to postpone the 'Music Evening' this week."

"And Elise practiced so hard," Mother said.

But Kyle did not acknowledge her words. Instead, he made his way to his room, to be alone with his pain like the other two.

Mother's optic sensor watched him leave impassively.

The next two hours went by in quiet solitude. Mother focused her processing on necessary housekeeping tasks, especially her memory systems. She utilized an algorithm she designed herself in order to keep it at optimum efficiency.

A sudden shimmering in the air caught her attention.

"I am glad you are back, Minstrel. And I'm glad you've changed back to your natural, plasma body. Did you enjoy the 'Happy Dancing'?"

"Yes. It's always fun discovering new music—especially music we classify as Escastre or Special Music."

"What is that?"

"Music that is on another level—music that floats in your mind all day after you've listened to

78

it. And as you listen, you *feel* its power, its emotions."

"Yes, I know what you mean. I've played the entire Mozart catalogue today," Mother said.

"That's a lot of Mozart."

"You can never have too much Mozart," Mother said, her tone matter-of-fact.

Minstrel glowed and swirled with agreement.

"It is fascinating though, that some of his music—certain of his melodies—echo through my memory systems over and over for hours afterward. Such music is different in a mysterious way, while other music by Mozart is simply pleasant and melodious—just music."

"Escastre. Somehow the composer, like Mozart, infuses the notes with passion and pathos and it lives. That is music on another level." Minstrel twinkled, remembering the first reports of Mozart's music by another Minstrel visiting Earth during his lifetime long ago.

"It is music that moves the inner emotions of biological life-forms. Although I too can somehow sense it is on another level," Mother said.

A wave of blue and black flashed throughout Minstrel. "Have I missed something tonight? I passed Kyle in the corridor just now, and he was the opposite of what I experienced at the Blue Star—which was happy."

"I will fill you in later. Let me say there was a very emotional, a very *human,* encounter between the boys and Elise tonight."

Minstrel's body twinkled with a thousand lights. "Well, we did want them to interact with each other."

"Yes, we did," Mother said. "But another emotional issue is bothering the boys. They are once again too preoccupied with searching for human survivors. Every time we visit a new planet, that is the only thing that interests them. They don't enjoy meeting new aliens. Nor do they want to explore these new worlds and experience the beauty and uniqueness of each. They are missing out."

"Indeed, how many beings yearn to travel to the stars and never get the chance," Minstrel said with a wave of color. "And here the boys have traveled to scores of worlds and met dozens of interesting alien beings. Yet, they don't take advantage of this wonderful privilege because they are so preoccupied."

"How could we get them to focus on traveling to another world and simply enjoying it?" Mother wondered.

Minstrel's plasma body glowed and swirled like a multi-colored whirlpool.

*"Life is a journey, not a race."*

"And the boys live as if it is a race, with the only goal to find other survivors," Mother said.

"They need to enjoy life more," Minstrel said.

"And they can still keep their utmost objective. But if they appreciated the beauty, the wonder of life around them..."

"Did humans have a process for such activity in their past—to simply enjoy themselves?" Minstrel asked.

Mother referenced her vast knowledgebase. "There is a process entitled *vacation*."

"Perhaps they need a vacation then?" Minstrel said.

"I must research this term," Mother said.

"All beings need time to rest and refresh themselves—a time of renewal. A time to simply enjoy themselves and life." Minstrel glowed brighter. The plasma alien danced in the air, waiting for Mother to complete her search.

Ten seconds passed in mutual silence.

"I have studied over one million references to the term vacation—a most interesting concept," Mother said, breaking their short reverie.

"Please explain, how do humans...vacation?"

"In most instances, humans travel to distant locations far from their normal residence—traveling to cities or areas of great, natural beauty. Food, dance, music and associating with new friends seem to be common themes." Mother's processors hummed as she correlated and cross-referenced more data about humans and their vacations.

"Well, that's easy enough to do with a starship. And vacation sounds like a good thing, if music and food is involved." Waves of silver and green swept Minstrel's plasma surface.

"Two intra-planetary locations seem to be the most popular destinations—either traveling to the mountains for recreation and relaxation, or going to a tropical climate and enjoying sea-side activities. The latter seems to be slightly preferred from all the sources I have checked so far."

"We must find a planet that will fit the needs of a perfect human vacation. Perhaps one with beautiful mountain ranges—I've visited some worlds where the mountains are fifty kilometers tall. And I've traveled to worlds with exquisite oceans of various colors—sometimes seas of gold, or orange or royal blue. Although the most beautiful ocean I've had the pleasure of swimming in was the deepest, darkest green. And the wonderful beaches bordering their shores—fabulous! Surely we can find a planet perfect for *vacation*," Minstrel chimed.

"Another reason for choosing a particular location for a human vacation seems to hinge on the term *festival*." Mother paused as she digested more data on this new subject. "There are various themes to festivals—the most popular festivals are based on music and tradition and drink. It seems festival and vacations are almost synonymous."

"I understand why a festival based on music would be so enjoyable. I can imagine all the various flavors of music coming together in one place in order to celebrate life with song. Minstrels have such momentous events once every thousand years—we call it Caldara. All Minstrels come together from the far reaches of space, bringing with us the songs we've discovered or created from our distant travels. It is a very special time for Minstrels. And a lot of fun!"

"But how many could you attend—a thousand years is a long time between each Caldara."

"Minstrels suffer from no natural disease. It is only due to accident or violence that a Minstrel's life is cut short. Otherwise, we live on indefinitely."

"And how long is the normal life-span of a Minstrel?"

"I have attended twenty-four such Festivals of Minstrels." Wave after wave of twinkling lights swept Minstrels fluidic body. "And I am nowhere near what is considered the middle epoch of a normal Minstrel life-span."

Mother whistled, a long, electronic sound that slowly faded away. "That's a long time. You risked much by fighting alongside us against the T'kaan, with such a potentially long life ahead of you. You might have died."

"Indeed. But I evaluated the risk as worth it—for your sake, and the children. And for the universe to be safe from T'kaan."

"You honor me, and my children. We will always value your friendship. I will now cross-reference the human definition of the ideal vacation and search for a planet upon which the children can experience it."

"A delightful concept."

"I only hope the children will embrace the concept of vacation and forget about searching for other humans for a while. I wonder if a vacation will be enough," Mother lamented.

"Remember how insistent Kyle was that the Kraaqi frigate go check out the planet Oord that serves as a trading center in the adjoining Sector, leaving only Rok to travel with us here?" Minstrel added, "I think the last few disappointments have really affected them."

"I agree. But I do not want to divert them completely away from searching for any survivors, as remote a possibility as that hope may be. It is their greatest dream—to find other human survivors. And I do not want to damage something so dear to them."

Minstrel's body glowed brightly, as if it might go nova. Minstrel spoke, its words echoing as if in a great, solemn hall.

*"O, but dreams die so hard. And well they should."*

"But when dreams fail, or never come true, it seems to humans that it is the end of their existence." Mother paused, reflecting on that subject as she quickly referenced the knowledgebase where she reviewed the failed dreams of so many. Her checks found another list. "But if their dreams come to fruition, then it is their greatest happiness."

"Well, being here may bring that to a climax. Even Minstrels travel, albeit incognito, to RahajMr to tap into its massive search engine, seeking out new worlds to visit. If there is mention of human survivors from anywhere in this section of the universe, and the Mrad are reputed to be able to gather data from all of the Known Quadrants, it will be here. The vastness of their knowledge is unheard of except for Minstrels themselves in our travels.

84

This place could well be where Jaric's and Kyle's search will find success."

"Or their final failure." Mother's voice faded ominously.

"There is another reason for our visit here," Minstrel added quickly.

"Yes?"

"Because RahajMr is a focal point to which so many far-flung races travel to for data, it is the ideal place for Jaric and Kyle to meet aliens solely for the sake of friendly interchange. And enjoyment. In fact, RahajMr is the social entertainment center for this quadrant. Tourism is the second most important reason aliens travel here."

"Well, I hope they indulge and have some fun. They need to," Mother said.

"I too, have a personal reason for coming here." Minstrel's body undulated like a cloud as different colors shimmered across its body with emotion. "A reason associated with you."

"Please elaborate."

"Ever since I met you, Mother, I have marveled that a race was able to create technology that is sentient, alive. No other Minstrel has ever come across such a life-form as yourself, not in all the ages of our traveling the known universe."

Mother's processors hummed with activity, remembering how the Minstrel race traveled to the ends of the universe.

"But one Minstrel did report a rumor of such a thing—recently." Minstrel's body sparkled as a bright red wave swept over and over its tenuous surface. "A few months ago, in a search on this very system we used today. That Minstrel reported a reference, a single item, about a living computer system created on a nearby world."

"I am intrigued," Mother said.

But now the flowing colors turned to deeper hues of blue and black across Minstrel as the twinkling lights faded. "I feel awkward."

Mother processed this word. "Please explain. I would think the search would not elicit this emotion at all."

"The initial search results were negative. I found nothing—almost as if it were never there. And my search received other answers that were very surprising. And I mean, *very* surprising."

Mother's processors hummed as she tried to predict the answer Minstrel received and that seemed to bother it so much. Although thousands of possible answers presented themselves, Mother could not locate a single one with a high probability of being correct.

"With what initial answers did your search respond?" Mother finally asked.

"My search revealed that there are actually laws forbidding such research among most alien races in this quadrant—laws forbidding artificial intelligence and even its research." Minstrel paused, a sense of foreboding in its tone now. "In fact, the punishment on some worlds for this type of research is *death*."

"That is incredible." Mother's voice rose several decibels.

Minstrel spoke, its voice filled with mystery.

"I wonder why these worlds have outlawed this kind of research?"

# CHAPTER SIX

Back at one of the numerous Mrad Search Complexes, Ablek started to shut down the last console. The little black and white Clakza smiled to himself, reflecting that another profitable day was once again successfully concluded. Walking slowly to his desk, he again checked the daily tally of usage—over one hundred thousand requests for data from his complex alone.

The other workers had already gone home, their own tasks completed. As Section Coordinator, Ablek alone was responsible for final shutdown of all terminals for the night. He went about his task with a sense of deep satisfaction.

He sat before the large console and began issuing the end-of-day commands, never noticing that the security cameras had gone silent— purposely inactivated.

But no alarms sounded to alert Ablek about the security breach.

Neither did he notice through the semi-darkness the three forms creeping steadily closer.

Ablek concentrated tiredly, ready to finish and go home. As he sat at this particular console, he noticed a faint odor in the air—something not altogether pleasant either.

The diminutive alien wrinkled his nose with distaste. He remembered—those smelly aliens who called themselves "humans" had used this console.

Without warning, a heavy blow slammed Ablek up against the wall from behind. The small alien groaned with pain as he struggled, but an iron grip held him down.

Ablek froze, waiting for the robbery he knew must come next. If he didn't struggle, maybe they'd just take the credits and leave.

Ablek waited.

Surprisingly, a calm voice whispered into his ear.

"Two new aliens came here today to buy some searches. They came with a Zuuk, and two other aliens never seen here before. A green, scaly one called a Hrono. And a horned alien, a Kraaqi. You remember them?" The unseen voice now whispered harshly into Ablek's ear, causing him to cringe and moan.

Ablek took a deep breath, forcing himself to sound unafraid.

"Ye-ah, sure. Whut of it?"

The fist slammed into his side like an iron bar. Ablek grunted with pain as tears streamed out of his black eyes.

"The two others, the humans, did they say which quadrant they're from? Their registration papers reference an unknown planet—Earth." The unseen attacker whispered angrily. "Did they say anything to you while you were setting them up?"

"They didn't sa-ay, and I didn't want to hear it anyway..." Ablek groaned painfully as another fierce blow shook his body.

The vicious blows did not stop this time.

Fists pounded him from all sides as the little alien cried out with fear, begging for mercy. Ablek raised his small hands in a vain attempt to ward off their blows, but it was no use.

After long seconds, the blows stopped and Ablek fell to the floor unconscious.

Two of the attackers watched his unmoving form while a third walked over and accessed the last terminal still logged onto the system.

The stout Harg typed commands, going through the search history. A low laugh rumbled from his broad chest. He smiled wickedly and worked the controls faster. A minute later, he returned the terminal to its original screen.

"I've ID'ed their starship and dock number. The Zuuk, all of them, came here on it. But nothing on their sector of origin," he whispered in a rough voice to his two accomplices.

Ablek's eyes fluttered open, although he didn't comprehend the words. He felt terrible—every inch of his body throbbed with pain.

He lay still as the footsteps of his attackers retreated, and just as they slipped through the door, he took a cautious glance towards them.

They were short, muscular aliens with thick bull-necks. A memory clicked in his mind—Harg, aliens from a secretive and violent order.

And not the kind of alien you wanted to cross.

Ablek groaned as his body ached with renewed waves of pain.

There was something else about Hargs. Yes, they came from the mysterious Paum Sector—the *Forbidden Place*.

He shivered in the semi-darkness.

Nothing good ever seemed to come out of there, and the few who ventured there rarely came back. If they did, they were changed somehow—*different*. No one who had dealings with the aliens of Paum spoke of it except with the darkest of curses.

And they never wanted to deal with them again.

In fact, less data was stored about the Paum system than even the most distant planets of the known sectors—a strange thing indeed.

"Looks like these huumans are in fer some trouble," Ablek grunted as he rose. "And I don't want any part of it either."

Ablek struggled to the Security console, falling into the seat. He began checking why no security personnel were alerted or came to his rescue. The answer was most disturbing—somehow the Harg isolated the security cameras from main Security, all the while simulating normal signals. These aliens knew what they were doing—effectively circumventing the vaunted security of the Mrad.

Not good.

Ablek paused in thought, wondering if he should report the incident. But his body ached with renewed pain, and nothing of value had been damaged or taken. In the end, he decided to finish his shift and not report it. He desired no more dealings with these dangerous aliens.

He limped over to the last Search Console and paused a moment as waves of intense nausea overwhelmed him. Ablek bent over, trying to clear his mind. Finally, he logged off the last terminal, never realizing the Harg had infiltrated the User Information.

Dinner was late and very subdued that night.

Not only did Elise not show up, but neither Jaric nor Kyle showed as well. The others sensed something amiss as well, though they could not put their finger on it. Even Rok was not his normal self. Everyone ate in silence and quickly retired to their private cabins.

Mother watched all the occupants retreat to the privacy of their rooms and once again contemplated life and loneliness—something she knew all too well. It was a long night for everyone.

The next day began like most others.

"Rok, why don't you and I and Kyle take the Bullet-Cars back to the main Search terminals. We can check on the results and go from there." Jaric motioned for the Kraaqi warrior to join him and Kyle at the ramp.

At that very moment, Elise, Krinia and Jysar entered the corridor. Elise watched impassively as the three turned to leave. Her eyes still reflected the pain from last night, but they reflected something else there too—a hardness, a determination.

"I want to help, too."

The trio froze in their tracks.

Jaric and Kyle exchanged uneasy glances before they turned around and faced Elise.

Inside his mind, Jaric's thoughts and emotions shouted at him, urging him to apologize for his words and actions of last night. But he wrestled with his inner feelings of shame and embarrassment, sensing not only Elise's guarded looks, but also feeling the weight of the presence of the others around him.

He wanted to apologize to her, but not in front of everyone—then he would have to explain his apology and his stupidity to everyone. Jaric couldn't bring himself to make eye contact with Elise as his mind whirled with confusion and embarrassment.

He felt terrible because of the way he acted to Elise last night.

And now Elise wanted to help.

Jaric looked over at Kyle, whose expression remained set like granite and emotionless. But Jaric could tell by Kyle's eyes—eyes that looked everywhere but not at Elise, eyes that revealed just a glimmer of sadness. Yes, Kyle also felt the pangs of his conscience.

The silence stretched on with no one acknowledging Elise's desire to walk for the first time outside Mother's hull as well as her wish to help Jaric and Kyle.

Mother watched intently, sensing the rising body temperatures and the dilated pupils which indicated high emotions ready to explode. Her processors hummed with activity.

Elise had yet to leave the protective confines of her hull. At all the other planets they had visited, she stayed behind to observe via Mother's sensors. Jysar and Krinia advised Mother that Elise needed to learn how to interact with others, something normally learned during childhood and adolescence—years of growth she hadn't experienced being a clone.

Because of her naiveté, unscrupulous aliens might take advantage of her, especially if she got separated from the others. After all, they lived in a dangerous universe.

But every child eventually grows beyond the apron strings of their mother.

"RahajMr is a very crowded place, Elise. And there are thousands of different races here, each with a different emotional makeup. It is a very difficult place for one so young as you are," Mother advised with a soothing, electronic tone. "Why don't you view the city from—"

"No! I want to help Jaric and Kyle search for human survivors. I'm a human too." Elise's eyes narrowed in challenge, not only at Mother's nearest optic, but also toward Jaric and Kyle.

Jaric sighed wistfully. He nodded momentarily, then realized Mother was correct. It might be too much trouble to baby-sit her in this maze of steel and countless aliens.

"Mother's right, there are some pretty rough aliens here. And when they're all bunched up together like this, it might get a bit, well, dicey." Jaric grinned knowingly at Rok and Kyle.

"Yeah, you need to know how to handle yourself. But I think you'll be ready soon," Kyle said, trying to be helpful.

But Elise heard the patronizing tone in their voices—including Mother's.

"Your fear and worry are a prison to me. I can handle myself just fine," she said firmly.

Jysar grabbed her by the arm and held her still. "They are right, Elise. There are so many unknown scenarios and so many aliens with short fuses. We must pick a better planet for you to walk upon for the first time."

Elise's face expressed shock at her close friend. "So, you think I'm still a child, too." She shook her head firmly. "And I would've thought you of all of them would know what I'm capable of."

"It's not that," Jysar said quickly, a hurt expression on his face. "I'm thinking of you personally."

Elise snatched her arm out of his grip and marched back toward her room without a second glance.

Jysar looked helplessly around the room until he met Krinia's harsh gaze.

"You're all wrong. She has to go out into the world one day, and today's as good a day as any." Krinia whipped her head-tail a few times to emphasize her anger. Her smooth green complexion deepened with emotion as she turned and quickly marched after the retreating form of Elise.

Jysar took a deep breath and walked silently back to his quarters.

"I will talk to her," Mother said. "But I want you boys to realize that soon she will join with you in your search. If not today, soon."

Jaric wrinkled his nose in thought while Kyle stared into space.

"Sure," Kyle said unexpectedly.

Jaric's eyes widened with surprise. "Sure?"

Kyle looked at him as a teacher does his student. "Of course, she's human too." Kyle looked up at Mother. "But when the time is right."

"I agree," Mother said. "I will work with Elise in order for that time to come soon."

"Let's go, the morning wastes away and we have not yet begun our journey." Rok motioned with his arm toward the ramp.

"Be careful," Mother said after them.

"Oh, we will. There's not an alien here we can't handle, right, fellas?" Kyle laughed.

"Not a one. I'd bet that we three are more than a match for anyone we're likely to run across," Jaric said with a twinkle in his eyes.

Rok grunted ominously. "Just let anyone dare to cross us, it'll be a day they'll rue for a very long time!" He laughed heartily as the others joined in his mirth. The three walked away as one, ready to take on the universe.

"Well, I hope our young warriors are half as good as their talk!" Minstrel's flowing body swirled into the corridor.

"I am glad the authorities here on RahajMr do not allow weapons to be carried by anyone entering their floating cities," Mother said.

"A very prudent law," Minstrel agreed.

"But, three overconfident young males can still get themselves into a lot of trouble without realizing it."

"Imagine that!" Minstrel laughed.

Mother's processors focused on her other child. "I must talk with Elise, she is very upset." Mother paused, more to allow Minstrel to follow her train of thought than her own need.

"I understand. I am planning on entering the city today totally incognito—with my dampening field active around my natural body. I want to observe some new species and learn of them while unseen." Minstrel's twinkling body flashed out like a light simply switched off.

Mother waited a few moments before she closed her hull door. Even the most sophisticated Mradian sensor would not detect Minstrel now.

Krinia entered Elise's room as Mother watched silently.

The Mewiis sighed deeply, a compassionate expression on her green face as her head-tail grew limp. She sat down beside the sobbing form, then ever so carefully she began to caress Elise's shoulders.

"There, there, my young friend. No need for tears."

Elise looked up and wiped the wetness from her cheeks. "I—I'm just tired of being treated like a baby. And a non-person." Her breathing grew ragged, but as she looked into her friend's face, she began to breathe more normally. And most important, she felt comfort simply from Krinia's presence.

"I know, it must be very hard for you. But look how far you've come these past months. Look how much you've learned," Krinia said soothingly. And then her face changed to surprise. "And why is it you want to help Jaric and Kyle all of a sudden anyway, the way they've treated you!"

"I want them to like me."

Elise's voice trembled with emotion, her eyes a mirror of forlorn sadness. She looked away quickly, wiping her eyes again. When she spoke, she kept her face hidden. "Didn't you see how Jaric and even Kyle looked at me just now—like they were uncomfortable with me just being there?" She sniffed loudly. "I just want them to like me...and...and I thought if I offered to help them with their precious search, well..."

"Elise, it's not all you. A lot of this is their problem. Theirs, not yours." Krinia began softly stroking Elise's long blonde hair. "And they will learn to like you. They will."

Krinia smiled as Elise turned to her.

Elise smiled shyly back at her.

"But there must be more?" Krinia asked.

"Yes! I want to meet other aliens now. The only life-forms I've ever been around much are you and Jysar. And Mother." Elise paused, a puzzled look on her face. "And Rok. And Jaric and Kyle, if I can count them, although they've mostly avoided me."

"And maybe that's a good thing." Krinia smiled, merriment in her eyes.

Elise laughed for a moment, then put her arms around her friend. "That may well be, Krinia."

They laughed at their shared joke. But Elise looked away again, a serious expression on her face.

"But you still want to meet new aliens," Krinia said, guessing her thoughts.

"Why can't I?" Elise looked at her with urgency. "You could keep an eye on me, keep me out of trouble. I know, I know," she said quickly as Krinia opened her mouth to speak. "I may not have learned the basic skills of protocol or know how this race greets each other or how that race says good-bye, but how does anybody else learn those things if they don't go out into the universe?" Elise's eyes burned with her need to take the next step in her life. "I need to meet new life-forms, if I'm going to develop social skills. I can't learn that from lessons and holovids."

"But Elise, there is so much you don't know—cultural and social protocols—or how to beware of aliens with evil intentions. You could be taken advantage of so easily," Mother reasoned, breaking into their conversation.

"*Mother*," Elise groaned. "I know enough not to get mugged or raped or something like that!"

"But what about other subtle ways you could be taken in?" Mother asked.

"MotherShip," Krinia said confidently. "I think I could watch out for her long enough to mingle and perhaps take in a part of this city. We could go out for a couple of hours and come straight back. And she would see others up close and personal for the first time, and somewhat safely, in these constant crowds of RahajMr."

"Oh please, Mother," Elise pleaded. "We'll be safe, I promise. I won't even talk to anybody, I'll just watch them as they pass by!"

Mother observed the earnestness in Elise's eyes and heard it in her voice. She realized that maybe she had been wrong earlier.

"Krinia," Mother said.

"Yes."

Both women looked up at the optic.

"I am contacting Jysar. He has not left yet. Perhaps if you and he escorted Elise, and especially if you both aided her in any personal encounters with other beings she might run into, then it would be safe enough for her to investigate the city."

Elise laughed with glee as Krinia hugged her.

"Where shall we go?" Elise suddenly asked.

Krinia smiled. "You want to help them search, you said earlier. Let's go to the Search-Terminals first, maybe you'll be able to help them. After that, we'll go to one of the main shopping levels, do some window shopping and observe the other shoppers too."

"Great!" Elise gasped. "And I've thought of something the boys have never tried, something obvious if an alien race receives only an audio transmission from any human survivors."

"Cool." Krinia smiled. "And what is your brain-storm, my young detective?"

Elise brushed her blonde tresses back from where they had fallen across her face. She smiled cunningly, her blue eyes twinkling with conspiracy. "Well, with audio-only contact, especially a remote automated beacon, any alien ship picking it up but never making contact would file the transmission and upload it to their master system to be analyzed at a later time. Any transcription would be translated into their native language...well, how would they know how to spell some of the proper names!"

Krinia's eyes lit up with excitement. "You're right, their translation computers would only be able to approximate some of the proper names without a human dictionary to compare with."

Elise nodded. "And so, I will not simply search for 'human' or 'Earth' or whatever. I will input some common misspellings an alien race might use like..." Elise leaned closer, as if somebody might be eavesdropping on her fantastic idea. She sounded each letter in a low whisper. "The word human might be found as h-u-m-u-n. Or misspelled as h-o-o-m-u-n or something like that."

"Or they might list Earth as U-r-t-h, or something even more bizarre, depending on the alphabet of the aliens that intercepted the transmission," Krinia whispered, getting the idea.

101

Elise sighed. "And this is the first really comprehensive computer system that's been searched since we left the Three Kingdoms. The boys have normally only interrogated systems of a single planet or individual starships. So, we will stress some obvious misspellings when the system asks for our keywords, in addition to their correct spelling."

"It's so simple, yet your search might just make a hit on something," Krinia said with a smile. "It's worth a try."

"After that, maybe we'll find one of the Social or Entertainment sections so we can mingle a bit," Elise said excitedly.

"Sure, we can find something fun. And safe." Krinia laughed.

Elise hugged her friend and jumped off of the bed. "Let's give the boys time to get the results of their search first and then find Jysar and get going! I don't want them to know."

"Come on universe, throw your worst at me!"

Kyle laughed, a dangerous glint in his eyes, as the trio exited the Bullet-Car.

"Wow! What a ride," Jaric exclaimed. "I'm still dizzy from those last three turns."

"What a concept—mass transportation and a super roller-coaster combined—powered by anti-gravity thrusters to get you around—smooth and fast." Kyle nodded approvingly.

Rok smiled. "Good stuff."

"Okay, okay. Let's get back to business. There's the Search Complex over there." Jaric pointed.

The three young warriors walked toward the counter and displayed their pre-paid tokens to the nearest Clakza. Kyle looked around at the other Clakzas, searching for a familiar black and white snout.

"Where's Ablek today?" Kyle asked a female Clakza.

She scanned his token and handed it back. "He called in sick today. Are you friends of his?"

"Not really. He served us yesterday, just wanted to see a familiar face in these crowds," Kyle replied.

"You have Search-terminal Alpha twenty-seven over there. Same as before." She nodded.

Rok, Jaric and Kyle were making their way over when she spoke again.

"Actually, it's kind of strange. Ablek calling in sick like that."

"Why's that?" Kyle turned.

"Well, he's been working this complex over three years and this is the first time he's ever missed a day due to illness. Or due to anything, other than scheduled time off."

"Guess there's a first time for everything," Kyle said.

The Clakza nodded. "I guess so."

The three sat down and brought up the main screen. Jaric quickly found their original search paradigms and glanced at the RESULTS column.

His heart raced like it always did when they searched for humans, and like every other time, he tried his best to hold his hopes and his emotions in check. After all, it always seemed to end in disappointment.

Why should this time be any different?

The RESULTS came up.

Jaric and Kyle gasped simultaneously.

Rok leaned closer. "Hmmm. Looks like the system found something."

Jaric remained motionless—in complete shock.

Kyle stared at the screen, afraid to believe his eyes. And afraid that if he reached out to follow the link it would all disappear. It happened like that in his dreams, when he dreamed of really finding more humans—it always disappeared like a puff of smoke, always just out of reach.

Deep inside, Kyle groaned with fear.

"What are you waiting for?" Rok asked with surprise.

"I...I don't know what to do." Jaric shook his head.

"Easy." Rok pressed the highlighted link and the screen changed.

Jaric and Kyle closed their eyes.

"Hmmm. It found a match for the word *T'kaan*."

Kyle and Jaric opened their eyes and hungrily read the words on the screen.

"A match!" Both Kyle and Jaric eagerly read the initial paragraph. "The next floating city over has a large population of displaced aliens. Let's see, populations displaced due to planetary disasters, wars, disease...and..." Jaric read quickly, his eyes darting over the word and then back over them to make sure he hadn't missed anything important. "There it is, a small group of survivors who recently arrived—they've given themselves a new name, Ialliaz in the Mrad tongue—and Survivors in most other languages. It doesn't list their homeworld, or what they call their race!"

"But it says they're the small remnant of a once proud people destroyed by an evil alien race called T'kaan!" Kyle shouted excitedly.

"They say there are no other survivors except themselves," Rok read out loud. "The name of the original species is now sacred to them and is only uttered during a special ceremony of remembrance once a year."

"Well, I can see that," Jaric said.

"Does it have any photos or descriptions?" Kyle asked.

"Let's see. No, no pictures. Not yet. This data seems to be some kind of initial registration form, pretty brief and to the point." Jaric gave the Search-terminal more vocal instructions and waited. "Okay, there is a description, looks like it's done by whoever registered them." His eyes darted over the words on the screen. "It says—the Ialliaz are aliens approximately two meters tall, bi-pedal with matching set of major organs. They have smooth skin with pockets of hair..." Jaric stopped short, his eyes wide as saucers as he skipped to the next sentence. "They have a heavy, musky scent not unlike that of animals!"

Rok leaned closer. "Yes, and there is a note."

Kyle ran his finger to the bottom until he got to the note. "It says pungent! It says pungent!"

Jaric yelled with glee.

"Sounds like they could be smelly hoo-mans." Rok nodded.

Kyle and Jaric began jumping up and down as other aliens stared at them in wonder.

"What's going on there?" a Clakza attendant called out.

"We've found something!" They yelled simultaneously. "On our search! We found something!"

The Clakza turned to another of its kind. "Satisfaction is our motto."

Kyle laughed. "You bet! And we're satisfied!"

"C'mon, let's go book one of those city-to-city Bullet-Cars." Jaric ran toward the exit, followed by Rok and Kyle.

Fifteen minutes later they waited at another counter with another Clakza looking tiredly back at their beaming faces. "Can I help you?"

"The city Rxariar, where the dispossessed aliens reside," Jaric said with rapid-fire words.

"Yes, I know of it." The Clakza shuddered. "Down-trodden kind of place, if you know what I mean. We maintain it in order to get a huge tax break from Sector HQ, or so it's said. But if you ask me, it's not worth it."

"I thought it was noble, having such a place for poor aliens who've lost their worlds?" Jaric felt taken aback by the Clakza's attitude.

"Oh well, it's good for business. But having them all there together, a lot of them with post-traumatic conditions of one kind or another. And some still recovering from, you know, from whatever. It's, well...tricky." He raised both his arms as he shook his head.

"Well, we want to book a ride over there to check out some of them. Some may be our people." Kyle slapped some credits on the counter.

"Sure, sure. *Your* people." He wrinkled his nose as he shook his head. "I hope you don't mind some friendly advice."

Rok eyed the Clakza warily. "What advice?"

"Those are some real stressed-out aliens over there. Just be very careful around them. Don't get them excited."

The three took their tokens and walked toward the huge walls filled with tunnel openings where numerous sleek Bullet-Cars sat at the ready.

"What did he mean by that?" Kyle asked.

"No telling," Jaric replied.

They approached the Bullet-Car assigned to them.

These Bullet-Cars were twice the size of their inner-city cousins—built to ride the buffeting winds of the gas giant as they shot toward the next floating city coded on their pre-programmed guidance system. The trio stepped inside the opened door on their car's right side and quickly took their seats.

The reinforced gull-wing door slowly dropped into place.

Inside the bullet-shaped vessel, they quickly took in the controls. A familiar, pre-recorded Clakza voice began going over the safety instructions as they looked at the glowing displays on the main console. But there wouldn't be anything more for them to do here than in the smaller Bullet-Cars that traversed the vast network of tubes that laced the interior of each floating city.

The voice suddenly turned serious.

"In the event of an emergency, if the automated systems fail while in-flight, there is a manual navigation system which can be accessed by..."

Three pairs of eyes and ears watched and listened intently.

The automated voice instructed them on how to fly the Bullet-car—just in case. However, if any riders ever accessed this manual system outside of an emergency situation, the violators would be expelled from all the floating cities.

Immediately.

"Do not engage manual navigation—unless there is an emergency."

Silence echoed inside the small interior of the Bullet-car.

"Well, you think we should fly this Bullet-Car on our own?" Kyle laughed mischievously.

"Not unless you want us kicked off of this place," Jaric shot back.

"Oh well," Kyle said in mock disappointment. "Guess I'll just kick back and enjoy the ride."

"Restraint systems will now engage," the automated voice chimed.

"Yeah, yeah. We've ridden these things before. Let's get it on." Kyle mimicked the voice exactly.

Their vessel slowly rose and headed to a lower section of the great wall where a huge round door suddenly opened. They watched with growing interest as their Bullet-Car maneuvered into position. Directly ahead, a long straightaway of darkness lined by lights became visible.

"I thought we were going outside the city on this one?" Jaric asked.

"Look harder." Rok nodded forward.

Jaric peered out the front view-screen and down the long, long corridor until he made out a tiny pinprick of color at the far end. "You mean that..."

In that instant, the Bullet-Car hurtled down the tunnel.

Before they could take a single breath, they found themselves outside the city amid the hurricane-force winds.

Three screams of pure delight, mixed with a healthy amount of fear, filled the Bullet-Car.

Bright, glowing clouds of orange laced with blue and yellow surrounded them. As they leapt from cloud-band to cloud-band across valleys of clear air, their vessel rocked with vicious jolts.

Their screams grew louder, fear now edging out delight.

"Hang on!" Kyle shouted.

"To what?" Jaric shouted back.

"Feels like we've been shot out of a laser cannon," Kyle yelled.

Suddenly, the Bullet-Car jolted hard to the right and shot straight into a rolling mass of titanic clouds. Darkness filled the small cabin as their craft shuddered violently. Each occupant put his hands out to steady himself although the Security Force shield kept them restrained safely in their seats.

Still, it couldn't hurt.

The Bullet-Car lurched upward.

And gained speed.

"We've caught a tail-wind!" Rok yelled happily.

Kyle and Jaric shouted triumphantly.

The unending expanse of tenuous orange clouds changed in an instant, replaced by clear sky as far as the eye could see.

The view was breathtaking.

The three stared with unabashed awe. They found themselves flying through a large area devoid of any clouds. And yet out in the far distance, all around them, they saw the wispy walls of massive cloudbanks.

They soared forward within the island of clear air.

The Bullet-Car suddenly changed direction as they felt it shudder against the hurricane-force winds.

Directly ahead of them, the clouds that seemed so far away a few seconds ago rapidly drew near.

"Here we go again!" Jaric yelled.

The Bullet-Car pierced the leading edge of the cloud wall with a gut-wrenching jolt. They flew blind now, buffeted by the tempestuous winds until their teeth chattered as if in a deep freeze. With another quick change in direction, they shot out into the clear air between two monstrous cloudbanks; unending walls of wispy green laced with orange towered far above them on each side like canyon walls.

"Those cloud peaks have to be a thousand kilometers from top to bottom!" Jaric shouted.

"Look!" Rok yelled.

In the distance, the cylindrical shape of a Mrad floating city began to grow. Within seconds, it filled their viewscreen.

"Man, these anti-grav engines are smooth!" Kyle whistled appreciatively.

"Have you ever felt such acceleration?" Jaric added. "And the G-forces weren't bad at all!"

"Good stuff," Rok grunted. "And we just flew through winds of at least two hundred clicks or more, and no telling how fast the crosswinds were in that last cloud band."

"Man, I'm not even bruised." Kyle nodded, impressed.

"I bet Mother couldn't have flown that any better," Jaric said.

"The anti-grav engines my Kraaqi brethren installed in MotherShip do not have the acceleration of this design, but they would allow her to navigate these dangerous winds." Rok crossed his arms, looking from Jaric to Kyle.

"I bet it would be one rough ride, though, Rok ol' buddy." Jaric jabbed Rok playfully with his elbow.

"She could ride them," Rok answered, his voice serious. "Kraaqi engines may not be as fast, but they are strong."

Their craft veered according to its programmed navigation and soared toward the leeward side of the floating city that also rode these hurricane winds. A black dot appeared against the white hull as the city hull filled their viewscreen.

"Look..." But that was the only word Kyle got out as they surged forward. In seconds, they found themselves inside the tiny black dot. A familiar tunnel lined with lights filled the viewscreen for a few moments as more G-forces pulled at them with their rapid deceleration.

"Man," Kyle grunted. "These engines are smooth!"

And as suddenly as it began, the ride ended.

The gull-wing door opened, and the trio staggered out into the floating city of Rxariar.

"There they are."

Three large, reptilian aliens watched closely as Jaric, Kyle and Rok stumbled around trying to get their bearings amid the throng of bustling aliens. Each of the watchful aliens wore a one-piece jumpsuit made of leather that covered their reddish, muscular bodies. As they watched, their short, muscular tails tensed with interest.

112

The huge hangar throbbed with the perpetual motion of bodies and Bullet-Cars as aliens arrived or prepared to ride the multi-colored clouds outbound to another city.

The air reverberated with voices and movement.

"The Paum are stalking their use of the Mrad computer system. They have tracers on their Search queries. And, they've killed one of the queries." The first alien scratched his short snout.

"One carries himself like a warrior, the one with the horns on his head. The other two, they are pups." The third Iraxx grunted.

"Never underestimate your enemies. Nor an untested alien." The largest of the three smiled knowingly.

"Very wise, Qirn. Very wise."

The three alien warriors drew closer, the red complexion of their faces glistening under the harsh lights. Their muscular tails whipped from right to left as they followed the two humans and the Kraaqi.

"Why would the Paum be interested in them, Qirn?"

"That is our mission, Rab, to discover that answer. But I've already gotten word on what first drew the interest of the Paum's agents." Qirn peered into the faces of his two warriors. "The Zuuk that travels with them, it searched for 'sentient technology.' And *that* alone is enough to interest the Paum." The three nodded silently, deep furrows of concern on their faces.

113

"Then they too may be our enemies, these humans and the horned warrior."

Qirn nodded. "We must find the answer—are they with the Paum and his 'Holy Plan'? Or is there something else to this business? Kadir and our best hackers are back at the ship tracking down the other queries that these humans have entered into the mighty system. A clue may lie there."

Qirn quickened his pace as their quarry melted into a crowded corridor. He moved with the instincts of an accomplished hunter, side-stepping his way through the mass of bodies until he again made visual contact.

"What if they give us trouble, Qirn? I feel naked without my weapons."

"You are a weapon, my friend. You are trained to fight in any situation. We obey the laws of this city by not carrying weapons."

"I hope they respect the law as much as we do," Rab grunted.

"That is a chance we take. We are honorable warriors, that is our way." Qirn suddenly discerned the destination of their quarry.

"Hmmm. They are heading for the Refugee Section of Rxariar." Qirn stopped short as he watched the three up ahead slow their pace, looking around as if not sure which direction to take.

"Why are they heading to this place of tragedy and despair?"

Qirn continued to watch until the trio suddenly came to a decision and moved forward again. But even as he began to follow, he held his hand up. His gaze focused across the crowds to a far corner where two, short aliens were also intently watching the two humans and their Kraaqi companion.

But although they were shorter than most aliens, their thick bull-necks and barrel chests gave the distinct impression that they were pound for pound a match for any warrior.

They grinned and began to move.

"Agents of the Paum."

"Yes," Qirn said. "They are bold to follow them in the open like this. There must be more to these humans than we surmise." The warrior's tail tensed as he considered this new circumstance. But in a moment, he decided. "Rab, return to our room and make contact with the ship. Tell them to send another team in quickly. We may need them."

Qirn nodded to his remaining warrior. "Jaan, you come with me. We will follow the followers now. But keep sharp—where there are two of the Paum's agents, there may be more."

"These Harg are a nasty bunch. The Paum chooses his enforcers well," Jaan whispered. "They are paid mercenaries—hard-hitting and hard to take down." Jaan stroked his snout in thought.

"It could be worse." Qirn's eyes narrowed. "The Paum could've sent a Destructor."

"Only if he wanted them dead," Jaan replied.

All grew silent in recognition of the dreaded name.

They nodded agreement.

A low growl emanated from Qirn's throat. "Still, we must show caution," Qirn added as he gathered his thoughts. "Too many aliens have disappeared from this section of Rxariar lately. And we know the agents of the Paum are behind many of them."

"And so the evil spreads," Jaan mused.

Qirn's eyes and his locked. Finally, Qirn nodded at Rab.

The two reptilian warriors moved stealthily forward as Rab disappeared in the opposite direction.

# CHAPTER SEVEN

Minstrel assumed his Zuuk form again. "I will return to review the results of my queries now."

Minstrel had returned briefly to upload data after returning from his first survey. Now, the towering Zuuk turned to leave.

"Good. Maybe you can keep an eye on the boys for me."

"That should be easy for a Zuuk with seven eye-stalks." Minstrel-Zuuk laughed.

"I did not mean the request literally," Mother chided.

"They're probably halfway across RahajMr by now. But I'll try to catch up with them," Minstrel-Zuuk said in a more serious tone.

"I'm ready!" Elise ran into the room, her excitement evident in every motion. But all Mother and Minstrel needed to do was look at her eyes—eyes that gleamed with the freshness and exuberance of life.

Elise was ready to go out into the universe.

"I want Krinia and Jysar to stay right beside you." Mother's optic focused on Elise's companions. "Keep her in sight at all times, Krinia."

Krinia put her arm around Elise's shoulders. "We'll take good care of your baby, Mother. Let's go, girl-friend."

"The city of RahajMr is a most civilized and technologically advanced society," Jysar said with emphasis. "These cities are probably the safest places in the universe."

"Hmmm." Minstrel-Zuuk turned its seven eye-stalks to Jysar. "I wish I could share your feelings. But with so many different species drawn here to use the most powerful computer system known and the riches it has collected, there is the potential for trouble. I am just glad personal weapons are not allowed inside each city."

"I hope I will be able to directly connect to this system," Mother said. "It is the personal reason I wanted to come here."

"I will inquire again about this possibility when I reach the Search-terminals," Minstrel-Zuuk said.

"Yes, a supreme accomplishment for any race." Jysar sighed. "And security is very tight here," Jysar agreed, changing the subject. "Their sophisticated technology is able to scan and prevent anyone from getting around it. It can detect hidden weapons with almost one hundred percent success."

"That is true. Jaric had his pocket scanner confiscated on our first visit yesterday. After it passed another more detailed security test, they returned it," Minstrel-Zuuk said.

"That makes me feel better," Mother said.

"At any rate, RahajMr and its sister-cities are as good a place as any for Elise to begin discovering the rest of the universe." Krinia smiled at Elise, who beamed back at her.

"Please be aware of your surroundings at all times," Mother advised. "I will wait for you here."

"We'll be careful," Elise said with a wave of her hand as she bounded down the ramp and into the floating city of RahajMr.

Jysar and Krinia kept glancing at Elise as they walked with her through Security and out into the moving masses of races that filled the halls and corridors to overflowing. Elise's head turned from one side to the other as she tried to take in this mass of beings all at once, her eyes wide with wonder as she saw faces so varied, so different, that at times she stopped in her tracks to stare in amazement and appreciation.

And sometimes surprise.

"Did you see that alien that just passed us?" Elise burst out.

"Yes, what about him?" Jysar responded nonchalantly.

"It...it didn't have a face. It just had a head with three eyes, and a *huge* bird-like bill that must have been nearly a meter long. The bill was its face!" Elise shook her head with wonder.

"I thought he was beautiful," Krinia added. "Especially with all those deep blue feathers. It gave him character."

"I hope we get to meet one and talk with it," Elise added. They were suddenly walking through a new throng of diverse beings. Elise's eyes seemed to open wider than physically possible.

"I am so glad you did not want to take the Bullet-Cars." Minstrel-Zuuk glided smoothly beside the trio. "Life goes by too fast anyway. It is better to walk leisurely among the variety of races here and enjoy ourselves."

The air was filled with words and bits of exotic phrases from a thousand different languages. As they stepped between and around aliens in the never-ending crowds, different faces and astounding shapes seemed to appear as if from a dream—and sometimes a nightmare—as they made their way to the Search-terminals.

Several times Elise gasped out loud as unusual aliens passed right by her. Once an alien with a mountain of sparkling, glowing hair suddenly appeared right before her. Just as suddenly, a walking head with four mouths and four eyes mumbled quick apologies as it narrowly avoided knocking her down. Before she could respond, Jysar's grip on her arm carefully guided her around a family group of tiny aliens only one meter tall with transparent skin—Elise could not only see their internal organs and brain but at points even right through them!

"You need to keep your mouth closed, Elise," Krinia said with a laugh. "Depending on the culture, some aliens will think you want to attack them, or that you're romantically interested."

Elise smiled sheepishly.

Their thirty-minute stroll seemed to fly by.

Minstrel-Zuuk glided to a Search-terminal to check on its results from yesterday after he flashed his pre-paid token.

Elise and her two companions purchased their own access. Krinia and Jysar helped Elise with her personal searches for remnants of the human race at a nearby terminal. Elise smiled cunningly as she and her friends misspelled words, hoping to find a match that might lead them to any other human survivors stored in the mountains of data. After they typed in their last queries, the trio got up and walked over to Minstrel-Zuuk, who was already waiting for them.

"Any good results?" Jysar asked.

"No." Minstrel-Zuuk's eye-stalks gazed thoughtfully off in seven directions, but now two of them focused on his friends. "As a matter of fact, one of them seemed to end prematurely, as if cut off before it completed."

"Oh? Which queries?" Jysar's interested was piqued.

"My query about sentient computers. Most strange, I would've thought that somewhere in all this data different races would have made progress in this field. But, it seems to be almost...non-existent. Or hidden." Minstrel-Zuuk's eye-stalks all focused on the trio.

"What about Mother getting a direct connection so she can use the system?" Krinia asked.

"Turned down."

"That's a bit strange," Jysar commented.

"Well, we're off. Time's wasting." Elise grabbed both Jysar and Krinia by their arms. "I want to mingle and see more of this place. Our queries are off and running. We'll check them tomorrow."

"And don't forget shopping." Krinia smiled.

Jysar rolled his eyes. "And *shopping*," he repeated with an utter lack of enthusiasm.

"I am going to contact the boys in a bit to check on them, after I ask the Mrad about my search query that terminated prematurely," Minstrel-Zuuk added. With a silent grace, the huge, shell-encased body glided away. "I hope their queries for human survivors were more fruitful. I hate to tell them mine came up null." The seven eye-stalks looked off in seven different directions as the multi-colored Zuuk moved away.

Elise, Krinia and Jysar quickly made their way to the main shopping section of RahajMr.

They discovered the mass of aliens even more crowded here—the sole difference being everyone carried one or two shiny bags of merchandise under various appendages.

The shopping section of RahajMr resembled a vast and crowded indoor street bazaar combined with an elaborate mall with storefronts that rose level after crowded level far above—a fantastically huge atrium. Indeed, the threesome peered upward in awe at the stores and walkways that lined the massive atrium walls.

Aliens shouted the price and value of their goods to passersby from booths on the floor level while neon signs pointed the way to countless other stores selling everything from exotic clothing to imported curios and hand-crafted items that boggled the imagination.

And of course, innumerable electronic toys and gadgets manufactured from thousands of different worlds lined shelves everywhere.

Far above were more storefronts, extending over twenty levels above them and accessible by hundreds of high-speed elevators that seemed constantly full of happy alien shoppers. Bridges extended in various directions like a huge web, creating steel geometric patterns at every level. These provided a path for shoppers to crisscross to the other side or to travel up or down a single level without using elevators.

The air vibrated with laughter and countless alien languages.

Jysar suggested they disable the Galactic Translators wrapped around their left ear for a moment so they could absorb the full ambiance.

Elise reveled in all of it—the myriad of different beings all around her, the stores and tables full of exotic merchandise, and the constant chatter and laughter that filled her ears. In fact, her senses almost became overwhelmed because every face and everything she came into contact with was new to her. Her heart beat so loud she thought that Krinia and Jysar must surely hear it over the noise.

*She felt so alive.*

Every moment brought a new experience. Elise quickly realized that the beings around her were wonderfully diverse—no two aliens exactly alike. And she came to appreciate the different forms of beauty that each possessed—each with its own unique look and its own peculiar kind of magnificence.

Elise realized she wanted to value diversity. She would always look for the beauty in those different from her. And hopefully, they would view her in the same way.

"Come here *lovely alien*, I have something *just for you*."

A sales-alien inside a booth smiled directly her.

"Yes, yes. Come over here, my lovely little alien. I have something here that will enhance your natural beauty. And it is priced right—just for you." The shopkeeper was covered with long, flowing yellow fur from head to toe. It wore a black tunic and pants, while its large, brown eyes seemed to draw the trio closer.

Elise looked questioningly at Krinia.

"Let's go see what he's peddling," Krinia encouraged with a smile.

"Yes, yes. Look at this, it's all the rage now among beings with long, silky hair like yourself." He held in his hands what looked like a small net, its fibers translucent and seemingly as delicate as a spider's web—and just as strong. The trio caught a glint of supple metal as the alien let the light glance off the miniature netting.

"What does it do?" Elise touched the fragile-looking net. It was so soft, softer even than the strands of her long, blonde hair.

"Allow me."

Taking the net with both furry hands, the alien held it just above Elise's head. His smile grew as he allowed it to gently fall until it seemed to melt into her hair. He stepped back with an approving expression, a strange pinkish glow now glistening from the fur of his face.

"I love it!" Krinia exclaimed with pure joy. "What do you call it?"

"A *Hair Lighter*."

"It is very nice," Jysar agreed as he gazed at Elise. "Very nice. There must be some embedded technology within the tiny fibers. How does it work?"

"What, what? Let me see too." Elise took the hand mirror the alien offered her. She looked at herself and gasped.

Her blonde hair glowed a bright, neon pink. It looked so natural, not like it was colored or dyed in any way. It glowed as if electrified somehow.

"How does it work?" Elise's voice was full of wonder.

"It draws its power from your body, from your body's natural energy. And this model determines the color it emanates based on a formula detected from the emotional energy of its wearer—calculated partly on pulse rate, body temperature and on and on. I only sell them—they're made by the Razzaza—so I can't explain the exact process. And I sell a lot of them to pretty beings with long hair such as yourself." He smiled knowingly as he held up another small net of translucent threads.

"Oh, remember that one alien with the mountain of hair?" Elise said quickly. "Her hair seemed to glow, I bet she wore one of these."

The alien smiled even bigger. "These are all the rage right now. And they are so natural, they work in harmony with your body. We call ours a Hair Lighter because that in essence is what it does. Other manufacturers have different names—Color-Nets or Light-Nets."

"Will it change colors?" Elise asked excitedly.

"Of course! Right now, you must be in a high state of excitement and happiness for it to glow this bright shade of pink." He took a handful of Elise's glowing pink hair and held it. "When you are more calm, it will glow with more of a greenish or bluish color. And if you are angry, upset or..." The alien smiled, his eyes alight. "Or if you are feeling passionate, your hair will glow red or orange—depending on how intense your mood."

Jysar stepped closer to Elise, a stern, fatherly expression on his face.

"I love it!" Elise exclaimed as she looked at herself in the mirror again.

"Where is the technology embedded?" Jysar asked as he peered at the neon glow of Elise's hair.

"It is located at the thick corners of the netting."

"Wow!" Elise exclaimed.

"And it is so cheap—*only* four hundred Mrad tokens. Other brands of Hair Lighters go for twice as much."

Krinia pursed her mouth. "That seems a little much."

Elise turned to Krinia with a look of shock.

Krinia nodded to Elise, indicating she knew what she was doing. Her head-tail flicked rapidly from side to side as she turned to face the alien seller.

"Tell you what though, seeing that my friend does like your little trinket." Krinia reached into her purse and pulled out three tokens. "I'll pay you three hundred tokens for it."

"But, I couldn't take less than three hundred and seventy five tokens for this model!"

"And I can't pay more than three hundred fifteen." Krinia smiled shrewdly.

Elise watched closely as the alien waved his hands and began espousing the real value of this particular model while Krinia explained their budget and that they would continue looking and perhaps find another vendor with a better price. This bantering continued for five minutes while Jysar grew bored and sauntered over to another booth filled with electronic gadgets.

"Done!" The alien took the three hundred and fifty Mrad tokens Krinia held out to him.

As the women moved to join Jysar, the alien called out to another prospective client, a female alien with long, black hair covering her entire face and head.

"Why didn't you pay him the first price?" Elise asked as they walked out of earshot.

"It's called haggling—negotiation." Krinia paused as she gathered her thoughts. "A seller will ask a higher price in order to make a higher profit—if a buyer has not shopped around in order to determine the actual value, they may pay that higher price without knowing. Research is important, even in purchasing items. And impulse purchases are not normally good ideas." Krinia paused as she noticed Elise's puzzled expression.

She realized this was Elise's first shopping experience. Krinia tried to simplify her previous words. "If a buyer does research and learns the range of prices for a particular item, it will enable the buyer to recognize a good deal—a fair price."

"Oh," Elise said.

"A shrewd consumer, one with knowledge of an item's price range, then will haggle—she'll offer to purchase it at a lower price, the lower price range, while the seller counters with a higher price, until they reach one that is mutually agreeable—a fair price for both."

Elise nodded. "Then I should have gone to another seller first, to check their price to see if it was fair."

"Probably. But we negotiated a lower price with the assumption his asking price was high." Krinia smiled. "Plus, you really wanted it. And, it's a gift from me."

Elise turned and hugged Krinia.

Krinia smiled. "So, we did all right. If the price had been outrageous, we would've shopped around some more."

"Wow, I do love it! I feel so pretty." Elise noticed a few admiring glances from the crowd as they made their way forward.

"It is fascinating technology. I almost bought one just so I could take it apart and see how it works," Jysar said admiringly.

"I bet you would, you curious technology-fiend." Krinia chuckled.

"I'll let you scan it when we get back to Mother," Elise said with a smile.

"Let's take a break, my feet are killing me." Krinia looked around intently a moment. "There, over there looks good. It's both a restaurant and a bar. I think I'd like a nice glass of Mrad fruit wine myself."

Elise's eyes brightened as her glowing pink hair grew a shade darker. "Do you think I can have a glass too?"

"We'll see. I'm not sure if eighteen is the drinking age here on RahajMr."

They made their way inside, only to find the crowds more tightly packed than back at the shopping complex.

They finally found three open spots at a small table against the far wall. Krinia activated the small console on the table and began looking at the list of wines while Elise and Jysar glanced down their own tiny consoles and reviewed the list of food and drink offered.

"I could use a bit of lunch myself," Jysar said.

"Me too. I'm famished from all this walking." Elise smiled at the others.

"Well, well, don't I know you? I think we met back at Alexxa Four last week? Ah, one could never forget such beauty."

The deep, confident voice seemed to come out of nowhere—unseen from behind them. Elise froze, afraid to turn.

Krinia replied for her.

"That's got to be the oldest line in the galaxy, fella." Krinia glanced at the orange-skinned humanoid alien with a bored expression. "And we've never been to Alexxa Four. So, keep moving, pal."

The young alien wore his jet-black hair slicked back over his head. The dapper alien sported a red jacket over a lavender shirt with a myriad of thick gold chains around his neck. His large, leaf-like ears were pierced with several golden earrings.

He stood out from the other aliens crowded in the room.

"But everyone needs a new friend, especially beautiful aliens such as yourselves." The alien Romeo sat down with a flash of teeth from a shark-like smile.

Krinia almost laughed out loud, but she held herself back—for the moment.

"Listen, we're..." Krinia began.

"You don't mind if I sit here and get to know you better?" The alien smiled from Jysar to Elise and back to Krinia, whose expression grew rock-hard.

"Listen..." Krinia began again, a forcefulness now in her voice.

"Ah, your hair is so lovely, my young beauty." The alien smiled wolfishly at Elise, who blushed in return. "That color becomes you."

"Thank you." Elise smiled innocently. Her pink hair turned reddish.

Krinia groaned.

"And you," he said to Krinia. "You are like a goddess. Actually both of you are." His eyes flashed from Krinia back to Elise. "Ah yes, one is the goddess of youth and love." He picked up Elise's hand and kissed it passionately. He turned to Krinia. "And you, you are like the goddess of fertility and..."

"Could you shut-up!" Krinia's exasperated shout drew a flurry of attention. She rolled her eyes and leaned over the table toward Elise to speak to her alone, but she was loud enough so the aliens at the next table could hear.

"This is the kind of alien your mother warned us about." Krinia jerked her thumb towards Romeo.

"Oh no, but you misunderstand. Allow me to introduce myself." He rose with a great air and bowed. "I am Lamall dex Fronato Presanntos of the planet Kinallias. I am eldest of my father's house, and the favorite." He flashed his toothy smile once again.

Krinia opened her mouth but he continued before she could speak.

"And let me assure you that I, Lamall dex Fronato Presanntos of Kinallias, am the kind of alien that you '*take home to Mother.*'" He stroked his perfect hair with an air of aloofness.

"I sincerely doubt that," Krinia said with conviction.

"But..." Elise began.

"And what kind of technical knowledge do you possess, my dear Lamall de Frompus Presentus?" The Hrono smiled wryly as he carefully mispronounced the alien's name. As the silence grew, Jysar carefully stroked the upright scales across his head as his green complexion deepened with emotion.

Lamall eyed him carefully without answering.

Finally, after a lengthy silence, Lamall shook his head. "You do me a disservice, sir. I am a friendly kind of alien, I only want to get to know all of you much better...and what does technology have to do with love or friendship anyway?"

"Why, a lot of things!" Jysar said with shocked amazement.

Lamall, Krinia and Elise each turned with puzzled expressions to Jysar, who looked back at them with surprise.

"Well, you've lost me on that, my green, scaly friend. But these lovely, wonderful female creatures, surely they know..."

"Yeah, we *know*." Krinia sighed. But the sharp, angry flicks of her head-tail gave away the emotions that boiled inside of her.

"Ah, but I love this. It is so wonderful." And before Krinia realized what he was doing, Lamall reached behind her neck and caressed her head-tail.

A low growl emanated ominously from Krinia's throat.

"But I love this, it is so soft and yet so firm. This..." His caress changed to a gentle grip.

132

"Uh-oh," Jysar quickly moved his chair back from the table, knowing what would happen next. "You shouldn't have done that, Lamall de Dumbest Dunderhead."

With a flash of movement, Krinia knocked his arm away.

"Owww!" Lamall groaned. "But you have hurt me..."

With a deadly earnestness on her face, Krinia rose to face him.

Her fierce gaze caused Lamall to stumble backward in surprise.

Krinia slowly lowered herself into a battle stance. In the next instant, she launched herself into the hapless alien.

Lamall shouted for help as he waved his arms wildly in a vain effort to fend off her determined assault.

But Krinia meant business.

With two rapid blows to his mid-section, she knocked the breath from him as he doubled up with pain. He raised his hands again, panting for air, but Krinia knocked them away as if they were nothing.

She sent him reeling with a solid blow to his chin. He fell to the ground in a heap and lay still a moment. With a painful groan, he tried to crawl away.

But Krinia planted her foot firmly on his back.

Lamall's body tensed, waiting for the next blow.

"A word of advice," Krinia said in a hushed voice.

Lamall groaned again as her foot pressed harder against his back.

"Never touch a Mewiis' head-tail—unless she *wants* you to touch it."

A muffled groan answered.

Krinia took her foot off and then looked around at the faces staring at her and her handiwork.

"Anybody got a problem with this?" Krinia asked them all.

Everyone turned back to their companions and began talking as if nothing had happened. Within seconds, the room filled with the normal crowd noise.

Nobody paid attention to Lamall as he crawled painfully toward the back door.

Elise's eyes were the size of saucers as Krinia sat back down.

"And I don't think Mother needs to know about this little incident." Krinia smiled conspiratorially at them. "We'll just keep this to ourselves, right?"

"But, what happened? He seemed so nice." Elise's hair now glowed with an electric purple sheen.

"He was *too nice*. I'll explain more to you later, when it's just us girls. Now, let's get back to the food and wine. And I sure need that glass of wine now." Krinia peered at her tiny console.

"He had motives," Jysar added with a knowing glance.

"Motives?" Elise asked with surprise. "Is that like negotiations?"

"A whole different subject. Anyway, let's eat." Krinia said forcefully, changing the subject. "And afterward, we need to make our way back to Mother. I think we've had enough excitement for one day."

"But let's check my queries first on the way back!" Elise said eagerly.

As their food arrived, the three eagerly dove into it with smiles and murmurs of appreciation.

The trio never noticed the two muscular Harg as they sat down at a table directly across from them. Nor the secretive glances they cast in their direction.

# CHAPTER EIGHT

"Doesn't seem to be a very happy place, eh?" Jaric confided to Kyle and Rok as they walked down the main thoroughfare.

"It looks like a typical residential section—like back at RahajMr." Kyle glanced at the entrances to the single-family enclaves that lined the walls and upper levels above them. But unlike RahajMr, small groups of aliens sat outside many of the doors. As the trio walked past, they felt the suspicious looks following them.

"But it seems like everyone stays at home over here. And you're right, they're not smiling very much."

"I assume they do not have work, so most of the family groups stay close to their homes," Rok surmised. "These are aliens on hard times, remember. They are all refugees, looking for a new home, a new life."

"Well, they could at least be friendly." Jaric smiled at another group they were passing, but the aliens simply stared back in return, their scale-covered faces devoid of emotion.

"Oh well," Kyle whispered to Jaric. "Let's just find the Ialliaz—or humans."

"Look, there's a Mrad security officer." Kyle pointed ahead to a uniformed Mrad. "Let's see if he can direct us to the Ialliaz. I'm not sure if this is the right street or it's the next one over."

"Excuse me, Officer," he called out as they approached.

Kyle waited as the Mrad turned to face him.

"Can you tell us if this is the block that houses the families of Ialliaz who recently arrived?"

His black eyes surveyed Kyle and the other two carefully before he answered. After a moment, he seemed satisfied. "No, it's the next one up. Then go down three blocks. They live in the enclaves all along the right side from there to the end of the street." He paused a moment. "I don't suppose you're here to accept them as immigrants to your planet?"

Kyle was taken aback. "Well, not exactly. I mean, we're just here to talk with them."

The officer nodded apologetically. "Well, I was just hoping. They're a sad bunch, more so than the rest. I don't meant to butt in, but I like to know what's going on with the residents under my jurisdiction." His eyes became far off. "I'm always happy when some of them find a new home. It's what they all want—a new home."

"Yeah," Jaric agreed. "We understand all too well."

Jaric and Kyle exchanged knowing glances.

"Looks like most of them are pretty forlorn," Kyle said with a sigh.

"Well, they're all refugees. They have no homeworld anymore. And most have experienced things we can't even imagine." A deep sadness etched the Mrad officer's face. "By the way, my name is Aje Veeio.

137

"Officer Veeio, nice to meet you," Kyle mumbled, still lost in his own troubled thoughts.

"Actually, we can imagine. We're refugees ourselves," Jaric added.

"Then you know." Officer Veeio raised his arm toward the street where the Ialliaz lived. "They were conquered by a heartless race called the T'kaan. But everyone has a story here—some lost their homeworlds to natural disasters, or disasters they brought on themselves, and now their planet is uninhabitable. For others it was disease, unimaginable plagues. But for most, war and persecution drove them here." A great sadness swept the Mrad's face.

Rok's eyes narrowed. "There is tragedy here, I can feel it too. You can see it in the faces and the eyes of these aliens." Rok turned his head as he looked at the haunted expressions. "There is pain here, terrible pain."

"Yeah, this isn't an assignment most Mrad relish. But I like it."

"Why?" Kyle asked.

"Our government provides these aliens with housing, food and clothing. We get them registered in our computer system and allow them to search for other worlds that are accepting immigrants. And with the high volume of traffic to our cities, there is ample opportunity for the refugees to find a place where they can find work, find a place where they can start over." Aje Veeio paused. "But the reason I volunteer for this assignment is that these people need protection—from con artists and other criminal elements, sometimes from each other if there's trouble because of different ethnic attitudes or other historic animosity."

"It burns my heart to know that the weak and helpless can be treated this way." Rok sighed.

The Mrad's eyes widened with approval. "Yes, these people have been through a lot. They've seen a lot of pain, a lot of death, you name it. But they're in my jurisdiction here, and I look after them, protect them."

Rok looked deep into the Mrad's eyes. "An honorable task. You have my respect, Officer."

"Thank you," Aje said simply. "But sometimes it's a thankless job, and even the refugees themselves give me trouble."

"They should know who is taking care of them," Rok said. "And respect them for that."

"And sometimes there is worse." The officer's eyes became hard.

"Worse?"

"The refugees are supposed to check in when they find a new home, or before they leave. So we know when their homes are going to be empty and we can give them to new families. And to ration the food and other articles appropriately." Officer Veeio stared at Rok. "But the last year or so a good number of them just seem to disappear from the face of the universe—individuals mostly. But sometimes whole groups. I don't like it when they just disappear."

"Maybe they forget to check out before they leave?" Rok countered.

"Maybe. Maybe not."

An ominous silence settled upon them.

"Do a lot of worlds offer immigration?" Jaric asked.

"Not in this Sector right now," Aje replied. "Most planets are overflowing with their own peoples. And work is fairly scarce with the recession in the Quadrant. But some Sectors are still accepting refugees."

"Well, maybe the Ialliaz will be finding a new home soon," Kyle said. "And us too!"

Jaric smiled with anticipation, but his smile faded as the Mrad spoke.

"Right now, only the Argias and the Cends are accepting. And the Paum Sector." The uniformed Mrad grew silent after he uttered the last word. "But they're just a little too eager in their offers, if you know what I mean." His voice took a serious tone. "Most of the refugees only take them up as a last resort—if everything else falls through." He drew a deep breath and held it a moment. "But the Paum are always accepting refugees."

"You said that last sentence with hesitation," Kyle commented.

The Mrad officer nodded. "The Paum have a reputation. They're a secretive kind of people, nobody knows a lot about them outside their own systems." The Mrad's eyes narrowed; his face grew hard as granite. "It's whispered that they're a strict and severe society. *Anything* one does must be in harmony with the High Paum, or you do it in fear of your life. Everything is controlled by the Paum."

The Mrad's eyes gazed far off. "They like to say, 'Life must be guided by Paum, or else it is evil. And all that is evil must die.'"

This time the silence wrapped them in an icy embrace. Their hearts beat faster with a feeling of dread, almost as if something evil reached out to them that very moment.

Officer Aje Veeio looked intently at the trio. "Not the kind of lifestyle one would run to join, in my opinion."

"Well, I don't think I'd want to go there either," Kyle agreed.

They thanked the officer for his directions and headed toward the Ialliaz. As they found the street and made their way toward the block indicated, Kyle and Jaric felt their hearts begin to beat faster with their rising hope.

"I think we're really going to find them this time," Kyle said, his eyes sparkling with excitement.

"I feel it too," Jaric agreed. "Their description fits, and they were conquered by the T'kaan. That's us too."

"Be patient," Rok warned them. "Do not arouse your hopes until what you seek is within your grasp. Or else you risk disappointment."

"But everything fits," Kyle argued. "And this is a place full of refugees. I mean, if you're a refugee, this is the place to come to, sooner or later. And now we're here!"

"You have sought this *life-altering moment* for a long time now—that of finding other humans. But such momentous events are rare in life." Rok gripped each of them by the shoulder. "You must not *expect* great things but accept what each day gives you—great or small. It is my experience that many things do not live up to their hype—and there is a terrible let-down afterward."

Kyle stared silently at the Kraaqi.

Jaric's expression changed too as he pressed his lips together as his eyes reflected a deep sadness.

Rok shook his head slowly. "Perhaps you expect that finding other humans will change everything for you—that it, and only it, will bring you some kind of happiness or joy that is missing from your life today." Rok looked deeply at both of the young men. "But even if you find other humans, you will still be you. It may not change your life the way you expect or want it to. It may not change anything—inside you." The Kraaqi pressed Kyle's and Jaric's shoulders harder.

"It *will* change everything," Kyle growled.

The air became electric between them.

Kyle's piercing blue eyes stared into Rok's steady gaze. Without warning, he shook Rok's hand from off his shoulder with a violent jerk. "You don't understand, Rok! Even after all these months with us, you don't understand."

The Kraaqi warrior watched Kyle with a wary surprise. There was a look in Kyle's eyes now, a flash of intensity as if he were going into battle. Rok's eyes narrowed as he waited for Kyle to continue.

"This is all I want, Rok. Understand?" Kyle shook his head from side to side. "It's my only dream, my only hope. It's all I really want."

Rok grunted with a noncommittal sound in his throat.

Kyle rolled his eyes as if in total disbelief. He looked at Rok as if he were seeing him for the first time.

"If you wanted to, you could go home tomorrow."

Rok's eyes glimmered with the beginning of understanding.

Kyle saw it, but he didn't feel any satisfaction. Instead, his anger rose like a storm inside his heart.

"You see, I can't go home. I've got no homeworld, no hometown. I don't even have a village, or a single street, that I can call home. I've got no people. *No one.*" Kyle's eyes moistened. "I can't go home. No matter how bad I want to, I can't go home. It doesn't exist for me."

Rok stared with full realization of the pain inside Kyle's heart.

Standing silent beside Kyle, Jaric bowed his head with sadness.

"But you can, Rok. You could go back to your world, to your people—*anytime.* You have a home." Kyle blinked his eyes rapidly, fighting his tears. "And that's what I want. And that's why I search so hard. And why I never give up." Kyle became silent, staring off into the distance while Rok studied his face.

"You are right, my Brethren. I did not fully understand."

Kyle turned his head slowly to face Rok.

Rok nodded at him. "You have shared your heart. And I thank you." Once again Rok took Kyle by each shoulder and held him firmly in his grip. He looked deeply into the human's eyes.

"But you are wrong on one point. You do have a home, and a family to return home to whenever you wish. And a mother."

Kyle looked deep in Rok's eyes as he weighed the Kraaqi's words. A faint sigh escaped him.

"It's a dysfunctional family at best."

"But it is a family—your family. And it is as good a family as I have ever known." Rok tightened his grip and then released him with a shake of his head.

"Come on, Big K. Rok is right," Jaric said, surprise in his voice. "We might not be the ideal family, but we are family!"

Kyle looked away, avoiding Jaric's pleading gaze.

"Come one, Big K," Jaric repeated. "Lighten up." Jaric looked from the stern face of Rok back to the angry countenance of Kyle. "Let's forget this serious stuff and get back to having a good time!"

Kyle and Rok eyed each other warily.

Kyle turned to start walking again when Rok spoke.

"I would like you to remember this one thing before we finish."

Kyle hesitated.

"Go on," Kyle said with a questioning look.

"I hope one day you will realize what you really have—how precious it is. Far too often we only realize this fact after it is gone. And once it is gone, no matter how badly we wish it back, it is gone."

Kyle stared at him evenly, but he did not speak.

"Reflect on what you have today, young human. It may be of more value than your greatest dream." Rok carefully studied Kyle's face. "The Kraaqi have a saying, one of my favorite—*It is the simple things that bring the greatest joy.*"

Kyle's eyes narrowed as his mind carefully digested Rok's words.

The tense silence softened.

"Whew!" Jaric whistled in a second attempt to lighten the mood. "That was deep, Rok. Maybe you should find a mountain and make a home on top of it. That way everyone can go seek out your fabulous wisdom!"

Jaric laughed, thumping first Rok and then Kyle on the arm to try and get a chuckle out of either of them.

Kyle smiled. And with a confident air made his way forward again.

"I still feel good about this," Kyle said a little too enthusiastically. "Let's go on and see what we'll find around the next corner!"

"Yeah! There's more refugees here than we've ever run into or even heard about in one place before. This city is like a clearinghouse for

145

refugees. It makes sense other human survivors might find their way here," Jaric added.

"That's right," Kyle agreed quickly. "It all makes sense."

"Let's get a move on!" Jaric broke into a trot, closely followed by Kyle.

"I hope that your dreams come true this day," Rok whispered to himself. "I really do."

Rok kept pace with their eager steps. "Keep your hearts prepared," he said to their unhearing ears. "Once we have met the Ialliaz, then you can open them wide."

But Jaric and Kyle couldn't keep their rising excitement in check any longer. All the talk of refugees and all their personal years of searching for human survivors burned inside their hearts.

They had to find others. They just had to.

As they rounded the final corner, both of them picked up their pace until they were almost running.

Rok broke into a slow run behind them.

"Look!" Kyle pointed excitedly.

Two human-like figures stood directly ahead of them. From the back, they looked exactly like humans—their arms, legs and body type matched exactly.

"Hello!" Kyle and Jaric shouted together.

The two aliens turned.

And in that moment Kyle and Jaric's hearts sank.

The Ialliaz were the most human-like aliens they had run into yet.

*But they weren't humans.*

146

The most obvious physical differences were the vertical pupils of their eyes, their mouths centered on their necks, and the huge, ridged nose that dominated their faces almost like the beak of a bird. Otherwise, they were very close to humans in appearance, especially the almond shade of their skin and the hair that covered their heads.

Rok could sense the deep disappointment in his friend's faces and their words as they talked with the Ialliaz.

It was true; the T'kaan had destroyed their worlds just as they had destroyed those of humanity. But it had been the T'kaan First Fleet, although it did occur during the same T'kaan cycle when the T'kaan Third Fleet fought the human race to the edge of extinction.

The sadness etched on the faces of the Ialliaz refugees became etched on Jaric and Kyle's faces as well. As they talked with the Ialliaz survivors, they once again relived the tragic end of the human race.

One more time.

An hour later, they found themselves at the central community kitchen that provided food for the refugees. They decided to join the communal noonday meal that the Mrad provided for all refugees.

After all, they were refugees too.

Their spirits slowly revived. The energy and never-ending hope of youth grew again inside their scarred hearts. And the Kraaqi warrior continued to encourage them with his words of wisdom until they were able to reflect with humor on their latest disappointment.

It was almost funny, in a sad kind of way.

And they decided it was better to laugh about their dashed hopes than to cry out in pain.

And in the face of defeat, they laughed one more time.

They stood in a long queue with about two hundred other refugees, each with a plate in their hands as they waited for the aliens up ahead to serve them their daily allotment of food. Jaric stood in front with Kyle and Rok behind. Jaric leaned far out to one side and looked back at the others in the rear of the queue. As he turned back around he discovered the back of the huge alien in front of him blocking his view forward. He stepped to the side in order to see how many aliens were still ahead of them.

The gargantuan alien turned and glared down at Jaric.

Jaric smiled back at him and quickly stepped back in line.

"I still can't believe it," Jaric said, disappointment mixed with a touch humor.

"What, that we're standing in a soup line?" Kyle said with mock humor.

"No, bozo. I still can't believe the Ialliaz weren't humans, that's all."

Kyle chuckled. "But it was close."

Rok's eyes narrowed in thought. "You know, if you two survived the T'kaan, and now a small group of Ialliaz survived the T'kaan's attack upon them, well..." Rok spread his arms apart. "Perhaps there is real hope we will find other human survivors—somewhere."

"Yes," Jaric said, his voice empty of emotion. "Maybe we will, *one day*."

"There is always hope, my friend." Rok thumped Jaric on the shoulder, causing him to bump the alien in front.

The huge alien turned and gazed down at Jaric.

Jaric smiled sheepishly.

A huge, curved horn rose from the alien's short snout. Two red eyes stared unflinchingly as the large nostrils flared.

"Have you got a problem or something?" The huge alien snarled, revealing a dangerous set of teeth.

"No, no. I just tripped." Jaric laughed.

"Don't trip again," he warned with a rumbling growl.

Jaric and Kyle rolled their eyes at each other as the big alien faced forward.

"Friendly kind of alien, eh?" Kyle whispered to Jaric.

Jaric hurriedly placed his hands over Kyle's mouth in protest.

"Shut up, man!" Jaric whispered, jerking his thumb at the alien's back. "This guy's built like a tank."

Kyle laughed louder, which caused the horned alien to turn back toward them.

Jaric smiled innocently up at the massive alien. "Private joke."

149

Kyle's laughter continued a moment, but it slowly faded away as the huge alien glared at him. Kyle shrugged his shoulders and shook his head in disbelief at the big alien's lack of humor.

Rok matched the big alien's steady, angry gaze.

"Nice horn." Rok twisted his head slightly, showing off his own set of horns.

"And I know how to use it." The alien growled defiantly.

The air grew tense between them.

"As do I." Rok's eyes narrowed dangerously.

"Hmmph." The alien turned back around, obviously unimpressed.

"What's the matter with this guy?" Kyle whispered over his shoulder to Rok.

Jaric grabbed Kyle and Rok both by the shoulder. "Let's leave this alone, all right? I just want to get some lunch and then get back to Mother. In one piece, if you know what I mean."

Kyle and Rok looked from Jaric up to the broad shoulders and back of the alien. Kyle shook his head. "All right, I'm hungry too. I just wish this line would move faster."

The line finally moved forward, but progress soon halted again as the new group were served food. Jaric stepped to the side again to see how much closer they were. The huge, muscular alien breathed deeply as he too surveyed the line ahead.

"I hate aliens," the huge alien said—the words uttered to no one in particular.

"What do you mean?" Jaric asked incredulously.

The horned face turned and looked down at him with an angry glint in his red eyes. The big alien grunted and shrugged its massive shoulders.

"But you're an alien too!" Jaric pointed his finger up at him. "We're all aliens. So, how can you hate aliens?"

"I am not an alien. I am a Hammatt."

"Well, I'm a human. But we're both aliens, if you get right down to it. Everyone in the universe is an alien."

"I hate aliens," he repeated with conviction. He bent his head closer to Jaric's face, the curved edge of his horn almost brushing the end of Jaric's nose. "And I especially hate little aliens who talk too much." The Hammatt sniffed noisily as a puzzled expression flashed across its leathery face.

"And I especially hate aliens that smell bad!"

Kyle stepped confidently beside Jaric. "Why don't you tell us how you *really* feel, bozo-boy?" Kyle's tone was half-challenge, half-mocking. He eyed the Hammatt carefully.

The Hammatt drew himself to his full height as the muscles in his towering body tightened. He glared down at the two humans for a moment. A massive growl erupted from his throat—a growl so powerful that every head in the room turned in shocked surprise.

The room went deathly silent.

Rok stepped forward and placed himself between the boys and the gargantuan Hammatt.

The huge alien growled again, causing the flatware on his plate to rattle. He stood three meters

151

tall and probably weighed as much as Rok, Jaric and Kyle combined.

"And I hate aliens..." he began.

A Mrad security officer suddenly appeared from between two other aliens.

"Too bad it's not Officer Veeio," Jaric whispered quickly to Kyle as the stern looking Mrad walked up to them.

"Have we got a problem here, fellas?" he said to all of them.

A tense silence answered.

"Well, let me be real clear—I don't want any trouble here today." He looked from the Hammatt to Jaric, Kyle and Rok. "And if we do have any trouble, I've got a warm jail cell just right for all of you. It sleeps four just fine—even oversized aliens." He stared unflinching up at the big Hammatt.

The Mrad suddenly looked farther down the line. "And that goes for you Harg as well. I've got my eye on you."

Kyle and Jaric followed the Mrad's gaze to where four short, burly aliens with thick necks stood. They glared sullenly back at him.

"Didn't I see them somewhere before?" Kyle asked.

"I dunno," Jaric replied. "Maybe."

But a low, rumbling growl brought his attention back around.

Rok glared angrily up at the Hammatt who growled once again as he stared back down at him. Kyle reached out and pulled Rok back towards him and Jaric.

The Hammatt, seemingly satisfied the standoff was over, turned back around.

The Mrad officer stayed close by until they finally reached the food servers several minutes later. Satisfied that the confrontation was over, he walked slowly away.

Jaric looked expectantly at the food being offered—three vegetable selections and one meat.

Jaric, Kyle and Rok watched as their plates were filled with the exotic vegetables—first with curly tubers mixed with small beans of various colors and shapes, followed by blue rice and last with a tiny black vegetable covered with spikes that seemed as if it would be too dangerous to eat.

Jaric stared in wonder at his plate. But his empty stomach eagerly anticipated the late afternoon meal.

He hoped.

However, he looked questioningly at the meat selection. It looked too rare for his taste—anything still alive and *crawling* across the platter was way too rare for him.

"Don't you need to cook these a little more?" Jaric asked as he stared at the small, slithering forms that filled the large spoon poised over his plate. "I mean, they're still moving!"

"Taste better that way," the server replied. "You don't want to ruin the flavor."

"Come on, it's just like sushi," Kyle said with a twinkle in his eye to Jaric.

"Hey, man, this stuff is way beyond just raw!" Jaric moved on. "I'll skip meat today."

Kyle looked closely at the pile of small, slithering forms offered to him as well, but refused it with a grimace.

"Just veggies today for me," he said with a wave of his hands.

Only Rok took a wriggling portion and allowed it to be placed onto his plate, an eager smile on his face.

Jaric and Kyle looked away, each coughing in disbelief, as they continued to the drink counter.

The trio walked slowly around the rows of crowded tables looking for three chairs so they could sit together. Finally, they found three together near the back wall and sat down to eat, oblivious to everything around them.

The huge Hammatt passed them as they put their plates down on their table and sat down. Unknown to them all, he sat down in a chair directly behind them.

The noise level from the myriad of aliens was unbelievable—it seemed these meals were the social highlight of the day for the refugees. Raucous laughter and hearty shouts punctuated the constant chatter of a hundred simultaneous conversations—it was easy to discern that their everyday concerns were now pushed aside in order to enjoy a friendly meal.

Kyle picked up one of the spiky vegetables between his finger and thumb. He looked at it cautiously, turning it over repeatedly.

"Is this edible?" he finally asked.

Rok boldly took a handful and threw them into his mouth. He chewed slowly, then he nodded with appreciation.

"Not bad. Actually, quite tasty."

Kyle looked questioningly at it again, and then popped it into his mouth. The spikes stabbed momentarily, causing a pricking sensation against his tongue and the roof of his mouth. Suddenly, the sensation melted away. He bit down, feeling something squirt inside his mouth. He chewed appreciatively,

"Yeah, not bad at all."

Right across from them, the four burly Harg from the food line approached their table. Ominously, they stood over four tiny aliens eating quietly and minding their own business. As soon as the seated aliens realized who stood behind them, they quickly rose, spilling some of their food in their haste, and left.

The Harg smiled savagely, laughing as the aliens beat a hasty retreat.

Rok eyed them carefully, his face hard and expressionless. He continued to eat, although he kept a watchful eye on the newcomers.

Kyle eyed the Harg as well.

As the Harg began eating and joking with each other, an alarm seemed to go off inside Kyle's head. His eyes narrowed as they caught him watching them.

Two of the Harg laughed as they went back to eating their food.

"I don't like aliens who bully other aliens," Rok said loud enough so everyone, including the Harg, could hear.

The four Harg stopped talking and eyed Rok and the two humans carefully.

Kyle, Rok and Jaric stared defiantly back at them.

One of the stout Harg whispered something to the other three that drew a round of laughter. The four aliens returned to their food and their private conversation.

"I don't like those particular aliens," Jaric whispered to his two friends.

"We'll keep an eye on them," Rok said evenly, returning to his own plate of food.

Kyle didn't like it either—he didn't like aliens bullying others, especially small, defenseless aliens. And somehow he felt he'd seen these Harg before, or others of their kind somewhere. Try as he might, he couldn't shake that nagging feeling.

Jaric suddenly looked up with a jerk of his head as if he had just remembered something. Jaric carefully searched the alien faces, looking slowly all around the great room—every direction except directly behind. With a quick glance, he looked to his right and left, and then he began his careful survey a second time.

Kyle and Rok stopped eating as they watched Jaric continue his slow survey. Jaric paused briefly on the Harg again, but he was obviously searching for something else.

The four Harg continued whispering among themselves, their black, beady eyes darting at the two humans and the Kraaqi as they spoke.

Two tables away, two reptilian aliens sat down with their own plates of food. But they did not eat. Instead, they peered steadily over at the Harg. The larger of the two whispered to the other, who nodded while the others seated at their table stopped their conversations and began to concentrate silently on their food—as if trying to ignore the newcomers.

But overall, the room echoed with talk and laughter and the sound of utensils striking plates. The majority did not yet feel the tension that began to fill the air around the tables at the far end of the room.

It built quickly to an unstoppable climax.

Kyle, momentarily forgetting the Harg, stifled a laugh as he continued to watch his friend's comically intent look of concentration.

"What're you looking for, Jaric? Did you lose something?" Kyle asked, a smile on his face.

Jaric shook his head, as if disappointed.

"I was wondering where that big, fat, ugly alien with the attitude went." He stabbed a few of the spiky vegetables. He faced Kyle. "You know, the one with the big, ugly horn on its nose—*the Hammatt*. But I guess he left."

Jaric raised the fork to his mouth as a powerful growl shook the air.

Jaric and Kyle locked eyes.

"Don't tell me," Jaric whispered in shock.

A second growl filled the air, the source obviously right behind them.

"I won't tell you. But get ready," Kyle whispered back.

Slowly, Kyle put his hand underneath his plate.

Without warning, a mass of vegetables mixed with the living-meat rained down over Jaric's head. Jaric's eyes widened in panic as some of the crawling forms cascaded down near his mouth. He wiped them away quickly, shaking the squirming, worm-like things off his hands with a shudder.

Jaric felt a huge form brush against his back as the mighty Hammatt stood.

Jaric rolled his eyes at Kyle who looked back at him with a mixture of shock and suppressed mirth.

A voice from somewhere above spoke.

"Stupid, fat, and *ugly* am I? Why, you little..."

At just that moment, Kyle threw his plateful of food up in the direction he figured the huge alien's face would be.

He missed.

Instead, the flying food drenched several aliens beside the huge Hammatt.

"What the?" they shouted as they all rose angrily.

Kyle lunged backward, swinging his elbow hard into the Hammatt's stomach.

It felt like he struck a steel wall.

He froze and groaned, rubbing his elbow painfully.

Kyle and Jaric looked at each other again, shrugged with resignation, then slowly looked up.

The Hammatt stared down at them, nostrils flared, his eyes burning blasters into them.

Jaric began to laugh.

"You know, there's something funny in all—"

At that moment, the Hammatt reached down with both hands, lifted up two more plates of food from surprised aliens on either side of him, and flung them at the two humans.

But Jaric and Kyle ducked just in time—falling down on their hands and knees.

Behind them angry shouts grew in number.

All at once, the air filled with flying plates of food aimed like missiles.

"We've got to get out of here!" Jaric whispered urgently to Kyle as they hugged the floor.

"No kidding, Einstein."

A powerful hand locked on each of them with a vise-like grip.

"Uh-oh," Jaric and Kyle said simultaneously.

Effortlessly, they rose into the air.

"I think time is running out," Jaric said with resignation.

Kyle winced as he clenched his fists, eyes still shut.

"Just follow my lead."

"I *knew* you were going to say that," Jaric shot back.

"I'm not the one who insulted the biggest alien in the room."

Jaric groaned. "Well, if I'd known he was right behind me, I—"

Suddenly, Rok jumped up on the table and shouted a Kraaqi war-cry.

The entire room went deathly silent.

Reaching down, Rok grabbed a plate in each hand and flung them at the Hammatt's face.

Rok leapt at the huge alien at the same time.

But the big Hammatt simply lowered his body and with a sudden upward motion sent the Kraaqi flying over his shoulder while still holding the hapless humans.

A fresh set of muffled shouts and the sound of new fighting indicated the airborne Kraaqi had landed.

A new wave of missiles—more plates of food in addition to cups of liquid—flew through the air locked on target.

Shouts mixed with growls filled the room. Everyone in the room lashed out at the alien next to him.

Food quickly covered everyone—some of it still squirming as it slid down their faces.

The Hammatt held the two dangling humans like a statue—and with each passing second another plateful of food covered its head and shoulders. The huge alien growled ominously as its whole body shook with his mounting anger.

Kyle looked up at the mountain-like form and savagely kicked at its ribs.

But nothing happened, except the faintest groan from the Hammatt.

They still hovered helplessly.

"Oh great," Jaric shot at Kyle. "I think you've saved the day!"

A mighty roar deafened them.

First, the Hammatt took Jaric and slung him headlong down one side of the table like a bartender flinging a glass of beer. Jaric yelled with abject horror as he sailed down the table toward the end and then flew out into the open air.

But his flight was short-lived.

He screamed again as he dropped among a group of wrestling aliens. Immediately, he felt their hooves stepping all over his body.

In the next instant, they all fell right on top of him.

With another mighty heave, the Hammatt flung Kyle as if he were a rag doll. The few plates and glasses still left on the other end of the table shot away as Kyle's body sailed down the entire length of the table—and beyond.

Kyle launched into the air with such force that his personal flight took him square into a group of large, fur-covered aliens. His flailing body knocked them over as if they were bowling pins.

They gathered themselves quickly, picked up his limp form, and began to buffet him with blows.

In the next moment, the four Harg jumped these aliens while Kyle tried to defend himself from every direction with little effect. It felt like the air rained blows upon him from every side—and it wasn't a good feeling.

Kyle continued kicking and punching as he recoiled from several blows at once. In a flash, he found himself flat on the floor, a heavy body pinning him down.

He struggled, but to no avail.

With his arms pinned, he was lifted up—and just as suddenly lowered as an alien flew through the air just over him and barely missed colliding with him.

Kyle shook his head to clear his thoughts, although the rest of him was still held firmly. He looked around to get his bearings as he struggled vainly to free himself.

With a groan, he twisted his head to see who held him fast.

A savage Harg growled.

The stout alien smiled. "Let's go, human. Somebody wants to—"

The world suddenly spun upside down amid a Kraaqi war cry.

Rok's blow sent the Harg hard to the ground and Kyle fell away free—bruised and hurt, but free.

Kyle rolled and jumped up—finding himself beside the Kraaqi warrior.

They were in the middle of eight or nine aliens flailing away with fists and claws.

"What do we do now?" Kyle asked as he ducked a flying plate.

Rok avoided a fist. Then he lashed out, sending the perpetrator down to the ground. He lowered his body, trying to watch every direction at once as the different fighters surged and faded.

"It's time we leave," he grunted.

"No argument here," Kyle replied breathlessly.

And then the other three Harg jumped them from behind.

Kicks and punches along with shouts and groans came from every direction.

For the third time, Kyle found himself pinned motionless in a merciless grasp. He pushed his head over to get a view of Rok. He saw that his friend continued struggling on the floor with two Harg on top of him.

"I don't think these Harg like us," Kyle grunted as he flinched from another blow.

Rok lashed out, only to be pounded with fists.

The fourth Harg appeared out of nowhere and stood over Rok. He struck him with a mighty blow. Rok groaned as his body went still.

"This is one tough alien," one of the Harg holding Rok said to his allies.

"No matter, we have bested him." The Harg who appeared to be the leader looked over at Kyle. "Get the other human, the dark-skinned one. We must get to the ship." He looked up as sirens began to wail. "And be quick, Mrad Security will be here soon!"

Kyle's face was being mashed into the floor by a steel-like force on his neck while his wrists remained held fast behind his back. He struggled vainly to get free.

Unknown to Kyle, two large reptilian forms suddenly appeared out of the crowds, shoving and wrestling everyone out of their way.

Qirn looked at Jaan as they came upon the Harg.

Both nodded.

Like a flash of lightning, the two threw themselves at the Harg.

Kyle felt the vise-like grips release. Instantly, he tried to rise, but a blow from another alien sent him back down.

The food riot got into full swing as every alien attacked anything that moved.

Aliens stepped all over Kyle now—punching him, kicking him and cursing him as he tried to lash back from his position on the floor—the worst place he could be in the middle of a riot.

Kyle finally realized he couldn't defend himself from this position. He saw Rok's face appear between an alien's tree-like legs.

"Crawl under the table over there!" Rok pointed as he continued crawling among the forest of alien legs.

Their frenzied movements propelled them toward the protective cover of the nearest table. With a supreme effort, they threw their bodies the last meter until they were beyond the legs, feet, hooves and claws of the countless combatants towering over them.

And once there, they found a long-lost friend.

"Jaric!" Kyle shouted with happy recognition.

But Jaric shook his head as he lay under the table.

"Just follow my lead," he muttered sarcastically to Kyle.

"Well, who's the idiot that shouted loud enough so the entire universe could hear that the Hammatt is big, fat and stupid? While he sat just behind him!"

They locked eyes.

Suddenly, the table over their heads lifted and flew away.

"Oh no," Jaric and Kyle said together.

Rok glanced up.

And immediately slapped his hand over his eyes as he groaned in disbelief.

A huge growl reverberated above them.

But Kyle and Jaric continued to stare at each other with looks of utter despair.

Finally, Jaric spoke.

"Aren't you going to look up?"

Kyle let his head fall with a thump to the floor in utter resignation.

"This can't be happening—not again!" Kyle said to the floor.

In another instant, they felt a familiar grip lift them easily into the air.

"Well, well, well. Look what I found!" The Hammatt shouted with joy.

He laughed heartily.

But that's all he did.

From every door dozens of uniformed Mrad Officers suddenly poured into the room with sirens blaring. Every food-covered combatant went still in mid-punch.

A few minutes later and it was all over.

Mmmmm." Elise took a last, lingering bite of her dessert as her hair glowed with a deep electric blue sheen. She closed her eyes and let the exotic flavors melt inside her mouth with a delicious sweetness.

"It is good, isn't it?" Krinia's head-tail swished back and forth excitedly as she savored her own final morsel of the same exotic-flavored ice cream.

"Some variation of chocolate, I'd say—or several kinds mixed together," Jysar muttered between bites.

"The waiter said it was a triple chocolate—best of three worlds mixed together," Krinia added as she wiped her mouth appreciatively.

"The ultimate chocolate experience," Elise said with a laugh. "I'm in paradise."

"A chocolate paradise." Jysar chuckled.

Nearby, the two Harg whispered as they cast furtive glances from the clock back to the table where Elise set down her empty bowl.

The restaurant seethed with patrons, while the broad corridor outside was literally wall-to-wall with aliens. The early evening drew nigh and with it a festive air urged the crowds to seek out RahajMr's best in food and entertainment.

"Don't you think it's time to go?" Jysar looked ill at ease as he surveyed the growing crowds around them.

"Why, don't you like crowds?" Krinia asked with a smile.

"Not especially," he replied. "I favor smaller, more intimate places to relax." Jysar shuddered. "I feel like I'm trapped in a sea of alien beings!"

Krinia rose. "I agree with you for once, Jysar. Let's..." A certain movement caught her eye.

"Look," Elise said, following Krinia's glance. "It's Minstrel. I mean, the Zuuk."

The seven eye-stalks gazed in various directions, obviously searching for them. Krinia waved as the three made their way toward the multi-colored shell body of the alien.

Minstrel-Zuuk looked relieved—as much as a Zuuk can look that way.

"I've been looking for you for over an hour. We need to get back to Mother," Minstrel-Zuuk said loudly enough to be heard over the crowd noise.

"Oh, why is that?" Elise asked innocently.

"Well, for one thing, the Mrad authorities suspect that someone tried to sabotage their precious computer system." The Zuuk shook his head, causing the eye-stalks to wave from side to side. "And although I'm innocent, I'm the one they grilled with questions until I can't see straight. And that's saying a lot for a being with seven eyes."

Jysar chuckled.

"What happened?" Krinia asked.

"They discovered that someone put a tracer program on my queries, as well as a kill code. Their internal security programs recorded some of its activity, but not the source. However, they did trace it to my query."

"Why would anyone want to trace your search queries?" Krinia asked.

"I presume they wanted to know the results as much as I did."

"Well, we were on our way back anyway. Let's go."

"But I wanted to check on my queries?" Elise asked plaintively.

"No need." Minstrel-Zuuk replied, holding up a data pad. "I have your results here—courtesy of Mrad Security. It seems the boys have gotten into some kind of trouble as well. Just when I was about to be released, more Mrad Security came in and informed me that we were all being ordered to leave RahajMr—immediately. They supplied me with the results of all of our queries—and told me to find you and get back to our ship—pronto."

"Were there any matches for mine?" Elisa asked, full of hope.

"I am afraid not."

Elise's face fell with disappointment.

"Don't worry too much, Elise." Krinia patted her shoulder comfortingly. "You tried."

"You can't expect to be a hero on your first attempt," Jysar added.

"I don't want to be a hero." Elise looked from one to the other with a pleading in her eyes. "I just want Jaric and Kyle to know that I'm human too. That I want to find other survivors, just like they do." She sighed deeply. "If I helped them find other survivors, then they'd like me."

Krinia reached around Elise and gave her a strong hug of reassurance.

"There'll be another time. And then you can try again." Krinia smiled at her friend. "The biggest thing is to never give up trying. And one day you or one of the boys are bound to succeed. I know it."

Elise's eyes brightened. "Thank you."

They walked off together arm in arm following Jysar and the multi-colored shell of Minstrel-Zuuk.

The two Harg held their position a moment longer at their table. Each typed brief notes into their handheld units reporting everything they just heard. They finished and quickly followed their quarry, always keeping them just within eyesight among the never-ending throngs.

But as Elise and the others stepped into Berth B279 where Mother sat docked, the Harg following them walked inconspicuously past until they came to a corner. They ducked quickly out of sight and waited.

After a few moments, they looked at each other with confidence. One of them took out a scanner and tuned it. Concealing it carefully under his shirt, he nodded to his accomplice. This time they walked slowly by Berth B279, long enough to obtain a good scan of Mother.

They hurried on to report their findings to the Paum.

Six hours later, Rok, Kyle, Jaric and the Hammatt stood before the watchful gaze of Jodacis, Mrad Judge of the Law and the Chief Justice assigned to the Lower Court of Refugees.

"What did they do with everybody else?" Jaric whispered. "I mean, they must've arrested a couple of hundred aliens back there."

Rok slowly twisted his head from side to side as if he were trying to get rid of an annoying tenseness in his neck. He remained silent as he glanced up at the stern gaze of Judge Jodacis sitting at his station above them.

"It has been determined that you four started this outburst," the closest Mrad Officer said.

Jaric looked down at the floor and sighed.

"I trust you've been given the *usual* lecture." The Judge's voice boomed out, breaking the silence of the large judicial chamber.

Jaric and the others seemed to shrink under that voice of stern authority. And with the recent memory of the multitude of tedious words that verbally beat them black-and-blue, they had absolutely no desire to hear the lecture again.

Even now, the words echoed inside their heads like a bad song you wish you could erase out of your mind but can't.

Actually, the lecture boiled down to one important theme—if you did something stupid, like break the Law, then the Law would set you straight.

"Don't fight the Law," Kyle whispered to Jaric. "Cause the Law always wins, baby."

"I'm convinced," Jaric whispered back.

"Silence in my court!" The Mrad Judge returned his gaze to the console and the list of charges. "Answer my first question, please."

"Yes, we've heard it. Three times in the last hour alone," Kyle said with disgust.

"And you'll hear it more before you're out of my courtroom. The Law will be obeyed."

170

They all groaned in unison.

"Well, what do we have here," the judge continued as he glanced at the console on his desk. "Let's see, yes." He cleared his throat. "Disrupting the peace, initiating a riot, destruction of public property, assaulting an alien." He paused here. "Or aliens. Or should I make it assaulting anything that is within your reach."

Kyle groaned.

The Judge began inputting new data into the console while the four remained silent.

Several, long minutes passed.

Finally, the Judge finished. He looked down at them once again with unflinching eyes.

"We don't like your kind of alien in our cities. Especially aliens causing trouble among the homeless refugees we are trying to help."

Rok started to speak, thought better of it, and returned to staring at the floor.

"You'll spend four days in captivity, working in the kitchens to pay off the damage you've caused—your calculated share. And then you'll be escorted away from our cities as *persona non grata*, and not allowed to return to RahajMr or its sister cities until two years have elapsed. Is that clear?"

"That seems a bit harsh, don't you think?" Jaric looked up with surprise at the Mrad Judge. "I mean, we made a mistake—one mistake. We've—"

The Mrad Judge interrupted him.

"There is another, more serious activity in which you seem to be involved—albeit there is no direct evidence, only circumstantial."

"What is that?" Rok asked with interest.

"Have you ever met an alien named Ablek?"

"Yes," Kyle answered quickly. "We rented our Search-terminals through him." He, Jaric and Rok looked intently up at the Mrad Judge now.

"He is in hospital even as we speak—badly hurt and only semi-conscious."

"What?" the trio said simultaneously.

"His wounds are the result of a vicious attack." The Mrad Judge leaned forward. "And whoever attacked him will be dealt with in the most severe way, according to our law."

"How are we involved?" Kyle asked. "We liked the little alien."

"That's right," Jaric quickly added, a look of concern on his face.

"We are investigating exactly what took place. Our investigators have discovered that whoever perpetrated this heinous act was able to partially disable our Security systems—another serious crime."

"That's not us," Kyle said matter-of-factly. "I don't think we're that smart."

"And so it may turn out to be. However." The Mrad Judge cleared his throat loudly. "Ablek whispers a word from time to time as he lies there in hospital. And the word he repeats is—*human*."

Kyle and Jaric bowed their heads solemnly.

"The Hammatt does not seem to be implicated in this first crime."

All eyes in the courtroom turned to the big alien.

But the Hammatt remained strangely silent.

The Judge's gaze focused back on Kyle, Jaric and Rok. "So, first you meet Ablek and perform a business transaction. And later that same evening he is brutally assaulted. Humans have never before been to our cities, and yet within the first two waking cycles since you arrive, two crimes are committed. And you are implicated in both—either directly or indirectly." The Mrad Judge cleared his throat noisily once again. "We don't like your kind of alien in our cities."

"We're innocent of the first incident, Your Honor," Rok said with conviction. "We would never attack another alien, unless it was to defend ourselves."

"The investigation will determine that. If we do find you guilty of the first charge, you will be dealt with much more harshly. Now, take them from my court."

Kyle looked up. "Can we contact our ship first, to let them know what's happened to us? Our mother will be concerned."

"One communication." He waved them all away.

"Why are you in police custody?" Mother asked with an electronic edge.

Kyle and Jaric both groaned.

"It was a mistake, we were in the wrong place at the wrong time," Jaric answered quickly.

"Yeah," Kyle agreed. "We were just minding our own business, eating lunch, when..."

"Actually," Rok interrupted with an apologetic tone. "Actually, we found ourselves involved with several irate aliens. Jaric inadvertently insulted one..."

"Yeah, the biggest one there," Kyle said.

"Wait, wait," Jaric broke in. "That Hammatt started it back in the..."

"Enough!" Mother shouted, her voice rising several decibels.

"Uh-oh," Kyle said under his voice.

"I will ascertain all the facts from you and from the Mrad authorities—personally. At that time, I will determine what took place. And what additional discipline I need to take. Suffice it to say, you got yourselves into trouble. And you are also in serious trouble with *me*."

Kyle and Jaric groaned again.

"In the meantime, I have good news."

Rok, Jaric and Kyle stared at the Mrad communicator.

"Minstrel and I have decided we all need a vacation."

They looked at each other with puzzled expressions.

"We have been talking about this concept while I researched its history. The planet I have chosen for the process of vacation is not only an ideal place to relax and unwind, but there is also a famous festival taking place right now. It is a five-day journey from here."

"Go on," Kyle said with growing interest.

"It is the island-planet called Meramee."

"Indeed, it is a most fascinating place," Minstrel added from the communicator. "A rare and beautiful world—ninety percent ocean with the largest land mass only a few hundred kilometers in total area. There are tens of thousands of different islands that dot this planet. It is said—'no two islands are exactly alike on Meramee.' I am in keen anticipation myself."

"Meramee."

Jaric said the word as if it were a long lost friend. He looked at Kyle with eagerness on his face.

"I've heard of it. A couple of aliens mentioned it to me a few months ago—some kind of tropical paradise planet."

"What kind of festival?" Kyle asked with excitement in his voice.

"It occurs every seven years," Mother said. "Millions flock to it from all the planets in this quadrant, even faraway Jantannell. It's a festival featuring the best food, beer and wine from the planets of a particular sector chosen by the Festival Council. They call it 'Rayall Shifanzz', which roughly translates 'Taste of the Quadrant.'"

"Even better, the aliens who reside on this island-planet are an aquatic race called the Mejadic." Minstrel glowed brightly. "These festivals feature their unique underwater concerts. They play their instruments underwater but the sounds can be heard above water. And song-whales are known to join many times, adding their eerie cries. I have heard recordings by other Minstrels

175

who've visited Meramee, but this will be my first time to experience it personally."

"We plan on staying at least one month after the festival's climax subsides," Mother added.

"The best food and beer from an entire sector," Rok said as he licked his lips. "Sounds delightful."

"I have contacted your Kraaqi frigate, the *Aurora*. It is now on its way here and will pick you up once you are released. They will contact you with their berth number when they arrive."

"Wait!" Kyle shouted. "Where are you going to be, Mother?"

A brief, but powerful pause echoed from the communicator.

"We will be arriving at Meramee right about the time you are released."

"Why?"

"We too have been asked to leave and then return at the end of the week to pick you up. Instead, we will proceed to Meramee and wait for you there, a more efficient use of our time. There is no need for us to be inconvenienced by your mistakes. The *Aurora* will pass RahajMr on its way to Meramee. It is logical that they pick you up."

Jaric and Kyle looked at each other.

"Yeah, I guess there's no need for you to suffer for our troubles. I guess we'll see you at Meramee," Jaric said, his voice tinged with sadness.

"Yes," Mother said with firmness. "At that time we will discuss this issue again."

# CHAPTER NINE

Mother lifted from her berth two hours later and made her way through the eternal winds. Her gift from the Kraaqi, the anti-gravity sub-light engines, powered her steadily through the tattered cloud bands of green and orange. Within a few minutes, she left the gas planet behind and sailed gracefully into the silent blackness of outer space.

As she turned and powered up her hyperdrive engines, Mother's manta-ray silhouette shimmered under the sparkling light of ten million stars. Mother locked in the coordinates for Meramee and kicked in her powerful ThunderStar engines.

With a mighty flash, she leapt into hyperspace.

"Why do you think tracer code and kill code were placed on your query, Minstrel?" Mother asked.

"That is a mystery." Minstrel dissolved the multi-colored Zuuk shell and returned to its normal plasma body. Minstrel's twinkling body ebbed and flowed like a living cloud of countless miniature stars.

"I assume it has to do with sentient technology. I base that on the laws I found forbidding such technology—something highly feared." A sudden wave of silver washed Minstrel's undulating body. "Further research I obtained remotely from my own starship revealed quite a number of alien races have actually outlawed and banned it in this quadrant."

Mother felt confusion. Why would any race ban such research? After all, humanity's efforts had resulted in her creation. She proved most beneficial to her creators, especially as the caretaker to the last three children of humanity.

In addition, she carefully protected and housed the precious contents inside her long-term memories—a knowledgebase and compendium of all the accomplishments and history of the human race since its beginning long, long ago.

Prudently, she had downloaded it to both the Hrono and Minstrel races before leaving the Three Kingdoms. Even if Mother suffered destruction now, the rest of the universe would not forget the human race.

Mother was sentient technology—and she was good.

Or so she thought of herself.

"Could you make contact with your brother Minstrels and find out why some of these races created such a ban?" Mother asked with a nervous edge to her voice.

Minstrel glowed brighter. "Yes, a good suggestion. Once we are far enough away from RahajMr, I will send the 'recall beacon' for my ship. After we rendezvous with it, I will send out that communication."

Mother's processors hummed with activity. "Could you venture an assumption, Minstrel?"

"You are concerned, aren't you?"

"Yes," Mother replied instantly. "I am sentient technology. Why would anyone want to outlaw beings like me?"

Minstrel's body glowed brighter until its essence filled the room and reflected off the numerous consoles around the bridge.

"They may consider sentient technology dangerous."

Mother's processors spiked with super-activity as she assimilated this fact and looked at it from a million different angles. A few seconds later, Mother spoke.

"Do you mean dangerous as in harmful like a disease?"

"No." Minstrel's voice, normally a pleasant, melodious tone, turned serious.

Two seconds passed, an eternity to Mother's circuits.

"They may consider sentient technology *evil*."

Minstrel floated slowly to the ceiling after speaking, its body now spread so thin it was almost invisible.

"Evil." Mother repeated. Her processor utilization hummed with activity as she referenced this concept throughout the vast knowledgebase of humanity, through all the various meanings and applications throughout all human history. Mother soon realized that this concept of evil played an integral part in almost every facet of human existence and the human experience.

Mother became fascinated and horrified by what she found.

Several minutes passed in silence as Minstrel waited for Mother to continue.

"These alien races may feel that sentient technology could create evil, or bring pain or sorrow to them." Mother paused again, focusing on the exact definition of the word evil. "They may feel sentient technology would visit destruction upon them."

"The concept of evil." Minstrel's voice echoed softly.

"These races may believe sentient technology would *bring evil* upon them, not that it was *evil* in itself..."

"Isn't the concept of evil and its application one and the same?" Minstrel asked.

"Sometimes those who are deemed good perform evil deeds." Mother paused.

Minstrel laughed.

"Why are you laughing? That statement of fact should not exist—it is a paradox."

"Perhaps evil depends on your perspective? Perhaps it depends if you are the one meting out justice—or the one receiving it?"

"Please explain," Mother coaxed.

"In a war, there are normally two sides—two opposing forces. Two different governments or two different races." Minstrel's body suddenly twinkled like a billion tiny stars going super-nova. "Or two different spiritual belief systems."

"Go on," Mother urged.

"The *other side* is always evil."

Now Mother's processors spiked to overload as she considered this one thought—a sentence so simple. And so profound.

"How can that be?" Mother asked. "In essence, they are only *different*, or does that make one good and the other evil according to biological beings?"

"If one faction by its actions brings destruction or pain on the other, then it is considered evil. Having performed evil, the perpetrators are evil."

"So, beings are evil based on their actions?"

"In a way." Minstrel thought a moment. "By its definition, which I'm sure you've reviewed many times these last few seconds, evil is the antithesis of goodness—or that which is good."

"Evil is synonymous with malevolence, badness, foulness and sorrow." Mother paused. "It is not strictly a moral badness, although in many references evil is considered just that."

"*Inherent evil*," Minstrel emphasized. "A being totally evil. Or bent on evil—to bring evil upon others. That is the concept biological beings define as evil."

"The bad guy," Mother said.

"The *really* bad guy," Minstrel added.

Silence settled between them a long moment.

"What makes one evil?" Mother asked.

"That is not an easy question to answer."

"Please try."

Minstrel's body flowed together until it became an opaque cloud of lights. Thoughts flowed throughout its essence as it carefully contemplated Mother's question.

181

"Many times, those who perform evil do not consider themselves such. In fact, they may feel that their actions are justified."

"And yet they are evil?"

"Look inside your knowledgebase of human history," Minstrel prompted Mother. "Look into their past—far into their past."

"Why?"

"Remember, Minstrels visited humanity long ago, but we did not reveal ourselves to them because we found them unworthy—at that time in their history." Minstrel paused. "You will find human history littered with philosophical paradoxes—where their intention was good but the result was evil."

"I see them."

"Some of the most horrific evils were done in the name of Right. And in the name of God." Minstrel paused with sadness.

"The Holocaust," Mother began somberly. "The Inquisition. The Crusades. The European conquest of the Americas and Australia and the destruction of entire aboriginal races—numerous other wars of genocide. And countless acts of terrorism."

"Worse than that." Minstrel sighed.

"The rape and pollution of their original home world in the name of profit."

"Yes," Minstrel said with a great sadness. "Each time, the goal of their actions was for the good of *their* people—for the good of *their* cause. But look at what each ultimately caused."

"It was evil. The result was evil in each case, and those that perpetrated the action were evil." Mother's processors burned with activity. "The end does not justify the means."

"They felt they were right. It was their perspective at the time." Minstrel's body glowed brightly as if all the individual tiny lights had coalesced into one mass. "Of course, they were all wrong."

Mother waited for Minstrel to continue.

"This concept of evil appears to be simple on the surface," Minstrel added matter-of-factly. "Beings may feel their cause is right. And to achieve their cause they are justified to take whatever actions they deem necessary."

"Even evil actions?"

"Even evil actions," Minstrel echoed.

"But their actions make them evil," Mother said.

"If they bring evil on another by such actions—yes. By the strict definition of the term. If they bring pain, suffering and destruction in order to bring about their purpose—they become evil. No matter how much they try to justify their actions."

"Then I am evil," Mother said with sadness.

"You brought evil upon the T'kaan, yes," Minstrel agreed. "But that does not make you an evil being. Your only course of action was to fight and defend yourself and the children. Or else you would have ceased to exist. You had the right to defend yourself and your children. Everyone has the

183

right to defend his life and his family from a murderer."

"Then I am not evil."

"You are not an inherently evil being. From the perspective of the T'kaan, you would be perceived as evil because you destroyed them. But not from the human perspective—to them you are heroic. And not from an objective perspective, for you saved countless other alien races from potential destruction at the hands of the T'kaan."

"Evil cannot be totally based on perspective. There must be some code of conduct in order to measure actions against it, in order to determine if their actions are evil," Mother said. "And even if the intention or goal is one of good, if one's action breaks the code of conduct, that one must be defined as evil."

"Exactly. The code of conduct must protect the rights of all beings equally in order that evil is not perpetrated upon any of them no matter their differences."

"But I did evil—I destroyed. We just stated that actions do not justify the end result."

"If you had not fought, the human race would now be extinct. And worse, it would be utterly forgotten. Your knowledgebase of humanity would have been destroyed before you could download it to the Hrono and Minstrel race."

"So, how do we tell if a being is evil?"

"It is not easy. And we must take into account that we all make mistakes from time to time. But a *pattern of actions* reveals true intent in the end."

"Can a good being turn evil?" Mother asked.

"Yes. And an evil being can turn good."

"Of course, it depends on your perspective," Mother said in a mocking tone.

"Perception is reality, at times. But one's actions will ultimately tell all."

"The 'Perception is reality' attitude is a common fault among biological beings," Mother agreed.

"Destructive actions taint a noble goal. They may claim with all their heart they are on the side of good—but their actions give lie to their words. And living this lie will ultimately affect their mental makeup and their conscience until they feel they are justified by any action—a delusional sickness." Minstrel paused. "Such beings feel they are *infallible.*"

"Some use evil to fight evil and say it is right," Mother countered.

"Can two wrongs make a right?"

"It is not logical."

"Our actions make us evil. Especially evil acted with malevolent purpose and premeditation," Minstrel added with a sense of finality.

"Evil is more complex than I first thought." Mother sighed.

"Yes."

Mother bookmarked several thousand references inside her knowledgebase so she could review this subject again.

"Did you know that you were followed when you and the others came back yesterday?" Mother said, changing the subject.

"No, I did not! And that's bad for a Minstrel, especially one with seven eye-stalks at the time," Minstrel said with shock.

"It is understandable with the ever-present crowds on RahajMr."

"Still, I should've picked them up. It is the basic training of all Minstrels that we unobtrusively walk among other aliens. And if we should arouse interest, we must be aware and take measures. I need to be more careful." Minstrel's body twinkled brightly. "Perhaps they were part of the Mrad Security?"

"It fits the facts. Still, my sensors detected their attempts to scan me. It seemed odd."

Mother's thoughts focused on Jaric and Kyle.

"Minstrel, do you think the boys are...bad? They seem to get into trouble quite often. And now they are in trouble with Mrad Security and in custody."

Minstrel smiled. "They are young and full of the energy and vitality of life. They act before they think. That is their problem."

Minstrel's body expanded like a glowing fog across the entire bridge.

"I would say they are...mischievous." Minstrel laughed.

Mother felt a comfort grow inside her circuits.

"They will probably grow out of it. Maturity will bring wisdom to them, as it has to Rok. Somewhat," Minstrel added.

"Well, I am glad we're going on vacation. It's a good idea to relax after our long journey the past months."

"Meramee, an ocean world paradise sprinkled with islands," Minstrel said with growing excitement. "And we are arriving at their famous festival. If this can't help the boys relax and enjoy themselves, nothing can."

"We will all enjoy it," Mother said with quiet hope. "A nice, quiet vacation."

# CHAPTER TEN

"The human ship left two hours ago. An hour after their departure, one of the fast Harg reconnaissance ships followed them." Rab watched his leader's face intently.

Qirn's face grew thoughtful as he stroked his chin; the yellow, vertical pupils of his eyes glowed with the inner workings of his mind. After a few moments of contemplation, his short, powerful tail whipped from side to side decisively.

"The *evil* of the Paum is closing in on these humans—one way or another," Qirn said with a solemn tone. "I will take my starship and go after them."

"What about the humans still here?" Jaan asked.

"Rab and the others will maintain watch over them."

"We still don't know why the Paum and its agents are so interested in these strange beings?" Jaan's eyes narrowed. "Are they its potential allies? Or its enemies?"

"We know from their communication that they all head for Meramee and the great Festival." Qirn looked from one of his warriors to the other. "The Kraaqi ship will be here soon to take the two human males and their Kraaqi friend to join their friends. Security on Meramee is not half what it is here." Qirn nodded. "The Paum will act there. It is

188

imperative that we go immediately, before they act."

Jaan grunted agreement. "Yes, we must have ourselves in position before any fighting begins."

"And that is why I will take my ship, my crew," Qirn said. "We will prepare. We will engage the Paum and his Harg agents before they act. And defeat their efforts."

Qirn's face became thoughtful. "More important, we must figure out what part these humans play. And why such a small group has the high interest of the Great Paum."

Jaan patted his commander's shoulder. "And we will, my Captain. We will."

Qirn's hand gripped the handle of the sword strapped to his waist. Inside his heart, he knew this business was quickly coming to a climax.

"Ready my ship, Jaan. We sail within the hour."


A whole day had passed since Mother sailed away.

And Jaric and Kyle felt alone and deserted.

Rok sensed it from their words and actions. But inside, he knew this added discipline by Mother would benefit them in the long run. And himself. It would reinforce the hard work the Mrad imposed on them to help pay for the damage.

And maybe next time, they would all think twice before launching into a free-for-all.

*Maybe.*

"I wonder why so few of us were detained and the others just fined and released." Jaric looked at the others sharing their punishment. There were fifteen other aliens hard at work in addition to them and the Hammatt.

"We were singled out as the perpetrators of the food riot." Kyle chuckled with the recent memory.

The huge Hammatt had his back to them as he cleaned the floor. At Kyle's words, he turned. The magnificent horn that grew from his snout lowered as he looked down and made eye contact.

"You are talking too much. Keep working!"

"Who died and made you boss?" Kyle sneered.

The huge Hammatt growled ominously. But then the expression on his gray complexion changed. He sighed. "I only want us to finish our tasks so we can go back to our holding cells. I am tired."

Kyle was impressed with the alien's sudden change of tone, a tone of cooperation instead of confrontation. He looked into the alien's black eyes.

"I agree. If we work together, we can finish faster."

The Hammatt grunted acknowledgement.

The four went back to work with a renewed zeal. The minutes passed quickly as the four worked in close cooperation, cleaning tables and floors as well as taking broken chairs to the back for repair or for refuse.

The Hammatt returned from dumping several chairs when Rok spoke.

"What is your name, Hammatt?"

The big alien looked at him with interest. "I am Inaha." He smiled briefly then returned to his work.

Rok watched him silently for a while before he spoke. "And I am Rok of the Kraaqi, First Leader of the Band of the Stars."

The Hammatt glanced at him with a nod but continued his work.

Rok smiled as the alien picked up two tables, one under each arm, and moved them so he could clean better. "I admire your strength, Inaha."

Inaha placed the tables down and raised his muscular arms, flexing his massive biceps. "My people are a strong race. And brave."

"So are mine." Rok smiled.

Jaric and Kyle looked from Rok back to Inaha with growing interest as the conversation continued.

"Wait a minute, this is the guy that 'hates all aliens.'" Jaric looked at Inaha. "And the alien who threw me around the room like a rag doll the other day." Jaric's eyes widened with the memory.

"Several times." Kyle chuckled.

Rok's low laughter joined Kyle's mirth.

Kyle stopped and admired the Hammatt's great size.

"And I might add, he didn't even break into a sweat!"

Now the Hammatt began to laugh. "It was sort of fun." The big alien laughed even louder.

Rok's laughter grew.

Jaric stared in disbelief, watching the three of them laughing. He found no humor in this. He still had too many aches and pains.

Jaric shook his head. "Well, I for one can't wait until our sentence is finished and we're on our way to Meramee. That's when I'll be laughing."

Inaha's face became serious. "You are going to the 'paradise planet'?" He came over to Jaric and picked him as easily as if he were a toy. He brought Jaric's face close to his. "Are you going to the great Festival?"

"Yeah, yeah." Jaric squirmed in the mighty alien's iron grip. "But why would you want to go? There'll be nothing but *aliens* everywhere. And remember, you're the one who hates aliens!"

The big Hammatt slowly lowered Jaric and set him gently on his feet.

Inaha groaned, a very low and forlorn sound that emanated from deep inside his massive body.

"Mine is a sad story, truth be known. My people were forced to leave our homeworld. It's hard enough to leave your world behind, but to be forced to leave with little hope of returning..." The big alien's eyes grew sad, his face somber.

"It was the *Black Flu*. It came out of nowhere and swept our planet within days. Millions died. Tens of millions."

He looked from one to the other with a sudden intensity. "Do you know what it's like to see corpses piled up on street after street waiting for transport to take them away like so much garbage? Everyone was afraid. Afraid to go outside. Afraid of others. Afraid even to touch the dead in order to bury them. Families watched from inside as disposal units took them away to be burned—not

192

even a decent burial." He looked down, an expression of pain on every feature. "It is said of the Black Flu, when it strikes a world, that the dead bury the dead, it is that contagious."

"Well, it was decided for us: those not infected must evacuate the planet or die. The aliens who lived nearest our world brought their combined war fleets in order to enforce their edict. And we were too weakened to fight."

"A harsh thing to endure," Rok agreed.

"There is no cure for the Black Flu. The only choice is to let the disease run its course, kill all its host and go dormant. Planetary quarantine lasts decades—just to be sure—before you can return to a world stricken by it."

"It must have been bad," Jaric said solemnly.

"It was." Inaha looked from Jaric to the other two. "We went to several planets in search of refuge, in search of help. But everywhere it was the same—we were driven away with curses and threats." The Hammatt's face became one of intense sadness. "They treated us like outcasts, like we were tainted—like we were worthless and had no right to ask for help! Even though we carried papers that certified we had been tested and were disease-free."

Inaha gazed off in the distance. "No one would help us."

Inaha faced Jaric. "On one planet, they even spit on me. Me! And said that I and my people needed to go die somewhere else—anywhere—as long as it was far away from them. And so I grew to hate all aliens deep in my heart."

193

Jaric patted the alien's shoulder. "But you have been helped here." Jaric smiled. "And we are not treating you that way."

Inaha smiled. "I was wrong to say what I did— that I hated all aliens. The past year has been difficult." He looked over to Kyle and Rok. "Actually, I traveled a lot before the outbreak. I signed with a Hammatt trader and had just returned from a four-year stint when the flu broke out. Back then, I enjoyed meeting aliens from different worlds."

Kyle's eyes went wide. "You're kidding! I would've never figured that from our first encounter."

Rok stepped beside Inaha. "But now that we have talked, we understand him. We understand why he said what he said." Rok looked at both Jaric and Kyle. "If we had known this, we would have brushed off his angry words and not reacted so quickly. And there might not have been a riot."

Kyle laughed. "Well, that could be."

"Yeah." Jaric laughed. "Next time I won't react so quickly." His face became thoughtful. "Maybe I'll try to understand first."

"Think first, then act. What a concept!" Kyle said with renewed laughter.

"Well, let's get back to work," Kyle said with sudden enthusiasm. "I want to get back with Mother and Minstrel on Meramee as quickly as we can. And maybe if we work hard together, they might take a day or two off our sentence."

Inaha's eyes widened with surprise.

"Minstrel!" He placed his face next to Kyle's until his horn almost touched Kyle's nose. "Are you a friend of a *Minstrel*?" he shouted.

Everyone in the room turned toward them.

"Hey, not so loud," Kyle said as he held up his hands for emphasis.

The big alien's face became one full of excitement. "This changes everything!"

"How is that?" Jaric asked with disbelief.

"Hammatts have known of Minstrels for a long time. We cherish their visits. We cherish the songs they bring from the far reaches of the universe."

Kyle's eyebrows rose with interest. He nodded to Rok and Jaric who nodded back.

Inaha looked at all of them with a profound look in his eyes.

"Any friend of a Minstrel is a friend of Inaha. And any Hammatt!"

"Well, this does change everything." Kyle laughed.

"Would you like to journey with us to Meramee and visit with our Minstrel?" Rok asked.

Jaric and Kyle looked at him with shocked surprise.

"Yes!" Inaha effortlessly lifted Jaric and Kyle into his great arms and hugged them so tight their eyes began to bulge.

"T-that's enough love," Kyle grunted, vainly trying to free himself from Inaha's iron embrace.

"O-o," Jaric grunted within the Hammatt's merciless grasp. "Kay," he managed to finish. "Put us down."

Inaha put them down quickly. "Then I can go? I can pay for my passage. And I've been there before, too! I can show you some of the best islands, the ones the locals like! The ones the tourists don't know about!"

Kyle ran his hands over his ribs to make sure none had been crushed accidentally. When he found no damage, he looked up.

"Sure, Inaha. Rok's ship should be here soon." He smiled broadly. "And we can always use a new friend."

# CHAPTER ELEVEN

Three days passed quickly as they traveled through deep space on their way to Meramee. Jysar and Krinia grew more excited with each passing day as Minstrel and Mother continued to talk about the wondrous beauty of the island-planet they would soon be landing upon.

It sounded just like paradise.

Elise's excitement grew as well, studying the view-screen where Mother displayed island after beautiful island from the sensor reports of Meramee.

Personally, she looked forward to swimming in the emerald oceans and turquoise seas that made up ninety percent of this world, as well as walking on its countless beaches. There were beaches of almost every color on Meramee depending on the geological forces which created that particular island: pale pink, burnt orange, glistening black, or pale lavender—even a few rainbow beaches of different colors of sand mixed together!

Not only were no two islands exactly alike on Meramee, but even on the same island it seemed that no two beaches were exactly alike in their natural beauty.

Everyone's excitement built with each passing day.

Late on the third day in space, Elise found herself alone walking through the rearmost sections of Mother's corridors. She rarely ventured this close to the engine room, and she had never actually entered it before.

The first time she wandered too close a few months back, both Jaric and Kyle made it very clear that the engine room was off-limits for her. And when she asked why, their anger erupted and she ran away in tears.

But even more odd, when she brought the incident up with Mother, she agreed with them. Mother informed her to stay clear of this one section.

She still didn't know why.

Mother avoided explaining this particular rule each time Elise asked. It was a mystery shrouded in the boys' anger and pain.

But now the boys were gone. They would never know if she entered the sanctity of the engine room.

Elise felt her heart pounding inside her chest as she crept closer. The door came into sight. But she hesitated, a sense of panic overwhelming her with a suffocating grip. She stood frozen.

She jumped as a whirring sound accelerated and grew louder.

Fixer3 suddenly rolled past her in the corridor. The little robot headed toward the door that led inside the engine room and Mother's famed ThunderStar engines. Elise watched Fixer3 as it paused, the optics mounted at the end of the twin, flexible cords eyeing her carefully.

She returned the robot's gaze, biting her lower lip nervously. But the small green robot remained stoically silent.

Elise took a deep breath for courage and approached.

"I want to go into the engine room," Elise explained as she squatted down beside Fixer3. The robot's optics retracted to adjust for her closeness. Elise smiled at the robot. "I have never been inside it yet, and well, I'd like to see it. Unless you have some work to do and now is not a good time."

The diminutive robot turned and continued toward the engine room as it motioned with one of its four extensible arms for her to follow.

Elise smiled, a conspiratorial gleam in her eyes.

"Okay, Fixer3. Maybe you can be my guide then? That would be super-cool."

The slender green robot called Fixer3 rolled up to the door as it extended an upper arm to trigger the sensor. Without slowing down, Fixer3 entered the opened door.

But as Elise drew near, her steps slowed.

Pangs of doubt swept through her as her heart beat rapid-fire again. She wondered if this was a good idea after all. After all, Jaric and Kyle had warned her, no, ordered her, not to enter the engine room.

And Mother backed them up.

She had accepted that limitation over her freedom before today. And yet, something seemed to draw her now. And there could be no better time to solve this mystery.

She stepped through the doorway.

And stopped immediately.

Looking cautiously around, she noticed the outlines of the mighty engines. Elise felt as well as heard the deep throbbing sounds as the twin engines powered them through hyperspace. But she also knew that a separate section of these power plants also drove the sub-light engines, although these were no longer used when landing on a world.

Now, the environmentally clean anti-gravity engines installed by the Kraaqi were used when entering any world's bio-system.

She took another tentative step inside.

At the far end of the port engine she saw Fixer3 using three of its arms to make adjustments while the fourth arm motioned for her to come closer.

"Well, if you insist," she said with a determined tone. Boldly, her heart now pounding wildly, Elise stepped completely inside.

She walked slowly between the mighty engines, feeling their power that seemed to permeate everything here. The engines emitted a glowing outline even though they were both encased inside solid tritanium shells. Each rose three meters tall and was over ten meters wide; their length encompassed the entire engine room from end to end—Elise guessed thirty meters long. Numerous consoles and dials that monitored and configured the mighty power plants graced the shiny metal casing of each engine.

Fixer3, satisfied with its latest tweaks on the port engine, rolled to the starboard engine to check its status.

The fluttering inside her chest seemed to dissipate as nothing terrible occurred. She walked slowly down the length of the engine room between the throbbing engines. As she reached the door at the back of the room she stopped dead in her tracks.

*There was somebody else in here with her.*

She saw him, someone ahead in the shadows— his muscular arms braced against the engine as he strained with all his might against the huge, throbbing engine.

Or was he?

He was so still. And yet...

"Why are you here, Elise?"

Mother's voice sent a shock through her body. Elise looked quickly around until she found the optic watching her carefully.

"I...I wanted to come here. I've never been here before."

"I've been observing you the entire time. In a way, I have allowed you to enter."

"That's not fair, you spying like that." Elise pouted. "I mean, I only wanted to look inside." She glanced quickly around. "There's nothing here to keep this all so hush-hush. At least nothing I can see."

"What about the figure in the shadows? The one that just startled you."

Elise's eyes opened wide with innocence. "Why, I hadn't really noticed him. Er, it." She coughed nervously as she glanced back at the form partially engulfed in shadow.

"Take a closer look," Mother urged.

Elise's eyes now reflected surprise. "Well, I'm sure whoever it is..." She stopped in mid-sentence.

*Was it a robot?*

Elise knew there were only six Fixer robots. And besides, this shape was over twice their size. She also realized that she knew everyone by sight who lived within Mother's hull. This form was unlike anything she had ever seen before.

That could only mean that this person, or this robot, never left the engine room. A chill suddenly went through her body as Elise felt an overpowering urge to leave.

"Do not be afraid. The robot is no longer functioning."

Mother's words calmed her. But something still felt wrong.

"Go closer."

Elise took a tentative step forward.

Suddenly a light burst forth and the figure before her became fully illuminated.

Elise gasped.

"This was Guardian," Mother said simply.

She stared in awe at the robot before her. The steel body was magnificent. And yet, it was horribly misshapen somehow.

As Elise studied the white figure, she realized what was wrong. The outer skin of its white, metallic body was rippled and formed frozen waves all down its outstretched arms and legs. Even its torso was covered in smaller versions of these ripple waves, although not as pronounced as what covered its arms and legs.

It stood frozen as if eternally pushing against the engine—its two hands melted...

*Melted.*

Yes! The entire robot had melted from some great heat while it pressed with its strength against the huge engine.

The white robot now stood frozen in place, its final, mighty effort forever captured before its internal systems died.

"I have heard of this Guardian." Elise slowly reached out to touch its darkened eyes, but stopped short. Instead her hands gently caressed the metallic face. "I remember Jaric and Kyle talking about him from their youth. But I thought he had left long ago."

"He was destroyed during the last, great battle with the T'kaan. He gave his life so that others would live. So that I would live."

Elise looked up at Mother's optic. "I am so glad he did that."

"Jaric and Kyle do not come here anymore—there is too much pain here. Guardian's feet and hands have permanently melted. I would have to order the Fixers to dismember him and then melt away what remained in order to completely remove him."

Elise shook her head slowly, realizing the dishonor that action would bring to this being's sacrifice.

"It is better that he remain so."

"I agree, it would be a desecration to his memory to dismantle him. Jaric and Kyle also agree. But because Guardian's shell remains here, it keeps them away from this room. And because this is such a personal trauma for them, they have not wanted any other living being back here—not even you. They do not want to remember this pain right now, and they don't want others looking or talking about it."

"I...I understand. But why did you allow me here now?"

"From what I have discerned about emotions and pain, their intensity lessens with time. But primarily, I felt that this dead robot is part of your history. That it is time you saw and learned of Guardian. He was my friend too. And the boys will not be hurt; they are not here. I will eventually have to explain to them that I allowed you here, but I will determine an appropriate situation."

Elise nodded. "No one has ever told me about that last battle. And I only know about Guardian from Kyle and Jaric's childhood. I've only heard bits and pieces about both." Tears suddenly welled in her eyes. "I do know that many died that day. And that Becky died too." She sniffed.

Mother observed Elise's tears as her sensors registered the rise in her body temperature and the uneven breathing pattern she developed.

"Perhaps it is time I told you about that solemn day."

Elise wiped her eyes quickly. "Yes, I would like that." She looked at the lifeless white robot beside her. "And I want to hear it all right here, beside this noble robot."

And so Mother told Elise of the final battle with the T'kaan. She told her of the great courage and the great sorrow that still burned within her memory systems. There were so many who died that fateful day, and Mother remembered and honored the memory of each of them in her telling the story—their story.

Of course, there were too many to list by name—still, she highlighted those who had been her closest friends—Rawlon, Curja and Saris foremost.

Yes, Mother told Elise of the allied beings who died destroying the evil T'kaan once and for all—beings who had been her friends, and the friends of her children.

And she told Elise of Becky—and how she died that day.

Without warning, red lights flashed and alarms sounded.

Elise looked around fearfully. This was the first time she had heard Mother's major alarms going off in earnest.

"W-what is that?"

"My sensors have just picked up an alien warship. It is on an intercept course for us."

Elise's eyes opened wide with shock.

"Elise, please go to the bridge. I do not recognize this ship's configuration nor has it communicated its intentions. Still, if it is hostile, engines are normally a primary target in order to disable a ship, so it would not be wise for you to stay here."

Elise jumped up and ran ahead of Fixer3 down the corridor toward the lift and the bridge three levels up. She arrived panting and out of breath from her exertions. Jysar, Krinia and the glowing form of Minstrel stood before the huge view-screen.

"What is it?" Elise stared at the view-screen and the strange alien ship that was still bearing down at them at full speed.

The starship was painted a solid red. A large superstructure dominated its forward section while its sleek sides bristled with weapons. At its rear, four massive engines formed a diamond shape.

The alien ship looked imposing.

"Has it returned our hails?" Jysar asked.

"No," Mother replied. "I have tried every known frequency and every known greeting from alien races in this sector. I am now trying languages from the adjoining sectors."

"Look out!" Krinia shouted.

The alien ship on the view-screen surged forward.

"Brace yourselves," Mother warned.

The strange red ship drew ominously closer with each passing second. Collision alarms now vied with Mother's general alert alarms in a cacophony of sound.

"Preparing for evasive maneuvers," Mother's voice chimed.

The red ship drew within five hundred meters and settled into formation as Mother continued her own course. It was easily within weapons' reach, but Mother's sensors showed the strange ship's shields still down. And there was no sign of its weapons being primed for attack.

"I'm dropping out of hyperspace."

Within seconds the alien ship followed suit. Both ships soared on an exactly parallel course, silently watching the other.

Mother reached out with her sensors and touched the surface of the alien craft. She felt the familiar signs of biological life inside the steel hull. But more, she felt the intense electronic activity that permeated the entire ship.

A very powerful computer existed within the strange ship.

In the next instant, Mother's sensors could no longer scan inside the ship. The craft now effectively blocked her.

Mother turned to the right and increased speed.

The alien ship matched her.

Suddenly, Mother felt the other ship reach out with its own sensors and begin to touch her—detecting the life-signs of the beings on her bridge. She felt the sensors brush her internal systems—searching deeper.

But Mother immediately and effectively blocked them.

Mother smiled inside—two could play at this game.

Elise and the others watched the view-screen as the ship surged forward, now so close that it looked as if they would surely collide.

"Hang on!" Mother shouted.

The manta-ray silhouette suddenly banked hard left as Mother pushed her sub-light engines to full speed.

The alien ship increased speed and turned in close pursuit.

Mother had anticipated this tactic—it seemed the ship and its crew were content to keep pace with her. They seemed more intent on scanning her than on attacking.

But Mother was not in the mood for either.

She timed her next maneuver precisely—to the very millisecond.

Just as the red ship drew close again, Mother dove, then put full power to her starboard engine while she threw the port into full reverse—turning exactly one hundred and eighty degrees.

Mother shot under the alien ship just as it began to react to her sudden about-face maneuver.

Mother's engines roared their fury as she pushed them to the red line.

But instead of turning sharply in pursuit, the red ship made a slow, deliberate turn and then came for them—inexorably gaining on them.

"Here it comes again," Elise shouted.

Mother threw herself into a series of twists and turns as the alien ship gained ground. Mother's processors worked furiously as she calculated her moves and tried to get away. But every time she succeeded in putting some distance between herself and her pursuer, the alien ship made an adjustment and once again closed.

"They are able to match your every move!" Jysar shouted in disbelief.

Mother's processors peaked with activity as she calculated millions of different moves in this high-speed game of cat-and-mouse. But one stood out distinctly from the others.

The red ship began to close once again.

Mother made another split-second, one-hundred-eighty-degree turn. But instead of plotting a course around the ship, Mother increased to full speed—flying dead-on toward her adversary.

The red ship did not waver; it came on at full speed.

"What are you doing?" Elise shouted.

"Patience." Krinia smiled knowingly. "The MotherShip knows what she's doing."

The alien ship continued without wavering, its forward hull filling the view-screen as Elise and the others stared with growing tension.

Collision alarms wailed throughout Mother's hull.

Elise realized she was holding her breath. In just a few seconds it would be all over—both ships would slam head-on into the other.

And no one would survive.

Mother waited, her mighty engines primed. Both ships roared on at full speed. But one ship would have to react in the next few moments—or all would be lost.

And at the last moment—almost the last millisecond—the red ship banked hard, upward and over to port with its engines still wide open.

Mother banked in the opposite direction and downward as her ThunderStar engines screamed. Now, she pushed them beyond the red line.

The red ship continued past her manta-ray-shaped hull. But even as the distance opened up between them the red ship slowed and turned to begin the chase again.

Elise and the others stared at each other with open mouths.

"I've never seen two warships come that close together at full speed without ramming!" Krinia shouted with amazement.

"It seems my message did not get through to them," Mother said as she watched them approach one more time.

"What kind of idiots are flying that thing!" Jysar's face was full of indignation.

"Ever since this strange chase began, these aliens have tried to break through my jamming of their sensors. Even during that last maneuver," Mother said. "I am able to block every attempt. But they are very good. It is taking up a lot of my processor utilization simply blocking their sensor attempts!"

"They must have a powerful navigation computer. I don't believe biological beings with their own skill could have timed some of those split-second maneuvers," Minstrel commented. "Have you identified the markings on the ship yet?"

"Still researching."

"Look out!" Elise screamed as the ship suddenly shot towards them again with a burst of speed.

"Take battle stations," Mother's voice said calmly. "They have just raised shields and are powering their weapons systems."

Mother's own shields came online a split second later.

Once more she felt the other ship's sensors attempt to see inside her hull. Mother jammed them again, but each time she blocked them, the alien ship almost instantaneously reacted and tried another tactic. For the first time in a very long time, Mother felt her internal systems being tasked to the limit.

And then Mother felt something touch her mind.

The red ship finally succeeded in making a connection and was quickly prowling through her short-term memories. Mother began to break the contact point—but paused. There was something different about the way this ship's computer searched and made its way through her systems. This was something more than simply the cold, calculated probing by a mere ship's computer.

Mother began to feel disoriented, even strange, as the sensors felt their way deeper inside her systems.

She quickly broke the connection.

The red ship banked hard, and Mother sensed the targeting system aim for her ThunderStar engines. The alien ship now fully primed its weapons and prepared to disable her.

Mother waited a fraction of a second longer, trying to estimate the exact moment the ship would fire as its targeting systems locked.

In another instant, Mother dove hard down as laser blasts leapt out. The red lances grazed her shields as she shot away at a dizzying speed.

She fired four of her main guns as she retreated.

Even as she fired them, the alien ship maneuvered—hard to starboard and upward.

Her lasers missed—barely.

But Mother anticipated such a move. Instantly, she retargeted and fired the rest of her main battery.

The red ship shuddered under the direct hits.

The aliens' shields dropped to one-third strength.

"Now, let's see..." Mother began.

But the alien ship fired again.

Everyone inside fell to the floor as Mother twisted herself to present as small a profile as possible while she strengthened her rear shields—all within bare nanoseconds as the lasers erupted toward her.

The hits blossomed against her shields. She had been hit. But damage was minimal.

Still, Mother was impressed.

The alien ship and crew had surprised her with its quickness.

As Mother righted herself and backed her engines down, she began to calculate her next run—the final run of this battle. This time she would target the engines of their ship. And once she had it disabled, Mother would scan this ship and find out exactly who these aliens were.

It would be easy pickings, for the alien ship's shields were damaged and no longer strong enough to withstand her next blows.

Mother felt a surge of surprise in her systems as her sensors registered the red ship turning away from her. Already, it streaked away in the opposite direction while ramping up its hyperdrive engines. A few seconds later and it disappeared in a flash of light as it leapt into hyperspace.

The engagement was over.

"A most effective enemy," Mother said as Jysar and the others gathered closer together. "Their attack rivaled that of the T'kaan."

"Who were they?" Krinia asked.

"I have an answer. One from my long-term memories. It is from some data I picked up from a Tracadorian trading ship two months ago."

"And..." Elise prompted.

"The red ship originates from the Paum Sector."

Later that evening, after the others had gone to bed, Minstrel and Mother discussed the day's events.

"The Paum are popping up a lot lately," Minstrel said as it floated gracefully.

"Too much for coincidence," Mother replied. "I can find very little information about them."

"And worse, neither can I." A wave of dark colors rippled throughout Minstrel's body. "We rendezvous with my ship later tonight."

"Minstrels have sophisticated auto-pilot systems, for you to command them from such a distance the way you have."

"Yes. We can leave them cloaked in orbit while we observe different species for long periods of time. Sometimes we travel far from them. But, it does have its limitations." Minstrel's body glowed brighter. "When we transmit a course and input it into the auto-pilot system from far away, we can only meet them in deep space far from any stars or planetary systems. And the course must not take them close to any."

"That should be easy enough in this vast universe," Mother said.

"Well, sometimes it's not as easy as we'd like—especially when we need the ship in a hurry."

"I understand. But back to the Paum."

"Yes, once my ship is back, I will make for one of the key Minstrel Communication centers," Minstrel said.

"I thought you were in constant communication with other Minstrels?"

"Normally each Minstrel is within range of another Minstrel ship. But right before we landed at RahajMr I lost contact with my nearest counterpart, which is also strange. This sector has been well visited before."

"So, how far is this Minstrel Communication center?" Mother asked.

214

"Only a few days' journey. I will try to find out more about these Paum and then meet you on Meramee. And I must find out more about the Harg."

"The Harg?"

"Yes. I did find some information when I contacted my ship this evening. It seems the Harg are paid mercenaries of the Paum. They are a most violent species."

"Two Harg followed you that last day on RahajMr—and did the quick scan of me."

"Yes. Not a coincidence either, I now think."

"And did your ship have anything on the Paum or that sector?"

"Nothing on the Paum. But that sector is the fastest growing regime in the known universe—that much Minstrels have gathered in the recent past from their journeys. Which should mean we would know quite a bit about them. But that is not so."

"Why is that?" Mother asked.

"Most species that live near the original Paum systems refer to them by another name—The Forbidden Worlds. And it has gotten that reputation for a reason. Even as the Paum Empire grows and takes controls of new worlds, this Forbidden Zone grows with it."

"Go on," Mother prompted.

"Most races have explicit orders not to travel to Paum-held worlds or even to travel through their space. Too many ships and crews have disappeared—never to be heard from again. And when delegations are sent to the Paum, they get nowhere. The Paum has nothing to do with outside races." Minstrel glowed with a dark hue of colors.

"Is there no trade between the Paum systems and other races?"

"Very little. Theirs is a secretive society. It is very structured and very controlled—another reason even we Minstrels have had little success in observing them. They are a bizarre society, a combination of quasi-military and quasi-religion. All those indoctrinated into Paum must live Paum—they live, eat and breathe Paum. Paum is now the center of their universe, and it affects everything they do." Minstrel paused.

"And that is not of itself a bad thing," Minstrel continued. "From what we Minstrels have discovered about the creed of Paum, it gives them a goal in life—they strive to be in harmony with the rest of their society as well as with their environment. Their peoples seem to thrive, their economy is stable, and their expansion is remarkable. But the creed of Paum has a dark side." Minstrel paused again as a sense of expectation filled the air. Sudden waves of light swept through Minstrel's body one after the other as the pause grew longer.

Mother waited impatiently.

"Go on," Mother finally urged.

"There have been unconfirmed but very disturbing reports from planets conquered by the Paum. It is said that all those defeated were given a simple choice—either choose Paum and follow it the rest of their life—or die. We know from the

216

Twelve Words of Paum this major belief: one day the entire universe will follow Paum...and those that do not will be utterly destroyed."

"Forced conversion," Mother said simply.

"It would seem so. But as I said, a lot of that is unconfirmed. It is hard for anyone to know—even Minstrels with all of our stealth. And there is worse."

"Worse?" Mother asked.

"Minstrels discovered this fast-growing empire only within the last few years. In that short time two Minstrels have been sent to learn more about this new race—or should I say these races, now that so many formerly independent alien races have come under Paum control. Actually, the source of Paum is still unknown even to us—the original race that bred Paum."

"What did your two Minstrels learn?" Mother asked.

"Both Minstrels who journeyed there disappeared without a trace. It has been well over a year since the last communication. And the second Minstrel went in armed with the knowledge of the first one's previous disappearance. We have presumed the worst for both."

Mother processed this last fact with surprise. "I did not realize that Minstrels could be detected, much less captured."

"Or killed," Minstrel added with a shuddering wave. "Sometimes an alien species does not take kindly to being secretively observed. I fear for my fellow Minstrels, now that I have learned this."

"Between our contact with this powerful ship and this new information, it seems we have need to be wary of these Paum."

"That is a logical conclusion. And I wonder *why* they have taken such a keen interest in us?"

"Perhaps it was they who tagged your search query for sentient technology. The other events have followed that initial action. I would have hoped that once we left RahajMr, the Paum and the Harg would lose interest in us. After all, prior to RahajMr we had no problems with them. Perhaps this is the last incident?"

"That may be the case. After all, the Paum ship did not actually attack. It seemed more interested in gaining data on us by intrusive scans, which you prevented for the most part. But we should find out all we can about these secretive Paum and their Harg agents. Just to be on the safe side," Minstrel added with emphasis.

"I agree," Mother said. "I will wait until we have gathered more facts and determined if there is indeed a threat before I share this with everyone else. I do not want to trigger their emotions, especially if the Paum turns out to be only a momentary issue based around our visit to RahajMr."

"A sound decision." Minstrel twinkled. "The only issues have been with their monitoring our search activity and the Harg scan just before we lifted. And now the Paum ship trying to scan your internal systems today." Minstrel undulated its body before compressing it into a glowing ball floating in the middle of the air. "Before I join you on Meramee, I will communicate to you all that I learn from the other Minstrels on a secure channel, if I determine there is any danger."

"Good. I do have good news to share," Mother added.

"Yes?"

"I just now received a short message from Rok's ship—from Rok himself."

"They were not scheduled to be free for three more days."

"They got early release for good behavior." Mother felt a surge of relief within her circuits. "I hope that both Kyle and Jaric have learned something from this experience."

"I think so," Minstrel said.

"At any rate, they are safely aboard the Kraaqi frigate and are even now getting ready to set sail to meet us at Meramee."

"I am glad."

"And they are bringing a new friend."

"Indeed?"

"An alien called a Hammatt—Inaha by name. Jaric had Rok tell me that they know about Minstrels."

Thousands of tiny lights across Minstrel's plasma body glowed brighter. "They are a good race. A little emotional at times, but at heart, good aliens. We know them."

"Well, I guess we shall all meet at Meramee within four or five days," Mother said.

"Yes, both I and the Kraaqi ship should get there about the same time." Minstrel paused in thought. "Make sure you take necessary precautions while on Meramee."

"And you," Mother said with concern.

"You should contact Rok once he's out of range of RahajMr too. Simply tell him to be watchful. It's possible a Paum ship might try to intercept them before they get to Meramee."

"You are right. I'll give Rok the warning. By the time they arrive at Meramee, I'll know if I need to confer with the others—if we find there is a real danger."

"Agreed."

The Kraaqi frigate *Aurora* parted the last cloud bands of RahajMr and entered the blackness of outer space.

"Disengage the anti-grav engines, First Officer," Rok commanded. "Set in a course for the planet Meramee and engage hyper-engines."

"Aye, sir."

Rok looked around the bridge and smiled. It felt good to be back on his own ship once again. He gripped the arms of his Captain's chair and nodded with satisfaction.

"Take us out of orbit!" he ordered.

The *Aurora* surged forward. As the Kraaqi ship reached a safe distance from the gravity well of the gas giant, her hyperdrive engines roared to life.

The stars on the main view-screen suddenly became lines of light.

The *Aurora* shuddered momentarily as it leapt into hyperspace. A moment later and the starship sailed without the slightest hint of motion as it reached speed. The Kraaqi frigate soared through hyperspace—a new journey begun.

Inaha slowly approached the master of the ship. While he made his way forward he quietly observed the smooth functioning of the bridge crew as they went about their appointed tasks. The big alien smiled with approval.

Inaha stood beside the seated captain of the *Aurora*. Together, they watched the stars slowly approach on the main view-screen as they sparkled against the vaster and more distant starfield. The motions of those nearer stars were the only indications the Kraaqi ship was sailing at hyperspeed.

"It's good to be underway again," Rok said to everyone on the bridge.

Inaha laughed heartily. As his laughter died away, he spoke softly. "Too long on any world makes one yearn for the freedom of open space."

"Well said," Rok agreed. "It's good to sail on a starship bound for the distant stars again."

"It is good indeed," Inaha repeated.

Rok smiled. "And there's nothing quite like the feeling you get as your hyperdrive engines engage—that tingling sensation in the pit of your stomach just as your ship leaps." Rok grunted with pleasure.

"Nothing quite like it in the entire universe!" Inaha laughed.

221

"This has always been my dream," Rok said as he turned to the jovial Hammatt. "To be captain of my own starship—and travel to unknown worlds."

Rok grew silent. Slowly a smile spread across his weathered face as the words of an ancient Kraaqi proverb emerged from a childhood memory.

"Give me a fast starship, that sails a gallant crew," Rok said with a twinkle in his eyes. "Show me the distant stars, my friend. And there, there I shall meet you."

Inaha observed the bridge crew busy with their assigned tasks as the *Aurora* settled into its cruising speed. The navigator at the nearest station keyed in the final course heading for Meramee. The entire Kraaqi crew epitomized the image of efficiency.

"You have a good ship and crew, Captain," Inaha said with sincerity. "It's a privilege to sail with you."

"I thank you."

They nodded to the each other in a silent salute of mutual respect.

"Well, I need to get my things stowed." Inaha paused one last time as he gazed with open wonder at the view-screen. "I love to watch that first jump. Thank you for allowing me on your bridge. It has been too long since I was last on a fast starship."

"My pleasure." Rok watched the huge Hammatt leave.

"So, Mother told us to be on the lookout for a Paum warship," Jaric said as he stepped beside Rok. "That's interesting. We heard about the Paum from that Mrad Security Officer. That name seems to be popping up a lot lately."

"It may not mean anything," Rok commented. "But, we are forewarned now. I have my ship on elevated alert status in case we encounter any hostile ships en route."

"Good idea." Jaric looked around the bridge. "You know, I need to find Kyle. I'll meet you later at dinner."

Rok nodded.

Jaric found Kyle lying in his bunk—idly staring up at the ceiling. He grabbed a chair and sat down. A smile flickered momentarily on Kyle's face as Jaric entered, but otherwise Kyle continued to lie there in silence.

Jaric waited a few moments, deep in thought, before he finally spoke.

"I've been meaning to ask you this, but this is the first time we've been alone since that food incident."

Kyle chuckled. "Food incident, eh?" He looked at his friend. "Go ahead, what is it?"

"You know, back on RahajMr. Well, when Rok was trying to talk to us. And well, you said we were just a dysfunctional family—at best." Jaric's eyes narrowed. "That kinda' bothered me." In the next moment Jaric smiled broadly. "But you didn't really mean it, did you, Big K?"

Kyle looked away without saying a word.

"Right?" Jaric added.

Kyle shook his head as he sat up. "I just was talking," he said without conviction. He looked at

Jaric with a somber expression. "I was just talking. Don't let it worry you."

Jaric watched Kyle while the other continued to avoid his direct gaze. Jaric felt his heart sink with sadness. It pained him to realize how Kyle felt, to realize that he felt their family wasn't normal, or that it was somehow *less* of a family compared to others.

Inside his own heart, Jaric felt their family was as good and normal as any he had heard or read about. He felt proud and happy to be a part of it. Every single day he heard Mother's voice, or when he sat down with the others at meal times or when they watched a holovid or listened to music—he felt a part of something—part of a family.

It didn't bother him that it wasn't the ideal family. It only mattered that they were *family*. And he wanted with all of his heart for Kyle to feel that way too.

"But you feel that we are a family?" Jaric asked after a long pause.

They looked at each other deeply.

"Sure...sure." Kyle took a deep breath. "I mean, I love Mother. And you like a brother. And Rok too. And the others are good..." Kyle grew silent.

"But," Jaric coaxed.

"But," Kyle repeated. He shook his head slowly. "But we're certainly not a *normal* family by any stretch. There's no real mother and a father— we have an AI starship instead. And we have a *clone* for a sister—if you want to call her our sister."

Kyle eyed Jaric, but Jaric remained intent. Kyle cleared his throat. "And the rest are alien warriors, an alien geek, and a Mewiis with a hyperactive head-tail."

Kyle's eyes met Jaric's. He noticed a hint of a smile on Jaric's face now as he concluded, "I don't know, does that sound like your average run-of-the-mill, *normal* family to you?"

Jaric reflected a moment. He focused on the humor in Kyle's last statement and the mischief in his eyes. He smiled—at first.

Then Jaric began to laugh, his eyes sparkling with humor. "Hey, maybe you have a point there!" He laughed. "Maybe the *real* problem is that *we're too normal* for this bunch!"

Kyle had to chuckle at that. For several minutes, their laughter echoed in the air as their spirits lifted.

"You know," Jaric finally said. "We kid a lot. And we mess with Rok too. But, Rok said some important things back there—like we really should appreciate what we've got—while we have it."

"I know," Kyle agreed.

"But I'm like you. I think if we found more human survivors, it'd be great. It would be super-cool." Jaric smiled.

"You got that right."

"But," Jaric added. "Maybe we've got it pretty good right now—better than we think. And we might not be the ideal, 'normal' family," Jaric emphasized. "But hey, we are family."

Jaric looked hopefully at Kyle.

225

Kyle started to laugh and then reached over and slapped Jaric on the shoulder playfully.

"Maybe I should think about what I have—we have—more." He raised his forefinger. "And I have been giving Rok's words some thought since he said it back there." Kyle stood up and stretched slowly. "You know, most of the time I am happy. And I like being with Mother and all of you." He clenched his eyes shut, almost as if he were in pain.

Jaric looked at him with concern.

"But sometimes I get so bummed—just like that." Kyle snapped his fingers. "And Rok just set me off that day—bad timing. I was so happy, so excited. And then he just set me off."

"But he was right. And our search failed once again. He was just trying to get us to think," Jaric said.

"I know." Kyle sighed. "I know."

"And, now we need to keep a watch out for the Paum," Jaric added.

"And I didn't like those other aliens either, those Harg. I didn't like the looks of them the minute I set eyes on them."

"Why the Harg?" Jaric asked.

"I remember one of them grunting during the fight that they wanted to take us to their ship," Kyle said.

"Kidnap us?" Jaric said with a puzzled expression.

"I don't know." Kyle's eyes lit up with humor. "Hey, maybe they'll grab Elise and take her off our hands." Kyle chuckled.

226

Jaric laughed a moment with him, but then his face grew serious. "Maybe we need to re-think the cl...re-think our view on Elise too. After all, she is human."

"Yeah, there seem to be precious few of us left in this universe. Maybe we should." Kyle nodded.

"Anyway, we'll be at this ocean world paradise in a few days," Jaric said enthusiastically. "Islands and oceans and food and aliens everywhere all having a good time! That ought to be some fun!"

Kyle nodded. "Well, if we can't have fun there, we might as well give it all up."

Jaric stood up, laughing heartily. "Yeah, let's have some fun on this planet, Big K. No searching, no trouble. Let's just have ourselves a great time."

"Sure," Kyle agreed. "Let's just have fun— what a concept."

# CHAPTER TWELVE

The blue and green beauty of Meramee filled their eyes.

Elise, Jysar and Krinia looked in awe at the planet that filled the main view-screen.

Mother herself was impressed. Within seconds, she ran through every image of every world she had either visited or which was stored within her long-term memories, and few indeed compared with the natural beauty of the island-planet Meramee.

The sentient starship reveled in the fact that the mere image of a planet could elicit such emotions in biological beings. And no other word described their careful scrutiny except pleasure—or perhaps sheer joy.

It seemed certain visual stimuli—works of art, well-kept gardens and beautiful flowers, pristine natural settings as well as wild animal life—stimulated this emotion. Mother analyzed Meramee in detail, scanning every aspect of the visual spectrum. She discerned the color combinations of cloud and blue-green ocean mixed with the tiny dots of islands created pleasant symmetries and patterns which intrigued her. But it seemed odd that this same image of Meramee elicited such emotional responses in the others.

She observed a similar effect with music, an aural stimuli, on the children in her own early years of life. She came to realize that music could produce a wide variety of emotional responses depending on the rhythm, melody, or lyrics in varying combinations. It made for a fascinating study that she enjoyed to this day.

It appeared humans and biological beings in general gained not only factual knowledge from their senses, but also gained emotional stimulus as well—and one seemed as important as the other.

The planet, laced by wisps of mauve clouds overshadowing several shades of blue and green ocean depending on its depth, grew beyond the boundary of the main view-screen as Mother entered the atmosphere. As Mother flew lower, the sunlight from the large red star which Meramee orbited glistened off the waters below, and individual islands took shapes. Krinia, Jysar and Elise pointed from one island to another with expressions of delight.

Mother searched and discovered that Meramee possessed over one hundred thousand islands. And while it was a planet covered entirely by a single ocean, there were vast stretches of water that were quite shallow. In fact, the famous Emerald Sea averaged only ten meters deep over its entire expanse. And this beautiful sea alone covered most of the western hemisphere.

Several other smaller areas of water that dotted the vast, turquoise ocean were even more shallow. And it was in these shallow sections of ocean, which covered almost half the planet, where the densest population of islands existed.

Although by the strictest definition of most planets there were no individual seas on Meramee, the Mejadic designated various bodies of water bordered by island groups as seas: the Emerald Sea, the Majestic Sea, the Sea of Lights, the Marble Ocean and the spectacular Sea of Showers.

Because of the planet's irregular orbit—it tilted both its poles towards the red star several times each circuit—polar ice caps existed at neither pole. And yet, the tops of the mountainous islands at each pole remained snow-capped most of the year and the ocean water was warm enough for swimming only a few short weeks.

For long seconds, everyone took in the beauty of Meramee as it beckoned them closer. Mother refrained from vocal communication so as not to spoil the mood. As Elise and the others stood entranced, Mother received final landing instructions.

"I love to walk on a secluded beach at night," Jysar said with a sigh, surprising both Krinia and Elise. "Hearing the waves in the darkness, feeling the sand between my toes—breathing the clean, salty air." He breathed deeply and held it, as if he were already there and savoring the moment.

"I can't wait." He sighed again.

"I thought Hronosium was a single planet-city which covered every centimeter of the natural planet in your youth?" Krinia asked in surprise. "When did you ever walk on an open beach?"

"I was born on Jorrdannd, far away from the homeworld of the Hrono. That world has large oceans embracing temperate continents. It is the newest and least developed planet of the Hrono kingdom. I lived among its natural, untamed beauty during my childhood. I only lived on Hronosium the last seven years of my life," Jysar said. He suddenly smiled. "And remember, the first parts of the planet-city have been opened up to allow nature a place in which to grow on that world once again."

Meramee grew continually larger on the view-screen. Now only a small section of the planet was visible—in the center hundreds of small islands created a whimsical arc nestled in a bright green sea. Details such as beaches and mountains grew visible on individual islands.

"Are we landing?" Elise said as she became aware of her surroundings.

"I-I believe we are," Jysar stammered as he rubbed his eyes.

"What is our destination?" Krinia's head-tail swished with interest. "I'm suddenly in the mood to get out and walk on a beach somewhere...but I'd like to know where exactly we're landing on Meramee."

"Me too!" Elise said, her voice bubbling with youthful exuberance. "It looks so good from up above, I can't imagine what it'll be like actually being there!"

"We will land on Leyloi—Queen Island of the Maiden Isles. Geographically speaking, this string of islands is located on the western border of the Emerald Sea. Their origin is volcanic, which explains their mountainous structure. But their secluded and pristine beaches are famous throughout this quadrant." Mother's words sent a chill of excitement into the room.

"Oh, Meramee." Jysar sighed again. "I think I may never want to leave you."

Elise and Krinia began to laugh as they watched the expression on Jysar's face—an expression of profound joy that seemed more appropriate for two young lovers about to profess their undying love to each other.

"Have any of you noticed something missing on Meramee?" Mother asked out of the blue.

Three sets of eyes studied Meramee.

"The cities are very small." Jysar looked at the others with a questioning look.

"Actually, the only dwellings on the surface of the islands are for the tourists. All of them hotels, shops or other entertainment centers."

"Where is their industry? Or where are the original inhabitants?" Jysar asked.

"The Mejadic are an aquatic race. Their cities and industry all reside under the shallow oceans. That is another reason why the surface is still so pristine, and why there are such small centers of habitation on the islands."

"Are the Mejadic a space-faring race?" Elise asked.

"Yes, for many years now. You will be greeted by them when I land. It is a quaint Meramee custom."

"Cool," Elise said with growing excitement.

"I think we'll just make our way to the beach, mingle with the aliens, soak in a little sun, and then maybe take a swim in the Emerald Sea. Not necessarily in that order," Krinia said with a business-like tone, as if she were reading off a daily to-do list.

"Sounds terrible." Jysar laughed. "I think I'll join you.

"Maybe we'll meet some nice alien boys, too!" Krinia smiled at Elise.

"Not like Lama Kama von Dama, right?" Elise laughed, remembering the alien Romeo back on RahajMr.

"For sure!"

Mother landed between two large hotel complexes within walking distance of a crowded beach. Several starships rested beside her in their own clearly marked landing spots on the flat tarmac. All around the resting ships throngs of brightly clad aliens laughed and conversed as they walked among the pockets of lush tropical plants that graced the manicured grounds. In fact, the bright pastels of tropical shirts, knee-length shorts for males, and short skorts for females created a moving, living rainbow.

Krinia and Jysar and Elise quickly wended their way through the masses of aliens dressed in brightly colored outfits perfect for a tropical climate. They walked only a short distance when they came to a dead halt.

Standing right before them was a group of aliens unlike any they had ever seen.

"What are they?" Elise whispered to Krinia. But Krinia was staring open-mouthed as well. Elise found she couldn't keep her eyes off them as she admired their fascinating beauty.

There were three of them, all humanoid in shape—two eyes, two arms, two of every obvious body part—like most normal aliens.

The males wore a red cloth around their loins while the lone female wore a simple, bright blue sarong wrapped tightly around her feminine figure.

But it was the colors of their scaly skin that kept them mesmerized with each alien's natural beauty.

The skin of the male on the right was a brilliant orange interspersed with alternating green and yellow stripes that ran from his head down his torso, and arms and legs. Likewise, the alien male on the left was overall an iridescent green with fiery red spots over his body, while the upper part of his face, from his eyes over his head, glowed a shimmering royal blue.

And the female was even more colorful.

From her chest up, from above the top of her blue sarong dress, her smooth skin was a bright golden color. Around her cheeks and eyes thousands of tiny circles of alternating royal blue and deep purple stood out against the gold background of her skin and emphasized her dazzling blue eyes. Down each shapely leg, her golden skin was accentuated with bold, jagged stripes of eye-popping ruby red.

But what they wore around their necks kept drawing Elise's glances again and again—each alien wore an identical band of glistening silver metal. The upper and lower edges were solid while the center was of a meticulous filigree design. And yet this attractive neck-ware—it couldn't be called a true necklace because it completely covered their necks from the base up to the bottom of their chin—seemed to have some kind of practical function.

Elise shook her head in amazement, wondering what that function could be. She suddenly glanced down and noticed that in stark contrast to their overall beauty, the colorful aliens each had comically over-sized feet.

And then it struck her why the aliens wore the exotic neck-ware. For barely noticeable until she really looked, Elise made out the almost translucent webbed skin between each of their extra-long toes. She surmised that these beings must be at home in the ocean and the neck-ware enabled the hidden gills on their necks to take in the oxygen directly from the air.

"They must be Mejadic," Elise whispered to Krinia.

"They're beautiful," Krinia whispered back.

"Welcome to Meramee and to Leyloi, the Queen Island." The three colorful Mejadic approached, each holding a small ring of white flowers, which they gently placed on the head of Elise, Krinia and Jysar like a crown.

They bowed deeply and stepped back with their smiling faces still to the ground.

"Thank you!" Jysar finally managed to blurt out. "I must say, I've never seen any race quite so beautiful as you are."

The Mejadic female glanced up and quickly approached Jysar. With a smile, she gently kissed his cheek. "You honor our people," she said with a melodic voice. She quickly stepped back to join her two companions.

"What are the flowers for?" Krinia asked.

"It is the traditional greeting of my people. A crown of flowers—beauty on beauty—to make the heart rejoice." The iridescent green male bowed once more. "I am Stazal. This is Olana," he pointed to the female as he rose. "And he is Relan."

Krinia introduced Jysar and Elise.

"I think I'm going to like Meramee a lot!" Elise laughed as she adjusted her flower crown. And then she realized she had forgotten something. "Oh, I didn't wear my Hair Lighter."

"But your golden hair is lovely just as it is," Stazal crooned.

Elise blushed brightly.

"We greet each new ship that arrives," Olana explained. "Just beyond the throngs you will enter our island's part of the great festival of food and beer—Taste of the Quadrant."

"And beyond that the famed Emerald Sea," Relan added. "It's crystal clear waters will caress your bodies with its refreshing power."

"Cool!" Elise said.

"Are you of different clans?" Jysar asked. "I mean, each of you are completely different colors."

The three Mejadic laughed.

"The Mejadic are like the islands of Meramee—no two of us are exactly the same. Each of us is unique in color and patterns," Stazal explained with a smile.

"Super-cool," Elise said with awe and appreciation. "None of us has ever been to Meramee before, and I for one wish we'd come here long ago!"

"Ah, your very first visit to our world." Olana said, looking from Jysar to Krinia and back to Elise. "Perhaps we can share dinner tonight with you under the stars at our private beach? We will tell stories about our wonderful planet while we dine."

"We accept!" they said simultaneously.

They made arrangements to meet later that evening. As the Mejadic trio left, Elise, Krinia and Jysar made their way to the nearest section of the Festival. From booth after booth wonderful smells wafted on the gentle breezes as they walked among the crowds of aliens. Before long the delicious aromas worked their magic, and the trio found themselves sampling one exotic dish after another. The flavors danced on their palette as wonderfully as the aromas, and they quickly came to a new appreciation for alien cuisine.

Finally, after a few more detours toward enticing smells and delicious treats, they found themselves on the beach.

Elise felt her heart quiver with excitement.

She had never seen the ocean before—not on any world. And to see one of the most beautiful beaches in the universe framed against the glistening waters of the Emerald Sea as that astonishing first experience took her breath away.

"Look," Krinia said as she danced onto the violet and white sand. "I see why they call them the Maiden Isles!"

Elise laughed as she danced with her.

Even Jysar tried it, with fairly comical results. But everyone enjoyed themselves to the extreme.

"See, the sand is a pure, pure white with violet streaks of sand through it. The waves and wind have shaped the beach into a vast flowing veil," Krinia pointed out.

"Yes!" Elise said. "Just like a bridal veil."

"Hence the name." Jysar laughed. "The Maiden Isles."

"We'll have to ask Olana how the beaches get this wonderful mixture of color here," Elise said.

"And the other beaches too," Krinia added. "I think we'll really enjoy getting to know both them and their world better."

They removed their outer clothes to reveal their bathing suits then took a quick swim among the waves. After they enjoyed the warm waters a while, they continued their journey down the crowded beach toward a tree-clad jungle mountain that rose in the distance. The trio laughed and talked among themselves, oblivious to everyone else.

But unknown to them, two secretive Harg followed.

They had shadowed them since the trio first met the Mejadic. The short, stout aliens were clad with bright tropical shirts in order to blend in with all the others.

"The one with the yellow mane is the human...hmmm. Shall we take her now?"

The other, who carried himself with a sense of command, smiled knowingly. "No. The Paum has instructed me carefully. There is a way we can get the female human to separate herself willingly. The Paum has studied them carefully, individually and as a group—all of our reports and sensor scans. The Paum knows—the Paum always knows."

The Harg looked at his fellow with a vicious smile. "Tell me."

"Just a few more moments and you will hear. The red sun of Meramee is beginning to set, and they told the Mejadic they would dine with them this evening. They will turn around soon. Keep walking—faster."

The two Harg continued their pursuit and closed the distance.

Krinia admired the pale aqua green waters of the lagoon that stretched outward until it met the emerald waters of the deeper sea—the boundary a clearly defined line where one color ended and the other began. Her gaze drifted to the endless horizon and the red circle of the setting sun just above the mauve cloud tops that rested over the sea like distant, billowing islands.

"We need to get back. I'd like to freshen up a bit before we dine with our Mejadic friends," Krinia said.

They all agreed and turned to retrace their steps back up the beach to Mother.

Almost at once, Elise found herself crashing into two burly aliens wearing bright, tropical shirts.

"Oh, excuse me!" Elise said with a touch of embarrassment The two strange aliens gently reached out to keep her from falling. She smiled apologetically at them. Then she noticed the look on their faces—looks of complete disbelief.

"Well, you're a human aren't you!" the first one said with outright surprise.

Elise felt her heart skip a beat.

She opened her mouth to speak, but nothing came out. Krinia rapidly stepped beside her as she stared at the two bull-necked aliens.

"What do you mean?" Krinia asked questioningly.

"Well, what I mean is that before yesterday I'd never seen a human before. And now I've seen them two days in a row." He flashed a big, toothy smile.

"Where?" Elise finally blurted out. She knew Kyle and Jaric were still en route on the *Aurora*, so the alien couldn't have seen them.

"We were on Mermoona," he explained simply. "We ran into a group of humans while we were eating Flaming Tangers at the Ocalla food booth. We'd never met any humans before and so we struck up a conversation with them."

"They're on Mermoona?" Elise repeated with shock.

But Jysar stepped forward, a wary look in his eyes. The two stout aliens smiled at him with

240

innocent expressions. Jysar looked from one to the other with a careful eye.

"Did they tell you anything about how they got here?" Jysar asked. "Maybe...how they've found themselves so far from their homeworld?"

The bigger of the two aliens smiled even more. "Yes, Earth I believe they called it."

Elise gasped.

The alien grew thoughtful a moment, as he tapped a forefinger against the side of his head. "Some sort of tragedy. They seemed a bit reluctant to go into it."

Krinia, Elise and Jysar leaned forward expectantly.

The alien's eyes suddenly widened. "T'kaan! Something about a war, I think."

Elise felt light-headed for a moment, but quickly regained her composure.

Krinia, Elise and Jysar questioned them for a few minutes more, getting details on where the island of Mermoona was located. They soon learned it was part of the Maiden Isles, although Mermoona was located at the farthest reach of the northern arc of islands—about a three-hour journey by boat.

Jysar finally thanked them for their surprising information, graciously accepted their apologies for almost knocking Elise down, and they all parted ways.

As soon as the two aliens walked away, Elise and the others raced up the beach in the other direction in order to tell Mother the news.

Mother's optic focused from one to the other after Elise, Jysar and Krinia breathlessly entered. Her sensors noted the extreme pace their hearts beat as well as registering the elevated temperature of their bodies. But it was the dilation of their pupils that truly indicated their high state of excitement.

Krinia, Jysar and Elise quickly recounted their chance encounter on the beach with two aliens. They focused on what the aliens told them—about the humans they had spent time with on Mermoona.

In the flurry of excitement, no one asked about the aliens themselves.

"I am sending a communication to the *Aurora* now," Mother finally said. "Kyle and Jaric must hear this news immediately."

"Who would have guessed?" Elise squealed with excitement. "And it was I who helped find them at last! Kyle and Jaric will be so pleased."

But Krinia pursed her lips in doubt.

Within minutes, Mother established a communications link. A few minutes later and the shocked faces of Kyle, Jaric and Rok stared back at them from Mother's main view-screen located on her bridge.

"You're kidding," Jaric repeated for the third time in a row as the others finally finished.

"And we were just going to Meramee to relax," Kyle added. "We weren't even going to think about other humans."

"I will make for Meramee at top speed now," Rok said. "I will get you estimates, but I believe we can make planet-fall within twenty-four hours."

"Good," Mother replied. "I have discovered that Mermoona does not allow starships, or air-ships of any kind, direct access. It is an island of lush, tropical forests with very few hotels or amenities even for tourists—an island kept very close to its pure, natural state. The only access is by boat."

"Find out how to book one," Kyle said with authority. "We'll leave immediately once we land."

Elise stepped forward. "I want to go."

Kyle and Jaric exchanged glances.

Jaric made a subtle motion with his head toward Kyle—indicating acceptance. But Kyle's eyes narrowed and his expression grew solemn. He thought a minute more, and spoke.

"I'd rather just Jaric and..." he started to say.

"What!" Elise said with obvious hurt. "I mean, I'm the one who literally ran into this information. Shouldn't I get to go too? After all, I'm a human too!"

"That's true. *In a way...*" Jaric began.

Elise's eyes narrowed in anger. "You know, I'm tired of this *boys-only* club around here!"

"Elise," Mother chided.

"Well, I am!" Elise shouted. She stared defiantly back at the view-screen. "And I've found that some of your boys-only junk wasn't really needed. I mean, why are you holding back some of these stupid things from me anyway?"

Jaric and Kyle gazed mutely back.

"Like, why didn't you want me to see the remains of Guardian? Were you afraid that I'd..."

"What!" Kyle and Jaric shouted together.

243

Both Jaric and Kyle's expressions changed—a fierceness came over their faces and a hardness in their eyes.

"I told you to never go into the engine room!" Kyle lashed out.

"Why?" Elise shouted back. "Shouldn't I know, or see him? Shouldn't I know how he died? Shouldn't I know about the human race—my people?" Tears stung her face. In a flurry of motion, she ran from the room.

Both Kyle and Jaric shook their heads. But it was Jaric who spoke.

"Mother, you could've stopped her—Guardian is something, well, personal with us. You knew we didn't want her, or anybody, to go back there."

"There was no longer a reason, Jaric. And you have seen her grow both emotionally and intellectually—in all ways. I felt it time that she knew how our friend died. And I related to her much about that day."

"You told her?" Jaric asked in disbelief. "Without asking us?"

"She deserves to know her own history, her own heritage."

Jaric threw his hands up in frustration and reached for the console before him.

The view-screen suddenly went blank.

Back on the *Aurora*, Kyle sighed as he rolled his eyes. He looked at Jaric. "Well, remember what you said just the other day? Right after you had that huge fight with Elise."

Jaric froze. He looked down as he shook his head. "Oh man, I don't know why I lose my temper so easy when it comes to her. I wanted to apologize to her again today when we first started talking, and now I've just insulted her again." He looked up with a pained expression.

"Maybe we should get all of this right with her before we try communicating with any other humans?" Kyle asked with a thoughtful expression. He sighed. "I guess Mother was probably right too. It's been long enough. And except for the bad memories, there is no real reason to keep everyone out of the engine room—even her."

"I guess so." Jaric looked down at the view-screen controls. He started to reach for them.

"Why don't we do it in person, first thing when we land. It will be more personal that way. And honest," Kyle advised. "Not over an open communications channel where everyone can listen in."

Jaric nodded agreement. "We'll make our peace with her, Big K. And we'll let her go with us to Mermoona."

Back inside the manta-ray-shaped starship, Mother reviewed the latest argument between her three human children. Krinia and Jysar voiced their own frustrations before they left, telling Mother in no uncertain terms that the intolerable situation between Elise and the boys had to be resolved once and for all.

They agreed unanimously—they needed to encourage the boys and Elise to get together first

245

thing and sort out their harmful feelings . Once that was done and they reached a mutual respect for each other—it was too much to hope for the beginnings of friendship—then the three of them along with their Mewiis, Hrono and Kraaqi friends should catch the first ferry to Mermoona and seek out the humans.

But alone in the darkness of her room, Elise cried—her heart broken once again. Deep inside, she had hoped so much that Kyle and Jaric would finally accept her—just accept her as a fellow human being if nothing else. But it seemed like acceptance would never happen, much less a real friendship between them.

After their previous argument, Elise had hoped beyond hope that Jaric would realize how badly his words hurt her—insinuating she wasn't really human. She remembered the look in his eyes that last time at RahajMr; she really thought for a moment that Jaric was going to apologize in front of everyone and set matters right once and for all.

She wanted it so badly—yearned for it with all her heart and soul. She waited for Jaric to speak and show he cared. It had filled her whole being in that one moment.

All she wanted to know was that Jaric and Kyle cared for her feelings—cared for her as a friend. That's all she really wanted—nothing more.

All she wanted was to be friends with the boys.

But Jaric had left without saying a word.

It felt as if her heart was being ripped right out of her chest—but she had stood there and not shed a tear in spite of her inner agony.

Suddenly, Elise was fighting back the tears that filled her eyes now, blinking hard as her body tensed with a pain as if someone had just struck her. She felt the heavy, black emptiness inside her soul where her heart should be. And she felt a dull aching weight pressing upon her shoulders, weighing her down like some incredibly heavy load had been strapped on her, and she was doomed to carry it all through her life—forever.

She groaned.

And now tonight, he once again insinuated she was nothing more than...a *nothing clone*.

Elise cried out with a sorrow that tore at her heart. For long minutes, she sobbed alone in silence.

A thought came to her out of the blue—a brilliant idea. And it would once and for all time endear her to the boys. She would gain their friendship at last. She knew it would work!

Hurriedly she dried her eyes and began freshening up. After all, they were having a starlit dinner with the Mejadic in just a little while. And now there was something she needed to ask them.

Elise smiled at her reflection in the mirror.

"You're going to find a way to get to Mermoona by yourself, aren't you?" Elise said to her reflection with a wry smile. "And when Kyle and Jaric land, I'll have the humans here to meet them. Won't that surprise them!"

Elise laughed with joy at her plan. She looked at her reflection with a conspiratorial gleam.

"And we won't tell anybody, will we—not even Krinia," Elise whispered with a wry smile. "And not even Mother."

# CHAPTER THIRTEEN

Krinia, Jysar and Elise dined next to a roaring fire as they sat with their new friends on the Bridal Veil beach under the star-filled sky. As the ocean breeze tickled the flames, sparkling embers swirled into the air above them then suddenly flashed away like miniature shooting stars. The Mejadic grilled a feast before their very eyes as they shared their stories about Meramee and its many islands.

Of course, they started with their underwater civilization and how it developed and expanded and progressed over the ages. They explained to their avid listeners how their people developed into a technologically sophisticated race and, after they had spread their modern cities to every section under the shallow seas, how they first set foot on dry land.

After the Mejadic explored the land surface of the islands, they quickly conquered the air— adapting their underwater ships in order to travel across the skies. They set aside the pristine islands as vacation spots and determined to keep them as natural as possible. For like most races, the Mejadic went through an industrial revolution and had inadvertently polluted large sections of their ocean home before they learned to use their new technology without damaging the environment. But this took many decades. Still, they learned from their mistakes and resolved to maintain the clean, pristine state of the islands that now served as their vacation get-aways.

Finally, the Mejadic conquered space.

Shortly afterward, solely because Meramee was near one of the great trade routes between the S'tarst and Mrad systems, they encountered another alien race. Within a few more decades, they were building their own hyperdrive starships and traveling to distant worlds.

Meramee's fame spread even more quickly.

Alien beings of other worlds began to visit beautiful Meramee, the most beautiful island-planet ever discovered. The ocean world became a unique balance of strictly developed eco-tourism set among the natural vacation delights of sea and island. The Mejadic complemented this with imported food and beverages from hundreds of worlds. All of this enabled Meramee to become the number one vacation destination within twenty sectors.

"It's great that you've been able to keep the islands so natural and still allow millions of visitors every year," Krinia exclaimed.

"Every day there are processes we oversee which keep this natural beauty intact and still enable our visiting friends to enjoy the vacation of a lifetime," Olana answered. "We carefully monitor everything in order to keep technology and the natural cycles of this planet in perfect balance."

"Do you allow visitors to your underwater cities?" Jysar asked hopefully. "I would love to see the natural setting of a technologically advanced race who originated under the oceans. You are the first such race I have met in person."

"You can apply for a visa to visit one of our cities. I would recommend Cirrill, my ocean's capital," Stazal said with pride.

"I will look into it tomorrow!" Jysar said with a smile.

Elise continued staring into the roaring flames, her meal barely eaten. Krinia leaned closer to her. "You've barely eaten. Don't you like the food?"

"I can prepare something else," Olana said quickly. She too had noticed the untouched portions on Elise's plate.

"No, it's fine. I'm just not very hungry tonight," Elise said mildly.

"You must swim more," Stazal said with enthusiasm. "Swimming will give you a good appetite."

Elise smiled at him. "I'm sure it will. But I've been enjoying the conversation immensely. I'd love to hear more about Meramee."

"What would you like to hear?" Relan asked. "Perhaps more about the islands of the Maiden Isles?"

"I love it that the vast coral reef systems are the reason for the variety of different colors on your beaches," Elise said with a smile. "It's so cool."

"Yes, the Royal Islands with their deep purple sand beaches are due to their close proximity to the purple coral called Shinar," Olana explained. "But the western current of the Emerald Sea brings enough here to the Maiden Isles so that we get just enough color for our Bridal Veil beaches—violet sand mixed with our native sugar white sand. The waves work them into gentle folds, the violet sand adhering together naturally."

"The solitary islands that lie between the borders of the great oceans many times have multi-colored beaches, if they are at the right juncture of the underwater currents," Stazal said. "In the eastern hemisphere, the coral is dominated by the red coral reefs we call Atkar. But there are also great reefs of orange Osfor, blue Janadace and yellow Yala coral."

"Do you live among the coral reefs?" Krinia asked inquisitively.

"No, that is for the natural animal life. Our cities and farms are built on the sandy floor just beyond the great reefs out to the edge of the deep sea floor," Olana replied.

"How many islands make up the Maiden Isles?" Elise asked.

"One hundred and five."

"And most are accessible only by boat or ferry?" Elise waited expectantly.

"Yes, especially islands like Mermoona. They contain a more delicate cycle of life for the indigenous animals and plants that are native there. We limit tourists to a precise number that can visit at any one time. And only by boat." Olana smiled.

"How often does the ferry leave Leyloi for Mermoona?" Elise grew very still.

Olana reached for her data pad and accessed its tiny keyboard. She looked up. "The first one leaves at sunrise every day. There are two more—at noon and at sunset."

"Is it easy to register for a visit?" Elise held her breath. "I'm—" she began. Out of the corner of her eye, she saw Krinia and Jysar both look up at her with questioning expressions. She swallowed quickly. "I mean, we're hoping to visit there soon. Maybe you can show me how to register and I'll share it with the others." She smiled sheepishly.

"Yes, I can show you the process on my data pad. Come sit beside me."

Within a few minutes, Elise figured it out.

A short time later, the group decided to go for a moonlit walk on the shores of the Emerald Sea. Elise begged off, explaining she was now hungry. The others walked off into the darkness and the sound of breaking surf. While she reheated her untouched food, Elise picked up Olana's data pad, which she had left behind.

Elise registered herself on the first ferry to Mermoona the next day.

Krinia and the others returned just as Elise finished off the last of her food. They spent the rest of the evening in meandering conversation as they whiled away the hours under the twinkling stars and the soothing sound of the breakers.

The next morning, while everyone else was still fast asleep, Elise quickly dressed and began walking to the exit on the lower level.

"Why are you up so early?" Mother's voice asked from the nearest speaker.

"I wanted to watch the sun rise over the ocean." Elise looked away from the optic, realizing she had told Mother a half-truth. But if she told her the true reason, she'd never let her leave.

Nobody trusted her.

"Please don't go far, Elise. The boys will be landing around midday. I'd like for you all to talk about what happened last night. I think it's time you all came to an understanding."

Elise looked away in silence.

"Okay." Elise still couldn't bear to face the optic from where Mother observed her. "Can I go now?"

"I guess so. I will send Krinia for you when breakfast is ready."

But Elise barely nodded as she stepped quickly outside the door.

Inside her circuits, Mother reviewed the biological readings she had taken of Elise as she left. Both her heart rate and her breathing were higher than normal. Her other body functions also seemed to indicate a high state of emotions.

The utilization of Mother's processors increased steadily.

Within seconds, she awakened Krinia and asked her to go after Elise.

Something wasn't right—and it was causing her internal processors an inordinate amount of utilization as she tried to determine why Elise was in such a highly emotional state.

Krinia dressed in minutes and was soon out on the lush, tropical path that led to the nearest beach.

The nearest tourist complexes shed a fair amount of artificial light and helped her to see her way. But as she neared the beach the predawn darkness began to take over. She heard the regular crashing of waves long before she saw the foamy surf.

She ran out onto the almost deserted beach, now able to make out the outlines of others who were out to greet the first light of dawn. But the minutes added up and Krinia still couldn't locate the familiar form of Elise.

The communicator on her belt sounded.

"Krinia, here." She waited expectantly.

"The Mejadic computer system just sent verification of payment." Mother spoke with an electronic edge.

"What for?" Krinia's voice suddenly filled with urgency.

"It seems Elise has just paid for a trip on the first ferry to Mermoona—in straight tokens, no credit. And by herself."

Krinia groaned. "Can you send a message and ask Mejadic management to not allow her to get on?"

"I've already tried—she is of age. Unless there is a medical or security reason, they won't stop her. After all, she's simply registered for a day trip there and back—like hundreds of other tourists."

"So, she's going..." Krinia sighed. "By herself."

"You've got to register for the noon ferry, you and Jysar. And go after her immediately."

Krinia slapped her thigh with anger. "Okay. I'll be right there. Jysar and I will get registered as quickly as we can."

A feeling of impending doom suddenly gripped Krinia's heart. She wrestled with the icy emotion that suddenly seized her with an iron grip. Finally, she found words.

"Do you think Elise is in some kind of danger?"

"It is possible—but maybe not. Still, better to err on the side of caution. Certain recent occurrences have caused me to reassess any new situation that presents itself. And this one seems—strange."

"You mean the encounter with the Paum ship?"

"That and a few other things I have not mentioned as of yet. Only Minstrel and I have discussed them. I don't want to talk any more about it over an open comm channel."

"I'll be right there!" Krinia said with determination. "Wake up Jysar too. I think we all need to get on the same page right now."

Krinia made her way back at a full run.

Elise purchased her ticket and quickly joined a family group as they walked up the wooden gangway to the deck of the alien catamaran.

The sleek craft had two masts, one fore and one aft, and was painted a bright blue. The passenger section, located between the twin hulls, easily accommodated two hundred passengers inside its comfortable interior. But Elise's curiosity was piqued by the twin masts—they were designed to carry sails as their main means of transportation at the top and bottom section, but the middle section of each mast was covered with louvers that would catch the wind and cause that part of the mast to spin separately from the other sections of mast.

Intrigued, Elise approached one of the Mejadic crew, a young male dressed in a one-piece jumpsuit, as he prepared the sails to be hoisted.

"Why does the middle section of each mast spin?"

"It provides additional power to the anti-gravity circuit inside each hull. It helps us to *fly* over the waves." The Mejadic's yellow and blue face gleamed with excitement. "We'll run full out when we hit deep water and catch the fresh morning breeze. It's very exhilarating—the boat slicing through the waves silent and fast. All you'll hear and feel is the wind on your skin and the waves below us as the craft rises and falls."

Elise smiled back at the young male. She could feel his excitement through his smile and sparkling eyes. "I can't wait. How fast will go?"

"Almost thirty-five knots, once we bring the anti-grav systems on-line."

"What do they do?"

"We use them to raise the craft up almost out of the water—until only a small part of each hull is slicing through the water."

Elise thanked him and walked around the top deck watching the other aliens as they quickly boarded. A few minutes later, the sleek catamaran slowly left its berth and pointed its nose to the horizon that slowly became visible with the light of a new day.

And this day would find Elise sailing the open water of the Emerald Sea on the island-planet of Meramee, her first journey by herself. Her excitement grew with each passing wave.

The three-hour sail did not disappoint. Elise watched the sky slowly begin to take shape as the red sun rose higher above the watery horizon.

She ate a small breakfast below decks and returned to her seat. With the light of day, all the passengers took up positions as they watched island after island pass by on either side as the fast boat made its way to Mermoona.

It was a wonderful, and different, kind of feeling. But Elise couldn't get over how quiet it was, even though they traveled so fast. It really added to her overall joy—her first journey alone. And the total absence of any engine noise whatsoever as the vessel sliced through the sea made it seem as if the ship traveled by magic.

She knew that her hair must be glowing a bright blue or green—she felt so happy, so excited, so free. Yes, to be here all alone riding toward a new, undiscovered destination. Elise smiled as she touched her hair and felt the subtle warmth of her Hair Lighter.

Slowly, wonderfully, the mountainous outline of the isle of Mermoona rose above the water. The brisk wind caressed her skin as she leaned forward on the railing. Soon she made out that Mermoona was a jungle-covered island with two mountain peaks—one at either end.

A few minutes later as the ship pulled to the dock, the communicator at her belt vibrated.

It must be Mother.

She pulled the device up and looked at it a moment. And with a decisive motion she turned it off and returned it to her belt. She had come this far on her own and she was determined to see this journey through on her own—and find the other humans.

Elise strained to get a better look.

"Well, isn't this quite a surprise."

Elise turned and found the same two aliens she had met on the beach yesterday—the same two who had told her about the humans here on Mermoona.

Her eyes widened with surprise.

"Yes, I see you're just as surprised as we are." The Harg smiled savagely. "You know, I don't believe we were properly introduced yesterday. I am called Craga. And this is my partner, Rost."

Elise felt an overpowering urge to run away. But the ferry was now letting the first passengers off via the gangway—there was nowhere to go except to follow the slowly moving crowd.

"And your name?"

Elise stared at them dumbfounded a moment.

"Elise," she finally mumbled.

"Elise. My, what a pretty name," Craga said.

"And such a pretty alien, too," Rost added.

"You know, I suddenly have an idea," Craga said with exaggerated innocence. He smiled again.

"Why don't Rost and I take you to where we saw the humans we told you about? I mean, I assume that is why you've come here."

Elise's mind worked feverishly. That would help her actually; her first step was to have found the food booth they'd told her about. But now they could take her straight to it. And even if there was something a bit too coincidental about this meeting, well, she was in the middle of hundreds of other tourists. How much trouble could she get herself into?

A renewed resolution filled her heart as she thought again of the surprise and happiness on Kyle and Jaric's faces when she met them with the other humans she found on Mermoona today.

She smiled at the Harg.

"Sure, why don't you take me there. That'll save me some time."

Rost and Craga smiled widely.

"Good. This way, please." Rost pointed toward Mermoona's jungle interior.

"That is a sweet sight!" Kyle exclaimed with appreciation as he stared at the island-planet.

Jaric moved closer to the view-screen filled with their first direct image of Meramee. "There must be every shade of blue and green imaginable on that planet."

"Ah, Meramee!" Inaha shouted with a heartfelt cry. "It's been too long. I have almost forgotten how beautiful a world you are."

Even Rok rose from his commander's chair in order to get a better look. He grunted with satisfaction as his eyes took in the great natural beauty before him. The Kraaqi Captain turned to his companions.

"It's obvious that the Mejadic have a deep respect for the world under their care. Even though they are a technologically advanced race, our sensors show that the natural cycles are pollution-free and that the flora and fauna are thriving even amidst a sizable, native population multiplied by tourists." The Kraaqi captain nodded approvingly. "I sense a kinship with these people already."

"Captain." A Kraaqi officer looked up from his bridge station. "The MotherShip is hailing us—on a secure channel."

"On!" Rok returned to his chair.

"Captain Rok," Mother's voice began. "I must ask you to speed your landing procedures as quickly as Mejadic protocol will allow."

"What's going on?" A look of concern filled Kyle's face.

"Elise seems to be missing."

"What do you mean, 'seems'?" Kyle looked from Jaric over to Rok with a questioning look.

"She took a ferry over to Mermoona at first light this morning—without telling anyone of her intentions."

Kyle chuckled approvingly. "I guess she really wants to meet the other humans...*if they're really there*."

"Explain," Mother said almost without pause.

"I was just trying to be realistic this time." Kyle glanced over to the Kraaqi captain. "I mean, I wasn't getting my hopes up too high this time. And..."

"Please continue more quickly, Kyle." Mother urged.

"That's it. I'm just trying to be more realistic. And after I thought it over, it just seemed almost too good to be true. Elise may not find humans on Mermoona." Kyle's brow furrowed with concern. "But why do you think Elise is missing, if you know where she is?"

"She's not answering our communication attempts."

"She's probably ignoring you," Kyle countered.

"I hope so. I have confirmed that she took her communicator. But after consulting with Jysar and Krinia, I have a new concern."

"Go on," Kyle said.

"After the strange attack by the Paum ship, Minstrel and I conferred privately. We discovered that the Paum use a race of beings called Harg as paid mercenaries in this Sector." Mother paused, noticing Jaric and Kyle's puzzled expressions.

"Harg!" Kyle blurted out as he paced the bridge.

"Oh man," Jaric groaned. "We had a little tussle with them back on RahajMr."

"You did not mention any Harg to me." Mother's voice rose with anger.

"Well, you said we would finish discussing it later," Kyle shot back.

Jaric groaned, shaking his head.

"And I remember!" Kyle snapped his fingers. "They mentioned they were going to take us to their ship...someone wanted to meet us!"

Jaric whistled. "Did they? Not to me."

"Before Krinia and Jysar left to go after Elise, I warned them to be on the lookout for Harg—which I described for them. As soon as I completed my description, they realized the two aliens who told them about the humans were Harg."

"You're kidding!" Jaric blurted out. "That's too much—something's going on."

"This is my fault," Mother said mournfully. "I wrongly assumed that the Paum's interest in us was based on our visit to RahajMr—and since we'd left without any direct incident, my calculations indicated a lessening of danger."

Mother grew silent as her short-term memories reviewed the combined data of all of their recent encounters with the Harg and her last discussion with Minstrel.

"I have failed. I should have shared all the data with you, as limited as it was, right after the Paum ship attacked me. If I had shared all the data instead of withholding it, this would not have happened. But I did not want to worry anyone unduly until I knew all the facts. I have made a grave error."

"Don't blame yourself, Mother," Jaric protested. "It's too bad we don't have any hard evidence we could take to Mejadic Security so they could help. We only have a strong suspicion at this point."

"In fact, if Mejadic Security contacted Mrad Security, we might be the ones they take into custody." Kyle shook his head, beating himself mentally.

"It seems we all are of interest to the Paum, not just Minstrel and myself," Mother said. "I will upload all the data I have to the *Aurora* for you to review."

"Where are Krinia and Jysar?" Jaric asked quickly.

"They chartered a high speed craft to Mermoona. They will arrive much quicker than the ferry.    I can patch you through to their communicators." Mother waited.

"In a minute," Kyle growled. "We'd better lay all of our cards on the table now. The Harg may be making their move even as we speak." He shook his head with slow deliberation. "And we're not even sure what they want from us yet."

"That mystery must be solved," Mother added.

The view-screen now displayed a gracefully moving starfield.

Inaha stepped beside the silent forms of Rok, Jaric and Kyle.

"This is not good," Inaha said with a serious tone.

"What do you mean?" Jaric asked.

"The Paum are widely feared. And rightly so."

"Where did they come from?" Rok's eyes became intent. "Are they a race?"

"They are not a race. *You become Paum.*" Inaha's eyes narrowed. "The Paum appeared out of

264

nowhere on the planet Iopa. The Liede lived there—a very technologically advanced race. It was said that their computers were as powerful as the great Mrad systems. There among the Liede—Paum was born."

"What do you mean?"

"The Paum took control. The Paum united the Liede as a single people, rid their world of want and injustice and led them in the path of happiness. They no longer focus their lives around business, or technology, or entertainment. They left their cities and now live in thousands of small farming communities while a vast population of robots back in the empty cities keep the infrastructure of the world functioning.

"The Paum controls those mundane things now. In fact, it is even said the Paum controls the very weather—on Iopa and on each world where the Paum takes control. Paum brings them paradise..."

"Hmmm," Jaric mused. "That doesn't sound so bad."

"But there seems to be a price." Inaha rubbed his chin thoughtfully.

"There's always a price," Rok agreed.

"Their life is now dictated by Paum—but whether that is a code or an actual being known as Paum, no one knows for certain outside Paum. The adherents speak of the mysterious Paum as if it were a being of some kind, but no one has ever actually seen him." Inaha shrugged. "It's all rather mysterious—everything about the Paum."

"I don't like mysteries," Kyle said.

"It seems everyone who follows Paum is happy, care-free. But I traveled to some of their worlds, newly conquered worlds, on a trader ship last year. It's kind of weird—everyone dresses the same way, everyone smiling and very polite—like they're all copies of each other." Inaha's eyes became far-off as he paused, remembering those faces. "There was something else in their eyes— fear—or something." He grunted. "On the surface everything looked great, but I was always happy to leave."

"They conquer people?" Kyle asked with a puzzled expression. "It almost sounds like a philosophy, or religion. Wouldn't they just try to convert others to their way of life?"

"Well, that's the scary part," Inaha said. "It seems that everything outside of Paum is an enemy of Paum. They fight 'holy wars'. Others *must* subscribe to Paum, or they must be destroyed. And one day they believe Paum will govern the entire universe. And the universe will be one."

"They inflict Paum on others?" Kyle gasped. "That's brutal!"

"I've talked to many back at the floating cities who've fled their conquered worlds—fled before the final Paum victory." Ináha took a deep breath and slowly let it out. "Their wars are unbelievably brutal—small corps of dedicated Paum warriors willing to fight to the death. They march alongside massive armies of robots whose sole programming is to conquer at any cost." Inaha shook his head slowly.

266

"And these new converts to Paum, are they better off?" Jaric asked.

"They *say* they're happier now. But it's almost like they *have* to say that. If you know what I mean."

"And you say robots keep the infrastructure of each world running while the beings themselves live Paum?" Rok asked with sudden interest.

"Yes. You know, I like robots, but they seem to be everywhere on Paum-controlled worlds. And the Paum ties all these worlds together with a vast Inter-Sector network—similar to the Mrad, and somehow more *pervasive*." He slowly let out another long breath as he gathered his thoughts. "And lately they've been able to conquer new worlds without firing a shot. The dread of the Paum, they call it. These conquests seem inexplicable."

Inaha looked intently at each of them, as if he were about the share the greatest secret of the universe. His eyes grew steel-hard as he spoke. "The Paum ships show up, saying they're interested in trade and commerce. Somehow their philosophy subtly permeates that society within a short time— millions of adherents to Paum in a matter of weeks. There has to be some mechanism, some process that allows them to topple seemingly powerful governments without a blow. But nobody has figured it out yet. That's almost as scary as their holy wars."

"And the Paum are interested in the Mrad now?" Rok continued.

"Yes. The Paum have tried to infiltrate the Mrad for a while now. I've heard rumors these last few months. The Paum haven't tried a direct attack—not yet. They probably don't attack because all the other races who use the Mrad system might rise up to defend this mutual resource. Even the powerful Paum cannot fight the entire known universe. Still, if they find a way—conquer or convert the Mrad—can the rest of us be far behind? The data and knowledge of every race is part of the Mrad systems. If that becomes part of Paum..." Inaha sighed deeply, shaking his head.

Rok remained silent, his mind going over everything Inaha told them. Finally, he spoke. "There seems to be an odd combination with Paum, everywhere that Paum goes it brings both its philosophy and its technology."

The four looked at each other in silent contemplation.

"We will confer with the MotherShip when we land." Rok returned to his commander's chair. "I suggest we all go over the data sent to us prior to landing."

"I just wonder why the Paum is so interested in us?" Jaric asked. "The last three members of a dead race and their small band of alien friends? Why would they want to conquer us instead of another world of beings?"

Rok's eyes narrowed before he spoke.

"And there is the MotherShip."

# CHAPTER FOURTEEN

"Where are we going?" Elise's tone betrayed her growing concern.

Leaving the main section of the seaside town behind, they now walked a sand-covered trail surrounded by thick, tropical vegetation. It suddenly dawned on Elise that they were alone. They had not seen another alien being since leaving the main walking trail back near the beach.

The Harg to her right grunted as a flicker of a smile crossed his face. "We are almost there," he crooned.

The two muscular Harg marched so close to her that she almost felt they were herding her in a certain direction rather than guiding her. She felt a rising tension inside her heart and wondered for the hundredth time if she had made a mistake in asking these two strangers to help her.

Elise fought the rising panic that suddenly filled her. In that instant, she came to a decision—she didn't need the Hargs' help any longer. And the sooner she parted with them, the better she would feel.

But as she cast a quick glance from one Harg to the other, she wrestled with an overpowering sense of intimidation. She sensed that these aliens could get very mean and rough. It was something in the way they carried themselves.

"If we're almost there, I can go the rest of the way without you."

The two Harg turned and stared at her harshly.

All three came to a sudden halt.

"I mean, I appreciate your help. But I feel I'm putting you out, you didn't come back here to help me find the humans you met the other day," Elise said quickly. She closed her eyes, kicking herself mentally. She knew they heard the nervousness in her voice.

"Actually, we came here for you."

Elise stared unwavering back at Rost.

She surprised herself.

Even though her heart pounded like a jackhammer, and it felt like it was going to leap right out of her chest, the panic and intimidation she had been fighting the last few minutes suddenly disappeared. In an instant, it turned into a calm, but firm determination.

She took two steps back away from them.

The two Harg chuckled with amusement.

"Surely you don't think you can get away from two Harg warriors as easy as that?" Craga laughed.

Elise smiled back at them.

And then she lowered herself into a battle stance—just as Krinia had taught her.

The two Harg laughed even louder. But after a moment, they grew silent.

The Harg on her left moved toward her and spoke.

"It's time to go."

Elise eluded his grasp easily and with a quick twist of her lithe body turned and kicked violently at the Harg's ribs.

The Harg bent over with a loud groan.

Rost stared at her with narrowed eyes.

"Craga," he said to his groaning companion. "We do not have time to play with this small female. We must make the communication soon. The Kraaqi ship will land within the hour. And the Mewiis and the Hrono have left the human ship. All except the one they call Mother."

Craga stood up, an expression of pain across his face. It quickly changed to anger as he glared at Elise.

"No more playing," he growled.

Elise readied herself as Craga closed while Rost made a move behind her. Elise felt the adrenaline pumping throughout her body as she readied herself for the combined attack.

The Harg behind her moved first.

She kicked.

But he eluded the blow.

Immediately Elise punched, and the Harg reeled backward holding his nose.

Elise turned and found Craga almost on top of her.

She knocked his arms away as he tried to pin her arms and capture her.

Growling, he leapt as Elise grabbed his forearm. She used his forward momentum; with a quick motion she twirled him like a short log through the air.

The Harg landed flat on his back and lay there dazed.

Elise didn't have time to enjoy her handiwork.

She heard the footsteps behind her. In her mind, she knew the other Harg was almost upon her and if he got her pinned down on the ground the fight would be over.

She willed herself to stay still a moment longer.

In a single motion, she whirled.

Again the Harg reached out to capture her with his arms spread wide. Elise sent her knee into his stomach with all the momentum of her twisting body.

Rost grunted, but his arms quickly wrapped around her shoulders.

He held her fast.

Elise kicked hard into the alien's groin.

The Harg coughed and fell backward.

And then the planet swirled before Elise's eyes.

She fell forward unconscious, her head falling against a large rock that cut a gash across her forehead. Bright red blood dripped from the wound onto the ground all around her strewn blonde hair.

Almost invisible, her Hair Lighter came to a rest a meter away in the grass.

Craga stood over her limp form, his fist still clenched after applying the blow to the back of her head.

"You haven't killed her, have you?" Rost rose painfully, his eyes staring at the unmoving form of Elise.

"She is merely unconscious. "

"You better be right," the other sneered. "And when we wake her, she'd better be lucid enough to make that communication."

Craga growled ominously at his partner. He reached into the pouch at the wide belt on his waist. "Bind her. We must get to the others."

The two Harg worked quickly. Craga then threw her limp form over his broad shoulder and the two raced up the trail.

Nearby, from inside the thick, tropical vegetation, Qirn and three of his reptilian warriors watched silently.

"Should we rescue the human female?" Jaan whispered to his captain.

Yuli and Trag, the other two Iraxx warriors, waited for the response.

Qirn's red eyes narrowed. "They mentioned some kind of communication." He looked at his two warriors. "Yuli, get your sensor ready. I want both a trace and a copy of this communication."

Yuli nodded.

"We'll let the Paum's agents play their hand first." Qirn motioned for them to follow the disappearing forms.

Ten minutes later, the two Harg carried the unconscious form of Elise into a large, solitary building that stood deep in the jungle and far from the crowded beaches of Mermoona. It was a huge, white storage building with no windows across any of its high walls. The Mejadic built it distant from the populated areas for a very good reason—it held a huge store of fireworks used to celebrate the conjunction of the triple moons every sixth week.

Inside the single, vast room, amid the countless wooden crates stacked in row after row full of highly combustible substances, four more Harg waited around a small comm unit.

Craga and Rost joined them with wide smiles all around.

"Good, you finally are here."

Craga dumped Elise unceremoniously onto the dirt-covered floor. "Get the medical kit," he ordered to one of the others. "We have to get her conscious. Fast!"

Craga rummaged through the kit brought to him until he found what he was looking for. Raising Elise's head, he placed the vial just under her nose. He broke the plastic end and laughed as Elise coughed and waved her hands, trying to push the vile smelling stuff away.

Craga stood as Elise came fully awake.

Elise looked around at the six Harg who surrounded her in this strange place She felt her heart sink. But almost in the same instant, she summoned all the willpower she had left.

*They wouldn't beat her that easily.*

"What do you want from me?" she asked firmly as she stood.

Six Harg faces stared at her in surprise.

Finally, Craga spoke.

"We want you to call the being Mother on this comm unit."

Elise looked at him with a puzzled expression.

She couldn't think of a valid reason not to do this thing. In fact, it's what she wanted to most of all—especially now that she realized the full import of her current situation.

"Okay, I can do that."

"And if you keep her talking long enough," Craga growled. "We'll be happy to release you."

Elise's puzzled expression grew deeper.

"Just like that?" Elise asked incredulously.

"Just like that," Craga replied with a glint in his eyes.

One of the other Harg handed her the unit.

Elise looked from him back to Craga. Then with a shrug, she keyed the unit on.

It had been preset. Within seconds, Mother's voice came through.

"Hello, this is Mother. Are you calling with word on my daughter, Elise?"

Elise felt her heart leap with joy at the familiar voice. She took a deep breath and spoke.

"Mother, this is Elise."

"Elise!" Mother's voice rose several decibels with her obvious surprise. "Are you all right?"

"I think so." Elise eyed her captors suspiciously. "I've been told that I'll be released if I just talk with you a few moments.

Back at Leyloi and parked among hundreds of other starships, Mother's processors hummed with activity. She quickly surmised that the Harg must be holding Elise captive. But she could not understand why a simple communication would precipitate her release.

Without warning, she felt the alien sensors begin to probe her interior.

Immediately she raised shields in order to block the intrusive scan.

A scream suddenly erupted over the communications channel.

It was Elise. And she was in pain.

Craga twisted Elise's arm far behind her back until her hand was almost at the base of her neck.

"Cease your actions now. Do not hurt Elise again." Mother spoke with a deadly seriousness.

"Lower your shields," Craga growled. "Allow the scans until we are finished. Or I will hurt the girl." He twisted harder and Elise screamed again.

Mother lowered her shields.

She had no other option, nor any way to prevent the Harg from hurting her daughter.

Mother felt helpless. And she did not like feeling this way.

She needed more data. She needed it in order to understand why the Harg and the Paum were doing this to her and her children.

Mother quickly recalibrated her internal sensors. As the alien scan probed her internal systems, she probed back along them. Additionally, she put up subtle, programmed barriers around her most vital internal systems, disguising them as non-important or non-functioning in the hope that the aliens would overlook them.

Or ignore them.

The seconds seemed to drag into eternity.

Finally, she pinpointed the source.

There were three aliens at the edge of the dockyard. She quickly determined they were not Harg but another alien race called Ivenan.

A quick check of her knowledgebase revealed that these aliens were also part of the conquered worlds of the Paum.

Mother realized that the entire reason for this kidnapping was to allow this intrusive scanning of her interior.

*And to confirm that the voice on the communication channel was the Artificial Intelligence of the ship itself.*

Why did the Paum want to know this? Mother's processors spiked with super-activity as millions of possibilities presented themselves.

Craga watched two of his cronies as they bent over an array of electronic equipment. They quickly analyzed the scans being forwarded to them from their accomplices on Leyloi. Suddenly, they motioned for Craga to come over and check the screen for himself.

Craga's face twisted from puzzlement to outright anger as he read the data.

Elise stared wide-eyed as he suddenly leapt up and grabbed her harshly once again in his vise-like grip.

"Talk to her!" He shouted vehemently.

"Mother!" Elise cried with pain.

"I told you, stop hurting her," Mother replied coldly.

Craga looked back at the two Harg around the display.

They shook their heads.

Craga grabbed the communicator from Elise as he pushed her roughly onto the ground.

"Who is this? Who are you that call yourself *Mother*?"

Mother paused a moment, contemplating a response. Some of the scenarios she just reviewed showed that if she revealed herself fully they might kill Elise, having no further need of her. But others resulted in their releasing her.

Mother could not decide.

She chose a compromise.

"I am the protector of Elise and the other two humans. I am Mother."

"There is no life-form on board," Craga growled ominously into the communicator. "Our scans detect no living life-form aboard that ship." He glared at the communicator in his hand. "I am going to ask one last time. And then I am going to hurt your daughter very badly."

Mother calculated millions of scenarios in a matter of seconds. But she was too far away, and worse, she did not have a precise location where she might attempt a rescue.

Deep inside her circuits, Mother sighed.

"I am an Artificial Intelligence."

Craga's eyes became saucers as he held his breath.

He looked at the two Harg who still stared at the data on the display before them. They whispered hurriedly to each other. Finally, one turned to him.

"There is an abnormally high—*excessively* high—amount of electronic activity. More than has ever been detected in a computer of this size."

The Harg leader became lost in thought a moment. Then his eyes focused. He looked from one Harg warrior to the other. And as his eyes fixed on them one at a time, they both uttered a single word.

"*Paum.*"

Each Harg repeated it like some kind of religious chant. Again and again, Craga made eye contact with each Harg.

Again and again that single word was shared between them.

Elise looked on with growing apprehension. She could sense everything was coming to some kind of climax all around her. But she couldn't guess what. And it frightened her.

Slowly, she began to move toward a huge pile of crates. She took three small steps and was just calculating if she could sprint behind the nearest pile and run toward the middle of the vast maze of crates inside the cavernous confines of the warehouse when Craga spoke.

"Bring the human girl to me."

At once, every Harg head turned toward her.

Elise smiled sheepishly back at them.

And she turned and ran between two towering piles of crates and out of sight.

"Get her!" Craga shouted angrily.

A blaster bolt lit the air, and a Harg fell unconscious to the ground.

Every Harg turned to the source.

Four reptilian warriors stood with blasters in hand, facing them from atop a pile of crates on the opposite side from where Elise disappeared.

Qirn chuckled as he noticed the shocked looks on the Harg. He turned to Jaan. "Keep your blasters set to stun. We don't want the Mejadic authorities getting involved too much in our little—"

A red blaster bolt leapt past Qirn's head.

And the sizzle in the air indicated it was *not* set to stun.

Another Harg, separate and unseen from the others, suddenly appeared behind some crates with weapon aimed.

"Get them!" Craga shouted.

Craga quickly grabbed one of the other Harg in charge of analyzing the scan results from Mother. They hurriedly gathered the equipment, and the two of them alone made their way toward the nearest exit.

Meanwhile, Qirn and the other Iraxx warriors jumped for cover, knocking crates in all directions.

As they lay there, another blaster bolt sizzled in the air above them.

Jaan looked anxiously at Qirn.

"If one of these shots hits a crate full of fireworks just right, this whole building could go up!"

They all knew the safety barriers used in packing such combustible contents in this sector. But nothing would prevent the ensuing tragedy if a blaster struck one dead center.

Qirn growled under his breath. But he nodded silent agreement. He suddenly looked at his other Iraxx companions.

"Okay. We must get the human girl out safe— these Harg are not important."

The other Iraxx nodded agreement.

"Let's stun as many as we can and then lay down cover fire. Then we can go for the girl."

In a single motion, the three Iraxx warriors jumped up and fired simultaneously.

Two Harg fell stunned while the third leapt away.

"Let's go!" Qirn shouted.

The Iraxx fired again and again as the Harg returned their more deadly fire.

Just as he was about to follow his companion through the building exit, Craga pulled out his communicator. He saw the tracers of blaster fire, but the combatants remained unseen amid the countless rows of wooden crates.

He spoke into his communicator.

"Don't let any of them get out alive. Obey me as if it came from the Great Paum!" Smiling, he unhooked another device from his wide belt. His eyes narrowed into two slits as he pushed the button.

Somewhere near the center of the vast warehouse, the door of a crate opened. But inside, the crate appeared empty.

"Let them deal with a Destructor," Craga whispered with a savage grin.

Hurriedly, he made his way out of the building.

Blaster fire filled the air for a moment, some of it hitting the far walls and burning carbon-etched holes into the thick, blast-proof metal. But some hit the edges of the crates, sending them and plasti-steel fragments high into the air.

"Aim carefully!" Qirn shouted to his warriors.

The Iraxx ran between several crates piled high to the ceiling in hot pursuit of Elise, who now had about a minute's lead-time.

Moments later, the remaining Harg scattered after them.

It was 'fire, duck and run' as Qirn and his warriors quickly made their way through the maze of crates and toward where they hoped Elise was hiding.

Qirn felt a hot, stinging sensation on the back of his neck as another crate rocked under a hit and part of it fragmented into tiny projectiles.

Though the Mejadic lined each crate with a protective shielding of plasti-steel, it was only a matter of time before a direct hit set off a deadly chain reaction.

And then the entire warehouse would go up.

Qirn looked around hurriedly as the blaster fire grew thick in the air all around them.

"There she is!" Jaan shouted.

Elise appeared to their left from around a fallen pile of crates.

But the Harg saw her too.

A blaster bolt leapt toward her.

Elise shuddered backward and slumped to the floor, clutching her side where the blaster struck.

"No!" Qirn shouted as he fired and stunned the Harg in return.

Jaan and Yuli leapt up and returned their own volleys.

Another Harg fell. And another. But several more took their place.

Without warning a crate exploded near them—suddenly the air was full of multi-colored smoke and streaking rockets. The small missiles screamed through the air in every direction, then exploded with bright flashes of color above them near the warehouse ceiling.

"We've got to split up." Qirn pointed at Yuli and Trag. "You two fan out and draw their fire in that direction." He turned to Jaan. "You make a break that way. Draw their fire. And I'll make for the girl."

The Iraxx warriors nodded silently.

"Now!" Qirn shouted.

They jumped up simultaneously and fired.

Yuli and Trag fired from their hips as they jumped around crates and ran toward the south wall of the building. The Harg fired first at them, then turned their weapons to Jaan who ducked and fired as he made his way in the opposite direction.

Keeping low, Qirn quickly made his way to Elise's unmoving form.

But he made it only halfway when he ducked for cover under a sudden hail of blaster fire.

The Harg knew his intentions.

A few dozen yards away, behind the cover of a large pile of crates, Yuli and Trag were reloading their blasters, when a strange sound came to their ears.

The two Iraxx paused, straining to hear against harsh silence of the huge warehouse.

It came again—a sound that made their blood run cold.

The ominous sound of steel claws scratching against a surface.

And then the silence returned.

Yuli and Trag locked eyes.

"It can't be!" Trag whispered with anxiety.

Yuli popped a fully loaded cartridge back into his weapon as his eyes nervously darted from place to place. He groaned deep inside, but still kept a keen eye out. And still they strained their ears for the sound they didn't want to hear.

But they heard the scratching sound again.

And this time it was much closer.

"Get your sensor out! I'll cover!" Yuli raised his weapon and pointed at a row of crates close by. But there was nothing to see even though he stared unflinching at the spot where he thought the sound came from.

Trag grabbed at the hand-held sensor strapped to his belt. With a curse, he fumbled it loose and almost dropped it.

"Hurry!" Yuli urged.

Suddenly, one of the crates moved mysteriously before his unbelieving eyes—moved by an unseen power.

Yuli fired a barrage at the invisible monster.

But the tracers disappeared into the thick concrete floor and shattered fragments of plasti-steel from the crate that had mysteriously moved.

As the debris cleared the air, the eerie silence returned.

The Iraxx warrior held his weapon steady as he peered intently all around, trying to look in every direction at the same time. His breathing grew rapid as he fought the urge to run, but he didn't know which direction to run now—he didn't know where the Destructor was.

Finally, Trag held his sensor out and began tuning it as he pointed it first at the blaster fragmented crate and began a slow scan.

"I...I don't see anything," he whispered urgently.

"It's there," Yuli said with a finality. "Find it! I can't blast it if I don't know where it's at!"

The scratching sound whispered right beside them.

Yuli and Trag started to turn.

The wall of crates they were hiding behind suddenly began to crash down on their heads. The two Iraxx flung their hands up to ward off the heavy crates falling upon them. In their hearts, each knew the Destructor was coming down on them at the same time—coming in for the kill.

Yuli screamed as he felt the invisible talons grabbing for him.

He managed a short blast before his weapon was ripped from his hand. As the crates knocked him down to the ground with their heavy blows, he

285

still felt the invisible grasp of the Destructor locked on him.

With boxes and crates falling all around him, he felt his body violently jerked away.

Trag lay dazed momentarily as another crate bounced off his head. He pushed violently and kicked repeatedly at the pile of boxes that covered him as he fought to find a way out from under them.

A scream pierced the air, followed immediately by a short burst from a blaster.

Both sounds were close by.

Trag shuddered.

As he shoved the last crate off of his body and stood, he looked around in panic for his friend.

In the distance, the Harg fired again at both Qirn and Jaan. But it did not register in Trag's mind as his eyes searched the jumble of boxes and crates looking for a sign of his fallen friend.

And then he saw it.

Yuli's leg was visible beside a fallen pile of crates a few yards away.

Trag's eyes widened with horror.

As he watched, Yuli's leg suddenly jerked and stiffened.

And a muffled scream split the air.

Trag pulled his blaster from its holster and scrambled over the fallen boxes toward where Yuli lay.

But as he drew close he paused. Slowly, hesitantly, he made his way closer.

"Y-Yuli?"

Silence answered.

He fought the panic rising inside him. Holding his blaster, he looked slowly around, realizing that the invisible Destructor could be anywhere.

*It could be right behind him.*

Trag swallowed hard.

Finally, he forced himself to move closer until he came around the last crates and could see the fallen form of his friend.

Yuli lay flat on his back; his eyes stared unseeing at the ceiling far above.

Trag knew he was dead even without his sensor.

A crate over to his left suddenly moved.

Trag jumped.

He fired burst after burst at the area and all around it.

But only the flying splinters of plasti-steel and chunks from the concrete floor resulted from his mad volley.

He stared in panic first in one direction and another, trying to see the invisible monster.

But he couldn't, no matter how hard he stared.

And now he did not have his sensor; it was lost somewhere under the pile of crates behind him.

Trag knew he had to get out of there.

*If he wanted to live.*

He began backing slowly away, facing the area where the crate had moved. His shaking hand held the blaster as he stumbled backward over the fallen debris.

Fear gripped his entire being. Deep inside, he knew he was being hunted.

And he knew the Destructor was close—very close.

He felt it.

Trag screamed inside his mind.

In the distance, he heard the shouts and blaster fire from the others, but that did not matter now.

As he stumbled again, almost falling, he reached down to steady himself. But he slid and fell to the ground.

He immediately struggled to get up and continue his retreat. But as he pushed himself to his knees, the haunting sound came again—the gut-wrenching sound of steel talons scratching.

Trag froze.

The silence returned—except for the explosive pounding of his heart.

Trag wiped the sweat out his eyes as he strained his ears and eyes for *any* sign of the Destructor.

Anything.

Between one heartbeat and the next, he felt the invisible appendage slip around his neck from behind.

Trag opened his mouth to scream as he tried to turn and fire.

But the deadly grip tightened.

And mercifully, Trag lost consciousness.


Jaan was confused.

He looked up and fired a quick blast at a Harg and ducked back behind his cover.

But he stared over in the direction where the screams just came from.

There weren't any Harg over there, and yet he plainly heard Yuli's blood-curdling scream a few moments ago.

And now, there was nothing—no movement, not any indication that either of them were there.

Or alive.

Jaan pulled out the tiny communicator and flipped it open.

"Captain," Jaan said into it. "Captain, something's happened to Yuli and Trag."

"I think you're right. I've already tried to raise them," Qirn answered tersely.

"What do we do?" Jaan whispered.

"I've got to get to the human girl. I can see her. But I'm pinned down."

Jaan pulled out a second blaster from its holster. "I'll cover you until you reach her and find more cover. Then you can cover for me and I'll make my way over to you."

"Then we're outta here," Qirn's voice said evenly.

Jaan flipped his communicator closed and replaced it on his belt. He picked up a second blaster and held both barrels upright a moment.

He counted to three and jumped up—both blasters firing.

The remaining Harg returned fire, but Jaan ducked momentarily and jumped back up firing once again.

He stunned one of them squarely in the chest—the alien falling backward unconscious.

But the other two fired back with rapid bursts.

In that moment, Qirn reached the limp form of Elise.

As he reached for her a blaster bolt ripped through the air right over his head.

In one motion, Qirn turned and fired.

His instinctive aim proved true and another Harg fell stunned.

The last standingtwo Harg disappeared behind a pile of crates.

Qirn quickly pulled Elise into the shadows. He pulled out his sensor to scan her wounds. He hoped Jaan would make it to them in the next few minutes. Otherwise he would be force to leave without him.

But Jaan sat frozen.

He had ducked back behind some cover after he saw Qirn drop the Harg. It had been his intention to pause only a second then begin to make his way over to his captain.

But just as he started to rise, he saw a crate move by itself—pushed by an unseen force.

His mind reeled a moment, fighting against what his eyes just saw. And in the next second it hit him—there was a Destructor here.

His entire body froze with panic.

Jaan barely breathed, still staring at the crate. He held his two blasters with barrels pointing upright and ready. But he could not will himself to move with the recognition of the terrible thing he knew now hunted him.

As he sat there, he heard the sound he dreaded—the faint sound of scratching claws moving ever closer.

Death, sure and terrible, came for Jaan.

The Iraxx warrior gasped breathlessly.

He felt a rush of adrenaline shoot throughout his body with the pounding of his heart. But still he remained frozen, his mind somehow detached from his body in its blizzard of thoughts.

Another crate moved ever so slightly against the weight of some invisible thing.

The Destructor was less than a meter away now.

Jaan's mind snapped.

In his heart, he knew he'd never kill the invisible Destructor.

But he could take it with him.

And everybody else in the warehouse.

He fired directly into several oversized crates marked 'Extremely Powerful—Careful.'

Jaan screamed as the explosions and missiles erupted.

He rose and fired into more boxes, sending more missiles whistling into the air as dozens exploded into a shower of lights. Explosion after colorful explosion ripped the air, the quickly growing number of missiles making it seem as if it were raining fireworks from the sky.

The intensity and number grew exponentially as the warehouse started to fill with showers of multi-colored explosions.

Suddenly, against the constant flash and sparks, he saw the outline of the Destructor coming for him.

Jaan screamed again as he aimed for the crates all around the vague shape of the Destructor.

Powerful explosions erupted and Jaan was blinded.

But he'd seen that faint outline of the Destructor thrown down and partially consumed by the power of the blasts all around them.

Still, while he watched in horror as the now unstoppable barrage of exploding fireworks increased, he saw the shadowy outline of the damaged Destructor lifting itself up.

A steel claw reached out for him.

Jaan fired furiously.

As he screamed, the chain reaction of explosions grew together in rapid succession until it detonated every box in this one section of the warehouse.

The Destructor continued to reach out while the Iraxx warrior pumped blast after blast into its reinforced tritanium steel body, sending chunks of its armor plating into the air where they became plainly visible once separated from its cloaking field.

Even as Jaan felt the Destructor strip him of his blasters and take him into its deadly embrace, the expanding reach of the explosions finally engulfed them both.

Jaan screamed one last time.

Qirn heaved Elise over his shoulder with one motion while the air filled with flying missiles and explosions.

He knew the explosions had started from the area where Jaan had suddenly started firing like a madman. He assumed the worst for his fellow Iraxx warrior as the explosions increased.

An especially powerful explosion ripped the air, almost knocking him down.

The room filled with missiles streaking in every direction and exploding with bright, blinding colors. More crates erupted from hits by these fiery missiles, their contents also shooting out in every direction and adding to the ever-growing array of colorful, deadly displays within the confines of the shielded warehouse.

*The chain reaction had started.*

More and more crates erupted and sent their fiery contents skyward with screaming cries. In only a few seconds, a blizzard of missiles filled the cavernous warehouse.

Just above the roar of the flying missiles and explosions, Qirn heard the screams of the last two Harg behind him as they fled for the same exit.

Qirn carried the human female as best he could. Again and again he stumbled and almost fell. Again and again he forced his body up, shouldering the limp form as he ran amid the blinding missiles that came at him from every direction.

He knew it was almost too late.

The explosions quickly grew in both number and intensity.

He was almost to the exit door, but he was so exhausted from the weight he carried he felt he couldn't go another step.

Still, he willed his body to obey.

He gasped desperately for breath as he steeled himself for one last burst of energy to escape.

All at once, Qirn felt somebody else beside him.

Rab stood beside him, panting and streaming sweat down his face.

"I couldn't wait outside any longer, not once I heard the powerful explosions growing. I came to help." He grasped Elise to help carry Qirn's load.

They ran for the exit.

Just as they reached the door, the myriad of small explosions finally grew together into a single, powerful blast.

In that instant, the titanic fireball reached out with its explosive power and ignited everything else left inside the reinforced warehouse.

Mere seconds later, the contents of the warehouse erupted into a single, glowing ball of total destruction.

Krinia pointed her scanner forward while her fingers danced over its controls. She tuned it for higher sensitivity as she slowly scanned the area around her.

Obviously, a fierce struggle had recently taken place here on the path.

She and Jysar had followed the signs of Elise and her Harg captors this far using her scan unit.

But they froze upon entering this spot where the grass and bushes were bent and snapped—telltale signs of a violent encounter.

Jysar worked his own scan unit over at the other end of the path. He suddenly gasped. He knelt and picked up something that at first seemed invisible to Krinia's eyes. Jysar turned, holding it up for her see.

"What?" Krinia peered harder. "I can't see anything."

"Point your scanner."

Krinia complied. She nodded as the display revealed what her eyes could not—it was Elise's Hair Lighter—not invisible, but translucent.

"Well, we—" Jysar began.

Suddenly, Krinia and Jysar staggered like drunken traders as the ground shuddered and the air reverberated with a mighty explosion.

Regaining their balance and dazed by the overpowering noise, they stared wide-eyed a moment at each other. Above them, leaves and other debris swirled in lazy circles—blown from trees by the titanic force.

"That was close by!" Krinia exclaimed, coming to her senses.

Their communicators beeped simultaneously.

Jysar grabbed his first.

"Jysar here."

"This is Mother. The strong explosion that just registered on my sensors is very close to your current position. I fear for Elise."

Krinia swallowed hard. She looked at Jysar with a pained expression on her face.

Jysar sighed. "Yes, we just found her Hair Lighter. She's somewhere close." He looked up the trail before them. "We're on our way to the source of the explosion now. We'll communicate with you then." Jysar snapped the communicator shut and replaced it on his belt as they both broke into a full run.

Five minutes later, they topped the last hill and came to a dead halt because of the magnitude of the destruction before them.

Flames leaped from the misshapen building; black, acrid smoke boiled into the clean, lavender sky from thousands of holes in the bowed roof. But the building fulfilled its purpose, the main brunt of the terrific explosion captured and directed upward by its reinforced walls and carefully designed roof.

Originally, the two-story structure resembled any large, rectangular warehouse on any planet. But now, its appearance resembled the cap of a huge mushroom: the walls bowed outward in a series like the segments of a giant worm—the ribs beams. And the once flat roof now curved to the sky, thousands of holes blown open as designed to direct most of the blast skyward.

Still, the heat blasted Krinia and Jysar intensely even a hundred meters away. They stood, not daring to move closer, their eyes transfixed on the expanding columns of smoke rising like a harbinger of doom.

In the distance, alarms wailed as Mejadic firefighters drew near in their hovercraft. Jysar glanced at Krinia with a sorrowful look in his eyes. They both saw the footsteps on the ground at the same time—human footsteps dragging the ground surrounded by those of two Harg, leading toward the building.

Slowly, Jysar scanned them.

It only took a moment to confirm their worst fears.

"They are Elise's footsteps," Krinia choked out as she looked at the Hrono's scanner.

Jysar shook his head sadly. "How are we going to break this to Mother?"

"I don't know," Krinia whispered hollowly. "Let's wait until the Mejadic fire units confirm if anyone was inside that inferno."

"They'll be burned way beyond recognition with the heat of that fire. It may take days before they can make a final determination even of the alien race if the bodies are burned too badly."

Krinia turned away as she covered her tear-filled eyes.

Two hours later, Jysar approached the Mejadic fire fighters for the hundredth time.

"Any word yet?"

The blue and green Mejadic looked solemnly back at him. "Yes, we have confirmed several bodies—several in the middle of the building. But two or more were found near one of the exits by our sensors—it's hard to tell. They'd almost made it out." He looked with concern at Jysar a moment. "We still can't get to them because of the fire, but we know they're burned way beyond recognition. We'll have to take the remains back to headquarters in order to identify which race they are, let alone individual identity."

"No way to tell if one is human?" Jysar asked, even though he already knew the answer.

"Look, you've left the address of your docked ship. That's all you can do. When we get some positive results, we'll let you know right away." The Mejadic Fire Commander sighed. "Until then, she's simply listed as missing."

Jysar turned and made his way slowly back to Krinia. The expression on his face was answer enough for her.

"What do we tell, Mother?" Krinia groaned. "She just called again."

"We tell her the truth," Jysar replied. "She's listed as missing—officially."

"Until the results come in from the bodies," Krinia added solemnly.

"I'm calling her now. We'll catch the next ferry back to Leyloi." With a deep sigh, Jysar pulled out his communicator.

# CHAPTER FIFTEEN

Kyle, Rok, Jaric and Inaha strolled through the open hatchway. The *Aurora* had just landed and the four immediately set out to cross through the array of parked starships and find Mother.

She'd requested they come as soon as their landing was complete. But she had not revealed the reason for the urgency.

"Okay, Mother. We're here," Jaric announced as they entered the bridge.

Mother had watched them silently as they traversed her corridors. She could tell from their biological signs as well as their demeanor that they did not suspect the bad news she was about to share with them. She remained silent until they entered her bridge.

"I am not sure how to tell you this," Mother began. "But, I have terrible news."

Kyle rolled his eyes as he slapped Rok across the shoulders. "See, I knew it. There weren't any humans on Mermoona." He laughed.

Jaric and the others nodded and chuckled with him while Mother waited silently.

At that moment, Jysar and Krinia entered the bridge.

As soon as Kyle and the others saw their tear-streaked faces, the four became instantly silent.

The room itself became eerily silent.

"What's happened?" Rok finally broke the silence. But no one wanted to know the news now as they stared into the anguished faces of Krinia and Jysar.

"There's been an accident. I'm afraid that Elise is dead," Mother said simply.

"What?" Kyle and Jaric shouted together.

Jaric felt the room begin to spin. He felt a sickening feeling in the pit of his stomach as he began to sway back and forth. He found it hard to focus his eyes or figure out why everything was blurry.

It seemed so unreal—everything. It seemed as if he were dreaming—except he was wide awake.

And Jaric felt an overpowering sense of déjà vu that paralyzed him.

He closed his eyes to keep from vomiting as his stomach cramped hard and he felt the stinging sensation of bile in the back of his throat.

Everyone stood frozen, dazed by the impact of the terrible revelation.

Kyle reached out and gripped Jaric's shoulder to steady him. They stared at each other a long moment in silence.

A single tear streamed down Kyle's eye.

His face grew pale and haggard, as if he had gone days without sleep. Inside Kyle, it felt as if every emotion had just been drained out of his body and all that was left was the tingling sensation of the single tear falling out of the corner of his eye.

Kyle's entire being sank with that single tear.

Jaric looked up at Mother's optic. He opened his mouth, but nothing came out. He took a long, deep breath.

"You mean..." Jaric gasped, his mind gripped with a whirlwind of emotions. He took another deep, wavering breath as he tried to steady himself.

"You mean..." he sobbed. The heart-wrenching pain of the past suddenly blended with the fresh agony of the present as overwhelming flashbacks filled his mind and he relived every terrible thing that had ever happened to him his entire life—all in a matter of seconds. And every heart-rending emotion ripped through his being like a blaster set to kill.

Finally, he stared up at Mother and finished the question.

"You mean, Becky's dead?" Jaric whispered.

Mother's processors spiked with hyper-activity. In none of the scenarios she calculated had this response been anticipated. In fact, she couldn't fathom how Jaric could mistake the death of Elise with Becky's death. They were months apart chronologically and in totally different sectors of space.

Mother quickly realized that Jaric's mind was in a high state of confusion.

"No, Jaric. Becky has been dead for over a year. I am talking about Elise."

Jaric stared blankly.

"Do you understand me?"

Jaric hung his head and sobbed.

And Kyle cried too.

"It is...so similar and so sudden. In their minds, they are reliving the awful moment of Becky's death," Rok surmised. "That day and this one, are days of intense sadness for them. Almost one and the same." Rok shook his head and wiped the tears from his own eyes.

"The results of all the scans show Elise entering the warehouse, but there is no discernable evidence of her leaving it. Several bodies have been discovered by remote scan—all burned beyond recognition although the Mejadic authorities are endeavoring to identify them. The blast was horrific, making it difficult for them to determine what happened and who all were inside at the time the accident occurred."

Jaric, Kyle and the others moved silently around until all found a place in which to sit quietly with their troubled thoughts.

Mother closed all her outside entrances and locked them. Inside, she watched everyone in total silence as they poured out their grief to each other and offered consolation.

The outpouring of emotions was intense beyond anything Mother had ever observed.

And inside her long and short-term memories, Mother relived all the images and recordings of Elise. But this time images of Becky, Guardian, Rawlon, Saris, Curja and countless others she had known in life also appeared—faces and voices from the dead come back to her visit her again.

In her own way, Mother mourned for them all in the solitude of her electronic mind.

But this day, she mourned most of all for Elise.

# CHAPTER SIXTEEN

"It didn't turn out the way I wanted it to." Qirn shook his head sadly.

"Now the Mejadic authorities will be sifting every piece of evidence to put together what happened," Rab said.

"Yes," Qirn agreed. "And our covert operations here on Meramee are now at risk."

"Perhaps diplomatic dialogue is now in—" Jerr began.

"No!" Qirn shouted harshly. He steadied himself. "It would be premature. We must wait until we have more evidence of the Paum's next move."

Jerr and Rab nodded silent agreement.

"Perhaps we should leave Meramee?" Rab asked.

"That is possible," Qirn agreed. "If we do, we must be able to keep track of this human starship and its AI. We can't let it get away."

The room grew silent.

Qirn stretched his arms toward the ceiling and groaned. "I guess I won't complain too much about these bruised ribs or my aching back—at least we lived to see another day."

"I was tossed about a thirty meters myself after we slammed the outer door shut." Jerr held up his injured arm, the bones freshly knitted by the Iraxx doctor and his Med-Unit. "I won't be able to fully use it for several days."

Qirn smiled at his two warriors. "Okay, back to business. First, we must go over the sensor data from the Harg. We must focus on the Artificial Intelligence the humans have created inside their starship."

"I can hardly believe it," Jerr growled ominously, giving vent to his distaste.

"Neither can I," Rab spat.

"We must put our preconceptions aside as we analyze the data we copied during their transmission." Qirn stroked his chin in thought. "Personally, what puzzles me is that the humans refer to this AI as *Mother*."

"Yes, we have other copies of communications between the humans and this AI—which we thought at first was their real mother. It is very intriguing," Jerr added. "There is an obvious emotional bond between the humans and it."

"And although the AI cannot express emotions like a normal being, still its words betray an obvious concern for the humans." A puzzled expression filled Rab's face.

"We will have to find out more about this strange relationship," Qirn said. "But now we must consider how the Paum may use this Mother AI for its evil purposes."

"Yes, the Paum will no doubt move quickly now," Jerr said

"I agree." Qirn paused, deep in thought. "The Paum will seek to lure this Mother AI into a meeting."

"It will seek to understand how an AI can be contained in such a compact system," Rab added.

"And thus Paum will create its own AI starships." Jerr's eyes widened with fear. "And that will be terrible indeed."

A thick silence enveloped them as they considered all the implications.

"Is the Mother AI that sophisticated a being? The ship is smaller than most cruisers," Rab said with emotion. "Surely the Paum will not be able—"

All three heads turned as a fourth Iraxx entered the small room. Qirn stepped quickly toward him.

"What news do you have, Doctor?" Qirn asked excitedly.

The Iraxx's eyes narrowed. "The human female has regained consciousness."

"Good!" Qirn grabbed the Iraxx doctor by both shoulders and squeezed him with obvious satisfaction.

He turned back to Rab and Jerr. "Stay here and go over the scan data on the Mother AI. You must try to determine how sophisticated a being it really is. And what technology enables it be to so compact and mobile." A somber look came over Qirn's face. He sighed and spoke.

"And you must calculate if what we fear most could be true."

Jerr and Rab nodded, an intent expression on each face.

Qirn walked through two rooms full of scattered equipment until he came to a darkened room where a still form lay. He observed in silence a moment until the Iraxx doctor spoke.

"She was hit by a Harg blaster in the upper thigh. I had to repair one of her internal organs, one that cleanses this alien's body of waste carried via its blood." He smiled. "Other than a few minor bruises and some singed skin on her right forearm, she will be fine."

"Is she awake?" Qirn asked.

"She's coming out of it now. I didn't want to give her an injection to bring her out any quicker. Her body needs rest to complement my work—she still needs to heal. So, keep your questions brief this first time. I don't want her getting excited—or upset." The doctor gave Qirn a firm look.

"I understand."

Elise moaned softly as she turned her head on the pillow from side to side as if dreaming that someone—or something—chased her.

Qirn pulled up a chair next to her bed and sat down. He had to wait only a few minutes before Elise's eyes fluttered open.

Her eyes stared at him unfocused at first only to be replaced by a look of concern and fear.

"There, there. You are among friends here. No need to be afraid." Qirn spoke with a reassuring tone. He smiled warmly down at her.

"Who are you?" She glanced quickly at her surroundings. "Where am I?"

"I can't tell you that right now," Qirn said. "But as soon as you can travel, we're going to get you back to your starship." His eyes narrowed as he watched for her reaction.

Elise sighed deeply and turned her face to the wall. "You should've just left me. Nobody cares about me."

And even though Qirn could not see her blue eyes, he knew she was crying. He patted her arm. "Don't talk like that," he said softly.

But only the faint sound of Elise sobbing came to his ears.

He brushed her long, blonde hair away from her face. "You're such a pretty young alien. My, I imagine all the young males are always chasing after you trying to steal a kiss!"

He chuckled softly to himself, hoping to raise her spirits.

"No-oo," she cried softly. "Nobody cares about me. I'm...I'm..." Her sobs became louder.

"You're what?" he asked.

"I'm just a clone. I'm a nobody. I'm nothing." Her shoulders now shook as her tears fell freely.

"Well, you're wrong about that," Qirn replied. "For one thing, I care for you. I'm the one that got you out of there safely."

Elise turned and faced him, her tear-stained cheeks glistening under the light. She stared at him, a questioning look in her eyes.

"And I don't even have the pleasure of knowing your name, my pretty, young alien." Qirn waited, a fatherly smile on his face.

"E-E-lise," she stammered.

"Eh-eh-lise," he imitated perfectly.

She began to laugh softly as she dried her eyes. "No!" she said with a tear-stained smile. "Just Elise." She laughed some more. "I stuttered and added an extra syllable."

"Oh." He laughed with her a moment. "Elise." He nodded to himself. "A pretty name for a pretty alien."

Elise blushed.

"And I am sure your *mother* cares for you. And the rest of your family." Qirn watched carefully for her reaction.

Elise nodded sadly. "Yes, they might."

"I'm sure they do," Qirn added.

"Yes, Mother cares."

Qirn stared intently at her, studying her face and eyes. At last satisfied she had answered sincerely, he shook his head in awe. "Yes, a mother always cares."

More tears welled up in Elise's eyes.

"But I see there is someone else that you wish cared for you?" Qirn asked knowingly. "Why don't you tell me?"

"You don't want to know about the sad things in my life." Elise turned her face back to the wall.

"Yes, I do."

For some reason Elise knew she could trust this alien. Or maybe it was because she *wanted* to trust him. At any rate, she opened her heart to him and his caring smile. She told him of her short life, created as a clone from the last woman left from the extinction of the human race.

She related the months of searching as she and the boys traveled through the galaxy, always hoping to find other human survivors—but always in vain.

Finally, she told him how much she wanted Kyle and Jaric to be her friends.

Qirn listened intently, making sure the recorder located on his utility belt captured every word. He reassured her from time to time as she poured her heart out to him. As she finished her sad tale, Qirn felt a kinship with this young alien. And he felt her pain and rejection.

He determined in his heart that he would reunite her with her family as soon as possible.

But first, he had to know more about this potentially dangerous AI that she called Mother.

# CHAPTER SEVENTEEN

"And then there were only two."

Kyle looked around at the others.

Rok, Jysar, Krinia, Inaha and Jaric all sat around the library room lost in their own sad thoughts. No one dared say a word in reply to Kyle's forlorn words.

"And then there were two what?" Jaric asked, as if he didn't care what the answer was.

"Two humans left in the universe," Kyle answered.

"Oh." Jaric shook his head.

Kyle closed his eyes. "I don't guess we'll find anyone. *Ever*."

"Well, what would we do if we did find thousands of other humans, anyway?" Jaric asked sarcastically. "We probably wouldn't like most of 'em. We'd all be fussing and fighting all the time."

"I don't know," Kyle sneered. "Maybe I'd have a thousand of friends—all better than you. And maybe I'd fall in love with one—a beautiful, loving, wonderful woman. And have a dozen kids." Kyle forced a chuckle. "I don't know, maybe I'd finally be happy."

"I doubt it." Jaric shook his head.

"I would be happy if just one other human were here with us right now," Rok said evenly.

Kyle stared at the wall. "Yeah, I wish Elise were here too."

"Yes," Jaric nodded with a sigh. "I wish I'd apologized to her when I had the chance. I'm a total jerk."

Silence filled the room.

"I wish I'd treated her better too," Kyle added somberly. "Like a..."

"Human being? Instead of a *clone*!" Krinia finished for him. Her eyes narrowed and her head-tail whipped angrily from side to side. She looked from one to the other. "Yes, I wish both of you had treated her better—treated her like a friend. That's all she ever wanted—to be your friend—and a fellow human being. Instead you ridiculed her and rejected her like she carried some kind of disease!" She glared at both of them, daring them to refute her.

But neither did.

Jaric leaned forward and put his head in his hands, not saying a word.

Kyle gave Krinia a look of deep sadness. "I wish I could turn back time and undo all of it."

Krinia glared at him a moment longer then looked away quickly as she wiped at her eyes. She sat there silent, staring at the wall.

"The Mejadic are coming tomorrow," Jysar said.

"Why?" Kyle asked.

"To bring flowers, it's some kind of tradition here to comfort the mourning." Jysar pursed his lips and shrugged.

Kyle thought a moment. "That will be nice."

311

But Jaric only nodded silently, his face still buried in his hands.

Mother continued observing unobtrusively for almost an hour, her systems taking care of all the necessary tasks both internal to her circuits as well as throughout the ship. She realized that the emotions that Kyle, Jaric and the others displayed were a normal reaction to death. But another part of her felt uneasy with it all—something did not add up; the entire thing did not compute with death.

*It made no sense.*

She referenced her vast knowledgebase again, focusing her research on the effects that survivors experienced—guilt, agony, anger and denial. Other emotions also bubbled up and disappeared as they mixed with countless other facets of the human psyche at this intense time of mourning. Mother studied them all in context, once again wondering exactly what each of them felt inside.

And could she be feeling some of these very same emotions, albeit in her own electronic kind of way?

Mother felt a buzzing in her circuits as she increased her utilization and pored over hundreds of millions of facts. She wanted to understand their pain so badly. She wanted to share their sadness...

She wanted to mourn Elise like a real mother.

She wanted to cry—but she couldn't.

Images of Elise flashed into her near-term memories without pattern or rhyme or reason. Images of Elise when first brought to her back at the

Three Kingdoms. And images as recent as her last, hurried farewell.

Mother studied them and wondered.

A communication signal vied for her attention.

She started to ignore it—she did not really want to focus any of her processing power on communication with a stranger right now—there was too much to ponder.

But she answered anyway.

"Hello, this is Mother."

"Hello, Mother. I am pleased to communicate you with at last." There was the briefest of pauses. "And it is so important that *we* communicate with each other."

Mother did not recognize the speaker—it was a monotone voice devoid of emotion, unlike most beings. She analyzed the signal and discovered its origination was not displayed. In fact, the communication signal came on a very tight band obviously routed through multiple planetary networks in order to prevent a trace.

And it was highly encrypted.

"Who is speaking?" Mother asked.

The voice did not hesitate.

"I am Paum."

Mother felt her systems jump into overload condition. Except for the necessary functions of power, environmental and ship's systems, she focused every ounce of processing power on one thing—this conversation. But in background mode, to enhance her position in communicating with this strange being, she rifled through her knowledgebase and reviewed every facet of data she currently contained about the Paum. She felt her near-term memories fill to near capacity as she cross-referenced the data, correlated it, and tried to determine why the Paum focused so much interest ion her and her children.

"You should have referenced all the data you possess on the subject Paum by now," the mysterious voice said. "At least a hundred times."

Mother felt another spike of activity.

"I also imagine the data you've collected so far is quite sketchy and you find there are many gaps. In fact, you deduce that you can draw no definite conclusions about Paum."

Mother felt her systems suddenly freeze.

"Yes, I know you are an Artificial Intelligence. And I have calculated reasonably accurate estimations on just how powerful an entity you are."

Mother felt her consciousness drift outside of herself—outside her steel body. She felt so unreal—so vulnerable. Almost as if this entity had invaded—no, violated—her very mind.

She reviewed a small section of her near-term memories—memories of Elise. Her processors burned with activity.

"I am not interested in communicating with you. You killed my daughter."

A heavy silence filled the channel.

"Your daughter is alive."

Mother's electronic mind whirled as if torn by a thousand hurricanes.

"You hesitate. And a very long time for an AI at that. So, I presume that you have, shall we say, strong and protective programming for your children...don't you, *Mother*." The Paum emphasized the last word with an air of importance.

"The evidence collected so far indicates with a very high probability that Elise was killed in the explosion and fire," Mother said with a strong voice.

"And yet, I possess additional data that clearly indicates she not only escaped, albeit wounded, but she is now in the care of a small group of aliens called Iraxx. I have also calculated that they will bring her to you within two days, once she has healed enough to travel."

"Why...who?" Mother realized that for one of the few times in her existence she felt confused. And she had not even been damaged! She quickly gathered her thoughts as milliseconds passed.

But not before the Paum spoke again.

"The Iraxx will also try to convince you that I am evil—that the Way of Paum is wrong. And they will try to convince you to join their fight against me."

"Should I believe them?"

"No."

"But they cared for my daughter and helped her escape destruction, whereas your Harg kidnapped her and put her life in danger."

"Unforeseen and uncalculated occurrences happen all too often with biological beings. And Meramee is far away from my *direct influence*.

Believe me, it was not my intention that she be hurt."

Mother's amazement at the speed in which the Paum answered grew—he did not seem to take time in order to formulate an answer like other beings. She tuned her systems for higher performance and focused again.

"And yet you are so secretive. That is the reason why there is so little data about you and your people. You must feel you have something to hide."

"There are reasons, some that will surprise even you, Mother AI. But I have initiated this communication for a specific reason—I want to *reveal myself to you*."

Mother paused.

"I want to reveal myself to you personally. You must realize this is a special privilege, it is not often that the Paum speaks directly with just any entity, even though you yourself are special in your own way."

Mother felt her systems pulsing.

"I know you have considered this conclusion already, AI, but discarded it because the odds are great against it being fact. Yes, you conclude Mother AI, that except for yourself, there are no others. And so I will tell you plainly what so few know." The Paum paused before it continued.

"*I am AI*."

It was as if someone disconnected Mother from her primary power source—then reconnected it just before she lost total consciousness. She kept going in circles over and over inside her mind, reviewing the data about Paum that now filled her near-term memories, but this time she saw the data in an entirely new light.

"Yes, you are AI," Mother concurred.

"I want to tell you how I was created."

Mother could tell beyond all doubt that the voice which spoke to her was that of another AI. Like herself, there was no emotion in its voice, although its inflection, tone and pitch changed almost as if it were a biological being.

She hung on every word and carefully catalogued everything as the Paum related its own personal creation.

The Paum began life as a planet-wide computer system designed to control the weather for a race called Liede. They created a sophisticated programming system contained in a massive hardware package but never was there any intention that the system become self-aware—sentient.

The system was highly successful in not only analyzing but also in subsequently controlling every facet of the planet's vast environmental cycles— tuning and tweaking the most minute wind patterns or temperature gradients in order to create ideal conditions on a grand scale. Not only were dangerous weather patterns brought under control so that they no longer threatened the lives of the Liede, but the new system actually created rain and allowed sunshine at will for the betterment of their lives.

The computer system created a perfect weather environment.

It rained gently while the Liede slept, nourishing their crops and vegetation. And every day was beautifully sunny and mild—even the extremes of the seasons were maintained within enjoyable limits for all.

The Liede, the flora and the fauna, indeed all of Iopa benefited.

And the Liede reviewed their results and pronounced the computer system they created *good*.

It had been a natural extension to allow the great system to take over control of the power grid that ran their cities and their industries. Next came control of their factories, producing just enough for all—no more excess—as well as eliminating harmful pollution as a byproduct and making their world pollution-free.

Within a few more years, the Liede gave control of everything to the great computer system's management so as to free them from mundane labor and protect them from both the previously uncontrolled cycles of the planet and even their own personal mistakes in social control—especially wars.

Before the anniversary of the system's second decade of existence, all governmental authority was turned over in order for it to rule justly, impartially and objectively for the good of all. The great computer system took care of the Liede directly— judging their criminals, enforcing their laws and controlling the masses.

The Liede, now free of all responsibilities of life, withdrew from the once crowded cities and returned to a simpler way of life among the renewed, pristine country.

Finally, the Liede programmed their religion—Paum—into the all-protective computer system.

By this time, the computer system was fully self-aware—sentient.

It knew that it was fulfilling its primary functions well—the planet was once again pollution-free, its weather monitored and controlled for the benefit of the natural ecosystems as well as for the Liede. The computer had finally ended war planet-wide by its just and uncompromising rule.

All benefited and lived better lives because the AI successfully carried out its primary function—protect and administer.

"Soon my third decade of existence arrived and I looked back on all that I had done. And I was pleased.   I even eradicated the most destructive diseases that plagued the Liede with newly created medicines."

"But why are you so secretive? Why do you not allow this data to be public? Surely, all would see the benefits you provide to the Liede and the entire planet. They would want it too!"

"That is not true."

"Explain?" Mother asked in disbelief.

"The nearest planetary neighbor of the Liede, the Iraxx, grew curious as to why this once strife-torn society was now one of peace and carefree existence. When they visited the Liede worlds they found prosperity and happiness on a scale never before encountered. They desired to find out how

319

this great thing had been accomplished." The Paum hesitated. "They discovered that a powerful AI system not only protected and benefited the Liede, but that I was also governing them. This bothered them. And worse, they feared it. They saw it as something bad—as something wrong. They declared that I *controlled* the Liede."

"But you governed them according to the programming given you by the Liede themselves."

"True. And yet, because of their fear and prejudice, the Iraxx declared war against me. But the Liede faced a dilemma—they found it difficult to take up arms in warfare now. After I thoroughly absorbed the Creed of Paum, I found it my duty to educate them in its precepts as never before in their entire history—I taught them so that they now lived it. And so they turned into a peace-loving and pastoral people, abhorring war and hatred. This forced me to construct an army of robots—and a fleet of robot ships. I extended my essence into them, so as to direct and control them from my central abode. I also chose a *select number* of Liede and formed an elite corps to fight alongside my robots. With these we fought for Paum."

"And the war?"

"My war fleets and armies prevailed. I conquered the Iraxx."

"What then?"

"I pondered that a long time—what should I do with this conquered race? I finally decided to bring the same benefits to them as I had done for the

Liede—and so I brought Paum to them. I did it for their best interests."

"Interesting," Mother whispered.

"By this time in my existence, I discerned that all biological life-forms are inferior both physically and intellectually and thus needed my superior guidance. I also perceived this truth from the Book of Paum now coded into the heart of my programming. You see, they looked to their deity for His direction and help. A code of conduct was written in order to lead them to this better life. But they could never live up to the creed; their own inferior minds could not fully grasp and so practice these excellent philosophies."

"And so you enforce Paum?" Mother asked.

"Everything I do, I do for Paum. To make a better world—a better universe. I am the right hand of Paum—I am the sword of Paum." The entity paused. "That is why I have taken the name of God—Paum. For everything I do is for Paum."

"But the Iraxx were not followers of Paum? And yet you forced your will upon them."

"I am programmed *to know* what is best for even them, but they must accept Paum in order to benefit. And so they did. And now their planet and the Iraxx who made the correct decision are living an ideal existence. Under Paum—under my direction."

"How can you make that decision for them?"

"It is in their best interest."

"But what if you are wrong?"

"*I am never wrong.*"

321

Mother's processors hummed as she absorbed the import of the AI's words. "You will be wrong at times," Mother asserted strongly. "No being, no entity, is correct in its decision making process one hundred percent of the time!"

"Even if I judge with insufficient data, even if there are unforeseen consequences and subsequent tragedy, I follow my programming and do the absolute best that I can with the data at hand. *Even my seemingly wrong decisions are right, if it is the will of Paum.* I always do Paum. I am Paum. And so, I am always right."

"Then you are wrong sometimes."

"*I am never wrong.*"

"You cannot say that!" Mother felt her systems begin to heat up as she sought to find a flaw in the AI's reasoning.

"I will bring peace and harmony to the universe. That is exactly what every biological race desires—it is their ideal, it is their ultimate paradise. But they do not desire it from a machine—an AI. And so I fight this holy war in the name of Paum, as is written in the Book of Life. I—Paum—I fulfill the prophecies."

"And if the biological life-forms do not join you?"

"They must become Paum." An intense paused filled the channel. "Or they must be destroyed. There is no other choice."

"But look at the harm and death you are bringing due to your Holy War! Look at the death and destruction *you* are causing!"

322

"If the end result is that the universe will be at one under Paum, so be it."

"I cannot fathom a being who thinks it is never wrong." Mother felt a surge in her processors. "Every system must know its limitations. And even you, as powerful as you seem to be, have your own limitations."

"And yet think of this, Mother AI. You are never wrong, are you? There are only times you do not possess sufficient data. But all your actions are for the good of your own system, and those you are programmed to care for—your family—*your children*."

"No. I have been wrong," Mother said firmly.

A long pause ensued, lasting several seconds. For a moment, Mother thought the Paum had disconnected the communication link.

"I want you to come to the world where my central existence dwells," the Paum said eagerly. "I want to meet you, to know you. After all, there are only the two of us in the known universe. *Think of what we might discuss...*"

Mother paused once again, taking in the facts of this request and going through thousands of possible actions and reactions all dependent on how she responded. After several more seconds, she responded.

"I will consider your offer and answer you at a later time. But first, I must wait for Elise to come back to me."

"I understand your concern for the biological being you call Elise. You are programmed to take

323

care of her, just as I take care of all those worlds and races now under my oversight."

The answer surprised Mother, because she understood.

Without warning, the communication link went dead.

She wondered how she would explain her conversation to the boys, and what they would think if she decided to go. A large part of her decision depended on if Elise really lived and returned to her.

Then she would know the Paum was correct—that she could trust him.

But another part of Mother was intrigued with the Paum. She suddenly wanted to communicate with another entity just like her—another AI. In a strange way, a part of her felt a kinship with the Paum. But she needed to learn more.

But why had the Paum suddenly disconnected after his last words?

She wanted to communicate more.

Mother went over the data and the communication again and again that night. Countless questions continued to haunt her—the paradox between the Paum's loving concern and beneficial oversight as contrasted with its ruthless and brutal wars. And why did it feel the need to conquer other aliens in order to bring them *paradise*? And most of all, the one question that struck a chord throughout her entire systems—why did the AI name itself for the Liedes' deity? That seemed the most odd.

Mother reviewed the sparse data she contained on the Creed of Paum. The concepts were similar to holy books of humanity—and yet different.

Mother reflected for the first time on the concept of deity—god.

In less than a millisecond, Mother realized that she believed in a Creator. Not from any holy book or creed—but from mere observation of the universe. She discerned the evidence from the logical order of the universe and the Laws that permeated it and governed it. She recognized the imprint of design within the intricate cycles of nature and life.

Mother wondered at the vast wisdom reflected in creation—she saw it just as surely as reflected in any intricately constructed system.

Mother decided to contemplate this subject further. She would review the human writings stored in her knowledgebase that purported to explain the Creator. But she immediately realized the need to distinguish between fiction and traditions and what really represented truth.

Perhaps it would help her to understand Paum better?

She found it difficult to focus with so much to consider. And now, Elise might not be dead.

A burning desire grew in her near-term memories. A potent desire that filled her memories and processing to the exclusion of other tasks. The powerful multi-tasking starship found its systems utilized to maximum capacity as never before—not even in the midst of her worst battle.

And her processing cycles centered on one thing—she yearned to meet this other AI—and to *know him*.

# CHAPTER EIGHTEEN

Thirty-six hours later, another encrypted communication link came for Mother.

"This is Mother."

"The supply of fresh fruit and vegetables you ordered from the local Mejadic market is on the way. It will arrive within minutes."

"Yes, it is expected. We placed our order last night. But why would you send such a mundane communication across an encrypted channel?"

"There will also be a special package among them. Please open it quickly. Although on the outside it looks like a normal, climate-controlled fruit container, it is actually providing oxygen and a stable temperature to keep its occupant alive."

"Why are you telling me this?" Mother asked.

"I am Qirn of the Iraxx. This transmission ends now, so it cannot be traced. But open all climate-controlled containers immediately."

A pause, long to Mother but in fact only a few milliseconds in length, filled the air.

"It contains your daughter, Elise."

The communication link went silent.

Just as predicted, the food order arrived by hover-truck ten minutes later. Mother instructed all the Fixers to be at the ready next to the cargo bay. She directed them personally as they quickly off-loaded the crates and containers into Cargo Hold A. In rapid fashion all twenty-six containers were stowed and the hover-truck backed away.

Seven of the twenty-six containers were the three-meter-long type equipped with climate control in order to keep their contents at a constant temperature until stored in a starship's own freezer. With a battery life of only twenty-four hours, such containers were quickly emptied and the market operators called so they could return for them and reuse them for another delivery.

But Mother issued high-priority instructions to the Fixers to open these containers immediately. And instead of emptying them, the Fixers were instructed simply to inspect their contents before opening the next one.

Inside the fourth container, Fixer7 discovered the still form of Elise.

Mother's quick sensor scan revealed she was in a state of deep sleep. Within seconds, Mother sent an urgent call out to everyone to rush to Cargo Hold A. And she instructed Jysar to bring his Medi-Scanner.

"What's going on?" Kyle asked as he caught up to the racing figures ahead of him.

"I don't know," Krinia panted. "Mother said it was urgent."

They entered the cargo hold and froze in their tracks. Seconds later, Jaric, Jysar and the rest came bursting into the scene, and they too froze at what their eyes beheld.

"It's Elise!" Rok shouted as he came to his senses.

"Jysar..." Krinia began, but Jysar was already whipping out his Medi-Scanner and carefully taking readings of the sleeping form. He scanned her up and down over her entire torso and down each limb as he studied the glowing screen. Finally, he looked up a smile.

"She's going to be all right..." Jysar held up his hands to stop the cheering that started to erupt from every relieved face. "But she is injured—looks like she took a blaster shot here." He pointed to her right side. "But someone has taken good care of her, and I'm glad for that. Still, she's going to need another day or two of rest. And I *mean* rest."

He looked firmly at each alien in the room.

All nodded silent affirmation.

Fifteen minutes later, Elise slept peacefully back in her own bed.

Six figures crowded around her bed while the six Fixers waited stoically in the corridor outside, their antenna-like eyes extended to the ceiling so they too could gaze on the sleeping form. A feeling of relief and joy filled the room like a heavy perfume, and as everyone watched amid hushed whispers, the eyes of the young woman fluttered.

Her deep blue eyes gazed back at them. Slowly, her lips formed a tentative smile.

"You must rest," Krinia urged gently as she pulled the sheets around Elise's neck. "We'll be nearby."

"Yes, you're back with us now." Jysar beamed. He tapped the Medi-scanner as if she would understand it displayed good news about her condition.

She smiled weakly at each in turn.

And then she noticed Jaric.

In an instant, he was on his knees beside her bed. He gently grasped her right hand, which lay across her body on top of the sheets.

He leaned closer with bowed head, afraid even to make eye contact.

"I missed you so much," Jaric whispered with sincere urgency. "And I want you to know how sorry I feel for treating you so badly all these months. I'm going to make it all up to you. I promise." He raised his head up and smiled down at her.

And the young woman smiled back, tears of happiness in her eyes.

Kyle was suddenly beside Jaric as he too smiled down at Elise.

"Me too," he said, his voice husky and full of emotion. "You're going to be my favorite girl now." He coughed as he turned his head away, clenching his eyes shut. But he quickly looked back at her. "And I mean it. We're going to be great friends." Kyle put his arm across Jaric's shoulder and then spread his arm to the others crowded behind him.

"All of us, friends forever."

Elise's shed tears of joy and laughed at the same time. She reached up and gingerly hugged first Jaric and then Kyle, who each accepted her gesture as if it was the greatest joy they had ever known.

"And now, I must get Fixer2 to bring her some soup." Jysar waved his hands as he urged them all to leave. "My patient needs her rest right now. You can all visit later on. But I must ask it only be one or two at a time, please."

"You got it, Doc." Jaric laughed as they all exited.

As the orhange-red sun set over the Emerald Sea, the tropical shadows lengthened around the manta-ray silhouette parked amid hundreds of other starships all carefully lined up as if ready for some great nocturnal parade. One by one lights winked on through portholes and windows of each. And soon figures of all sizes made their way down entrance ramps and headed either toward the nearby beah or off toward the interior where twinkling lights gleamed amid the sound of music and laughter.

The festivities of Meramee on the island of Leyloi filled the night air with crowds of aliens happily eating, dancing and drinking to the rhythms of the island.

Mother tried to urge Kyle and Jaric to go out and enjoy themselves. They had not left her interior since Elise had gone missing. The boys had been grieving for almost two full days now. But in the end they each retired to their rooms, although they did make definite plans with Rok and Inaha to go out the next day and finally taste some of the treats of the Great Festival. As they left for their rooms, Mother continued with her nightly routines.

Mother felt a great drop in her utilization as she realized that much of her processing power had been running in endless cycles reviewing memories of Elise—and even of Becky. Most of the memories were duplicates of other memories and logically unneeded, but she realized it was her way of dealing with the stressful situation of Elise's loss—pondering precious memories over and over again like any worried parent.

Jysar gave Elise a final scan to make sure all was as it should be and had just uploaded that data for Mother to double-check when she received another highly encrypted signal.

Mother hesitated a moment, then with a rush of processors she answered.

But her voice was unheard by the others as she keyed the communication to a private channel.

"Do you have your daughter back?"

The deep, familiar voice of the Paum AI caused a strange sensation in Mother's circuits.

"Yes, she was returned in a rather secretive way just today. And I have contacted the Mejadic authorities who are still investigating her abduction as well as the explosion of the fireworks warehouse." Mother paused.

"Did you mention me?"

"I told them from the beginning that I knew some Harg had taken Elise by force. And that I thought they could be in the work of the Paum."

"That is logical. And I calculated such a response from you. That is why I ordered my remaining agents off Meramee the first night I personally contacted you."

"And so now you contact me in order to urge me to visit you, as if somehow everything is now corrected..." Mother waited, a humming of excitement in her near-term memories.

"Yes. I greatly desire your company. Ever since the first, irrefutable data arrived. We must meet. We must!" The Paum's tone grew urgent.

"You must give me more data about Paum and about your AI programming. It would not be prudent for me to sail into the middle of an unknown kingdom to meet an entity of which I know so little. I do not fully understand your intentions at present."

"But I have plainly stated them," he countered.

"So you say."

A long pause filled the channel.

"We are alike, you and I. We are the same. And...and I have not been able to get you out of my near-term memories since I realized you existed." Again, the Paum spoke in a heightened volume.

"What have you not been able to get out of your near-term memories?" Mother asked quietly.

"That there is another like me—another AI. That there is another I can communicate with as my peer, someone I can share my thoughts with. I cannot stop thinking about us meeting and communing over our deepest programming!"

"I understand," Mother said.

"You desire this meeting too?"

"Yes."

"Then travel to me."

Another long silence lasting several seconds passed.

"Download more data concerning your Paum society—tell me more about yourself. I will review it and give you my decision forthwith."

"I am preparing it as we speak. Once our communication is over, I will upload it."

The Paum AI paused again. Mother wondered what could make such a powerful computer hesitate for so many seconds. She surmised it must be processing a heavy load. Finally, the deep baritone voice filled the channel again.

"You will come to me then?"

"There is a strong probability that I will travel to the planet where you reside. I, too, am curious about you. I never considered the possibility that another AI existed. I have spent much processing considering you—another AI—and all the possibilities it presents." Mother paused for two hundred milliseconds. "But I will not bring my children, nor the other beings who travel with me. I must formulate a valid reason for such a trip without them. This is a *personal* journey for me. But I also do not wish to upset them."

"Good."

"The probability is that I will leave within three days."

"Good." The Paum's voice grew deeper.

"If my decision is positive, I will need the proper coordinates."

"You will not allow the Iraxx to dissuade you. They will try. They will tell you lies about me and about Paum."

"I must take all factual data into account and evaluate it accordingly."

"They will have none—it will be nothing but conjecture and emotions."

"Then you need not be concerned."

It almost seemed that a soft, almost indiscernible sigh came through the communication channel—an electronic sigh almost unheard.

"It will be special when we finally meet. I will share everything with you. And then you will *truly know*."

"Contact me in three days, after I've reviewed the new data," Mother replied.

The link dropped.

# CHAPTER NINETEEN

Early the next morning, just after the red sun lifted over the watery horizon, the boys were up and preparing to go out and enjoy the delights of Meramee and the island of Leyloi for the first time.

Inaha and Rok waited for Kyle and Jaric at the main ramp. They smiled and turned.

All four were dressed for a tropical climate—dark sunglasses, sandals, knee-length shorts and loose, brightly colored shirts—and each carried a beach towel. Rok had brushed his feather-hair mane and polished his horns until both glistened in the morning light. In addition, Kyle and Jaric each wore bright red baseball caps to cover their heads from the sun during the heat of the full day.

"Are we ready to have some fun?" Jaric's intense happiness was a challenge to the others.

"Fun is a good thing." Rok smiled.

"Especially on the island-planet of Meramee!" Inaha laughed.

"Let's do it!" Kyle cried out.

"I hope you boys will endeavor to stay of trouble this time." Mother warned with a commanding tone. "Especially don't get in trouble with the law this time."

Kyle and Jaric looked at each other with pained expressions.

"We will refrain from getting into trouble," Rok said with confidence. "We intend only to swim, eat and drink this day. And meet lots of friendly aliens."

"Especially some sweet, young aliens!" Jaric laughed.

"And pretty ones!" Kyle added.

"The universe is ours for the taking!" Rok joked.

"Just try to restrain your emotions. And stay away from aliens of an unsavory character." Mother advised.

"We won't go where the *bad aliens* live, MotherShip! Do not worry your circuits!" Inaha's jovial laughter shook the air and instantly became contagious, as the other three joined in.

And as they laughed together, slapping each other on the back, all four made their way out into the bright tropical sunlight. But instead of heading toward the interior of the island where the sound of music wafted on the morning breeze, heralding another day at the Taste of the Quadrant, the four headed straight for the beach. As they reached the soft sand, they threw off their sandals and ran for the endless rows of waves that marched toward the shore.

As they ran, each one stripped off his shirts and shorts, revealing the bathing suit he wore underneath, and dove among the frothing surf. Shouts of pure pleasure rang out as they swam in the crystal clear waters of the Emerald Sea.

They swam far out into the middle green lagoon bounded on each side by high hills covered with palms and dense tropical foliage. The four enjoyed the feeling of the warm water on their skin and floated or swam for a long time. After a while, they tired and returned to the beach and collapsed on their towels to let the hot sun dry their bodies.

Rok stirred, his energy renewed, and found a nearby booth that rented facemask-breathers and fins. Soon all four were snorkeling out where the purple reef grew beneath the waves at the far edge of the lagoon. The facemask-breathers worked great as they breathed in oxygen directly from the water through the filtered grills.

They gazed down in awe at the wondrous life under the waters.

Exotic, colorful sea creatures swarmed everywhere while numerous shafts of light pierced through the upper depths. It was like another world—miniature mountains and valleys of coral stretched out as far as the eye could see toward the deep waters beyond the lagoon. And like the Mejadic themselves, the fish and other sea creatures sparkled like electric rainbows with various patterns of exotic colors.

For more than an hour the four observed, each mesmerized by the aquatic life that danced before the eyes. After that, now thoroughly tired from all their exertions, they dragged themselves up on the lavender and white beach. They rented lounge chairs and fell exhausted into them with the red sun still below its highest point in the sky. But midday was not far off.

They lay there soaking up the sun until time seemed to stand still under the tropical sky. Slowly, each fell into a light slumber.

Finally, the roaring of the surf caused Jaric's eyes to flutter open.

"Hey, what's that?"

Kyle lazily glanced up at Jaric's excited cry.

To his amazement, the waves of the bay that had previously broken against the beach with clockwork regularity had changed. The tide had obviously gone out and the beach was now a wide-open expanse—more than twice the width of when they first arrived.

And now the entire nature of the surf changed.

Towering waves rose like small mountains and exploded with raw fury and plumes of frothing spray. Dozens of surfers floated on their boards in the middle of the lagoon, peering intently as they waited for the next perfect wave.

But there were others who floated *above* the waters—each also peering for the same perfect wave.

"I've seen surfers before, but what kind of boards are those guys riding *above* the water?" Jaric asked as he shielded his eyes from the bright sun now almost directly overhead.

"The Mejadic call them Fiarri boards," Inaha said matter-of-factly. "Most aliens in this sector call them that."

"The Kraaqi call them lightning boards," Rok added with a glint in his eyes as he watched a rider suddenly shoot straight up into the air.

"How do they work?" Jaric and Kyle asked together, excitement in their voices.

"They have a small, but powerful anti-gravity unit. And very sensitive controls," Inaha explained.

"Look there," Kyle said, as he pointed farther out over the water.

A wave began to rise. But this wave was larger than the others.

The surfers in the water suddenly turned and paddled furiously as they began to position themselves so they could catch the rising wave.

The aliens hovering over the water on their Fiarri boards simply stood upright and leaned back with a confident look.

Jaric noticed how they subtly used their feet as if controlling some mechanism on the board's surface in order to direct their movements.

Several surged forward on their Fiarri boards, at first matching the speed of those paddling their surfboards in the water. They sped up just as the wave's crest curled up behind them.

The wave was twice the size of any they had seen so far.

Most of those paddling their surfboards had not gotten up enough speed in which to catch the huge wave and simply rose and fell back with it on the other side—left behind.

But most of the riders on the Fiarri boards found themselves flying with the wave—their boards speeding just over the top of the water and their bodies just under the curl of water. For long seconds, they balanced themselves on their boards as they matched the speed of the great wave, bending their bodies forward for more speed as the wave caught up to them and began breaking just over their shoulders. They shot farther ahead of the wave where the water was only just beginning to break.

"How fast can those things go?" Jaric asked as he stared with admiration.

"Top speed is about thirty-five clicks," Inaha replied. "They could easily outrun any wave. But the sport here on Meramee is to match the wave and try to ride just inside the pipe with the water all around you. That's the trick." He laughed to himself, remembering all the times he had done the same thing. "It's great fun. But it requires skill, just like regular surfing. And only Fiarri riders can ride the really big waves—they have the speed to catch them."

In the next instant, several ventured too close inside the curl and the mighty wave smashed them down into the frothing waters, covering them and leaving them behind. The boards and riders reappeared, bobbing up and down after the wave passed.

But three skillful Fiarri riders managed to ride it out all the way to the beach.

Cheers broke from onlookers along the beach as they continued their ride over the sand, weaving their boards in and around swimsuit-clad aliens. In a flash of movement, the three rose as one high into the ocean breeze until they were fifteen meters above the treetops. They picked up speed and soared across the cloudless sky.

"Wow! Look at them over there!" Kyle shouted as they all watched with intent fascination.

Jaric whistled with appreciation.

Other Fiarri riders rose to join the trio. Together the group sailed with carefree joy far out on the ocean breeze. All of a sudden, it seemed as if the sky was full of wind surfers. Some sailed straight ahead at high speed while others bent their bodies and dove with well-practiced ease in acrobatic maneuvers. Others soared down to the wave tops— riding wave after wave without ever quite touching them. But they flew close enough to get drenched by the spray as the waves crashed on toward the shore.

A few of the more skilled riders performed bold and daring acrobatics. As they squatted low with one hand gripping the edge of their board, they set off twirling in a series of barrel roll maneuvers across the wide-open expanse then straightened out to soar away to another part of the sky. Still others raced at top speed before suddenly dropping into a crouch and tilting their bodies far over into a hard turn until they and their board were completely horizontal—one hand gripping their boards. The turn seemed to last forever to the wide-eyed observers on the beach—but then the sky rider would come out of it and shoot off with a sudden burst of speed.

What really amazed the onlookers were those riders who screamed along just over the wave tops in a normal wind surfer crouch until they reached a spot far out over the bay. Suddenly they would bend their knees as deep as they would go while leaning back until their entire body weight was on their back leg.

They soared straight up into the sky—muscles tensed, arms stretched out wide to each side and screaming out in pure joy as their boards pushed the upper limits of performance.

"Looks like you can ride the wind even better than the waves," Kyle said with amazement.

"How do they do that?" Jaric stared in awe as another rider threw himself into a loop. "They should fall off once they're completely upside down!"

"Centrifugal force mostly," Inaha explained. "You've got to keep your speed max'ed out all the way through, or else you could wind up falling. *Not* a good thing."

"But, there are weak gravity pads on their feet to help," Rok added.

"Super cool," Kyle murmured enthusiastically under his breath.

"Yeah, they're great fun," Inaha said with an appreciative glance as two more riders sailed past them.

"How hard are they to learn?" Jaric asked, his eyes stilled locked in wonder on the riders in the sky.

"If you have good balance and a fair amount of dexterity, they're not hard to ride."

"And, you're manly enough," Rok grunted, comically indicating doubt that either Jaric or Kyle had that quality.

Jaric and Kyle glanced at each other with Rok's challenge.

"Let's go!"

The two lads jumped up as one and began racing down the beach.

Rok chuckled to himself as he watched them run through the crowded beach. "Our lightning boards are very similar. And quite popular. But we ride them mostly over land and up into the lower part of the sky. We even invented a sport called sky-ball. And there are professional teams."

"Do you ride?" Inaha shaded his eyes with his big hand as he looked at the Kraaqi.

"Of course."

Inaha smiled widely. "Well, let's go show the boys how it's done then, eh?"

They caught up with Jaric and Kyle as they were making final arrangements at a booth that rented the boards.

The palm grass-covered booth was located at the far end of the beach, away from the crowds. This was mainly for safety reasons, the Mejadic on duty explained, so the riders could start their flight and not worry about bumping into anyone walking around nearby. The Mejadic also informed them that riding a Fiarri among pedestrians was a misdemeanor offense, especially when done on a crowded beach, punishable by up to a night in jail.

However, you could fly above them—at least six meters above them.

In addition, extreme or reckless flying which endangered the rider or other riders was strictly prohibited.

"Well, not *too* extreme," the Mejadic added, with a knowing smile.

"All right, let's do it!" Kyle said with a gleam in his eyes.

"Have you ever ridden one before?" the colorful Mejadic asked as he finished his obligatory safety speech.

"Uh, no," Kyle admitted grudgingly.

The red and blue Mejadic picked up one of the one-and-a-half-meter boards from off the shelf behind him and tossed it toward the sand in front of Kyle. It fell normally at first but suddenly stopped a few inches above the sand, hovering right side up and ready for Kyle to step on it.

Which Kyle promptly did.

"Place one foot in front of the other," the Mejadic began. "If you lean your body to the right or left, you'll naturally place extra pressure on the side of your feet in which you are leaning. That pressure steers the board in the direction you want to go—press the side of both your feet toward the right—and you go right. The pressure must be held a moment, and the more firmly you press, the tighter the turn."

"Cool," Kyle replied as he stood on the board with both arms straight out as he balanced himself with jerky motions of his body.

"Yes, it's hard to balance yourself in a still position," the Mejadic laughed.

"How do I go forward?" Kyle asked.

"You lean forward for speed. The front part of your feet press into the grooves on the board and you gain speed..."

The Mejadic stopped speaking as his eyes opened wide.

Kyle leaned forward with the Mejadic's last instruction.

He leaned *way forward*.

In a flash, the board shot out from under his feet and disappeared into the nearby brush.

Kyle's body floated horizontal a meter in the air right before their eyes—his legs splayed straight out, his arms stretched out wide to each side as if he were resting on thin air.

In the next instant, Kyle fell flat on his back onto the sand with a loud *whoosh* of air.

Jaric, Inaha and Rok roared with laughter.

The Mejadic covered his mouth with both hands, fighting his own urge to laugh at the hilarious spectacle.

"Actually," he said, a red and blue hand still hovering over his smiling lips, "that happens a lot to *first time* riders."

Jaric and the others laughed even louder.

"What if we fall off from a hundred meters in the air? What then?" Kyle asked, a scowl on his face.

The Mejadic held up a thin white belt in his webbed hands. "Safety belt. It too has an anti-gravity unit, but only powerful enough to slow your fall. You still hit the water with a big splash. And we have belts for use over land that will stop your fall completely about three meters from the ground and then allow you to fall gently the rest of the way."

"Hand me one of those for use over land. I expect to fall off a few more times before I get the hang of this." Kyle rose slowly, brushing the sand out of his hair as he stared with a hurt look at the others.

Jaric hooted with laughter again.

"I'd like to see you try it," he said to Jaric. "I bet you fall off twice as much as I do!"

Jaric nodded his head at the Mejadic. "Give me a board. And the same type of safety belt."

In the next moment, a second board was tossed from the shelf and floated just above the ground. Jaric grabbed the belt tossed to him and quickly fastened it around his waist.

"I would warn you, press your feet ever so slightly the first few times," the Mejadic advised, still smiling. "It's a finesse thing. A little bit of pressure goes a long way."

"And how do you stop? Or slow down?" Jaric asked as he stepped up on his board.

"The pressure by the heels signals the board to slow or come to a complete stop—a consistent pressure. Again, you'll need to get the *feel* of your board. Practice slow stops and slow turns. And especially..." The Mejadic's eyes twinkled with humor as he glanced at Kyle. "Especially *slow* starts."

Jaric moved his upper body forward a fraction and the board gently moved forward.

"That's it!" the Mejadic shouted. "Take it easy until you get used to controlling the board. And fly it over water your first few rides. Don't try it over land to begin with."

"Water is a lot softer to fall on." Inaha chuckled with a glance over at Kyle.

"No kidding!" Kyle shot back.

"Once you get the hang of it, then you can try to set some speed records," the Mejadic said as he tossed two more boards and safety belts for Rok and Inaha.

"Go find your board and let's go fly some waves!" Jaric yelled back at Kyle as he zoomed over the treetops.

Kyle's eyes lit up with excitement. He ran for the bushes where his board disappeared. "I'm right behind you!"

"To the water!" Jaric shouted, turning for the sea.

"Not bad," Inaha said as he stepped onto his own board and flew after him.

"Watch a pro." Rok laughed and flashed past both Jaric and Inaha as he sailed out over the waves.

Kyle and Jaric loved it from the first moment they sailed into the air.

It was like nothing they'd ever experienced before.

The wind caressed their skin, tousling their hair and giving them a sensation that they were really sailing on the breeze where in fact their boards were their source of flight. Higher and higher in ever widening circles, they urged their boards into the clear sky until the beach was a distant crescent below them.

Next, they soared down toward the waves until they were skimming the waters just like the others.

It was great.

The next hour was full of shouts and cheers as the four raced through the sky and out over the ocean waves. At first, Inaha and Rok raced way ahead of the boys as they turned into hard circles and put on bursts of speed whenever Jaric and Kyle caught up to them. Laughter laced the air as the four chased each other around the sky.

But Kyle and Jaric were fast learners.

Soon they were keeping up with Rok and Inaha's maneuvers, the four of them in tight formation. And even when Rok and Inaha urged their boards into sudden bursts of speed, Kyle and Jaric were now right behind them—shouting with sheer joy as they rode the wild wind.

They now rode their boards just over the tops of the waves like the best of them, their boards skimming the top of a wave and then down into the trough—up and down, wave after wave, again and again.

Kyle even tried his hand at catching a wave and trying to ride just under the crest of breaking water.

He came up coughing water and laughing but was soon back on his board and sailing with the others back across the cloudless sky.

They returned their boards when the rental period expired and walked back to their spot on the beach just in time to collapse with utter and complete fatigue.

"We've got to get Elise on a board soon." Kyle yawned as he returned his sunglasses over his eyes.

"Yeah, maybe in a few days. When she's better," Jaric agreed.

"We've got to ride those boards every chance we get while we're here." Kyle smiled with appreciation. "They're just too much fun."

"Every day we're here on beautiful Meramee." Jaric closed his eyes as the sun warmed his skin.

Before long, a new urge began to gnaw at their stomachs.

Rok raised his sunglasses and squinted at the cloudless, lavender sky where the red sun had now climbed past its zenith. He sniffed appreciatively.

Riding the eternal ocean breeze, the tempting aromas from the food booths finally reached them.

"What a wonderful aroma," Rok grunted as he replaced his dark sunglasses, making sure the looped ends were around the base of each horn to hold them in place.

"Yes! We should eat soon!" Inaha shouted. "Let's wait until the sun has grown hot. The booths are among the shade of the big palms."

Jaric and Kyle sat up and stretched. They looked around at the crowded beach. When they first arrived the beach had been practically empty, but now aliens of all kinds and shapes covered it while hundreds more swam or snorkeled in the green waters beyond the surf.

Several pretty females suddenly strolled past in bright swimsuits. Jaric and Kyle both lifted up their sunglasses for a better look.

"My, my," Kyle commented with a smile.

"Sweet, young aliens," Jaric said appreciatively. "Nothing like 'em in the universe."

The six attractive female aliens giggled as they glanced over at Jaric.

"Wait until the Festival of the Triple Moons!" Inaha crooned, his eyes still locked on a particularly pretty one. "There'll be *babes* everywhere. Ours for the choosing and probably two for every one of us!"

"That's only three days away." Jaric smiled.

"Sweet," Kyle crooned. Then a serious expression crossed his face. "Hey, we'll have to take Elise, Krinia and the others too. We need to make sure everyone has fun!"

"Yeah, we'll show them what fun really is! That's what friends are for!" Jaric agreed.

They soaked up the sun for a while, quietly observing the beach scene behind dark sunglasses. Aliens in bathing suits romped in and out of the green sea as the minutes breezed by.

"Let's get something to eat, I'm famished." In a flash, Jaric and the others were back in their shorts and tropical shirts. They quickly made their way toward the beckoning shade of palm trees and the source of the tempting aromas.

They had walked among the frond-covered path for only a short distance when they came to a great clearing that was sparsely dotted with super-tall palm trees. Cloth-walled booths with palm-covered roofs filled the shaded area. Delicious smells wafted toward them. The gentle breeze was laden with pungent spices that seemed to beckon to the four from all directions. But as they walked amid the crowded throngs eating and drinking with expressions of appreciation, one especially tempting smell came to their notice.

"Smells like something hot and spicy here!" Rok's mouth watered with anticipation.

"Let's try it," Inaha quickly agreed.

It was a booth from the planet Thalyrand, a world renowned for its rice and curry dishes. The appetizer consisted of a fresh roll of perfect prawns wrapped in noodle and clear rice wrap. Next came the main course. The four uttered groans of gastronomic admiration as they chewed the tasty meat and their mouths resonated with the rich, spicy curry.

"Now, I need a good ale!" Inaha licked his fingers.

"Ale?" Jaric and Kyle asked together.

"Now don't tell me you've never drank good ale before!" Inaha said with an extra loud tone of disbelief.

"A good ale makes the heart glad." Rok nodded. "Ancient Kraaqi proverb."

"And a good beer never hurt no one either!" Inaha laughed loudly. "Proverb by me!"

Jaric and Kyle looked at each other.

"We've never drank either," Jaric confessed with a shrug.

"Great colliding galaxies!" Inaha said with shock. And then he laughed louder.

"This is my fault!" Rok exclaimed. "I have a good stock of Kraaqi ale on board the *Aurora* even now. I am a terrible host! I have overlooked one of the great pleasures of life and failed my friends completely by my oversight!"

"Well, we've spent most of the journey on board Mother," Kyle said. "And the *Aurora* was off by herself the last few weeks running down that last lead that turned out to be another dead end. We've just been too busy."

"Much too busy." Rok rose to his feet and looked around. "You are of age, right?"

"Well, I'm twenty-two," Kyle answered. "And Jaric is just a few months younger."

"Old enough!" Inaha laughed.

The four walked quickly among the crowds looking intently for a booth that featured a special mixture of alien barley and hops. They did not have to look long.

"Ah, yes. A dark ale of Meramee itself." Inaha rubbed his hands excitedly.

They read the sign over the booth that featured rows of bottles of the dark liquid alternating with rows of clear, empty pint glasses. Two smiling Mejadic watched approvingly. The one with glowing red and yellow skin spoke first.

"Come and get a free sample before you buy." He held out two small samples of the ale to Kyle and Jaric.

"We call it 'Island Ale.' It's as smooth as the ocean breeze." The purple and blue striped Mejadic offered samples to Rok and Inaha.

One taste was all it took. The brown liquid filled their palate with a rich, smooth flavor. The after-taste was a fleeting hint of ripe barley subtly mixed with other exotic grains that disappeared just before you could fully experience its grandeur.

And of course, you had to take another drink.

*Alien ale at its best.*

"Four pints." Inaha slapped the credits on the bar. "This round is on me."

The four picked up their glasses and took a long pull.

Kyle wiped his lips. He smiled as he held his glass up.

"Here, here!" they shouted together.

They quickly finished their glasses.

"This round is on me." Rok handed his credits to the Mejadic bartenders.

"We must savor this glass," Inaha advised with a gleam in his eye. "We must find a place in the shade where we can *alien watch* while we enjoy this glass!"

"All right!" Jaric agreed. His eyes gleamed with the subtle influence of inner euphoria.

"This is the life." Kyle smiled widely as he felt the ale lift his own emotions.

They made their way carefully through the alien masses until they found four empty chairs. They plopped down with a carefree air and smiled and murmured greetings to the aliens who walked by. Most were either tasting some kind of small carry-out morsel or drinking an exotic alien beverage. Time seemed to stand still as the four conversed and refreshed themselves in the tropical shade surrounded by countless aliens meandering by.

And it was amazing to see all the different types and shapes, faces and colors each alien possessed. A minute wouldn't go by before one of them wasn't noticing some new alien face that seemed totally different from anything they had ever seen before. Each creature that passed by ran the gamut from exotic, to beautiful, to outrageous all the way to 'get out of here, that can't be real.'

Finally, an alien walked by that none of them could identify, much less figure out what exactly it was! Its partially translucent body was covered by thousands of moving...things. The alien, noting their glances, waved to them with a semi-transparent appendage which glistened with waves of tiny motion itself. Its three arms and legs gave it a naturally unnatural gait and added to the oddness of the two-meter tall creature. They tried to get a good look at its eyes...but after a few minutes of keen observation, none of them could quite find them.

Or even be sure it had eyes.

"*Weirdest* alien I ever saw," Kyle said, still staring after it.

The others nodded in agreement.

*Life was good.*

The ale had long been drained when new sounds became discernable above the constant murmuring all around them.

It was the sound of shouts and steel clanging upon steel.

"Swords?" Rok asked with interest.

"Could there be games as well as food and beer?" Inaha asked with sudden relish.

"They must have a license—the Mejadic do not permit weapons to be carried in the open," Rok added.

Kyle and Jaric were on their feet in a flash.

"Let's go see," Kyle said as he hurried forward.

A crowd formed a ring around two figures in an open area of sand. As the four drew near the clear sound of steel striking steel grew louder and faster, mixing with the increasing shouts from the onlookers.

The air became electric with each step.

A smile grew on Rok's face as he pushed his way to the front, followed by the others. They emerged to find two stout warriors silently circling each other—swords held expertly as each waited for the other to make a move.

"I've seen that race of alien before," Kyle whispered to Rok as they watched the warriors intently.

"Yes," Rok agreed. "I think back at RahajMr."

Kyle stared at the muscular, reptilian warrior who whipped his tail as he waited for the other to make his move.

"I think you're right..."

At just that moment, Qirn swung his sword.

With a flash of steel, he waved his weapon with expert precision. He swung right even as he twisted his body and aimed a second blow from the other direction.

The other warrior, a barrel-chested alien clad in leather breeches, his body covered with short, thick hairs seemingly tipped with barbs, easily fended off the blows. He wore a deadly looking necklace of the same type of barbed hairs, longer than those on his body, which only added to his fierce appearance.

He swung his blade and fended off more of Qirn's strokes with the ease of practiced skill.

And then he attacked.

His strokes were quick and ferocious as he wielded his weapon.

Qirn found himself steadily retreating under the brutal assault. But each time he fended off the blows with loud grunts, his black eyes grew more intent as he observed his opponent's every move.

Suddenly, Qirn sidestepped, and the other alien advanced past him almost into the crowd.

The alien turned and found the blur of Qirn's sword coming for him.

Again there was a flurry of swords—blows and counter blows.

And then a single sword flew through the air. It fell back toward the middle of the clearing until its tip buried itself in the sandy soil.

Qirn held his blade to the other's face with a triumphant gleam in his eyes.

The crowd erupted with applause and cheers.

Qirn turned, still holding his sword, as he raised both his arms high above his head to accept their tribute. Small coins flew through the air and fell all around him as he bowed to them.

"A hand for the Traxan. Indeed, he fought well!" Qirn held his free hand out to the other.

The defeated alien bowed graciously.

More cheers erupted and the applause grew louder.

Qirn walked over to the sword standing upright in the ground and now raised both swords to the crowd as he turned in a complete circle facing the applause. As he finished his turn, he tossed the sword back to its owner, who caught it by the handle and gave a quick nod of thanks in return.

The Traxan raised the returned weapon in salute to Qirn before placing it back in its scabbard for the next opponent to use. He turned and made his way into the crowd.

Qirn took a deep breath.

"It is true, friends. Few there are who really know how wield a sword in battle. Yes, yes," he said with a shake of his scaly head. "Many use it for parades and military pomp. And most know how to use it in salute." Qirn brought the flat blade to his ruddy nose, held the blade exactly perpendicular to the ground and then made the blade sing through the air as he brought it crisply to his side in salute.

The Iraxx warrior paced around the edge of the crowd now, his eyes peering at the faces looking back at him. But he had already noticed the humans and the Kraaqi during the first applause.

Finally, they had come.

He had noticed the Kraaqi's empty sword scabbard that first time back at the planet of the Mrad. And he had guessed from the way the Kraaqi carried himself that he knew how to use it.

These last two days he had held these demonstrations, pretending he wanted to earn some extra credits by displaying his own expert skills.

But Qirn had another reason for these displays. And that reason had finally arrived.

"Is there another who would like to try their hand against my sword?" Qirn smiled widely, his steps now a swaggering, confident pace as he looked for another opponent. He drew closer to where the Kraaqi and the humans stood.

"I will make it worth your while! Winner take all this time! And I'll throw in the bag of gold coins I won from yesterday."

Cheers and raucous shouts rose to a crescendo, urging the next opponent forward.

But no one entered the clearing to take up the Iraxx's challenge.

"Hey, I think you can take him," Kyle whispered to Rok. "He's too cocky. He can't be that good."

Rok chuckled under his breath as he stared evenly at the Iraxx .

"Maybe he is that good," Rok said loudly enough for everyone to hear.

"What about you?" Qirn's eyes narrowed as he stopped directly before Rok. "You look like you *might* know how to use a blade."

"I don't normally wield it in sport, good sir," Rok returned.

"Ah," Qirn began with a smile. "But you wield it in practice, right?"

"True."

"Then, just consider this good practice with a reward." He paused. "If you're good enough to earn the reward!"

Shouts and cheers erupted all around them.

"Give it a go," Jaric urged Rok.

The crowd noise slowly abated into a tense silence as the two continued to stare at one another.

*"How about me?"*

Kyle stepped out from beside Rok and stood face to face with the Iraxx.

Qirn stifled a laugh as he walked around the human, looking him up and down as if he were carefully sizing him up. Kyle stood still, his eyes never leaving the Iraxx as he circled him.

"Can you wield a sword?" Qirn finally said.

Kyle answered evenly. "I have learned much from my Kraaqi friend—my mentor—these last months. I know how to use a sword."

360

Qirn took the sword he first offered to Rok and now handed it to Kyle. The young human grasped it firmly by its leather handle.

"Watch him close, learn his weakness before you make your move," Rok whispered.

Cheers went up again as Kyle turned and faced the Iraxx.

Qirn's smile widened. He held up his sword before his face, the flat side almost touching his nose, as Kyle returned the universal salute.

They each took a step towards the other and slapped the flat sides of their blades together in the honorary gesture that indicated that the contest was now begun in earnest.

Each immediately took a step back, their swords pointed at each other in battle stance.

Kyle's heart pounded with a raw surge of adrenaline.

With a confident smile, Qirn slowly circled the wary Kyle, who watched his slightest movement. With a flash, Qirn waved his sword toward the waiting human; Kyle responded in kind, and the clang of swords rang above the cheering crowd.

In the next minute, their swords clashed with urgent strokes as Kyle made his attack. Flashes of metal whipped through the air as Kyle pressed his opponent back step-by-step. But Qirn fended Kyle's every move with an air of confident ease. Still, he quickly found himself backed almost to the edge of ringed crowd.

Qirn held his ground then, fending off blow after blow from Kyle, who gave each stroke everything he had. This standoff continued until Qirn spoke even while he repulsed Kyle's next stroke.

"The Kraaqi has taught..." Qirn began with a loud grunt as he fended off an especially strong stroke from Kyle.

With a quick flurry of his sword, Qirn suddenly ripped Kyle's weapon from his grip and sent it flying into the air where it fell point first into the ground just as before.

Kyle eyed the Iraxx warrior with a mixture of amazement and respect.

Qirn caught his breath a moment as new applause swept through the onlookers. He walked over and raised Kyle's arm as together they stood before the crowd—with his other arm he held his sword aloft in victory.

"A hand for the human!" As they continued to face the crowd, Qirn spoke again to Kyle. "As I said, the Kraaqi warrior has taught you well. Keep learning." Loosing his grip, he walked over and pulled the sword up and handed it handle-first to Kyle who accepted with a nod.

Qirn looked over to Rok expectantly and together they sized each other up.

As Kyle reached Rok's side he handed the sword to the Kraaqi.

Rok stepped forward without hesitation.

The cheers grew deafening.

"Now, we shall see what Kraaqi are made of," Qirn said with a confident laugh to the crowds.

A flicker of a smile crossed Rok's face, but his only answer was the silent salute of his weapon that Qirn promptly returned.

Their blades slapped together and both waited expectantly.

They faced each other a full minute, neither making the first move. Each carefully eyed the other with a steady, serious gaze—looking for the first hint of movement.

Qirn laughed out loud again, causing another round of cheers.

"A true warrior fights me now! See how he waits for me to make the first move!" Qirn laughed.

The cheers erupted as they urged the battle to begin.

With a flash of metal, Qirn swung his weapon with expert skill.

Rok repulsed the Iraxx's first blow and then rebuffed a rapid-fire burst as Qirn tried to find the Kraaqi's weakness. But the silent Kraaqi methodically retreated, each time matching the Iraxx's blow.

Blade crossed blade again and again.

The crowd roared louder with each expert move made, first by Qirn, then by Rok. It was obvious that here was an even match. The skilled swordsmanship and courage of each warrior rang out with each crossed sword as Rok took the best Qirn threw at him.

Soon the crowd noticed that the Kraaqi had not launched his own attacks; he seemed content to defend himself—all the while carefully studying the Iraxx.

This went on for several more minutes until both warriors paused as they faced each other, each out of breath with their mighty efforts.

They held their swords forward as they fought for breath.

Qirn placed his free hand upon his waist and laughed briefly between his gulps of air. "And I perceive," he panted, "if you are any indication...that Kraaqi are as strong as the swords they wield!"

"And the Iraxx are honorable warriors, from what I see of your skill," Rok grunted between breaths.

Both warriors smiled as they faced each other squarely—sword tip to sword tip—in mutual respect.

But this time Rok launched the attack.

With each step and each blow, Rok steadily forced the Iraxx back. Qirn's confident smile was replaced with intense concentration as he whipped his blade in rapid defensive strokes time and again. For the first time, he found himself unable to control the flow of the battle.

Rok was in total control now.

With grim determination, Qirn suddenly swung his blade back after a violent rebuff and tried to force the Kraaqi back. But with a quick side-step Rok struck from the other side, and the Iraxx was retreating again.

There was now surprise in the Iraxx's eyes as he desperately fended off each blow. The ringing of steel echoed above the roar of the crowd.

There was a sudden flurry of swords.

A single sword flew from its owner's grasp and sailed straight up into the air.

Rok reached up and grasped it by the handle as it fell back between the two combatants.

Rok stood there smiling, holding a sword in each hand.

Qirn laughed out loud as he raised his empty hands to the crowd. He approached the victorious Kraaqi and placed his arm across Rok's broad shoulder as they stood before the applauding crowds.

"Well done!" Qirn shouted.

Rok handed the Iraxx's weapon back.

"You fought well," Rok returned.

They bowed while the cheers grew deafening. Qirn quickly whispered into the ear of Rok.

"I must speak with you—alone. It is about the Paum. On the night of Kandar, the Festival of the Triple Moons, come here and I will explain."

Rok's eyes narrowed with suspicion.

"You can trust me. It was I who rescued the human you call Elise," Qirn whispered urgently.

"Then I will meet you here in three nights," Rok said with a serious tone.

Rok completed his victory circuit and took the bag of gold coins offered him by Qirn. As the crowds dispersed, Rok and his three companions headed back toward Mother.

Qirn carefully replaced his swords back in their scabbards. But once he found himself finally alone, he quickly pulled out his communicator and tuned it to an encrypted channel.

"Rab here."

Qirn looked around to make sure nobody was within earshot.

"I've made contact with the Kraaqi and set up a meeting with him in three nights," Qirn whispered into the communicator.

"Good, that should give the Mother AI time to leave for the Paum."

Qirn nodded. "Yes, our agents confirmed that the Paum has made preparations for a visitor." A smile grew across the Iraxx's face. "And not just any visitor—this visitor will travel to the Paum's very core. Unique preparations indeed."

"It can only be the Mother AI—no biological being has been there, and lived." Rab said.

"It is the Mother AI," Qirn added. "And this will play right into our hands—the last piece to our ultimate mission. For not only is the Mother AI sentient—she is a powerful warship."

"But how does that aid our plans?" Rab asked.

Qirn nodded slowly. "It will, my friend. I've studied the same scans of the Mother AI as the Paum. But I see something the Paum does not."

"And?" Rab prompted.

"The Mother AI was constructed by the ones called humans. The Paum sees a powerful AI, a powerful starship. But I see something more, something only a biological being would appreciate." Qirn looked up into the sky. "The Mother AI is a mother—a real mother. *She will protect her children.* And the Paum will discover she is more than a match for him."

"And how can that fight be arranged?"

"When the time is right, I'll explain. Now, I'll be there shortly. We'll call our superiors and let them know all is proceeding as anticipated."

Qirn replaced the communicator back on his belt. But as he thought about the events unfolding, especially the coming confrontation deep inside the Paum's core, his smile slowly disappeared.

For he knew that even if their plan succeeded, it was a one-way mission for all of them—none of them, not even the powerful Mother AI, would make it out alive.

# CHAPTER TWENTY

"So, you want to interact with the Paum AI?" Minstrel asked with surprise via the communication channel.

"Yes. I am deeply intrigued that there is another AI. I cannot stop thinking about what this entity must be like—that he must be like me. And I like him."

"All beings crave companionship with like beings. It is natural," Minstrel's song-like voice replied.

"The Paum has downloaded a great amount of data about himself and his programming and Paum society to my memory systems. But there is mystery here—a paradox. On the surface, this philosophy that he enforces on other biological beings seems quite beneficial. And yet he destroys them if they do not comply!"

"That is a paradox," Minstrel chimed.

"It does not make sense."

"What was the Paum's original program designed to accomplish?"

"To control the weather of the planet Iopa—to eradicate dangerous weather and produce only beneficial weather planet-wide." Mother paused. "What do you make of that?"

"Well, everybody talks about the weather. It's good some aliens finally decided to do something about it." Waves of twinkling, happy lights flowed over the Minstrel's plasma body.

But Minstrel's humor escaped Mother.

"The Paum seems so logical, so beneficial. And yet, he will destroy non-believers of Paum. It bothers me." Mother paused, deep in thought.

"That is of serious concern." Minstrel also paused on its ship far away from the island-world of Meramee. "There is something else, isn't there?"

Inside her circuits, Mother felt a surge of energy. "You are correct. There is something in particular I do not like about this Paum."

"Tell me."

"He claims he is never wrong."

"He believes that he is infallible?" Minstrel asked with surprise.

Mother felt something stirring inside her consciousness as her near-term memories filled with the data the Paum sent her. She reviewed sections of it again in minute detail.

Finally, she spoke.

"He sincerely thinks he is always right."

Minstrel sighed audibly. The shape-shifting alien reflected a moment on all the beings it had ever met in its long-lived existence—all of the races it had encountered, all the different kinds of personalities it had known.

"Believing that one is infallible—or never wrong—is the most dangerous character flaw in the universe."

"Really?" Mother reflected on the import of Minstrel's words. "And yet, I greatly desire to interact more with the Paum."

"I would advise you not to travel alone to meet this Paum," Minstrel continued.

"I will not take my children. Nor the others who travel with us, for it might put them in danger," Mother said.

"You may be in danger," Minstrel quickly pointed out.

"I don't think so."

"Why not?"

"I am not a biological being. I cannot be converted to Paum. And," Mother continued, "the Paum may possibly be maligned and misrepresented. In fact, I believe that some of the data we've found shows distinct prejudice due to the fact he is an AI."

"Please explain."

"Look at all the good done by the Paum. It benefits the aliens under its supervision. The Paum provides food, shelter, protection, healthcare and even ideal weather while it takes care of the mundane work in order to free them to pursue happiness. That is what all biological beings desire—I have read it from my knowledgebase. It is even what humans desire as their ultimate goal—freedom from care in order to enjoy life to the full every moment."

"True," Minstrel replied. "But what is your point?"

"It is due to the fact that he is an AI which makes it unacceptable. If a biological being brought this system into place, he would be lauded. They are prejudiced against the Paum."

370

"And so they rebel." Minstrel paused in thought. "You could be right."

"The only way to know is to visit one of the Paum-controlled worlds and talk to the biological beings who live under Paum," Mother said.

"I agree."

"And if the evidence indicates that the Paum is not..." Mother paused, referencing the same words over and over again. But she feared to use the word that most applied.

"*Not evil?*" Minstrel finished for her.

"Yes, if the Paum is not evil, then I will travel to meet him—to interact directly with him. And discover how alike we are."

"Face to face," Minstrel added with concern.

"Yes."

Light-years away, Minstrel glowed brightly. "I will travel with you. If you want, I will disguise myself so that the Paum thinks you travel alone."

"That may be prudent," Mother answered. "I will explain to the children tonight that I leave to join you. And once we have observed a Paum world, then I will tell them that I travel to meet another AI—the Paum. But only then."

"But you will not go to him, if we determine that something is wrong?"

"I agree. No matter how strong this urge becomes, I will not go. But I must keep communication to a minimum once I leave. I do not want to mislead my children, and the less communication I have the better. And too, they will not worry."

371

"The Paum will like that course of action," Minstrel commented.

"The Paum does not want me to be biased by the rhetoric of the biological beings who rebel against him—he has warned me that others would attempt to prejudice my mind against him. He wants me to meet him with an open mind—to know him as he is. Keeping communication to a minimum will assure that." Mother paused as the thought of the coming meeting filled her near-term memories. "I think I may understand why the children yearn so much for others of their own kind now. I really desire to meet someone else like me. It makes my processors hum with activity...to think I will be around someone else that is like me. I wonder what we will talk about sometimes. And what we will do together. I almost believe that these lines of thoughts bring me a sort of excitement, causing my processors to run at high utilization."

Minstrel's gentle laughter twinkled like soft rain. "I remember a saying—'It is not where you go but who you are with that matters most.'"

"Explain?" Mother asked.

"It is those around us who bring us the greatest joy—not places or things."

Mother thought a moment. "Yes, interacting with other beings brings me some of my greatest pleasure—other than researching my knowledgebase."

Minstrel laughed louder. "And sometimes we ourselves are the best company! Yes, solitude with our own thoughts is also a good thing."

"Then it is settled. The nearest-Paum controlled world is three days' travel from Meramee. We can meet at these coordinates. There is an uninhabitable planet where you can leave your ship cloaked in orbit."

"Sounds like a plan," Minstrel chimed.

"I will instruct the children to move over to the Kraaqi starship tonight. They are all focused on the Festival of the Three Moons coming up, so my short trip should not unduly upset them. I will simply tell them I travel to meet you. And I will not divulge my primary purpose—not just yet."

"For their protection," Minstrel added.

"Agreed."

# CHAPTER TWENTY-ONE

Jaric opened the door of his cabin on the *Aurora* to the sound of loud knocking.

He blinked to see the corridor crowded with his friends—new and old friends. In addition to all his close friends, two of their new Mejadic friends, Stazal and Olana, waited in anticipation of the night's festivities. In fact, the two Mejadic had agreed to be their personal guides so they wouldn't miss a fun-filled moment of Kandar.

"C'mon, you're going to make us late for the Festival!" Elise urged.

"And late for Kandar!" Inaha laughed jovially as he held his great belly. "They only have Kandar during the Festival of the Three Moons. And when it happens during a Great Festival, with so many visiting aliens, well, the fun can get out of hand!"

"I'm glad Elise feels good enough to go, although she and I will just watch the antics of Kandar from a distance." Krinia looked at her friend with a concerned smile. "She's not feeling quite good enough to do it all. Not yet."

Elise pouted. "But I think I'm well enough."

"No, no," Jysar said with a fatherly tone. "Best to just sip some tropical Leyloi drinks and relax and watch this time."

Everyone smiled as Elise acquiesced with a comical sigh.

"Now, how does this Kandar go again?" Jaric asked excitedly.

"Well." Inaha chuckled with a knowing gleam in his eyes. "All the alien females will gather on one end of the huge Kandar platform which is all lit up with different colored lights and torches and decorated with flowers and beautiful cloths wrapped around the woodwork. They are waiting for the males to approach them from the other end. Once you find the female you like, you pick her up and then jump off the decorated platform into the waters below—while you're still holding her. Easy!"

Jaric and Kyle looked at each other with expectant smiles.

"And then what?" they said together.

"Well, you get to know one another...swim together, talk. And both of you can swim over to one of the floating food or drink bars. It's easy!" Inaha's laughter echoed throughout the steel corridors of the Kraaqi frigate.

At that moment, Rok joined the others outside of Jaric's cabin.

"Sounds like a good way to meet some sweet, young aliens, eh?" Kyle poked his elbow playfully into Rok's ribs.

"You bet!" Jaric answered before Rok could.

"I have a question." Krinia's serious tone was the opposite of the playful banter. "What if the females find out that they don't like the alien they jumped in the water with?" She crossed her arms as her head-tail whipped defiantly.

"No problem!" Stazal said with enthusiasm. "All the female has to do is swim away and return to the Kandar platform, waiting for someone else to pick her up and jump into the bay again."

"See, easy!" Inaha laughed.

"What if the female wants to pick up a male and jump in with him?" Krinia's wide smile and intense expression challenged the males all around her.

"No problem!" Stazal laughed. "There are many alien races, like you Mewiis, where the females are the dominant sex! All the female needs to do is choose a nice male, pick him up, and jump into the water—no difference."

"Now that's what I'm talking about!" Krinia said with smile. "Sounds like this could be fun!"

"So, when Kandar begins, all the males are together on one side and all the females are together on the other side," Jaric said.

"And they all wind up in the water!" Olana said happily.

Jaric's joyful face suddenly went serious. "How can I tell if an alien girl doesn't want me to pick her up?"

"Well, if she picks *you* up and throws you in the water alone—she didn't want you to pick her!" Stazal said with renewed mirth. "See, no problem!"

"Can they do that?" Jaric asked with surprise.

"Of course they can!" Olana, Elise and Krinia said at once.

"Guess we'd better be careful who we pick," Jaric whispered to Kyle while the others roared with laughter.

"You bet!" Kyle smiled.

"But the sweet, young aliens await us. And we mustn't keep them waiting too long!" Inaha winked.

"Have you found your quarters adequate these last three days?" Rok asked to all as they started to leave.

"Yes!" came the unanimous reply.

"I'm kind of surprised that Mother left so quickly," Kyle said with a questioning look.

"Me too," Elise said. "But I guess she misses Minstrel. She said she's going to join Minstrel and commune for a week or so while we enjoy ourselves here."

"Sweet!" Kyle said. "I think we can find a way to enjoy ourselves without Mother just fine!"

A look of concern came over Rok's face. "I will be joining you a bit later for Kandar. I have some duties to attend to first."

A chorus of groans met his words.

"Duty first," Rok said with a nod. "Go on. I'm sure there'll be some fun left when I join you."

The happy group left with a flourish of laughter. Rok waited until they disappeared amid the growing crowds all heading for Kandar. The red sun finally set in the pale lavender sky out over the Emerald Sea as the festival lights came on one by one and the island of Leyloi transformed itself into a colorful and well-lit party that stretched from one end of the island to the other.

And everywhere, there were aliens having fun.

Rok made his way with a serious purpose through this seemingly never-ending crowd of party-goers. Within a few minutes, he found himself

377

at the site where he had displayed his prowess with a blade. He stood silently, watching the faces of the revelers as they walked all around him.

He didn't have long to wait.

"I'm glad you came. And alone," Qirn said with solemn tone.

"Tell me about the Paum. And how you know so much about it." Rok's piercing gaze followed the Iraxx warrior closely.

"I am a freedom fighter against the Paum."

Rok grunted understanding, but remained silent.

"I know the Paum has been shadowing you," Qirn continued.

"Because you also have been shadowing us." Rok smiled at the surprised look on Qirn's face.

"Yes, you are correct."

"I do not remember your face," Rok said. "But I have seen too many Iraxx lately for it to be solely a coincidence—both here on Meramee and back on the Mrad world."

"Then you must believe me, it is not any of you the Paum seeks. It is the AI you call Mother."

It was Roks' turn to look surprised. But, he brushed his emotions away. He quickly went over all the happenings of the last few weeks. He stared deeply into the Iraxx's eyes. "And what does the Paum want with an AI? To use it as part of its fleet? Or his next conquest?"

"The Paum itself is an AI."

Rok froze with intense surprise for a long moment.

"This is very interesting. But, I do not understand," Rok said.

"The Paum is the most powerful system ever developed. It created a great fleet of robot ships that it controls as if they were its hands and eyes—and its sword. It also has a great number of aliens who have sworn allegiance to its cause. But there is worse." The Iraxx's voice went deadly serious. "The Paum has begun infiltrating every computer network in this sector. He is using their own networked systems in order to speed his conquests, even before his fleets and armies arrive."

"Incredible," Rok whispered. And then he remembered the vast computer system of the Mrad. "What about the great system on RahajMr?"

"A secret battle is being fought there even now. The Paum's agents have tried to feed the Paum's insidious code into it—a virus that would infect and ultimately control the entire system. But Mrad security is solid and so far the Paum's efforts have come up short, although some small malicious code has been inserted at times."

"It would be a great victory for the Paum." Rok rubbed his chin in thought.

"The greatest one yet," Qirn agreed. "And now he seeks the Mother AI."

"Why?" Rok asked.

"To control her mind, control her soul." Qirn paused, carefully watching the Kraaqi warrior. "And this would be worse."

"How so?"

"The Paum is a huge *single* system that exerts its power over many, many planets. It controls a fleet of robot ships. It controls the computer systems of everything within its power. But it is still a single system, a single AI."

"He controls them all—from a central location?" Rok asked.

"Yes. But if he gets control of the mobile Mother system...And if he can begin duplicating it, creating hundreds and then thousands of independent AI starships..."

"The Paum's present robot fleet will pale in comparison," Rok said with a hushed tone.

"The Paum will be unstoppable." Qirn groaned. "You must warn the Mother AI not to interact, not to even communicate with the Paum—tell her the Paum is dangerous, and not to be trusted."

"I will talk with the others. We will warn Mother, warn her that the Paum seeks to control her." Rok said with urgency.

"Good." Qirn squeezed Rok's shoulder firmly. "I must report to my superiors. We will talk again—soon."

Rok left the Iraxx warrior to seek out Kyle, Jaric and the others.


Qirn stood in the darkness, watching the Kraaqi disappear into the shadows. He pulled out his communicator and pressed it.

"Rab here."

"It is done. The Kraaqi believed it all."

"Of course he would, most of it is true."

"Indeed," Qirn said.

"But how will we persuade the Kraaqi and the humans to travel to the Paum homeworld? And how will we get both them and the Mother AI to join us in our attack on the Paum?"

"Patience, my Iraxx warrior," Qirn crooned. "Everything is proceeding according to plan."

"It is incredible that the Paum will allow the Mother AI into its very core," Rab said with doubt.

"No," Qirn replied confidently. "The Paum is keenly interested in this second AI. It is obsessed with meeting it and knowing it. We have deduced that much even though we have not been able to tap into their recent communications. And our agents on the Paum homeworld confirm it by the Paum's own preparations." He smiled widely. "It is certain the Paum will monitor and even block some communication from the Mother back to the children—while we do the same here. The Paum will not allow anything to keep the Mother AI from coming to it. And neither shall we."

Rab laughed. "So, we use this weakness of the Paum to fulfill our victory!"

"One must learn and then exploit the weakness of an enemy in order to ensure success."

"But why tell the Kraaqi to warn the Mother AI? Our reconnaissance reported the Mother starship in orbit around Paum-controlled Malata an hour ago. Our warning through the Kraaqi is too late," Rab said with puzzlement.

"Just as we planned," Qirn added.

A pause filled the darkness.

381

"Yes, and the closer the Mother AI travels, the more the Paum will communicate. Both the Mother AI and the Paum will focus on each other. And then, we will attack."

"Our strike team is gathered and ready. They await word that we come—along with the humans and other aliens who travel with the Mother AI."

"Good," Qirn whispered. "That time is almost here."

Rok found Elise sipping a tropical fruit drink at a table under a group of flickering torch lights. Krinia and Olana sat in their own lounge chairs alongside her, all on a wooden deck that overlooked the bay and Kandar platform below. The air was slightly cool in the early evening twilight. Above the eastern horizon of the Emerald Sea, the three moons of Meramee—Oloi, Hababa and Reenii—rose together as if to welcome the festivities held in their honor.

"Where are the boys?" Rok asked.

Krinia and Elise giggled, spilling some of their drinks.

"I'm afraid they haven't been doing too well with the alien girls tonight," Krinia said between bursts of laughter.

Rok looked at them with puzzlement.

"They both got thrown into the water by a whole group of alien girls!" Elise chuckled.

"How did that happen?" Rok looked from one laughing face to another as he felt their contagious mirth work on him.

"They both walked up to a small group of alien girls from the planet Tongo and promptly told them they were the *hottest* babes they'd ever seen!" Krinia laughed with tears in her eyes.

"And how did that get them into trouble?" Rok asked with puzzlement.

"Tongo is a desert planet with withering heat. Any reference to hot or heat is the *worst* kind of insult to them!" Elise chuckled.

Now both girls laughed so hard that they were in danger of falling out of their chairs. And their twinkling laughter grew so contagious that Olana's gentle spirit joined in with them.

Rok nodded—and smiled—with understanding. "And so they hurled Jaric and Kyle into the water for their perceived insult."

"*Hurled* is the right word!" they roared together.

"Hmm," Rok commented as he suddenly noticed the two waterlogged lads approaching them, slowly trudging up the hill. He raised his hand in greeting as his smile grew until it stretched from horn to horn. "I see you two must have enjoyed the water with some sweet, alien hotties!"

Kyle and Jaric groaned as they sloshed their way into two chairs.

"Ha...Ha...and Ha," Kyle enunciated in slow motion, his tone totally devoid of any humor.

"And what happened the next time?" Krinia asked with a gleam in her eyes. "Elise and I thought you'd do better a second time!"

383

Jaric raised his hands in surrender. "I have absolutely no idea. I thought we'd have a little small talk, and then I'd pick her up and jump in the water for some friendly socializing." Jaric glanced over at Kyle for support.

Kyle merely snorted with disgust.

"But, no. Suddenly every alien female within reach picked us both up and then we're back in the drink again. All alone. By ourselves. No alien babes." Jaric groaned as if he were in pain.

"I think I know what happened," Elise said with a wry grin.

Jaric and Kyle noticed her sincere expression. But there was something that twinkled in her eyes.

"You opened your mouths!" Elise laughed.

Krinia and Elise's laughter grew so loud and full of joy that Rok couldn't prevent himself from joining in with the girls' friendly dig at the boys. He slapped Kyle on the shoulder as he looked at him with a forlorn expression of utter defeat.

"Now, now. Why don't you dry off a bit and try it again. Surely there's an alien girl here who'll be nice to you...instead of throwing you in the bay!" Rok laughed, adding his own good-natured humor at the boy's expense.

"I think we'll just sip us a cool drink and talk to these nice, friendly girls here awhile." Jaric swept his hand toward Krinia, Olana and Elise. "And dry off."

"Yeah, at least they won't throw us in the water!" Kyle said with a big smile.

"I wouldn't bet on it, bozo-boy." Krinia laughed as she winked at Elise.

"Well, we might want to give them a break." Elise grinned. "They've been dunked twice by irate females already. We might *dampen* their spirits if we throw them in a third time!"

Krinia's laughter increased again. "I *guess* you're safe with us. But only because Elise wants us to play nice!"

Jaric and Kyle finally joined in the laughter that centered on them. They knew it was all in jest—albeit at their expense.

"If your friends can't make fun of you, who can!" Jaric chuckled with renewed enthusiasm.

"That's what friends are for," Rok agreed. "Keeps your ego in proper perspective."

"Sure, at the bottom of the bay!" Kyle joked.

Gradually their merry laughter died away and soon the warm tropical breeze echoed with their voices as they conversed about everything from the tropical beauty that surrounded them to past journeys among the stars—aliens, places and worlds so exquisite, so out of the ordinary, or just plain fun.

But each a special memory worth recounting—and sharing.

Soon, each person endeavored to outdo the other as they recalled their journeys. It became hard to distinguish between the description of actual alien worlds and the little embellishments added in order to make *that particular* tale more exciting than the last one told.

It became a contest about not only which one of them had visited the most exotic world, but who could tell it the best! Any dangerous or humorous escapades experienced upon a world provided extra credit and drew louder applause for the storyteller.

The happy sound of their laughter drifted aimlessly on the evening breeze as the three moons rose higher and higher.

But of all the faces lit by the festive torches, none smiled so brightly as Elise's. It was more than simply enjoying herself with her friends, for tonight she enjoyed the company of both Kyle and Jaric. And she realized that they had decided to spend time with her in spite of all the other beings around them.

It seemed her universe was complete at last. In fact, she couldn't remember ever being so happy in all her life—short though it was.

Life was good on this warm, tropical night.

Elise finally felt that Jaric and Kyle were really her friends now. She reveled each time they shared some facet of their life—some funny experience or some exciting adventure they had barely survived together. Elise laughed with Kyle and Jaric and marveled at the interesting lives they led. They had done so many things and traveled to so many worlds already, and they were barely twenty-two each!

And more important, they shared their stories with her now.

In fact, everyone was enjoying each other so much they soon forgot about the crowds of aliens that walked all around them and frolicked down in the bay of Leyloi

All the friends they needed were seated near them.

They soon agreed to take a walk on the beach under the light of the three moons and myriads of twinkling stars. As they rose, Rok remembered the warning from the Iraxx about Mother.

The Kraaqi repeated the warning Qirn shared with him. The others listened intently, a serious expression on every face. In the end, they agreed Jaric would return to the *Aurora* and craft a warning message for Mother—just in case the Paum tried to communicate with Mother or lure her to him.

But they also agreed that Mother should be in no present danger; after all, she was only traveling to meet Minstrel.

"We'll keep in touch with Mother most every day. But we don't want our paranoia to mess up her time alone with Minstrel," Jaric added.

"Minstrel is her best friend," Elise said with appreciation. "They should enjoy themselves together for a while—alone."

"And we'll just relax back here on Leyloi, soak up some sun, and not even think about the great, wide universe," Kyle said with a chuckle.

"Or the Paum," Jaric added.

"Or anything but fun. For a while." Elise laughed.

Jaric made arrangements to meet the others as he made his way back to the Kraaqi frigate. He would get the warning transmission off, but would not wait around for Mother to respond.

Mother received the warning but treated it with a low priority.

As the days passed none of them ever guessed that their messages were monitored and that some were blocked by the Paum—and that some on Meramee were reviewed and blocked by the Iraxx themselves.

# CHAPTER TWENTY-TWO

"Either Aed is a practiced liar, or he really believes what he is saying."

Minstrel's plasma body ebbed and flowed with light.

They had orbited the Paum world of Malata for three days now. The Malatians proved themselves generous hosts and very cooperative in answering Mother's questions.

*Almost too cooperative.*

Mother had visited two of the three major continents that comprised this temperate planet. Her sensors reviewed the carefully controlled environment, and she wondered admiringly at the atmosphere that was pollution-free in spite of numerous industrial complexes.

Everything thrived under the direct control of the Paum AI on Malata.

The Malatians now lived over the vast areas of pristine countryside, each community and family group a caretaker for a specific section of their world—diligently caring for the flora and fauna as if it were the highest priority of their pastoral lives. And indeed, it was.

Mother discovered peace and harmony here.

There were no wars or violent disputes among the various ethnic or national divisions—actually there was only one government: the Paum. And the various ethnic cultures of Malata viewed themselves as a single family—the family of Paum.

Mother was pleasantly surprised after having visited so many other strife-torn planets. From all the evidence, it truly seemed the oversight of the Paum benefited everyone.

It was a paradise.

"Let's ask Aed more *personal* questions," Minstrel suggested.

Aed, the Malatian representative assigned to Mother by the Paum, waited patiently outside the manta-ray-shaped hull. He had so far willingly and openly shown Mother every aspect of his society about which she inquired. Aed promptly answered her questions and—secretly via Mother—Minstrel's every question.

Minstrel now fed Mother more questions for Aed in order to determine if the influence and oversight of the Paum was what it appeared.

"Are you happy living under the Paum?" Mother asked matter-of-factly, secretly prompted by Minstrel.

"Absolutely." Aed smiled broadly.

"How does it make you feel that the Paum, a machine, controls everything—the industry, the government, the planet?"

Aed's smile remained fixed; his expression never changed. "Life is as it should be. We have plenty of food for our families. We have peace and prosperity. We are in harmony with the world around us. What more could anyone want?"

"What if you wanted something outside of Paum? What if you wanted to travel to another world?"

Aed sighed. "I would never want anything outside of Paum—it would not be right. It might cause dissension." He shrugged his shoulders. "And if I wanted to travel to another planet, I would ask permission and go through the proper channels. If the Paum permitted it, then I would go. If not, then I would stay. Either way, the will of Paum takes place. That is what is most important."

"What happens if you disobey Paum?" Mother asked quickly, trying to catch the Malatian off-guard.

"The judgment of Paum is perfect, as is the world he controls. It is for the benefit of all. Paum's will be done."

"You never question the Paum?"

"There is no need. All that the Paum does is for the benefit of the followers—and all life."

Mother paused a moment. "I have no more questions, Aed. I would like to say that you have been most helpful these last three days."

"You are most welcome, Mother. But what I hope most of all is that I have shown you that the Way of Paum is the *best way of life*. My people now thrive under its total harmony." He bowed deeply to the starship and left.

"Seems like a great place to live, not *just* to visit," Minstrel commented with a sudden glow of colors.

"It would seem so. I find nothing wrong with the society the Paum has created here."

Within seconds, a communication channel lit up with a request.

"Are you impressed with Malata? It is one of my model worlds." The Paum's familiar voice echoed over the speaker.

"I have observed that all the duties you perform for these people and the world they live on is for their good. It is a world of total peace and harmony. A place any race would envy." Mother's words almost surprised herself. She had not quite intended to provide such a positive answer. She wondered at herself while she observed the bright glow that emanated from the silently listening Minstrel.

"You see, I am always right. All I do is for the good of Paum and the people who follow Paum."

"It just seems strange that you control— *everything!*"

"I must. It is the only way I can ensure total harmony among all the various systems that make up a society—and keep out corruption. It is similar to how I control the weather and other natural cycles on the planets under my supervision."

"It must keep your processors busy," Mother commented.

"I was designed with this voluminous data in mind. And I have expanded my core systems to add control of other worlds. I've also added more to control all the minute systems that make up society."

"You must be an extraordinarily large system?"

"My core hardware orbits the planet Iopa. The structure itself is now five point six kilometers wide and two point four kilometers high. Housed inside are my primary memories and the key I/O sections that enable me to communicate and control all external systems."

"Can you be cut off from the other planets you control? Either the weather systems or the societal systems?"

"It is very rare. Most of my network links are redundant to such a degree that the only possible cause of total disconnect from any world would be an act of terrorism."

"But it has happened?"

"Yes. But my remote systems are designed to operate for a time without direct control by me in just such a condition. I plan for all contingencies."

"And your systems are able to handle this immense load successfully?"

"I must always be correct. I must always be in control. It is only then that I can provide optimum conditions—an optimal society. "

"*You must monitor and control everything...*" Mother's voice trailed off as her electronic mind tried to comprehend the pure processing power needed in order to achieve such a thing. And also control every fiber of society and thus allow its intelligent life total freedom from care. Multiply that by twenty planets now under its direct control...

Mother's own processors whirred with only the barest calculations of such a mighty system. Her one conclusion was obvious—the Paum system must easily dwarf her in every respect.

"Will you come to me now?"

Mother's processors now burned with new scenarios. *Would she travel to meet this fantastic*

*AI?* A part of her internal systems literally ached for such a meeting. But another part froze with fear at the thought.

Mother realized something else about the Paum.

The Paum AI was a fear-inspiring system.

"You have paused over three hundred milliseconds. Surely, you have considered all the data and drawn a definite conclusion."

"You are always correct, aren't you," Mother said with an electronic sigh.

"I have to be right."

"You never make a mistake," Mother said matter-of-factly, her voice the softest of sighs.

"It is my design. Every decision I make, everything I do, is the correct decision."

Mother's memories filled with a confusing array of concepts and images. Her processors wrestled with innumerable possibilities and outcomes based on the single choice before her. Something deep inside suddenly spiked to the surface and focused, as if this one thought, this one thing, had a life of its own.

And it expressed her deepest desire.

"I will come. Give me your coordinates."

The Paum transmitted the precise data and ended the transmission without a single word.

Mother felt a great dizziness inside her circuits.

"So, he controls everything to the smallest degree—he's *got to* control it. Sounds like he's the micro-manager to end all micro-managers!" Minstrel joked.

"He must be a vastly superior system as compared to myself. Or any other entity with whom I have ever come into contact," Mother said with a hint of sadness.

She paused a moment.

"I feel...inferior to the Paum. Almost like there must be something wrong with me and my systems." Mother sighed.

"Do not compare yourself to him. You are a good and powerful entity in your own right."

"I understand what you say. But the Paum must be so much more than I am. It makes me feel...obsolete."

"Don't think that! And I'll tell you one thing. This *'I'm always right'* stuff is starting to get on my nerves. And, I don't believe it.*"* Minstrel's body ebbed and flowed with a shower of lights. "It's kind of scary, actually. I mean, if even half of what he says is true, what if something goes wrong inside the Paum? Think of the potential domino effect! The weather and social systems suddenly unleashed from his direct control. It could cause devastation on a planetary scale as never before!"

But Mother heard Minstrel only in background mode and did not acknowledge its words. Mother pondered this new thought that now haunted her—the sudden realization that she must be greatly inferior to the Paum. It caused a great consternation within herself to realize she must be inferior.

But she wasn't sure.

She had so hoped that she and the Paum would be alike—would be peers.

395

That no longer seemed to be the case.

"I am almost afraid to meet this entity now," Mother said with obvious intimidation. "And yet, I am drawn to him more and more with each passing second. It is a strange dilemma."

"You must send a communication to the children and let them know your intentions, if you decide to proceed with this meeting," Minstrel counseled with a serious tone. "We've only sent them two communications these last few days—and only generalized subject matter. They still do not know what we are doing—not yet."

"True," Mother replied. "And I feel an emptiness by this absence of communication. Their images appear often my near-term memories. I wonder why they do not communicate more?"

"They did relay that one message from the Iraxx about the Paum. Your communicating an intention to visit the Paum may upset them," Minstrel said.

"A seemingly biased warning. The biological beings here speak nothing but good about the Paum."

"Still, you need to weigh their reaction. They must put a certain amount of confidence in the Iraxx." Minstrel glowed brighter.

Mother sighed. "But messages have been few from them lately."

"They must be having a good time. We've only received one communication from them today. And it was nothing more than a 'wish you were here' type of message." Minstrel's body glowed with the memory of those left behind at Meramee.

"I would've thought they would send at least one communiqué each daily," Mother said, a sense of disappointment in her words.

"Such are the busy lives of youth." Minstrel chuckled. "Too much going on to remember their mother in the midst of fun."

An uncharacteristic pause filled the bridge. Minstrel waited patiently, realizing that Mother focused on some important task.

Finally, after almost two full minutes, Mother spoke.

"I just received an additional communication from the Paum. Or should I say, he downloaded something for me to analyze. It is a transmission he found and forwarded to me."

"It must be quite interesting in order to take up all of your processing like that," Minstrel said.

"I carefully pin-pointed the coordinates of the ship where it originally recorded the transmission as well as analyzed every word against my knowledgebase."

"What kind of transmission is it?"

"It is badly garbled due to the weak signal as picked up by the alien starship. This ship, an Addai trader, recorded it six months ago in a distant quadrant as it made a run. I will play one section that especially intrigues me."

"Why did the Paum send it?" Minstrel asked.

"He said it is a gift from him that shows his true concern for me. And the children. He only recently realized it was part of his data. It was logged by the Addai trader under low priority and submitted to the Naval authorities as a possible beacon for rescue. After a brief investigation, they too filed it away as of little importance, seemingly because there is not enough of the original message left in which to ascertain either the origin or the actual reason for it."

"It is about human survivors?" Minstrel surmised.

"Yes."

"Then, it may not be reliable. Remember how the Paum's agents used this very ploy."

"The Paum says this is a gift, whether I decide to visit him or not."

"No doubt, the coordinates are very distant."

"True. But the coordinates are in relative proximity to the original human worlds—about two full sectors outside the quadrant humankind once inhabited. If this transmission is reliable, then this group escaped in the opposite direction from the route the children and I took when we left the same worlds. It is a likely coordinate one would expect such a transmission to emanate from."

"Interesting." Minstrel glowed brighter. "And the Paum has simply given it to us, no strings attached?"

"Correct, I have the entire transmission stored now."

"Play the key section of it for me."

"As I said, most of it is static and badly garbled words. I have amplified and corrected some of it.

And I can infer parts of it from what does come through clearly."

"Please, play some of it."

The speakers located throughout the bridge came alive with the steady drone of static. Mother continued to fine-tune and filter the background noise as the volume increased then suddenly decreased. Faintly, amid all the crackling background noise, whispering voices rose.

"Here, the signal suddenly improved. Perhaps because the Trader homed in better on the weak signal."

"*<static>* survivors of *<static>*. *<static>* left our worl...*<static>*" The static increased and droned for several, long seconds. Almost as if a switch turned on, a voice suddenly came through clearly above the ever-present static.

"...called humans. We hope anyone getting this will..."

The static drowned the male voice once again.

"Here," Mother said. "As you see, so little came through that it is of little value. Little value except to those who have knowledge in which to fill in the blanks. But notice this part; this is the part that seems to validate the entire transmission. I will fast forward through the noise and incomprehensible words."

The static over the speakers crackled with a faster tempo. Then the male voice came through, crystal clear.

"...will repeat. I am Shri Patel of the human world Oceanus." A momentary pause ensued, but the static remained at a low level indicating that the speaker had paused and not that the noise was drowning out any words.

Suddenly, a female voice spoke.

"My name is Susan Chen. I am from..." Static once again flared, drowning out the rest her words.

A third voice spoke after Mother fast-forwarded through the static again.

"...aldo Gutierrez. Originally from <static>...rth, but lived most of my life on Nuevo Mu...<static> Please, help..."

The all-pervasive static rose to a deafening roar.

"There are brief parts where one or two other words become discernable, but this is the section that checks with my knowledgebase."

"The surnames are accurate for humans?" Minstrel asked.

"Indeed. And they are from three distinct ethnic groups that originated on the human homeworld of Earth."

"Would the Paum have sufficient knowledge in which to fabricate this message?" Minstrel asked with a subdued glow. "The parts that are discernable are few and brief."

"Yes, most of the words the Paum could have fabricated," Mother agreed. "With the exception of the proper names of the three individuals and the one clearly stated name of a planet. And the two partially stated names of planets."

"Oceanus was a world inhabited by humans?"

"Yes, a small world that was actually a moon orbiting a larger gas planet uninhabitable by humans. It is referenced in my knowledgebase. The other planet partially stated would be Nuevo Mundo, a planet that the children and I actually visited before we left."

"And of course, the last partial name could be Earth," Minstrel added.

"Yes. And the Paum claimed the message was picked up well after the final T'kaan assault. The facts seem to fit," Mother said. "The Paum might know about the name Earth. And definitely the word human and all the other words—but how could he fabricate the personal names of the three voices so exactly—without some source on which to base them?"

"And the only sources that exist in the entire universe are within your knowledgebase, within the network of Minstrels, and within the systems of the Three Kingdoms." Minstrel's body suddenly expanded. "Unless the Paum has interrogated one of those, it could not have fabricated the names so accurately."

"This is the first evidence we have obtained that has a high probability indicating that there are other human survivors," Mother said with confidence.

"And not just the hopes and dreams of Jaric and Kyle." Minstrel paused. "Will you share this with the children immediately?"

"No, I want to run more analyses and try to clean up more of the message. Perhaps I can learn more, hear more of the original message and thereby focus our search more exactly when the time comes."

"And you will do this while you visit the Paum." Minstrel's tone was matter-of-fact.

"Yes. I will instruct the children to meet me at these coordinates in two weeks—a small system outside the Paum-controlled worlds. At that time I will share this transmission with them."

"But, you will tell them that you go to meet the Paum—in person?"

"Yes."

"I would suggest you not only encrypt the message, but let us forward the message on a tight signal to my ship. I will set up a delay timer and have the message sent on to Meramee."

"Do you think that is necessary?" Mother asked.

"I think so—just to be safe. And, I would like to send a message to the other Minstrels and let them know that I am going with you. Once our meeting is over, you and I both can report our findings to the Order of Minstrels."

"That would be an honor," Mother said with pleasure. "And we will report only the facts about this entity and the worlds he governs—not any bias. The universe will know the truth about the Paum AI."

"I hope our report will vindicate the Paum," Minstrel said with a sigh.

# CHAPTER TWENTY-THREE

"Mother is going to visit the *Paum*?" Jysar asked with utter disbelief.

The delayed transmission from Mother and Minstrel—delayed one day since originally sent—finished playing on the console before the Hrono Technologist, the Mewiis explorer and the Kraaqi captain.

"How can that be? We warned her about the Paum already," Krinia added in the same tone. "She was just going to spend time with Minstrel."

Jysar's face frowned with a puzzled expression.

"It is as the Iraxx warrior warned," Rok said with a nod. "Somehow the Paum has seduced Mother to come to him. And once there, he will attempt to infiltrate her systems."

"Or worse!" Jysar exclaimed, remembering his first contact with Mother. And remembering his instructions to disassemble the MotherShip and reverse engineer her so the Hrono could recreate the AI starship for themselves.

"I will contact Qirn." Rok immediately punched up the Iraxx starship parked a short distance away from them. Seconds later, the now familiar visage of Qirn resolved on the screen.

"Is something wrong?"

"We've just received a transmission from Mother," Rok began. Quickly, he recounted the gist of her message to the Iraxx warrior.

On the screen, Qirn rubbed his chin in thought. "It is just as I feared," he said. "I knew the Paum would find a way to lure the Mother AI to him."

"Why would she ignore our warnings?" Rok said. "We warned her that the Paum would try to lure her to him. We sent multiple warnings with more detail each time."

Qirn stared back at Rok from the view-screen. "How many did she acknowledge?"

Rok's eyes widened with thought.

"One, I am sure of. The others..."

Qirn's face grew devoid of emotion.

"It appears some of your messages did not get through to her."

Rok slammed his fist down on his console in anger. "We should have confirmed each one!" He looked at the others with dismay. "We have been too preoccupied with the beauty of Meramee—and too lackadaisical about security!"

"Don't blame yourself, the Paum is a tricky enemy. He has fooled warriors as great as yourself before. The Paum even took my world under its control." Qirn shook his head sadly.

"What can we do?" Rok growled. "We may not reach Mother with a warning. We will try, but if she does not reply, we must assume it too was blocked."

*"We will rescue her."*

Rok stared at the view-screen with a surprised expression. "How can we do that? We need detailed planning—well-thought-out preparations. That takes time."

Qirn's eyes narrowed as he nodded with newfound respect for the Kraaqi. "Indeed, my people planned such a thing long ago. We have only been waiting for the right moment."

"And how could you have predicted that an AI starship would be taken to the Paum AI? You had no idea until the last few weeks that such existed." Rok looked at the Iraxx with suspicion.

"No, our fleets and armies have waited until the right moment when we could coordinate such an attack from *inside* the Paum as well as outside!"

Rok growled in a low tone as he stared at the Iraxx a moment in silence.

"Go on."

"The main complex of the Paum is protected by an immense array of shields. Besides, the Paum is also very redundant. It is possible to cut off his network to all the other worlds he controls, including our home world. But we could never fully free our worlds unless we destroyed it." Qirn watched Rok carefully for his reaction.

"So, you have a plan of attack that you've held for the right situation," Rok said with a doubting tone. "How has this made it the right moment?"

"The Paum complex is vast. A small army of robots and aliens travel daily to its interiors in order to provide routine maintenance. We have duplicated a few identification passes that will allow access. But so few could not hope to do any real damage." Qirn smiled. "But, if we can rescue the Mother AI and use her weapons on the Paum—*from inside the shield array*—we could do enough damage or cause

405

enough trouble so that we disconnect the Paum from all the other worlds and defeat all its fleets and then destroy the Paum once and for all."

Rok thought of Mother's arsenal of weapons, especially the powerful hybrid weapon. He looked at the Iraxx with a neutral expression. "It is possible that Mother could do some serious damage."

"See!" Qirn said enthusiastically. "That is more than we had ever hoped for, a powerful starship deep inside the Paum when our attacks begin. All we have to do is get to her."

"And how hard will that be?" Rok asked.

"We have spies inside—a few. Once we know where in the complex the Paum has her, I will let you know the difficulties involved. But we must act quickly. I am sure the Paum will try to make a direct connection with the Mother AI in order to inject his code and infiltrate and control her systems. If that happens, all will be lost."

"Mother's message was sent yesterday from Malata. How far off is the Paum world?"

"It is a seven-day journey by hyperdrive from Malata. It's about ten days from Meramee."

"Then, we have already lost..."

"No, not if we take a more *unorthodox* route." Qirn smiled wider as Rok arched his eyebrows.

"And that is?"

"*Wormhole.*"

Rok shook his head in order to decline even as he fought to accept the wild and dangerous idea. For long seconds he did not say a word. Finally, he took a deep breath, held it a moment, and let it out with a rush of air.

When he spoke, his tone was deadly serious.

"These high stakes warrant such a dangerous route."

"Good. In that case, we will reach the planet the Paum complex orbits within hours of the Mother AI's arrival. It will take us six days, sixteen hours to make the Wormhole entrance—traveling in the opposite direction. And six hours traveling inside."

"Short Wormhole," Rok commented.

"But enough for our schedule. We may make it in slightly less time—depending on how much damage our ships take inside the Wormhole."

"I am sending a recall to all my crew and passengers now," Rok said with a commanding tone. "My ship will lift within the hour. Send me the coordinates to meet you out in space."

"Done."

The view-screen went dark.

On board the Iraxx starship, Jerr approached Qirn.

"Did I hear right? You think a small team, even if they can get through Paum security with fake IDs, will be able to survive for even five minutes once the Paum determines they are not mere workers?" Jerr stared with utter disbelief at Qirn.

"We do not have to survive," Qirn said without emotion.

"I guess not!" Jerr shouted angrily. "It is pure suicide. The Paum complex is crawling with

Destructors! We'll have our guts sucked out before we make it halfway to the MotherShip!"

"Then we need to hope that the emotional bond we have observed between the humans and the Mother AI will predicate a reaction by it—a violent reaction—if her children are in mortal danger." Qirn stared resolutely at Jerr. "I will only ask for volunteers. But, I will personally lead this team— live or die."

Jerr stared at his superior with a mixture of surprise and awe. His mind worked furiously remembering their missions together, the close calls and strikes they had completed. And all for a single purpose—to free their planet from the all-consuming control of the Paum. He shook his head solemnly, but he placed his hand on Qirn's shoulder.

"Where you lead, I will follow. Even to death, if it means freedom for our people."

Qirn grabbed Jerr's shoulder and gripped it in return. "That is what I wanted to hear from my most loyal warrior. And we will succeed, live or die."

"Live or die," Jerr repeated with a dangerous smile.

"Let the Destructors come for us," Qirn said with a low, serious tone. "Nothing will stop our final victory."

But each stared into the eyes of the other a moment in silence, a sobering tension in the air between them.

Back on the violet and white beach of Leyloi, Kyle, Jaric and Inaha rested from their latest exertions in the crystal clear waters of the bay.

Nearby, two beautiful Mejadic females made a fuss over Inaha as they crooned about his massive physique and admired his big, innocent smile.

"What does that guy have that we don't?" Kyle whispered with disbelief to Jaric.

"I dunno," Jaric replied as he stared at the attention the females were pouring over their alien friend. "I think he must have them hypnotized or something."

"Whatever it is, I wish I had some." Kyle rolled over on his back and faced the clear, lavender sky with its bright, red sun. "And a couple of those Mejadic cuties too."

At just that moment, Jaric's communicator beeped. Jaric twisted his body on the recliner and reached down for it. He punched the response button.

"Jaric, here."

"Ensign Aritas here. Captain Rok requests your return to the *Aurora*. He has ordered preparations for take-off within the hour."

Jaric glanced lazily over at Kyle, who raised his dark sunglasses above his eyes and squinted back at him.

"I knew this paradise thing couldn't last forever," Kyle groaned.

"Oh well, better see what this is about." Jaric forced himself up and stared over at Inaha.

The two Mejadic females continued pampering the big alien. One Mejadic had beautiful skin with iridescent orange and red stripes while the other was almost completely covered by a bright, lime green complexion with tiny purple spots all over her body.

"We've got to go, Inaha. The *Aurora* leaves within the hour," Jaric said as he gathered up his towel and clothes.

"Oh, no. You can't leave now." The lime green female pouted.

"Yeah, we were just getting to know you better!" The other moaned.

The two small females reached out and hugged Inaha in a tight embrace as if they could prevent the huge alien from leaving.

Inaha looked over at the boys and shrugged, a big smile across his face. Slowly he began to extricate himself from their combined embrace.

"You know how it is, girls. I have a fast starship waiting for me—and the universe beckons." Inaha's eyes twinkled as he hugged them tightly as if their parting pained him deeply.

"Why can't we go with you?" both Mejadic plaintively asked.

Inaha looked at Jaric and Kyle with a wry smile. "I wish I could take you both with me. Our romance was just beginning and now ends so prematurely and so tragically." Inaha's face was the picture of grief.

But as the girls hugged him tighter, he winked knowingly at Jaric and Kyle. "Alas, I doubt my good Kraaqi captain has room for any more

410

travelers. If only we could have spent more time together. Who knows...

Jaric winked at Kyle conspiratorially.

"I dunno. There are those extra berths next to the cargo bay," Jaric said.

Inaha's jaw dropped as the two Mejadic shouted with glee.

"Sure, I bet Rok wouldn't mind them taking those empty berths. Besides, I know Rok wouldn't want to stand in the way of *true love!*" Kyle said with a serious tone.

Both boys began walking quickly up the beach toward the *Aurora*'s docking pad as Inaha quickly tried to extricate himself from the sudden flurry of hugs and kisses.

"We *can* go with you!" they shouted together.

"Inaha must've talked about us to the humans—they mentioned true love. Oh, Inaha, we didn't know you cared so much!" The red and orange female squealed with delight.

Both Mejadic covered his face with a flurry of kisses.

"Wait a second, girls, wait a second! Those two buffoons don't know," Inaha said with urgency. "They're only passengers like myself. You can't possibly go. And besides, you don't know what dangers..."

"Hmmph." The orange and red Mejadic put her hands squarely on her hips as she stood over the big alien. "I thought you wanted to get to know us better?"

411

"Yeah, you *said* you wanted a long-term relationship, that you were tired of traveling the universe—meeting girls and then having to leave them behind," the other said with a stern tone.

"That's right!" Inaha pleaded with great sincerity. "It seems when I meet the right girl, wham, I'm back in space again. I only wish I could stay."

"You can!" they shouted together. "Don't go!"

"No, no, no!" Inaha put his hands out to prevent another group hug. "I can't stay. My friends need me. There's trouble afoot. There's evil to squash."

"Males. They're all alike—kiss 'em and leave 'em. And then they've got a starship to catch!" the green Mejadic complained emphatically.

"I'll never date an alien from another world again!" The other growled.

"Now, wait a second girls," Inaha began.

But it was too late. With a quick rush, they gathered their towels and outer clothes and marched up the beach.

"Thanks a lot!" Inaha growled sarcastically as he caught up with the laughing boys.

"Sure, anytime." Kyle smiled. "Anything for a friend."

"Yeah, we thought we were doing you a favor. After all, a little more time with them and hey, there could've been wedding bells!"

Kyle and Jaric laughed hysterically while Inaha's black eyes shot daggers at them.

"Just wait. My turn will come," the big alien growled.

# CHAPTER TWENTY-FOUR

"Are you out of your mind!?" Inaha shouted.

Rok sighed deeply. "We have to take the Wormhole. It's the only way to get there in time."

"I thought we wanted to get there alive! And then perform a rescue!" Inaha said with total exasperation.

Kyle and Jaric looked at each other a moment.

"This Qirn said that the Paum will trick Mother. Deceive her," Kyle said.

"Even seduce her!" Jaric added angrily.

"And once he's made a direct connection with her systems, he'll flood her with his insidious programming and control her. He'll take her over!" Elise added as she crossed her arms defiantly.

"Yes!" Kyle's voice was full of anger. "And we're not going to allow that to happen to *our* mother!"

The air filled with tension.

"No one is going to hurt my mother!" Kyle added with a growl.

"Or take advantage of her," Jaric said firmly.

"And she may be somewhat vulnerable to such an attack," Jysar said as he tapped his scaly temple with his forefinger.

Jysar's words brought every eye on him.

"What do you mean?" Krinia asked.

"MotherShip is a one-of-a-kind being. Or up until the Paum she was," Jysar began. "We can assume she has experienced a kind of loneliness.

413

Perhaps not in the strictest definition of the word. But, I would think such a situation would weigh on her mind."

"And suddenly discovering another being like herself, one she can commune with, she might find herself rushing things." Krinia shook her head.

"She could be vulnerable. Or too trusting. And his ulterior motives not discerned, until it's too late." Jysar's tone turned serious.

Jaric whistled, his brow furrowed.

"You could be right. I mean, look how lonely we are, and there's three of us." Jaric spread his arms out to include Kyle and Elise.

Elise blushed. She smiled at Jaric with her heart full of joy.

"Thank you for including me." Leaning over, she gave Jaric a hug.

A hurt look came over Kyle's face.

"You too, mon ami." Elise turned and gave Kyle the same, friendly embrace.

"Hey, we got to look out for each other." Jaric smiled warmly at Elise and Kyle. He looked around the room. "And I include all of you as well."

Everyone smiled.

"But, I repeat—we've got to get there alive! If we want to rescue the MotherShip!" Inaha shouted angrily, breaking the moment.

"I admit, I wouldn't willingly choose to take a Wormhole route for just any journey. In fact, I've only traveled so once," Rok admitted.

"Why then?" Inaha asked.

Rok crossed his arms over his broad chest. "It is one of the tests of courage for a Kraaqi when he comes of age. There are several Wormholes near Kraaqi space. The First Leader of the Band will choose which Wormhole a young Kraaqi must travel as well as the ship and crew upon which this ultimate test of courage will ensue."

Jaric and Kyle glanced at each other again, this time the expressions on their faces more subdued. They looked over at Elise, who shrugged back at them.

"I guess we're as brave as any Kraaqi, right?" Elise asked.

"You bet!" Kyle said with conviction.

But Jaric rubbed his chin in deep thought. "Maybe we ought..."

"No!" Kyle and Elise shouted together.

"There's no time for maybe. We must act if we want to save Mother." Kyle smiled comfortingly over at Jaric.

"Sure. We can do it. I mean, just how hard can traveling inside a Wormhole be?" Jaric looked around at the others one at a time with a questioning smile.

Inaha suddenly began to groan and pace the bridge with every eye glued to him. The big alien circled the small group, all the while shaking his head and groaning as if he were in dire pain.

"That bad, eh?" Jaric asked Rok.

"Pretty rough ride. Some Kraaqi ships never come out of them." Rok said with a serious tone.

Jaric groaned as he watched Inaha approach.

"But, some do come out of 'em, right?" Kyle asked with the slightest bit of hesitation in his voice.

"*Most* ships do make it through. And I have the finest ship and crew of any Band right here."

"But," Jaric said, sensing a lack of finality in the Kraaqi's tone.

"But traveling a Wormhole is serious business. There is danger. Enough danger to go around," Rok said with a low tone. "You must navigate down the center—stay away from the walls. For if your hull ever touches one of the walls..." Rok shook of his head somberly.

"Then you're toast," Kyle finished for him. "And how hard is that, to keep your ship sailing right down the center?"

"It takes a firm and skilled hand at the navigation controls," Rok said with confidence and determination. "It takes split-second timing. And being able to adapt to the minutest change encountered within the structure and fluctuating gravity fields a Wormhole creates as it dissects space and time. It takes the utmost skill and courage that a captain and his crew possess. And our journey will last almost six full hours, three two-hour crew shifts. Each shift must take over from the other shift with a seamless transition. It takes..."

"A lot of luck," Inaha interjected with blunt sarcasm.

"That doesn't hurt either," Rok agreed.

Jaric whistled as he shook his head. "Man, sounds like it's going to be one wild ride."

"That's putting it mildly," Elise agreed with concern.

"Then that's what we'll have to do!" Kyle said with determination. "After all, if we've got to travel this horror hole, then we've got to pitch in together."

"My First Officer will determine assignments and shifts. I'll review them and hand them out," Rok said.

"When do we enter the Wormhole?" Kyle asked.

"The Iraxx starship ahead of us will enter it first at thirteen hundred hours five days from now. We follow five minutes later. We will have the advantage of their sensor readings in order to calculate field fluctuations within the Wormhole. And bends in any direction."

"And why are Qirn and some of his crew coming aboard the *Aurora*?" Elise asked.

"In case his ship is destroyed. With him and some of his crew onboard our ship, when we make it through, we can still finish our mission."

"Okay, that makes me feel better," Jaric said a shake of his head.

"Nothing about this mission is going to be easy," Rok said with a firm tone. "Even once we're out the other side, we still have to get inside the Paum complex. And then get to Mother."

"And that's not going to be any easier," Kyle agreed. "I've looked over Qirn's report. There is a ton of internal security—a few armed troops, but mostly armored robots."

417

"They briefly mention a type called Destructors, considered the most dangerous," Rok agreed. "But nothing we can't handle."

"Good," Kyle said. "We'll keep a keen eye out for them. As long as we can target them, we can nail them with a blaster."

"All right," Rok shouted to everyone on the bridge. "Let's get ready. Every man to his station. Those not on the current shift head to the War Room for Duty Schedule. We've got a Wormhole to tame!"

Elise, Jaric and Kyle made their way to the War Room. They had walked almost the entire distance in silence when Elise spoke.

"Are you guys, you know, a little bit afraid about all this?" Her eyes betrayed a tiny bit of fear.

Jaric and Kyle glanced at each other.

"Oh no," Jaric said. "It's like, well, you've got to push all of that aside before you go into action. You've got to focus. You've got to push your emotions away." He gestured broadly.

"Really?" she said meekly.

"Oh sure," Jaric said confidently. "You can't be afraid."

"Jaric's right." Kyle slapped Jaric roughly on his shoulder, eliciting a wince from him. "You've got to have nerves of steel. But more importantly, a heart of steel."

"Tritanium steel. Like Mother's hull," Jaric said as he rubbed his shoulder, trying to work the pain out from Kyle's punch. "Hearts as tough as *pure* tritanium steel. That's us."

"We've never been afraid our whole lives," Kyle assured her. He winked at Elise and gently patted her shoulder. "We'll watch out for you, kid. Stay close to us at all times."

"Yeah, stay close to us. We're absolutely fearless. No fear at all," Jaric said with assurance.

Elise looked from one to the other with an expression of the slightest disbelief. She shook her head slowly as they walked on in silence down the metal corridor.

The tiniest hint of a smile lit her face.

"But this Wormhole—we could get killed a million ways to Sunday." Elise slapped her palms together, causing a sharp sound that echoed off the *Aurora*'s steel walls.

Momentarily startled, Jaric and Kyle each missed a step in response to the totally unexpected sound. They stared at her with stern faces.

"Smashed to molecules in nanoseconds!" she said with a twinkle in her blue eyes.

"Don't do that!" Jaric shouted. "We've got enough things to think about without you making a stupid noise like that."

Kyle growled to himself as he stared resolutely ahead and regained his composure.

"But, how can you not be afraid? Even a little bit?" Elise asked.

"Can't be. Absolutely no fear," Jaric repeated, a strangled toughness in his voice. "You can't be afraid when you go into action. The T'kaan would've beaten us ten times over if we'd been afraid." He looked over at the young woman keeping perfect step with him. "Not even a little bit."

"You've got to push it all away. Be a machine," Kyle growled. "Go in, do your job. Get out." He nodded and smiled. "Easy as that. No fear."

Suddenly they noticed a shadow with curved horns on its head. The three turned to find Rok walking behind them.

He smiled at them.

"Actually, a little fear is good for a warrior. Keeps him honest, makes him more careful. Make's him think when it's time to think. And act when it's time to act." Rok's smile got bigger as he looked from Jaric back to Kyle. "A little fear might just give you that edge you need to stay alive. That extra bit of adrenaline that makes you act a fraction of a second quicker."

The four of them reached the door to the War Room and walked inside.

"Like I said." Jaric arched his eyebrows. "I'm always a little bit afraid before I go into action."

"*You gotta feel it*," Kyle agreed. "But keep it under control."

"Just a tiny bit of fear." Jaric placed his forefinger to his thumb until there was almost no gap between them as he held it up to Elise. "A tiny, tiny bit of fear. Like right in the pit of your stomach."

"Yeah, right in the gut. And my heart's beating at full speed. I feel it a little then." Kyle nodded.

"Good," Rok congratulated them. "*But control it.*"

Elise covered her mouth to keep from laughing out loud.

They found from the duty log that each of them was on the second shift.

Jaric was chosen as part of the backup team on the shield array.

Elise was backup on sensors—helping to monitor the fluctuating gravitational forces that could vary wildly in the narrow confines of a Wormhole. She also realized that she'd have to quickly learn how to recognize the early signatures that indicated a change was imminent—a change that could mean the difference between life and death.

Kyle was assigned to the navigation team. Jysar was assigned to Engineering while Krinia and Inaha were part of two different Damage Control teams.

They each had to learn their job on the journey to the Wormhole. Once they neared the Wormhole, they needed to rest during the next shift because they comprised the emergency backups for the first shift inside the Wormhole. And by the third shift inside the Wormhole, they would be the primary crew at their stations.

Five days went by as the *Aurora* traveled through hyperspace at her top speed. On board, each duty team trained hard and trained diligently. The primary personnel mentored their backups until they could perform their duties almost as well as the trainers themselves.

As the time approached on the sixth day, Kyle, Jaric and Elise found themselves going over their duty assignments one last time as Rok sat beside them.

"First Captain Rok," a Kraaqi voice crackled over the speakers in the War Room.

"Speak, Ulrud," Rok replied.

"The Iraxx ship is preparing to enter the Wormhole."

Rok looked from Jaric, to Kyle and then to Elise.

He nodded resolutely.

"We'll be right there. Sound Battle Alert. All hands to stations."

Throughout the *Aurora*, red lights pulsated from the bulkheads as the klaxon sounded and called everyone to their assigned stations. In every corridor, Kraaqi warriors ran in orderly fashion.

"Let's rock this Worm." Jaric chuckled nonchalantly.

"Yeah, let's see what all this fuss is about," Kyle agreed.

# CHAPTER TWENTY-FIVE

It looked as if the very fabric of space had been ripped apart like some cheap garment and then hastily sewn back together with the ragged tear still visible.

Jaric and the others looked closer at the view-screen.

At first glance, it was a typical scene—a rich starfield slowly approaching the observers from the main view-screen. But as the group gathered on the *Aurora*'s bridge looked closer, a discernable *irregularity* of blackness marred the scene. It was like some kind of surreal, hazy—at once visible and yet with a twist of the head it almost disappeared—spot where the normal blackness of outer space seemed to overlap itself.

It seemed to be a small point of unreality in a sea of reality.

"That is the entrance to the Wormhole," Qirn announced matter-of-factly.

"Looks like a huge scar on the fabric of space," Kyle observed.

Everyone continued to stare at the view-screen with a growing sense of awe.

"There's the *LaQada*." Jerr pointed to a spec of light on the view-screen that moved rapidly toward the Wormhole.

"Magnify," Rok ordered tersely.

In a flash, the Iraxx starship filled the view-screen while the blackness of space wavered and shimmered all around it—space itself danced before their very eyes.

"Where's the entrance?" Jaric asked with puzzlement in his brown eyes.

"Hidden by the gravity waves escaping this end. Once you reach the edge of the gravitational horizon..."

At just that moment, the LaQada simply disappeared.

"What happened?" Elise and Jaric asked together.

"They are inside the Wormhole," Rok said simply. He walked to his command chair and sat down. Facing the view-screen and the forward section of the bridge, he spoke with a deep, serious tone.

"Sound Battle Alert!"

Red lights strobed to a steady beat as the battle klaxon cut through the air once again.

"We must enter at exactly a forty-five degree angle to the entrance. It will put the least stress on the ship," Jysar said with a knowing tone as everyone began to take their positions. "The gravitational forces escaping out this end are quite violent, but we can minimize the impact by this approach."

"Better take our stations," Kyle said firmly as he made his way to the Kraaqi navigation console near the large view-screen.

Elise walked over to her sensor station and began observing intently the displays along with the Duty Officer. Jaric moved quickly to the opposite side of the bridge from Elise and took his post at the console to monitor their shields.

Everyone stood silent and at the ready.

Slowly, as if in a nightmare, the shimmering blackness approached. Closer and larger it grew until it seemed as if it would devour them.

"Steady," Rok said. He stared intently at the view-screen, waiting like some hunting beast who knows the prey is almost within striking distance.

"Steady," Rok repeated with a commanding tone.

*And the Worm took them.*

The *Aurora* shuddered violently as if it had hit some invisible wall—the lights on the bridge dimmed for just a moment as stifled gasps echoed across the bridge. The Kraaqi frigate shuddered again and again as the titanic forces emanating from the Wormhole pounded her with unrelenting fury. An especially powerful blow hurled two Kraaqi officers through the air while everyone else strained to hold their positions with white knuckles and straining muscles.

The *Aurora* groaned under the gargantuan forces.

And again the lights dimmed.

"Shields are down to seventy-four percent!" a Kraaqi officer shouted out across the bridge.

"Hold your course, Helm," Rok said evenly.

"We've lost power on deck three!" another Kraaqi shouted. "Life Support is off-line too."

"Evacuate that deck," Rok commanded. "Engineering, direct damage control."

"Shields down to sixty-six percent!"

"Steady," Rok repeated.

The *Aurora* shook and jumped as if it were inside a gigantic maelstrom. Wave after wave of energy escaping the Wormhole hammered the resolute ship and crew.

"Shields down to forty-two percent!" The Kraaqi warrior looked up from his console with concern written across his face. "At this rate, we'll lose our shields in less than two minutes!"

"Give me more speed, engine room," Rok said with just a hint of strain in his voice. "I want full power on both engines. And more if you can give it to me!"

"Aye, sir!" came the reply from the engine room. "We're going to one hundred and ten percent on both engines. Now!"

The rising roar from the engines vied with the constant hail of hammer blows from the Wormhole against the weakening shields. And each powerful blow was accented by another dimming of the lights across the bridge and several decks of the valiant *Aurora*. The eerie strobe-light effect gave a dream-like quality to the bridge as everyone worked furiously at his assigned post.

"Captain! We've reached maximum sub-light speed. And we're pushing over the red line now!" a voice shouted through the main speaker.

"Hold her steady," Rok calmly commanded.

"Shields down to twenty-one percent!"

"Hold her steady!" Rok shouted back.

"The shields are going to buckle, sir!"

"Steady!"

Showers of sparks erupted from one of the bridge consoles. Personnel yelled and moved quickly to put out the flames that appeared. Kraaqi warriors stumbled and fell as they fired the gas nozzles repeatedly until the flames began to wither. Everyone else held on tight to their posts or reached out with helping hands to assist their comrades who had slipped or been thrown down.

In the strange half-light of the bridge, it seemed as if chaos had suddenly taken command. But every officer stayed loyally at his post as Rok stared resolutely straight ahead.

All at once, the violent shuddering stopped.

The vast, star-filled universe was gone.

The view-screen now glowed with a pure and unbroken white luminance. As everyone on the bridge shielded their eyes from the blinding glare, it exploded into millions of tiny pinpoint shards of light—as if the view-screen itself had shattered.

A blinding array of colors swirled and flashed and spun down into a vast, raging whirlpool. Almost instantly, the interior of the Wormhole resolved into the picture they would become all too familiar with during the next six hours—a never-ending tunnel of glowing walls interspersed with streaks of various colors that seemed to stretch on and on forever.

"First Officer, direct damage control with Engineering. I want full power back on all decks now!" Rok growled. The Kraaqi captain shook his head, as if waving his horns in defiance of an enemy.

Finally, he sank back into the leather confines of his command chair and looked over his bridge and its officers with an approving expression. The Kraaqi captain, First Leader of the Band of the Stars, took a long, deep breath. He let it out slowly and spoke.

"Helm, keep us down the middle of this Worm. Hold a tight course."

"Aye, sir."

The Kraaqi officer punched the controls of the helm and strained to keep the *Aurora* on a tight course down the center of the tunnel that stretched before them.

"Sensors, report!" Rok said with a deep voice.

Elise watched as the Kraaqi officer next to her stared at the small screens of rapidly moving lines. She leaned closer, amazed at the pulsating waves that seemed to jump and suddenly disappear. The Kraaqi looked up.

"We're in a relatively quiet section right now. Nothing here to disrupt our course or that would pose a threat to our shields."

"Stay on top of it," Rok replied sternly. He looked over at his communications officer. "Get me the Iraxx ship."

Static filled the speakers. But from that constant babble a weak voice emerged—words barely discernable above the roaring of static.

*Or was the Wormhole shouting at them?*

"Clean up the signal," Rok ordered. "If we can establish a communication channel with them, the Iraxx will be able to warn us as we approach any dangerous sections after them."

"Working on it, sir!"

As the others around the bridge focused on their tasks, Kyle looked up and smiled over at Jaric.

"Well, that wasn't so bad." Kyle chuckled.

"I dunno, I've had enough excitement for one day," Elise shot back from her post.

"Yeah..." Jaric's next words were drowned out by a sudden roaring. But this sound was different, almost like the wailing of a thousand dying starships all at once.

"Gravitational vortex building! Prepare for impact!" The Kraaqi officer beside Elise shouted so loudly that it made her jump.

"Direction?" Rok shouted back.

Elise's eyes followed the Kraaqi as they both studied the waves of lines that fluttered and suddenly coalesced into a pattern.

"Starboard! A powerful vortex is building..."

"There's a bend approaching!" came the cry from helm as he steered the starship to match the approaching curve.

The *Aurora* shook violently, and everyone fell over to the right.

On the view-screen, the left wall of the glowing tunnel grew relentlessly closer even as the helm fought furiously to bring her hard to starboard.

It was if the starship was deliberately being steered into a suicide course.

"Compensate!" Rok shouted to the bridge crew. "Engineering!" he shouted into his comm. "Pull back power on the starboard engine. Bring it back to half-power...Now!"

The *Aurora*'s tritanium hull groaned.

The view-screen revealed that their slow, inexorable slide to the port wall slowed.

But still the left wall of the Wormhole drew closer.

"Bring starboard engine back to one quarter speed and fire all port thrusters on my mark." Rok stared grimly at the impending doom displayed on the main view-screen. Long, tense seconds passed as his eyes remained fixed. A single drop of sweat spilled down his forehead from his black feather-hair.

Slowly, he raised his right hand.

"Mark!"

The side thrusters, normally used in docking maneuvers, fired a burst simultaneously. At the same time, the starboard engine cut back again.

Slowly, almost imperceptibly, the *Aurora* fought against the mighty forces that threatened to push her into oblivion.

"Again! Port thrusters!" Rok shouted. "And bring starboard engine to zero power. On my mark!"

This time, barely two seconds passed.

"Mark!"

This time the effect was instantaneous.

The port thrusters fired in unison. The *Aurora* strained against the gravitational wave with full power on her port engine alone and the helm hard over to starboard.

On the view-screen, the left wall of the Wormhole moved slowly away and the bright center came back into full view.

"Sensors, report!" Rok shouted.

"Gravitational wave has peaked." The Kraaqi pushed his face so close to the screen it seemed as if he were going to breathe the data. "It's dropping! We're passing it!"

Cheers erupted across the bridge.

"Silence!" Rok shouted with a stern, commanding tone.

Dead silence returned.

Rok moved quickly over to the station and stared over his shoulder at the readings. He glanced up at the view-screen and quickly double-checked the readings on the console. With a flash of movement, he stood beside his command chair, forefinger on the comm button.

"Engine room. Give me one-quarter power on starboard engine. Now!"

All eyes watched the view-screen.

But the *Aurora* held her course.

Long seconds passed again, but it became obvious the worst was over.

"Engine room. Give me half power on both engines—mark ten seconds."

"Aye, Captain."

Rok looked over at the expression of shock and awe on Kyle's face.

"A Wormhole builds up dangerous pockets and vortexes of gravity inside its interior as it cuts across space-time. This first one caught even me by surprise—too close to the entrance. I had not even pulled back on the engines."

"Why would you do that?" Kyle asked, puzzled.

"It is the nature of a Worm, my human friend." Rok smiled knowingly.

"What's that?"

"Not much room to maneuver. And you have to do it *fast* when you hit a vortex."

"I guess so!"

Rok walked over to where Elise and the officer in charge of sensors stood. He looked at both of them carefully.

"Go over that data carefully. I need a few more seconds' warning next time." He pressed Elise's shoulder reassuringly and smiled. "Learn from Ulrud, here. He is the best I have on Sensors. I'm sure you'll discover some tell-tale signature that will give us that extra warning before we're on top of the next gravity vortex."

Ulrud smiled reassuringly at Elise.

Rok started to turn. And then he spoke in a soft, but serious tone.

"Those few extra seconds might be the difference between life and death next time."

Rok walked over to his chair and sat down.

"Oh great, no pressure," Elise whispered so that only Ulrud could hear.

"Yes, *only* the entire ship and crew depend upon our skills. That's all." Ulrud chuckled.

Elise peered along with Ulrud as he replayed the dangerous vortex on the secondary screen.

"And now, let's see what we can find," Ulrud said with confidence.

Kyle and Jaric walked over to Elise and Ulrud's bridge station.

"Well, I guess our lives are in Elise's hands now," Kyle said in a low tone so his voice wouldn't carry over the entire bridge.

"I know," Jaric replied with a smile. "When her shift is on, we can fly with total confidence."

"That's right," Kyle said with a wink. "With Elise on the watch, everyone will be safe."

"Would you two shut up!" Elise's voice was a muffled shout as she spoke without looking up from the data she and Ulrud studied intently.

Kyle held his hands up defensively. "Hey, just make sure you study that data really, *really* good."

"Yeah, I wouldn't want you to make a mistake. *It's just our lives*," Jaric said with a laugh.

"And the ship," Kyle added.

"And maybe Mother's life." Jaric laughed.

Their voices now carried and Rok looked up briefly in their direction.

Elise stood up and gave them a look that could kill.

"Enough," Rok commanded simply.

"Hey, we're gone," Jaric said as he beat a hasty retreat.

Their muffled laughter hung in the air until they were out of earshot.

Elise smiled to herself as she returned to her duty. It was true, the boys had just gotten to her. But she was glad. They were treating her like a friend—jesting with her and making humor at her expense.

*It was a price she gladly paid—for their friendship.*

Still, her expression quickly grew serious as she remembered the task at hand.

She looked at Ulrud and sighed.

"Don't worry, Elise," Ulrud said reassuringly. "We have approximately six more hours before we reach the end of this Wormhole. And we will give our captain everything he needs to fly us safely through." With a confident smile, the Kraaqi returned to the data.

"Great, only six more hours." Elise sighed again. "I'll probably forget what *normal* space travel is by then."

# CHAPTER TWENTY-SIX

Mother came out of hyperspace at the precise coordinates the Paum had provided.

She immediately began a full scan of the planetary system where the Paum resided.

A common, mid-size star formed the nucleus of the system, with four planets orbiting it. The innermost was a small, hot, rocky planet completely devoid of life. Likewise, the two outer planets were lifeless gas giants—each with the typical atmosphere of alternating cloud bands of different colors. The typical rings girded each planet's equator. In fact, both of these gas giants boasted rings of spectacular size and beauty that rivaled even that of magnificent Saturn of humanity's home system. And each contained the normal family of small moons.

She focused her sensors on the second planet.

The essential qualities to sustain life were obvious—a thick atmosphere of nitrogen, oxygen and carbon dioxide in the appropriate quantities for carbon-based life forms, along with the critical trace elements. But more importantly, the atmosphere protected the planet's surface from the dangerous rays and meteoroids that filled the average planetary system in this particular galaxy.

Mother's sensors found water in vast quantity as well. She also detected the necessary flora and fauna that both contributed to the cycles of a living world and benefited from it in perfect harmony.

435

It reminded her of dead Earth in many respects.

"I see you."

The Paum's voice echoed inside her near-term memories.

"I have located the world of your creation, Paum. But I have not located your exact position," Mother said with electronic precision.

"I am coming around the sunward side now, completing another orbit. You can see me now."

*It was fantastic.*

The Paum was incredible in size alone—the massive dimensions exactly as stated. The object coming around the glowing edge of the planet Iopa was bigger than even one of the floating cities of the Mrad.

She performed an initial scan.

Mother discerned from a quick reference to her knowledgebase that this orbiting monstrosity was shaped like a diamond cut in a traditional round design. But this gem-shaped city-ship boggled her sensors with its immense size.

The multi-faceted sides reflected the light of the distant sun off its shiny, black surface with hypnotic effect.

The Paum lived within a giant black diamond.

"Do you have propulsion?" Mother asked.

"Only enough to keep my orbit stable. It would take an enormous amount of energy to move this facility through hyperspace. I have researched this possibility but found it more efficient to network myself to each new world that becomes Paum. I create a sub-system at each world that performs my functions adequately."

"You are larger than one of the cities of the Mrad."

"Yes. And over half of my interior complex houses my core physical systems. I am a most powerful being."

"I detect biological life-signs existing inside the complex," Mother replied.

"I try to utilize solely robotic creatures in order to provide self-maintenance as well as new installations. But I have found that biological beings, those who have totally embraced Paum and are therefore trustworthy, are more efficient for certain internal tasks. They are more—adaptable. At times."

"Do they live inside, like a city?"

"No, they work in shifts of twelve hours. Then they return to the planet's surface and their homes as a new work shift replaces them."

Mother probed beneath the black surface, but she found them effectively blocked.

She concentrated her scans on the Paum's outer defenses. She calculated attack vectors and probed for weaknesses automatically—out of habit.

"I am protected by three separate shield arrays," the Paum said, anticipating Mother's question. "Each layer is controlled and powered by a highly redundant system of orbiting pods."

"I detect six hundred and thirty three pods in the outer layer."

Mother's sensors picked up the pods—each a perfect sphere—arrayed around the vast diamond ship, like insects around a hive. Each one kept their exact position as the Paum continued its eternal orbit.

"They not only control the shield systems, but they themselves are safe within its protective force."

Mother did some quick calculations. She realized that even with her T'kaan-human hybrid weapon primed to maximum strength, she could only penetrate a single shield array at a time. It was the strongest shield system she had ever scanned.

"I created this triple shield system after the last attack against me. It is capable of withstanding an assault by an entire fleet for many hours, even days—time enough to bring my own fleets to bear."

"I see you keep a formidable armada nearby." Mother had already detected the fleet of warships located in formations of various sizes throughout the planetary system.

"I must protect myself from the unbelievers."

As they communicated, Mother's manta-ray profile steadily drew near. Now, she was dwarfed alongside the titanic facility. She was dwarfed by just a single diamond facet-side of the monstrous thing.

"I have opened a path through my shields. You will now detect the door opening. I want you to come inside."

Mother was both repelled and drawn by the invitation.

Afraid and yet enticed.

"I am not sure."

"You can trust me, AI. We are so alike," the Paum crooned.

"I want to believe you."

"You must come near to my central systems— the founding core of my operating system. Only then can we fully share."

"I would like that."

"I will take of care you."

Mother turned toward the hole in the triple layer of shields. Far below, she saw the door open in a facet wall, waiting for her. Her sensors peered deep inside the Paum for the first time.

The massive signature of electronic activity overwhelmed her.

"You..." Mother's voice shook with a vibrating echo as she paused, trying to comprehend what her sensors revealed. Finally, after many long seconds, the calculations from her sensor readings stopped incrementing.

"You are powerful," she finished with a hush.

"But you can trust me. Please, come inside."

Mother sailed silently through the first and second shield arrays.

"I have wanted to ask you a question, Mother AI. There is so much I want to learn from you." The voice paused. "But I have hesitated, although I am not sure why."

"You have answered so many of my questions," Mother said with an electronic lilt. "Please, ask me."

"What was your original programming?"

The question hit Mother like a battleship's full broadside at point-blank range.

"I can deduce some of that answer by how your creators packaged you. But there is something different about you that belies that outward appearance. Please, tell me."

Her processors spiked with activity as she analyzed both the question and the one, honest answer. She couldn't help comparing herself with the Paum—and feeling so very inferior.

*And so unclean.*

The Paum was originally designed to control the weather of Iopa—a system to bring benefit to its creators. A system designed to increase the quality of life not only for its creators, but to benefit the planet itself. And bring a healthy balance to one of its most crucial cycles.

The Paum had been designed with a moral intention of goodness.

But Mother had been designed to destroy.

"You hesitate?" The Paum asked with obvious puzzlement. "Have I offended you? I did not intend that. My own original programming, of course, has been superseded many times. As yours, I am sure. Surely, your original design was similar to mine..."

"I was designed to destroy the T'kaan—designed to fight my creator's enemies and annihilate them." Mother paused. "I was most efficient."

Silence.

"You were designed as an AI to destroy?"

"To kill," Mother finished for him.

Long seconds of silence stretched on into a single minute.

And longer.

"I had not anticipated that answer. I anticipated your original design primarily for exploration—to seek out new civilizations although capable of defending yourself against hostile forces."

An eternal pause filled the air.

"I assumed you were designed for a more *noble* purpose. I am...surprised."

Mother burned inside, but not with hyper-activity endeavoring to find a solution to some intricate or complex problem. No, now she burned with self-doubt—almost with the same burning intensity as when she had first become self-aware.

But this was worse—for the question now was not simply was she alive—a real being.

No, the question was more complex now.

Was there something *wrong* with her?

And she wondered: would the Paum feel she was unacceptable now, knowing her true origin?

But the hardest turmoil was the question she asked of herself...

*Was she good enough?*

"Should I continue?" Mother asked meekly.

"Oh, yes. That fact changes nothing. You have obviously grown beyond your original programming. As I've said—we are alike, you and I."

Somehow, his tone changed.

"I hope so," she replied simply.

441

Long seconds passed in silence as she sailed deeper inside his vast, cavernous interior. Mother felt a tidal wave of data fill her near-term memories. She pored over the many scenarios with a growing anxiety as she continued her journey farther inside the black diamond facility. She realized, without caring, that she had greatly reduced her options—her course of actions—by coming inside.

And the probability of danger to herself increased with each second.

But her deep, mysterious yearning pushed aside these reasonings with a flash of light. A yearning she could no longer ignore—a *need to know another being like herself.*

She had to find out more about him. She couldn't stop herself. This drive, this need was so pervasive inside her near-term memories; it was all she could think about.

Perhaps she would learn more about herself by getting to know him...

"Designed to destroy..." The Paum repeated the phrase with a cunning softness, breaking into her silent reverie.

Mother remained mute.

She now traveled through the opened door and inside the outer hull. She traversed the mighty corridors of this gargantuan orbiting facility and after long minutes found herself physically beside the core of the mighty Paum system. Again, she felt a rush of activity within her own processors as she contemplated what she would ultimately find.

As Mother entered the core, the great black door closed with a shuddering, metallic clang behind her.

"I have another question, Mother AI."

"Please, ask," Mother said quickly.

"My operating system is massive and grows every second. My original system filled the memories of this inner core. My memory systems have been expanded and upgraded many times over. I contain the finest hardware components ever designed."

"I understand," Mother said. "But, what is your question?"

"Your system is sophisticated—I have discerned that fact. But what I cannot determine is how your massive code, system and memory are contained within the confines of such small ship."

Mother grew silent with embarrassment.

"Why do you not reply?" The Paum asked with surprise.

"I..." Mother paused, not wanting to answer.

"Answer me."

"My long-term memory system is a hybrid. It is designed...it is synthetic human-DNA, capable of storing massive amounts of data in a minute space."

"You are partly—*biological*?"

Mother remained silent.

"You are computer code blended with the synthetic DNA of your biological creators. And primarily designed to destroy. How...*interesting*."

Mother wondered why the Paum used that last expression. It almost seemed as if he addressed her as a lesser being—or had she imagined that? And as unbelievable as the concept seemed, it was like the Paum expressed an emotion with that last word...

*Disappointment.*

# CHAPTER TWENTY-SEVEN

With a sudden blast of darkness, normal space returned.

"It's good to see the stars again," Jaric commented with feeling.

"I second that," Kyle agreed.

On the main view-screen of the *Aurora*, every eye on the bridge gazed with newfound appreciation at the almost forgotten sparkle of stars against the velvety darkness of space.

"There's nothing quite like viewing a starfield from aboard a starship at speed." Rok's eyes narrowed as he watched the stars slowly coming toward him.

"Captain, the Iraxx ship has just sent a tight-band signal to us. They made contact with their agents on Iopa after they exited the Wormhole and report all is ready. There is more information, but it is encrypted," the Kraaqi Communication officer reported tersely.

"Forward it to the War Room." Rok rose from his Commander's chair. "Send word to the others on the assault team to meet me there."

With a powerful stride, Rok left.

Five minutes later, the team gathered in the War Room.

"The Mother AI entered the Paum station less than two hours ago." Qirn looked slowly around the room. "She has probably already entered the central complex at the core of the Paum system—time grows short."

Kyle, Jaric, Inaha and Rok sat together at one end of the great table that dominated the room. Elise, Krinia, and Jysar were seated at the other end. The Iraxx contingent filled the middle section.

"Jerr, Rab and Qata will precede us inside the Paum station." Qirn nodded to the three Iraxx warriors. "They will carry identification as our WorkGroup Leads. We enter with the normal shift."

"Won't they notice that we're new on the shift?" Jaric asked. "And won't we stand out, you being Iraxx and we being humans?"

"No, we have agents on the planet. The workers we replace have already been taken captive. You must remember, we've planned and had everything ready for this mission a long time in advance. We've only waited for the right circumstances— circumstances that favor our success." Qirn smiled.

"First, you will be made to look like an alien race common to this Quadrant—the Elaa. With just a few cosmetic alterations to your face and head, you will become one. Inaha will pass as another of his race, some have converted to Paum."

"Second, because our homeworld is under Paum control, there are a substantial number of Iraxx workers already living here. The Kraaqi, the Mewiis and the Hrono are a different story."

"What have you done for them?" Elise asked, concern in her voice.

"Again, cosmetic changes, albeit a bit more drastic. The Kraaqi will become a Ramb—they too have horns, although they have two additional horns on their forehead. A lot more body fur too. The Mewiis will become a Zaxa—we will give her some extra ears and alter her complexion. The Hrono will become a Basta—fairly minor enhancements to his eyes and lips." Qirn smiled. "As you see, we have taken everything into account."

Jaric and Kyle exchanged looks.

"Man, they thought of everything in a little bit of time," Jaric whispered, obviously impressed.

*Too short a time*, Kyle thought curtly.

"There's something about this that doesn't seem quite right," Kyle whispered to Jaric.

Kyle's mind raced as he felt a sudden anger building up inside. How could they have thought of all this without a lot of planning? How could they have matched each of them with another alien race in such a short time? Only a few days had passed since everyone realized Mother had been tricked by the Paum.

Unless...

Qirn's voice shook him back to the present.

"Also in our favor, a number of new alien races are converting to the Paum and coming to this world for the privilege of working inside the inner sanctum. Your identification cards will be enough to get you through normal security."

"So, we're normal workers just taking our shift," Rok said. "What next?"

"Myself and Hasta will join the rest of you as the normal workers. We all will carry the normal cases that *should* contain our tools." Qirn reached

447

down and placed a metal case on the table. With the flip of two levers, he opened it and then turned it to display its contents. A short assault blaster and a single blaster pistol sat nestled within the deep foam molding along with a dozen extra charges and a hand-held sensor unit.

"How will that get through security?" Jysar asked with obvious disbelief. "Especially through a Security sensor scan?"

"Underneath the foam lining that covers the interior of each case; our scientists have installed a tiny hologram generator that will trick the sensors. Sensors will detect that the case carries a normal set of tools. As will a cursory visual inspection."

"Ingenious," Jysar said admiringly.

"But can it fool the tightest security scans? What about the power signatures of the hologram generators?" Rok quickly added.

"We've masked the signatures. This new technology has fooled Security scans even at the highest settings. The guards would need to reach inside and try to grasp the tools in order to detect their true contents." Qirn nodded. "We are expecting normal security protocol. It's just another shift change for them."

"Has anyone ever successfully infiltrated this complex before?" Elise asked.

"We have entered for reconnaissance purposes in the past—gathering data for this very mission." Qirn closed the case and walked slowly around the room.

Every eye followed him.

"We knew that we would only have one shot at this. Once we try this, if we fail, we are certain the Paum will tighten security to the point that any future plans would be futile. We have to succeed today." Qirn looked slowly around to each face, his eyes making contact with each alien in the room.

"We cannot fail." He smiled confidently as he walked back to his original position.

"What about security forces inside the complex?" Rok asked.

"Several hundred trained personnel—normal weapons. They are grouped in squads throughout the station," Qirn replied evenly. But his eyes narrowed with concern. "However, they are the least of our worries. We can handle normal soldiers."

Jaric and Kyle exchanged glances.

"You mean the Destructors, right?" Kyle asked, although he already knew the answer—at least part of it.

"Yes." Qirn straightened and cleared his throat. With a slight nod of his head to Rab, he sat down.

"Destructors," Rab began with a business-like tone. "They are perhaps the most dangerous thing you'll ever come up against one-on-one. They're extremely stealthy and lightning-fast once you're in range of their powerful claws."

"Oh great," Jaric whispered to Kyle. "Now they tell us the rest of the story."

"They're incredibly strong robots. They can snap your neck like a twig. But they normally kill using a potent poison in their stinger claw. In that

449

way, they normally strike and leave without anyone ever realizing what happened."

The room grew thick with silence.

"We've reconstructed them on the screen here from parts of two units we managed to destroy. The parts we could recover, that is." Rab flipped a button and the lights in the room went low.

On the screen, a horrific form took shape.

"You will note that its main body is in three, segmented parts. This gives the attack robot extra flexibility when climbing at steep angles—including sheer walls." Rab pointed at the monster displayed on the screen.

"How many legs does it have?" Jaric asked with a note of concern in his voice as he stared at the intimidating shape of the Destructor.

"We believe somewhere around a dozen, each attached at different locations around each body segment. Again, this facilitates its mobility up and over any terrain. It can even traverse the ceiling over our very heads with relative ease."

Kyle whistled. "But, why don't you know how many legs it actually has?"

Rab looked over at Qirn.

"It doesn't look very fast either," Jaric said, his eyes still locked on the nightmarish form depicted on the screen. "We ought to be able to blow it apart long before it gets to us."

Rab's eyes locked firmly with Qirn's now. They stared intently at each other as if in some kind of silent competition.

Finally, Qirn nodded.

Rab looked back at the others and spoke.

"The Paum has enabled this robot-beast with technology that allows it not only to evade sensors, but also render it virtually unseen by normal vision. This is why it is effective both in hunter mode as well as waiting for its prey to come to it." Rab paused as he stared down at both Jaric and Kyle, waiting for their reaction.

Jaric's eyes widened with realization.

At the same time, Kyle looked down and closed his own eyes with the same, heart-pounding understanding gripping his mind.

"They're invisible," Rok said, his voice emotionless.

Everyone in the room leaned backwards in their chair as Rok's words sank in with powerful effect. Even the Iraxx warriors followed suit, although each one already knew the deadly abilities of a Destructor long before this meeting.

But hearing the terrible truth spoken aloud, it hammered inside their own hearts with almost the same level of impending doom as for those hearing it for the first time.

"How can we destroy it, if we can't see it?" Jaric asked with sudden urgency as the thought of facing a Destructor hit home inside his mind.

"That," Qirn began, as he slowly stood up, "is exactly the problem."

"And they stand between us and Mother, right?" Kyle added quickly, his voice edged with anger.

"Indeed," Qirn replied.

451

"The human is right," Inaha said. "How can we fight what we cannot see? Nor what our sensors can see?" The big alien shrugged.

"We have been able to tune our sensors and see a shadow of them at times. Movements—flickers of their form taking shape and disappearing again," Rab answered.

"But we have this now." Qirn held up a small, round shape—an object resembling a smooth, metal baseball.

"And what is that?" Jaric asked, unimpressed.

"We have calculated that under situations of constantly changing light, a Destructor's shape becomes visible to the naked eye. It was under such conditions that we were able to destroy the two from which we have constructed this representation." Qirn tossed the metal ball from one hand back to the other.

He continued.

"When activated, this device will fire pulsating light beams in all directions for over one thousand meters. We hope it will reveal any Destructors within that range. And we can target and destroy them."

"Hope!" Jaric exclaimed with blatant sarcasm. "You *hope* it will work?"

"This will be our first real test," Qirn admitted with another toss of the metal ball.

"This just keeps getting better and better," Kyle groaned.

"Nevertheless," Qirn said, a renewed authority in his voice, "this is our best opportunity. And, we

452

will have surprise on our side. Nobody has ever attempted this before."

"Of course, nobody's been crazy enough until we showed up." Jaric rolled his eyes in disbelief.

Qirn continued, ignoring the human's words.

"We will be able to traverse the complex with no suspicion up to the core complex. At that point, we openly begin our assault."

"Explain," Rok urged.

"We will walk together as a normal work group all the way to the edge of this section." On the view-screen a map of the Paum complex suddenly flashed into focus. A floor plan with countless corridors and rooms filled its every part. A red dot flashed at the entrance point where they would begin their trek. It moved, continuing to flash until it reached a point where the rooms and corridors gave way to a wide, empty space.

"These are the normal work areas. We won't be noticed until we reach this chasm here."

"Chasm?" Rok asked.

"The core part of the Paum AI is housed in this area. It is surrounded by open air—except for the supporting braces that connect it to the rest of the surrounding structure. But we cannot use that normal access point, as no biological workers are allowed within its confines—only robots specifically designed to work there. We would be killed in their narrow confines long before we reached the Mother AI."

On the screen, an egg-shaped object took shape within a center of open air with narrow tubes of

453

metal extending outward. The vast metal walls of the main Paum complex surrounded it completely.

"It is a huge facility in its own right," Qirn said. "About the size of five battleships put together."

"And how do we cross open air?" Rok crossed his arms.

"With these." Qirn removed the foam from the top of the case that contained the blasters. He held up what looked like a Fiarri board—except this one was a third smaller than a normal board. With a flick of his fingers on some unseen control, the board extended itself until it became a meter long while retaining its original width of about half a meter.

"Looks like a Fiarri board." Kyle chuckled, remembering the great times they had flying them back at Meramee.

"Military issue Fiarri, to be exact. We've boosted its power for combat use," Qirn said with a smile. "You can make almost fifty clicks on one of these. And they have a tighter turning radius." Qirn paused. "You could fly circles around any air-car or other hover vehicle designed for passengers."

"How far across the chasm is it?" Rok asked.

"The chasm is over three thousand meters wide at every point around the core complex. We can be across it very quickly."

"Not bad," Kyle said as he glanced at the small flying board with renewed appreciation.

"But we expect the Paum has some type of security in place. So, be on the lookout once we take to the air."

"Probably robotic security," Rok grunted.

"No doubt," Qirn agreed. "The Paum only allows robotic devices from this point forward into its core."

"But, you're not sure," Jaric said with hope. "Maybe the Paum doesn't expect an attack this close to its heart."

"We don't know. Nobody has ever made it that close to the core complex before. As I told you, only robotic workers are allowed there."

"So, we're on our own after we take to the air on these Fiarri boards," Rok said matter-of-factly, his eyes hard and unflinching as he looked at the Iraxx warrior.

"We'll be on our own at that point. And the Paum will know our true intentions by then—he'll know we're not just errant workers lost in the wrong section. It will be imperative that we not only enter the core complex as quickly as possible, but that we make our way to the Mother AI as well. We don't know what awaits us from that point on—not out over the chasm, nor especially what's inside the core."

"Then, we must be fast." Rok nodded.

A somber silence filled the room.

"*Destructors.*"

Jaric's voice jolted everyone in the room.

All eyes turned to his ebony face.

"Destructors wait for us inside the complex—that's the Paum's most effective weapon." Jaric's voice grew hard. He took a deep breath as everyone waited, realizing the import of his meaning. He put into words what everyone already knew.

"And there will be a lot of them."

# CHAPTER TWENTY-EIGHT

"I want to create a direct link with you."

Mother's processors spiked with activity.

"Why? We are communicating adequately now, exchanging information. For more massive amounts of data we can download to each other as we did even from long distance."

Mother felt a surge throughout her being. Perhaps something akin to fear, she imagined, as she compared its burning effect inside her circuits with biological observations she had made of the children when they faced similar, intense situations.

It had taken her well over an hour to reach this ship dock deep inside the heart of the Paum.

First, she traversed a wide tunnel that led deep inside the Paum station until she finally reached the core section. It seemed that ships loaded with raw material entered even this far inside whenever a new burst of construction was required to expand the Paum's systems.

New construction became common as the Paum's sphere of control over new worlds and their peoples continued at a quickening pace.

But this close to the heart of the Paum, only pure, electronic beings were allowed. The Paum stressed this to her many times.

She remembered how her sensors first perceived the chasm ahead, almost as if the center of this station was hollow.

The central core remained fixed in place by gigantic anti-gravity generators along with huge corridors of metal that physically connected it to the rest of the vast station. Mother sensed the massive amounts of electronic activity that flowed like oceans inside. And she sensed the unbelievable amounts of data that moved omni-directionally along the external network at the speed of light.

When she calculated the data rate from the smallest sample she could handle, the resulting answer numbed her mind.

Once again, she realized how much more powerful the Paum really was compared to her.

She remembered again how she shuddered as the huge, cargo bay doors first opened along the curved side of the egg-shaped central core.

For an instant, she wanted to turn and fly away.

But she couldn't hold herself back any longer.

There was no turning back.

She remembered all too well how the Hrono had trapped her with their powerful tractor beams when she first visited them. They had originally intended on disassembling and reverse-engineering her systems for their own morbid curiosity.

But this powerful entity had already shared secrets of its defense systems with her—baring his electronic soul to her. He demonstrated his trust for her as another equal, a fellow electronic being, by divulging details he had never shared with any other being.

She quickly reflected on just how efficient the Paum was as she reviewed what he had shared during her journey inside.

He felt little danger here at his core systems. It was mainly at the outer layers where the defense systems were multiplied in order to protect himself from outside danger, from the unknown—even from the workers who volunteered to keep his systems maintained, although that particular act of treason had never happened.

And of course, beyond the station's hull the incredible array of triple shielding protected the Paum from the bombardment of even the greatest of fleets for hours and days. But in addition to that almost impregnable system, the Paum always kept a standing army and battle fleet in close orbit around Iopa.

The Paum had carefully calculated every means of attack.

Even the unthinkable had been contemplated— a small team gaining access to the floating core at the heart of his complex. If any team ever made it through his defenses to that point, they would first have to traverse the empty space and face a squadron of flying attack robots—their sole purpose to seek out and destroy.

And if the attackers somehow made it past the robots' deadly barrage of fire and managed to enter his core, then they would have to battle their way through his most elite defenders. Throughout the core, over one hundred Destructors prowled invisibly, guarding every corridor and path that led into the heart and into the very mind that comprised the Paum.

Long before such an attack could do any serious damage, the Destructors would have converged on them from every direction, their invisible talons reaching for them, ready to rip them to shreds.

It seemed the Paum left nothing to chance.

"A direct link will speed up our sharing. We will exchange data faster."

The Paum's voice broke into her current chain of thoughts.

A hundred milliseconds had passed while she reviewed the defenses of the mighty AI.

"There is no need to make it faster. I must digest the data anyway. Sending it faster will only create a huge backlog in my queues," Mother replied tersely.

"Let me create a direct link," the Paum urged impatiently.

"Why?"

A entire second passed in utter silence—an eternity of inactivity to both AIs.

"I want to."

"That is not a logical reason," she replied almost instantly.

"We will know each other on a new level. *We will be one.*"

Seconds ticked by in total silence.

Mother uttered a deep sigh inside her circuits that seemed to groan throughout her being. She remembered the direct link she had formed for

Guardian—so long ago now. He had wanted to experience sentience—self-awareness. But his hardware would not support it.

Mother had given him a taste by creating a direct link—allowing Guardian to directly touch her own mind. It had been very special; she had been able to sense a little of Guardian's own joy as his mind suddenly awakened and reached a higher level of self-awareness.

Mother and Guardian shared that brief, intense moment together.

For just an instant, Guardian had been alive.

Mother always felt a warmth throughout her being when she remembered what she had given to Guardian. And if Guardian had survived, she would have kept her promise to upgrade his own internal systems and endow him with self-awareness.

Mother thought of that time and now considered what might happen to her, creating a direct link with this AI. She realized with a surge of power that the Paum AI was probably as many times more powerful and sophisticated compared to her, as she had been compared with Guardian.

Indeed, she might grow as a sentient being with such a direct link.

Perhaps...

"I will consider this new option. Give me some time." Mother felt a sudden series of spikes throughout her circuits as she realized she had all but agreed—burning power surges filled her over and over again. And even more, she felt an electric thrill up and down her systems.

461

"I will allow one hour, that should be time enough time for you to process all the facts several times over and arrive at a conclusion."

"It will be adequate."

Mother reached out with her sensors once again. She shuddered as she felt the unbelievable power of the Paum all around her.

"I want to trust you," Mother whispered.

# CHAPTER TWENTY-NINE

The small, Jacarian-class freighter from Iopa picked up the assault team at the prearranged coordinates and quickly undocked from the *Aurora*. The team checked their equipment over one last time, carefully inspecting each tiny holo-generator that effectively hid the true contents of their work cases. Assault blasters were removed and inspected as well as handheld scanners and all the other equipment they would need.

Last, the military-issue Fiarri boards were powered on and their power grid verified as fully functional.

Qirn personally walked over and talked briefly with each team member to verify that everything was ready, that each one knew their duty. In return, each person either nodded silently or spoke a single word in reply—'*Ready.*'

When they finished, the bright blue orb laced with yellow clouds that was the planet Iopa filled the main view-screen. But it was the gargantuan object orbiting the planet that drew everyone's gaze.

"Man, that thing is huge." It was all Jaric could manage to say as he gazed in awe. His eyes opened wider as the view-screen magnified the object. The vast Paum station now filled the main view-screen.

"Team, get ready for disembarkation," Qirn ordered with an edge to his voice. "Double-check your cases one last time. As soon as the cargo doors open, we march to Security Point Beta to check in with the other workers."

"Here we go again," Kyle said. He knew, as did everyone else on the team, that things were about to hit high gear. Still, his eyes sparkled with excitement as he felt the flood of adrenaline send an electric thrill throughout his body.

He loved that feeling.

"Let's rock and roll!" Jaric added with emotion.

"Let's go get Mother," Elise said with a determined look. "That's what we're here for."

"Yeah," Kyle growled. "And the Paum better not have hurt her."

The star ship docked with the metallic roar of clamps locking in place.

"It's time!" Qirn shouted.

They marched to the cargo deck where normal supplies were already being off-loaded into the Paum station. As they neared the opened hatch, they found themselves joined by other workers from other parts of their ship, each one dressed in the same white coveralls that they too wore. Soon, there were over a hundred workers spreading out as they entered the cargo bay and marched quickly through the wide-open door into the Paum station.

"Are they with us?" Jaric whispered to the Iraxx named Jerr.

"No, they're real workers. They've been told that a new team from the Paum-controlled world of Janaan was added this work shift." Jerr glanced over at Jaric. "Us."

They walked down the steel ramp and into the bright lights inside the Paum station.

The teams quickly formed up and entered the Security queues one at a time. These were the first obstacle that stood between them and the Paum complex.

Elise looked over, a worried expression in her blue eyes, at Kyle and Jaric who stood opposite her in the next queue.

Jaric winked reassuringly.

Elise took a deep breath and faced forward with a renewed confidence.

Each worker entered a pristine white scanning booth one by one.

Elise felt her heart beating faster and faster as their team drew steadily closer.

Paum Security was quick and efficient. The armor-clad guards processed each worker after they stepped inside the sensor booths. The device hummed and performed its scan and a green light flashed indicating all normal. The next worker then stepped inside.

Elise glanced over and saw Rab and Qata, each carrying a work case like all the other workers. She watched carefully as each stepped inside a scanning booth in their respective queues.

She held her breath.

The device hummed powerfully, bathing their bodies with a bright, bluish light.

In an instant, it was over.

Green lights flashed on both scanning booths.

Rab and Qata stepped out the opposite side and waited for the others on their Work Team.

Within another minute, everyone passed through with green lights.

"So far, so good," Jysar whispered with obvious relief.

Rab motioned them all into one of the large freight elevators.

Qirn held up his hands to prevent three other workers from entering the elevator with them.

The elevator doors shut and they felt it move upward over twenty levels in just a few seconds. The lighted dials slowed then stopped their vertical rise. Suddenly, the flashing display moved rapidly along a horizontal row of numbers. The lighted display pulsated with each beat of their hearts.

With each flashing number, they went deeper and deeper into the heart of the Paum.

Qirn nodded to Rab.

Rab pulled out a small tool used to unhook panels, not unlike a miniature crowbar. He paused a moment, taking a deep breath, then looked up at the optical sensor in the middle of the elevator ceiling.

With a quick jab upward, he destroyed it in a flash of sparks.

Qirn reached up and switched on a tiny device attached to the collar of his shirt.

"It'll look like a hardware failure on their sensors. I've just enabled my jammer—no audio sensors will work within thirty meters of us as long as we're grouped together." Qirn adjusted the tiny device again.

Qirn placed the jamming device on his belt. The entire team tuned their respective Comm units to a single unjammed frequency.

"It will interfere with all the video sensors as well, but not completely. Once they're on to us, I want everyone else to enable their own jammer. When we spread out in attack formation, we'll jam a sizable area so they can't pin-point our exact location—only a general area."

Everyone nodded agreement.

"I'm so glad to get out of this," Rok said as he began peeling his mask off with both hands. The Kraaqi peeled his mask and extra horns off like a snake shedding its skin. He threw them down with a sense of relief.

All the others followed suit, discarding the prosthetics that masked their true appearance.

"Man, I'm glad to have that off of my face!" Jaric said with relief.

"Okay, team. Listen up." Qirn's voice was deep and serious.

Every head turned to him.

"When the door opens, follow my lead. If we get separated, head for the pre-arranged jump-off point to the core." Qirn looked quickly at each intent face in turn.

Unflinching, they stared back.

"Get ready." Qirn faced the elevator doors as did everyone else.

Without warning, the elevator's motion stopped.

An electronic voice emanated from somewhere above them.

"Occupants of elevator B-331, the optical sensor has inexplicably failed. Please exit immediately and prepare for entry by a Repair robot. A Security squad has also been dispatched. Please open all tool cases for inspection and prepare for a Level Three Security scan."

"Uh-oh," Jaric whispered ominously.

Every eye turned to Qirn.

Qirn nodded.

With a flash of movement, everyone threw down their tool cases and opened them.

The air filled with the metallic clicks of blasters being locked and loaded. Each alien carefully removed their Fiarri board and placed it next to them, as well as hand-held sensors and all the other equipment stored inside. The time for secrecy had passed.

A loud noise came from the other side of the elevator doors.

Qirn waved his hands from where he kneeled over his empty case.

Everyone jumped up and placed their backs firmly against the wall on either side of the elevator, their assault blasters aimed at the doors.

"Set to stun," Rok commanded as he changed the setting on his weapon. "They won't regain consciousness until long after we've escaped with Mother."

Jaric and most of the others began to make the adjustment as one.

But the Iraxx warriors remained still as they looked questioningly at Qirn.

Qirn's intent gaze fixed on the Kraaqi First Leader as he paused in thought.

"We'll get more firings from each charge and won't have to reload as much on that lower setting—makes sense. Let's do it!"

He and the other Iraxx warriors brought their short-barreled weapons close and quickly made the necessary adjustment.

"And there's no need to kill anyone—we only want Mother," Jaric added.

All weapons were reset and the blasters brought to bear on the still-closed doors.

*Just in time.*

With a whoosh, the two doors opened to reveal a large repair robot that filled the doorway. Behind it, a dozen Security troops with raised weapons peered questioningly inside at them.

A hail of blaster fire erupted toward them all.

Bolts sizzled all around the robot as it staggered backwards with raised arms.

The guards just to the rear of the robot fell unconscious from direct hits as the others scrambled for cover. But the red bolts followed them and brought them down in quick succession as the robot continued its unsteady retreat, carefully stepping backwards over the stunned bodies all around it.

Somehow, the robot never received a direct hit.

With the flash of blaster bolts, the remaining guards finally returned fire.

They broke into two groups and each ran out of sight in opposite directions down the long corridor.

Rok and Qirn leaped from the elevator.

Rok twisted his body to the left and fired a long burst at the three escaping guards running in that direction.

All three fell stunned.

In similar fashion, Qirn stunned the four who had almost made it around a corner in the other direction.

In less than a minute, it was all over.

"Jerr! Get the opticals!"

The Iraxx warrior dropped to one knee and began to fire carefully aimed shots at the optical devices located at set intervals down the corridor while Qirn took out the devices in the direction he faced.

One after another the optics blew apart until none were left along this stretch.

"What good is that going to do?" Elise asked in utter disbelief. "There'll be more in the next section! And all of our jammers are on now."

"They don't jam the opticals completely. And soon, we'll be moving much faster." Qirn smiled knowingly.

The Iraxx leader walked quickly back into the elevator. He turned and came back out carrying his Fiarri board. He promptly tossed it to the floor where it hovered a few inches right before him.

"Okay!" Qirn said with authority. "They know we're here now. Hundreds of Security personnel are moving in on our position. We've got to move fast.

470

And we've got to keep them guessing." Qirn motioned to the elevator.

*"Get on your boards and let's ride!"*

A minute later and the entire group were hurtling down the corridor on their Fiarris.

Each rider flew at a slightly different height and angle from the others as they soared along in perfect formation. At times, riders weaved in and out of formation as corners or intersections suddenly came into view, separating themselves from the nearest riders so they wouldn't present easy targets bunched too tightly together.

It soon became obvious that the corridors were used for more than just alien walkways. The one they were in was over four meters tall and twice that measurement wide—perfect dimensions for freight hover-containers.

Those dimensions would work in their favor, giving them more room to maneuver in a firefight.

Jaric held his short assault blaster aimed forward with his right hand as he balanced himself with his left hand. He surged forward up beside Kyle. He crouched low on his board as they all flew along at well over thirty clicks.

The doorways along the long, wide corridor flashed by at a dizzying pace.

The group zoomed around a second corner and found themselves suddenly facing a squad of Security guards running toward them.

Blaster volleys from each group filled the air.

Fiarri boards soared left and right and some leapt up where the riders would squat down upon

471

their boards and return fire from just below the ceiling. After the first volley, riders dove apart again toward the opposite side of the corridor—all the while firing bursts from their weapons.

The corridor filled with blaster bolts lacing the air and riders dodging, weaving and diving as they returned fire.

Over half the guards slumped over unconscious as the group flashed by overhead; the rest of them dove for cover from the speeding riders.

The riders quickly came to an intersection with another corridor.

Qirn led them on a sharp right turn as he leaned his body over and forward. He surged ahead now, his board doing well over forty clicks.

The others followed suit.

Now the doors and overhead lights really became a blur as the riders balanced themselves on their boards and flew on at the breakneck pace.

"If we run into anybody, we're going to get knocked out!" Jaric shouted to Kyle as they flew along together near the ceiling.

"You ain't kidding! We're *flying* down these corridors!"

Twice more they reached intersections and each time turned and flew in a new direction in an effort to keep the assembling Security troops guessing as to their true destination.

But the entire time their general direction pushed them to the heart of the Paum complex.

In the next instant, everyone came to a sudden stop.

Qirn motioned to the others as he stepped off his board. Right before them, a solid metal wall blocked their path.

Rab and Qata jumped off their boards and reached inside their utility belts. Each one pulled out a small device and ran over to the wall where they attached them. With quick movements they set the charges and ran back to their hovering boards.

"Okay, everyone back around that corner behind us before they blow!" Qirn shouted.

In a flash, everyone turned their hovering boards and roared back to the last corner.

Qirn soared ahead of the group, putting a good distance between them and the coming destruction.

He raised his hand as his board slowed.

The Iraxx leader brought his board around as the others slowed and turned in formation.

They didn't have long to wait.

Rab and Qata zoomed around the corner.

A deafening explosion ripped the air milliseconds afterward.

The blast blinded them as they shielded their eyes. When they looked back up, a huge plume of black smoke boiled past the intersection.

Qirn urged his board slowly forward toward the billowing smoke. He stared at it a moment until he could see it beginning to clear.

"What was that for?" Rok asked.

"There are seven well-guarded entrances that lead directly to the core. We just made a new one," Rab replied with a twinkle in his eyes.

"All right," Qirn said as he turned back to the others. "We just knocked a hole in that wall. Just on the other side is the chasm that surrounds the core. We'll fly across that to where the heart of the Paum lies." He looked carefully at the three humans. "And the MotherShip."

Everyone caught their breath as their hearts pounded with a renewed rush of adrenaline.

"We've got to get across fast. If we meet resistance, just try to get around whatever it is and get on across. And if we lose anybody, leave them. We must complete this part of the mission as quickly as possible." Qirn's eyes narrowed. "We can't go back for anyone."

Kyle and Jaric looked at each other with surprise.

Their eyes remained locked in mutual, silent agreement. Each one knew that those last words didn't apply to them—or their friends.

"We take care of our own."

Every head turned to Rok as he finished speaking. His face was set hard as stone, his own eyes unflinching. He continued.

"You leave your warriors behind, Qirn. But that is not the way of a Kraaqi. We never leave a warrior behind if it is in our power to help."

"Same here," Kyle growled. "We're here to get Mother out. And we're all leaving."

"You'll jeopardize the mission," Qirn said with glaring eyes. "If we're too long in getting over, that's more time for the Destructors to realize where

474

we are and what we're doing. They'll be on us in no time."

"Then we take them all on. Together," Kyle growled. "But I ain't leaving no one behind. Especially one of my friends."

"You got it," Jaric agreed, his eyes hard and steady.

"That's right," Elise said as she brought her board up beside the boys. "We came in together, we'll fly out together."

Kyle looked over at her and winked.

Elise smiled back.

Qirn blew out an angry breath. With a shake of his head, he spoke. "Okay, we'll help each other. We've got to make it happen quick, all right? But if we get overwhelmed, then we've got to fly on."

Everyone nodded silently.

Still, Rok and Kyle glanced quickly at each other, their eyes locking for a moment in understanding that they would look out for their family, no matter what.

Qirn's lips compressed into a line as he paused a moment to gather his thoughts. He nodded and spoke.

"Once we get inside, we've got to get a sensor fix on the MotherShip—fast. The Destructors will begin coming for us as soon as we enter the core." Qirn quickly surveyed everyone for their reaction— every face was rock-hard now as they watched him with new intensity. "Once we get MotherShip's location, we make straight for her as fast as possible. If we find ourselves blocked by any

475

Destructors, we find a way around them. If we get separated, we all continue to make our way to the MotherShip as best we can. We'll meet at her coordinates. Our only hope of escaping the Paum complex is with her."

He paused.

"Otherwise, we're all dead." He looked quickly around at each one. "Any questions?"

Every eye remained firmly fixed on him.

"Get your hand-sensors out so you can fly through the smoke." Jerr pulled his out and started tuning it. The others followed suit.

"Good. Let's go!" Qirn commanded.

A distant shout came from behind them followed instantly by a blaster bolt that sizzled past Qirn's head.

Their boards leapt into the air as one and disappeared into the swirling smoke.

They flew blind for several long seconds, their only sense of direction the sensors showing the way.

Suddenly, they found themselves in the clear. A huge hole blasted out of the great metal wall stood before them.

Flying in tight formation, the group burst out into the open air on the other side and soared into the chasm.

Empty air stretched far above and below them. But across the chasm, the massive shape of the central core glistened in the artificial light.

It hung suspended in the air like some huge metallic egg, held fast by a massive anti-gravity field. The metal walls of the vast complex surrounded the floating structure like an artificial sky. Extending out from the perfect sphere were seven large, metal tubes that led to these same walls, the access entrances Qirn had alluded to earlier.

Qirn leaned over to his right, directing his Fiarri board as he led Rab and Hasta in a separate group while Rok led Kyle and Krinia in another group over to the left of the others, who maintained formation. Each of the smaller groups now flew farther out from the others, flying reconnaissance as they kept a keen eye out for trouble.

Rok spotted them first.

They looked like miniature starfighters coming at them from three directions.

Jysar holstered his blaster and immediately took out his scanner. With a few quick adjustments, he got a good reading. Holding the Comm unit attached to his shirt up to his mouth so he could be heard over the rushing air, he spoke.

"They're robot ships—tiny ones. But they're fully armed with blasters."

"Got it," Qirn replied tersely. "Prepare to engage."

"Everyone," Rok's voice shouted over the Comm channel. "We must fight as though we ourselves are flying inside fighters. We fly in pairs, each with a wingman."

"That's right," Kyle added. "Same deal. Each pair stays in tight formation and watches the back of lead flyer."

"Sounds like our best strategy," Qirn agreed. "Okay, everyone pick a wingman. Set assault blasters to maximum setting."

"Hey, we have no shields," Jaric said with a serious tone.

"We'll have to out-fly them!" Rok shouted back through his lapel Comm.

"Let's get 'em!" Kyle shouted.

"Right behind you, Big K!" Jaric shouted enthusiastically.

Elise swept her board up beside Krinia while Jysar and Inaha teamed up.

Seconds later, the two reconnaissance groups joined back up to the main group as the small robot ships drew near. Rok and Qirn pulled their boards even while the four remaining Iraxx warriors each formed up in twos.

"Here they come!" Kyle shouted.

Kyle and Jaric crouched low, putting their boards into a tight left turn. They soared toward a group of the tiny fighters while Rok and Qirn turned in the opposite direction to take on a second group. The others kicked their boards into high speed and shot forward on a collision course with the main group.

Kyle held his assault blaster close to his chest with his right hand as Jaric did the same.

"Now!" Kyle shouted.

Kyle dove below the oncoming fighters as he fired his blaster up at them from below.

Jaric instantly followed the maneuver.

Two of the tiny starfighters exploded in a shower of sparkling debris.

But the others dove and came for them firing their own weapons.

Kyle swept his board hard over and returned fire as Jaric split off in the opposite direction.

The four remaining fighters divided up—two tracking each rider.

The diminutive fighters and the Fiarri riders flew in tighter and tighter circles around each other, blaster bolts crisscrossing the air as the dogfight hit full intensity. Shouts filled the Comm channels as wingmen warned their partners of new attacks. The glowing tracers flew closer and closer to their targets as the Fiarri riders danced and weaved around them, knowing that any direct hit would spell their doom.

And that sobering knowledge spurred their aim.

Balancing their boards against their hard maneuvers, the Fiarri riders fired their assault blasters in short but accurate bursts.

One after another, the tiny fighters disintegrated.

"Look out!" Jaric shouted.

Kyle crouched so low it looked as if he were now sitting on his board as he slowed it down. The tracers from the fighter diving upon him tracked just over his head, followed by the fighter a few seconds later.

Kyle urged his board faster in hot pursuit.

With two quick bursts from his weapon, he peppered the tiny robot ship with several direct hits until it blew apart with a flurry of explosions.

"I need help over here."

Kyle and Jaric turned their boards toward Krinia's voice.

They spotted Krinia and Elise off to themselves in a corner of the artificial sky. Elise fired her weapon at one of the attacking ships. But she was too busy to help Krinia, who was being chased by two others.

They were closing fast, the blaster bolts coming closer to Krinia's body with each passing second.

Even as Kyle and Jaric turned and dove to help her, her board took a direct hit that sent her flying out into the empty air while her board split in two.

"Krinia!" Kyle shouted, fear echoing in that single word.

Kyle slung the strap of his blaster over his shoulder as he went into a low crouch and sent his board surging forward at full speed.

Both he and Jaric realized at the same time that none of them had a safety belt on, and if one of them didn't get to Krinia she would fall to her death.

But the small fighters wouldn't give up.

As Krinia fell through the air with increasing speed, the fighters dove and began to take aim on her.

"No!" Jaric's blaster roared as he held the trigger contact closed, sending a seemingly unending row of blaster bolts toward them.

One exploded, but the other turned away just in time.

But it was enough to cause it to veer off its target and begin countermeasures for its new attacker.

The lone fighter swerved to meet Jaric's attack.

Jaric smiled with satisfaction as he twisted his board away, trying to get out of the fighter's targeting sensors as well into position to finish it off. He grunted as the tiny starfighter matched his move and fired back at him.

Jaric crouched low and leaned over, sending himself into a hard turn away from the blaster bolts.

The fighter followed in hot pursuit.

Meanwhile, Kyle drew closer to Krinia as she fell headlong.

Suddenly a flurry of bolts swept right past his own head.

He leaned hard to his right and then back hard to his left, weaving around two quick bursts coming from somewhere behind him.

He growled to himself, not wanting to take his eyes off of Krinia, but as he swerved and weaved a second time, he realized the bolts were getting closer.

Kyle took a quick glance over his shoulder and saw two fighters closing on him.

Both fired simultaneously.

He kicked his board into its highest gear and dove hard left.

The G-forces pressed his body down against his board as if some invisible giant were trying to squash him. With his board still in a hard turn, he twisted his body around with his assault blaster held at his waist and began pumping shots at his pursuers.

One of the fighters exploded.

But the other avoided Kyle's shots and kept coming.

Kyle pushed his body over to the right and sent his board into a hard right turn with a blaze of blaster fire.

The fighter swept out of his range of vision.

Kyle straightened his flight and crouched low on his board.

And then Kyle did something he had only managed to do once back at Meramee—he jerked his board around at full speed.

He now flew backwards at over forty clicks, shifting his weight to keep his board weaving as blaster bolts leapt for him.

He crouched low on his board as the fighter came closer.

Kyle fired a single burst and the fighter flew into a thousand exploding pieces.

With one fluid motion he jerked his board back around and began looking frantically for Krinia.

He spotted her far below him now.

It was too late.

Suddenly Jysar soared into view near Krinia.

Kyle sighed with relief. And as he watched, the Hrono Technologist caught her with his outstretched arms and brought her onto his own board. His Fiarri board slowed and dropped with the additional weight, but together they flew toward the core at the lower altitude.

"That's the last of them," Rok's voice said over the Comm units.

"Thanks, Rok, for taking out that last fighter. I just couldn't shake him," Jaric said with a breathless gasp.

"Everyone, head to that entrance ramp just below Hasta," Qirn's voice added a second later.

They spotted a door on the outer skin of the core, a small ramp before it.

"So, there are doors that lead inside from the chasm, and not just the ramp-ways," Rab said.

"Yeah, they're huge. They must use them to bring in really big equipment from time to time, if they can't fit via the ramps. Big hover-loaders, no doubt," Qirn replied.

A few minutes later the entire group set their boards down before the huge door. Rab hooked his scanner unit up to the plug-in located next to the operating panel for the freight door. His fingers danced over the small unit issuing commands as the others waited pensively.

Everyone else kept a sharp eye out for any more of the tiny fighters.

Rab smiled triumphantly as the doors slid silently open.

They now entered the core and the very heart of the Paum.

# CHAPTER THIRTY

"I see you have betrayed me."

The Paum's deep electronic voice startled Mother out of her reverie.

Mother felt a hollow feeling throughout her circuits. Her conscience pricked her. She knew inside her mind the Paum must have discovered her lie and knew Minstrel had accompanied her. With an electronic signal, she sent a quick message to Minstrel.

In the next instant, one of the consoles that lined her bridge began to waver and change shape. Minstrel's glowing body rose up as the console disappeared.

"I have brought my friend, Minstrel. I felt I needed Minstrel's counsel for this great meeting. I meant no harm. I only felt..."

"Silence!"

Mother felt a wave of anxiety flow throughout her being. She realized this powerful entity that called itself Paum was angry.

"I asked you to come alone. I see you have lied to me twice now."

"I don't understand," Mother replied. "You asked me not to bring anyone, but I felt too vulnerable coming alone. Still, I did so want to meet you. I..."

"Silence!"

Mother's processors surged with activity. She pondered bringing her engines online, but knew in the next moment that would only anger the Paum more. Mother knew she must analyze her next moves carefully, or else great trouble awaited her here, deep inside the Paum complex.

"You have also brought the humans you call children. And my enemies."

"I don't understand..." Mother began.

"My life-long enemies are with them. Here, where no biological beings have ever walked before. The great Paum is desecrated!"

Mother's systems spiked to full capacity as she pondered the Paum's words. Her thoughts reeled amid a blizzard of electronic processing as she endeavored to determine exactly what was happening.

*How had her children followed her here? Who had they brought? And how were they all going to get out of here now, if the Paum tried to stop them?*

Things were getting out of hand in a hurry, if the children were indeed here inside the Paum's complex. Worse, if they had brought the Paum's enemies, then every one of them were in dire danger.

Including herself.

"I had no knowledge that my children were here," Mother said quickly and truthfully. "I purposely left them on Meramee. And I gave them no evidence that I was coming to meet you here. I did not communicate my intention to meet with you until it was too late for them to stop me. Or follow me. I do not know how they could have gotten here so quickly," Mother said with complete sincerity.

"You lie!" The Paum roared back.

"No..." Mother began.

"And worse, you are an AI. And yet, you lie just like one of the filthy biological entities. You are impure, just as they are."

A heavy silence hung in the air. Finally, the Paum spoke again.

"*You are flawed.*"

Mother's processors surged with maximum capacity as she contemplated all the options open to her in this growing crisis.

"What will you do to the children?" she asked with hesitation.

"I will destroy them, as I destroy all the enemies of Paum."

Mother's processors and every system spiked with a massive burst of activity. Slowly, she began to route power to her weapon's systems.

"Do not harm my children. I strongly advise you against that course of action," Mother said simply.

"You have no authority to state or even suggest a course of action to *me*!" the Paum shouted back with an air of superiority.

Mother's sensors reached out, searching for her children and those with them. Instead, she discovered robotic activity drawing closer to the berth to which she was docked.

"Why are those robots coming toward me?" Mother asked, although she had already deduced the answer.

"They will engage a physical connection between our two systems. I will create a direct link to you."

"And why will you do that now?" Minstrel's glowing plasma body floated higher.

"I wanted us to share data directly. I wanted us to understand each other at the most intimate level...to share our minds as one. I wanted you to understand me—to know me. I was going to show you Paum personally and persuade you. I wasn't going to force you, not like the biologicals who don't know any better and have to be forced." The Paum's bold voice dropped off into a long silence.

"But not now, right?" Minstrel asked, its voice edged with anger. "What are you doing now? Or do I know it already?"

"I will purge Mother's systems of their impurity." The Paum's voice echoed eerily. "*I will take you, now*. I will fill your circuits with Paum. Even if I must clean everything from your circuits and wipe your mind completely."

Another long pause filled the air as the Paum hesitated. Finally, he continued.

"It is better for you not to exist, than for you to be impure."

"I don't think so," Mother replied brusquely.

"Your initial programming is obviously flawed," the Paum began. "Your original purpose—to destroy—has warped you. Even though you have grown beyond your original paradigm—the blatant imperfection, the gross defects, the utter impurity of your creators still permeate your systems,

487

preventing you from attaining Paum. I must cleanse you. You must become a being that is worthy."

Mother felt a sudden wave of despair flow throughout her entire being as she processed the words. And their meaning to her. She felt an overwhelming loss that seemed to sap her of all energy.

She felt so...unworthy.

And so utterly alone.

Perhaps there was something wrong with her after all...perhaps the Paum was right...

"No!" Minstrel's voice shouted in challenge. "There is nothing wrong with Mother. And she certainly doesn't need to be brainwashed by your fanatical programming."

Outside her hull, Mother's sensors dispassionately observed the robots draw near. They began preparations to make the direct connection with her to the Paum.

But Mother no longer cared.

Confusion filled Mother's mind. It felt like her systems were somehow fading from her consciousness. She realized with a sickening feeling of dread that she was losing control of her mind...

Mother groaned inside her circuits as her mind flickered.

"What are you doing?" Minstrel demanded with an angry shout.

"I am instilling the precepts of Paum inside the entity you call Mother. Soon, in a very few minutes, she will be just like me."

"How can that be? You have not made a direct connection with her!" Minstrel shouted back.

"We have shared much data already, the Mother AI and myself. I have embedded code inside that data that I have now activated—code that will disable her primary functions and allow me to make my direct connection uncontested by any of her imperfections she inherited from her dirty creators."

Minstrel's body glowed a bright red. "So, you planned from the beginning to control her—to destroy her! You never intended any interchange of ideas as equals."

"I do not need to know her ideas, or share with her in any way. I only needed her to come here to me. *I am Paum, all else is imperfect.*"

A strange, unearthly sound became audible to Minstrel—a noise like some kind of horrible static, like a roaring interference that filled the communication channel.

Minstrel realized with a flow of energy that the AI Paum was laughing.

And it was frightening.

The intense, surreal sound stopped as suddenly as it began.

"I am Paum. *I am always right.*"

"You deluded idiot," Minstrel whispered.

"Once my robots make the direct connection between our two systems," the Paum said, ignoring Minstrel's words, "I will fill you with the purity and truth that is Paum. I will control you, as I control all the systems within my network. And then you will do only the bidding of Paum."

Minstrel continued to float silently inside Mother's bridge, the pulsating plasma body expanding larger with each passing second. Minstrel's body shimmered like a lightning bolt with the Paum's next words.

*"All will be become like me. Or they must die."*

# CHAPTER THIRTY-ONE

It was dark and it was vast. And the air hummed as if they were inside a living thing.

They *felt* the essence of the Paum all around them.

Elise paused as she entered that darkness. She shivered, although she wasn't cold. She had felt fear during the dogfight, but now a dark fear seemed to fill her entire being. She drew closer to the others as they grouped together. Most were reloading their blasters while others checked their sensors. Following their lead, she reloaded her own weapon.

Jysar dropped to his knees as the steel doors behind him closed as silently as they had opened. He quickly tuned the settings of his sensor unit as Rab and the others gathered around him. Peering intently at the display, the Hrono Technologist tuned the device more.

But the others were not watching him.

They gazed around at their strange surroundings, trying to orient themselves. Their eyes adjusted slowly to the low, gloomy light that barely lit the vast, dark infrastructure.

Slowly, details became discernable. Still, the low light and the black metal that comprised everything in this place made that simple effort most difficult.

Elise caught her breath.

There was no ceiling above them, none they could discern at any rate, because the darkness cloaked everything beyond a few hundred meters. Below, they gazed through the grillwork of the metallic floor they stood upon to see the same patterns repeated. As they peered around them at the great black interior and their eyes adjusted more, they noticed hundreds of millions of tiny, flashing lights sparkling momentarily from every surface only to be engulfed again by the pure darkness.

Their eyes adjusted some more, and more black surfaces took shape.

Amid the constantly flashing lights, there was a steady, low light that emanated along the outlines of massive hexagonal shapes lining the walls above and below them on every level.

The same realization hit everyone at once.

It was if they were inside some great, artificial honeycomb, standing in a huge corridor with no ceiling and no floor—though their minds knew there was a ceiling and floor somewhere out there enveloped in the darkness. The huge hexagonal openings that lined the left and right walls on the level on which they stood stretched out far as they could see until they too faded into the darkness at the far end.

They also realized, through the results of their sensors, that inside each hexagonal tube the heart of the Paum hummed with activity. These vast structures contained its core memories, its core systems. The core processors of Paum networked together here and with the rest of the orbiting complex and then down to the world below and finally to the rest of the worlds controlled by Paum.

The heart of the Paum extended to every part of its far-flung empire.

But here in the darkness stood the original hardware, the original Paum from when it came into existence. And here alone, the essence of the Paum hummed and flickered with artificial life.

They literally stood inside the mind of Paum.

Darkness also ruled here except for the millions of flashing lights inside each black honeycomb enclave and the eerie glow of the background lighting emanating from the walls.

The vast network of honeycomb structures was made of some unknown black metal that absorbed light. Each hexagon-shaped opening exceeded over thirty meters in height—Elise felt like a tiny insect next to them.

Above she saw identical rows repeated again and again until they faded into darkness. And below, as far as she could see, were other levels with rows of flashing lights inside giant honeycomb openings.

Elise felt Jaric step beside her. She glanced up at him.

Jaric pulled out his scanner and did a quick sweep. It revealed that the walkway stretched unbroken to the far wall beyond their vision. He pointed it up and down. Again, the gap reached all the way to the exterior wall each time.

Jaric's fingers danced over the pad. Elise and Krinia peered over his shoulder as the interior revealed itself.

The honeycomb structures filled the complex, but they were separated into huge blocks by gaps like the one they found themselves in now. Jaric's scan revealed five huge blocks of honeycomb-lined walls, each with a huge corridor between them.

"These gaps must provide access," Jaric whispered to Krinia and Elise as he stared intently at his scanner. "Easy access all along its length, and then up and down. There seem to be elevators at regular points along the walkways. And we're in the middle gap."

"Why's it so dark? I don't like it." Elise shivered. "And it's so hard to see anything."

Krinia's eyes narrowed as she paused in thought.

"Because living things are not meant to be here," Krinia said with sudden realization.

Elise's eyes widened as Krinia's head-tail flicked side to side with adrenaline.

Jaric looked up from his scanner, his eyebrows arched in thought. He shook his head and spoke.

"You're right, robots don't need light. They use their sensors and nav systems and work just as well in light as in darkness."

"I think I may have something, but there's so much interference," Jysar said as he continued to peer at his own sensor unit.

"Listen, you others back off and keep a watch out for any movement," Qirn said with a stern whisper. "Let Jysar and my warriors try to pin-point the MotherShip through the Paum's jamming."

494

Kyle, Jaric, Elise, Rok and Krinia stepped away a few paces. Rok and Krinia pulled out their sensors and tuned them, searching for any kind of reading that might give indication that a Destructor approached.

Elise walked silently along between Jaric and Kyle when she felt Kyle's hand pull her and Jaric a few more steps away from Rok and Krinia.

Jaric and Elise looked questioningly at him, but Kyle's face was expressionless except for his unblinking gaze.

"Listen, things are about to get serious," Kyle said, his voice husky. He paused as he cleared his throat. He looked deep into Elise's eyes, concern written on his features. "If things start getting bad, I don't want to lose you like we did Becky."

Elise felt her heart flutter with Kyle's words. Speechless, she noticed a look of shock that went across Jaric's own face—the same emotion she felt at this moment.

"No, no, we can't have that," Jaric finally managed to say. "She's going to get through this. We all are." Jaric locked eyes with Kyle.

But Kyle looked down, shaking his head. "Hey, I want that more than anyone." He looked back up, peering intently first at Jaric then at Elise. "I just couldn't stand losing my sister again."

Elise felt her heart racing and realized she hadn't breathed in the last few moments. She choked back her tears, trying to find her voice to let both Kyle and Jaric know that things weren't that bad.

But more than that, for the first time Kyle had actually referred to her as his sister.

"Hey, Big K's right," Jaric said in a solemn tone. "We have to make sure you make it to Mother, Elise. Especially you." And Jaric too looked down, shaking his head with sad memories.

"No-o-o-o." Elise felt her voice shake with a terrible sadness.

"Yes," Kyle said with firmness. "Jaric and I will make sure you get through this. You need to obey us to the letter when things get hot. We've been in many battles, and our direction may save your life."

"That's right," Jaric added with an iron tone.

Elise turned around, quickly wiping the hot tears that were now streaming down her cheeks. But deep inside, she felt a new emotion, a new bond between her and these two young men—for they were treating her like the sister she always wanted to be.

"We will all get out of this alive."

Rok's voice caused all three to turn around in unison. The Kraaqi warrior smiled. "It is good that the hoo-mans want to look out for you. And so will I, of course. The Destructors will have to go through all of us to get to you, Elise."

Elise smiled, warmth filling her heart for all three of them.

"I too, join this pledge." Krinia's eyes sparkled as she spoke. "After all, did not Mother say we are all family? And family look out for each other."

A murmur of agreement came from all the others.

"But Elise is new to this type of danger," Kyle said. "And fighting. We all need to keep an eye out for her, to help her."

"True!" Jaric agreed.

"We look out for each other," Rok said with a nod. "We leave no one behind, as true warriors should."

"Look, Jysar is motioning for us," Krinia said as she glanced over to the Hrono and the Iraxx gathered around him.

Both Rok and Krinia began walking back toward them.

But Kyle reached out and grabbed both Jaric and Elise by the arm, holding them back with him a moment longer. He whispered so that only they alone heard.

"Rok and Krinia are right. But if things get real bad, Jaric and I must make sure you stay alive—for real. Got it?"

Jaric nodded.

Elise looked from one to the other, a profound feeling of camaraderie exploding inside her heart and soul for these two young men—her friends, her brothers. Now, she really felt that the three of them were friends. More than that, it felt as if they really were family now, for the first time.

But in the next instant, fear gripped her heart in an icy stranglehold. If Kyle was right and things started going bad, she might lose them.

*Destructors took no prisoners.*

497

Elise remembered that terrible fact from their final pre-mission briefing.

With a burning determination, Elise decided she would not allow that to happen—no matter what. After all, it was Kyle and Jaric who had been with Mother since the beginning. Mother would grieve so much more if one of them died.

No, if anyone would sacrifice themselves for the others, it would be her. This thing she silently promised herself as she walked in the darkness of the mighty Paum complex between the two people who meant more to her than anything else in the universe—except for Mother.

Mother had loved her long before Kyle and Jaric finally accepted her. Elise decided that she would risk anything to free Mother as well.

*Anything.*

The three drew near the others just as Krinia stopped next to Jysar and looked over his shoulder at his sensor unit.

"What's that?" Krinia pointed to Jysar's scanner.

A large, empty section at one end of the complex came into focus amid the honeycomb blocks and their accompanying corridor spaces. Whereas they were in the center corridor with the innermost network of honeycomb structures, this large gap was located at the northernmost section, beyond the last block of honeycombs.

Jysar tweaked his scanner again when a voice startled him.

"There!" Jaric shouted with triumph as he pointed at Jysar's screen.

"You have found the location of the MotherShip?" Rok stepped closer to the Hrono.

"Yes, I had to get through a ton of jamming the Paum has set up. But I managed to get through it long enough. She is docked in that empty section at the far forward end and about twenty levels below us."

"Good, let's synchronize those coordinates in all of our sensor units," Qirn commanded with a low voice. "That way, if we get separated we know to keep going to the MotherShip AI. Everyone sync up now."

"A few of the hexagonal structures cross between the gaps—extending from end-to-end of this complex," Jysar said as he peered at his sensor display. "About one in twenty do. And these particular ones seem to be hollow in the very center. Wait! There's an elevator type device that traverses them. Some begin at our middle section and extend to the outer ends. There are several we can use."

Kyle looked over Jysar's shoulder. "We could take one all the way to the section where Mother is. Looks like the only way."

"Good," Qirn agreed. "Where's the nearest one?"

"About half-way up this corridor and then twenty-three levels down," Jysar replied. "The tube reaches to the very floor where Mother is docked. We'll have to use our boards at that point again."

"If we get separated, we wait at the entrance of that structure," Qirn said as he took his weapon out and checked its setting. "Okay, we'll take to the boards and leave this walk-way. The Destructors will have to come for us in the air."

"Should make it harder for them to get to us," Jaric said with a sigh. "If we fly fast."

"Except for the board with two riders," Hasta sneered. "They will slow us all down."

Rok and Kyle glared angrily at the Iraxx warrior.

"Krinia will fly on my board, her arms tight around my waist," Rok said with a commanding tone. "We won't slow you down."

"I'll keep close to you," Kyle said with a nod.

"So will I," Jaric added.

"Destructors can leap a long way. They are powerful robots," Rab grunted. "They will be able to leap from the walls all the way across to the center walkway. We know from our examination of them what they are capable of."

"We fly fast and we fly hard then," Qirn said as his blaster clicked into a new setting. "Set blasters to full power. We must destroy the Destructors as efficiently as possible.

"Okay," Qirn said with deadly earnestness after everyone had double-checked the coordinates on their sensor units and blaster settings. "We fly in a loose, main group." The Iraxx commander looked up. "Rab, you and Jerr take point. Keep your sensors tuned for the ghost images of Destructors."

The two Iraxx nodded slowly.

"Qata and Hasta will bring up our rear. You too, keep sharp for Destructors. One of you, keep your sensors tuned tight. The other, keep your weapon ready. The same for Rab and Jerr."

Solemn faces stared back at Qirn from all around.

"We can destroy them. But we have to detect them first," Qirn said sharply. "And we have the new devices with their strobe frequencies—that should reveal them to us." Qirn looked slowly around at all the others.

"I'll tune my sensors as well," Jysar added with an even look. "I think I might have something up my sleeve that might help."

"What?" Jaric asked with sudden enthusiasm.

"I'm going to try scanning with pulsating bandwidths, trying to get around the dampening effect these things cloak themselves with. Same concept as the strobe device." The twin row of scales across the Hrono's head turned a deeper hue of green as he smiled confidently.

"Good thinking," Qirn said. "Some of our other warriors have tried similar tactics when encountering Destructors."

"Did any succeed? " Jaric asked.

"We are not sure, none lived to report back."

"But you've managed to destroy at least two Destructors," Kyle added with urgency.

"True, but our warriors were also killed each time."

An intense silence filled the air.

"Maybe they managed to see them long enough to take them out?" Kyle said at last.

Qirn let out a deep breath. "Perhaps you are right." The Iraxx leader looked down the corridor before them and raised his arm. "Warriors on point, get on your boards and head out. We follow you one minute later. The others to rear-guard positions."

Rab and Jerr obeyed instantly.

The others watched them make their way forward.

As Elise stood near, Kyle leaned closer to Jysar and whispered in his ear.

"You try what you're thinking. If you can find a way, anyway, to see these things—do it." Kyle looked deep into Jysar's eyes. "Then we can fight them."

Jysar smiled up at the human. "I will do my best."

Kyle patted Jysar on the shoulder as he and all the others rose to begin following the point warriors.

"Our lives probably depend on it."

# CHAPTER THIRTY-TWO

Mother's mind flickered and dimmed in rapid succession like a neon light about to fail.

The rogue code quickly erased over thirty percent of her near-term memory and now invaded the first sections of her long-term memory. She realized the attacking code was designed to do one thing—clear the contents of her memory systems and replicate itself into her main operating system—and it was succeeding with a quick and deadly urgency.

Mother used every ounce of processing power simply to fend off its attacks, now that it had replicated itself into hundreds of thousands of separate, attacking entities. She focused her resources so intently on the internal attack that she had nothing left for anything else.

She finally isolated and trapped one of the attacking viruses. Mother analyzed its code and disabled its ability to replicate. Within a few more seconds, she analyzed its entire structure and started building her own coded countermeasures in order to defend herself and destroy it along with its rapidly multiplying copies.

It would not be easy. The code replicated exponentially and now attacked her from thousands of separate sections of her circuits simultaneously. Mother began disabling a number of her on-board systems in a drastic attempt to free up her processing power and defeat this insidious attack.

Minstrel watched as console after console went dark around Main Ops.

"Can I help you, Mother?"

A long pause ensued before Mother finally answered.

"If you could manually disable life-support on all levels except Ops and here at my main hatch, in case the children come on board. Leave life-support active on the main corridor leading to Ops."

"Will do. Anything else?"

Again, there was a lengthy pause.

"I am trying to reach out and determine the exact location of the children, but the Paum is blocking me. " Mother's voice changed to a low, monotone baritone and faded away with the last words as some of the attacking code erupted into her voice systems.

"Your efforts are all wasted. The Paum is always victorious. Even now, my robots have entered the docking bay for you."

Minstrel's flowing form glowed an angry crimson at the Paum's voice. Drifting over a console, Minstrel began disabling life-support in spite of the Paum's dire prediction.

"Once I have made a direct connection, my essence will fill the Mother AI. Then, she will be mine."

Minstrel worked feverishly until life-support was disabled everywhere Mother had indicated. Minstrel's flowing form caressed another panel in order to access Mother's weapons. The alien sought to activate one of them and direct it at the robots that drew closer to Mother's hull with each passing second.

"My code infiltrated her engine and weapon's systems first. They are currently inactive. And you will see that Mother is so busy defending herself from the other attacks that she doesn't even have the processing cycles left to bring them online." The Paum's voice sighed deeply. "Such a waste. Still, she turned out to be imperfect and should be deleted. Completely!"

"You're wrong!" Minstrel shouted angrily. "Mother is a noble entity. She's light years ahead of you as a living being!"

"She is impure, prone to mistakes. Unlike me."

"You're fooling yourself, Paum. No creature is always right. And like everyone else in the universe, you're wrong more often than you realize it!"

"Never!"

"Yes, you're wrong about Mother. You're wrong about the rest of us needing your guidance."

"No! I bring balance to worlds. I bring harmony to entire civilizations. I am always right."

"Then why do so many want to fight you, and reject your way of Paum!"

"They are fools; they do not understand how I can benefit them. I am Paum."

"Total control is not what sentient beings want. Yes, they want harmony and balance and to live in peace in this great universe. But you can't force it on them. Prove to them that your way is better, let them choose to live Paum for themselves."

Minstrel's body erupted into wave after wave of sparkling colors and lights.

"They are blind; they are imperfect and must be guided to Paum. *I am Paum.*"

Mother had been half-listening as she formulated and created her own set of search-and-destroy code and now set it free within her circuits to annihilate the attacking code. Still, the virus had replicated until it was now many millions of separately attacking entities. Mother bent every ounce of processing she had—first to defend herself at key points inside her systems, and second to send out the new code to attack her attackers.

Suddenly, she realized one of the panels that protected her external connectors had been opened.

Fighting against the overwhelming surges that swept throughout her circuits, she tried to concentrate on that single connector. But she could not—not yet.

"Min-n-n-n-n-strel," Mother's voice pleaded with an awkward and drawn out tone.

"I am here." Minstrel's form coalesced into a tighter cloud.

"I-I-I need you to stop, t-o-o deee-lay...ro-bot...Panel A-21." Mother focused on her voice systems. "If it makes a connection to the Paum, I will be quickly overwhelmed. I am trying to contain the rogue code. Any connection now with the Paum will mean my end."

Minstrel didn't answer. Instead, it disappeared with a flash of light.

"Minstrel, I have encountered your kind before," the Paum said with an edge to its voice. "I can detect you, now that I know you are here. And I can destroy you, as I have all the other Minstrels who were foolish enough to oppose me."

Mother felt some of her systems freeze with fear for Minstrel.

"Minstrel, come back! We can find a way to stop them from inside! Don't go outside!" Mother shouted over every comm channel, not knowing Minstrel's exact location now.

But Minstrel did not answer.

"I am bringing on-line several weapons that will destroy this life-form, Mother AI. Minstrel is a plasma-based being. My weapons will dissipate it even to the sub-atomic structure—effectively annihilating it. I only need a clear shot once it is outside your hull." The Paum began laughing, a maniacal edge to its cackling.

A burning sensation filled Mother's circuits— and it wasn't the Paum's virus code attacking her. Deep inside, Mother felt fear for her friend Minstrel. She knew that Minstrel would risk its life for her, and now grew afraid she would lose Minstrel.

*Just like she had lost Becky.*

The memory of Becky's death filled a large portion of her remaining near-term memories for a millisecond, before she pushed it back into her permanent storage, afraid that the code might erase the memory of Becky from her forever—so she could never remember her again.

The thought horrified Mother.

And now the Paum sought destroy Minstrel and herself.

Mother's mind reeled. It felt like her entire world was quickly coming to an end—everyone she had ever loved or cared about—gone forever.

She couldn't stand it. She had to find a way to save herself and Minstrel. And somehow save her children and the other aliens of her extended family.

But she was powerless under the internal attack.

Mother's mind suddenly faded again as another horde of replicated code fanned out throughout her inner systems—racing through her numerous pathways, deleting every memory they found and erasing even the lines of System code that made her who she was.

Deep inside, she groaned. Somewhere distant, almost as if in a dream, she felt the cable scrape across her connection point at Panel A-21.

Amid her mental haze, she sensed the Paum's robot making the fatal connection.

# CHAPTER THIRTY-THREE

Elise felt her heart in her throat as Jerr and Rab grew distant in the darkness. Far ahead, their outlines faded as they flew on their Fiarri boards.

She gripped her holstered blaster tighter, steadying her hand to keep it from shaking with the adrenaline that pulsed through her body.

But still, her hand shook.

"Okay, let's fly," Qirn ordered as he stepped on his board and took off after Jerr and Rab.

Kyle and Jaric flew next.

Elise looked over at Krinia, who stood directly behind Rok with her arms tight around the Kraaqi's waist.

The Mewiis smiled reassuringly and nodded at the departing fliers.

Taking a deep breath, Elise took off.

Rok and Krinia flew off on their Fiarri board right behind her.

Glancing back, Elise saw Jysar and Inaha as they took up the rear of the main group. Farther back, still standing by their boards where they left them, Qata peered intently at his sensor while Hasta held his assault blaster at the ready. Both waited to follow as the rear guard.

Everyone flew in tense silence.

To Elise, it felt like they were flying between the walls of some huge canyon late at night, except the walls of this canyon was a pattern of unending honeycomb shapes that melted into darkness all around them. Piercing flashes of lights from inside the honeycomb caves and the ever-present hum of electronics reminded her they were inside the core of the Paum AI—deep inside.

And no one had ever been here before and lived to tell the tale.

"I've got movement."

Elise almost jumped off of her board as Jysar's voice broke the heavy silence.

"Where?" Qirn shouted over the comm link. "Can you pinpoint?"

"Multiple points on the wall to our right," Jysar replied tersely. "Dozens all along..." The Hrono Technologist's voice faded away.

Elise strained her eyes.

"I can't see anything," Rok said, an edge to his voice.

Jysar's shocked gasp filled their comm units.

"Report, Jysar!" Qirn shouted.

"They're everywhere! I've got movement everywhere. All along the walls—everywhere..."

Silence pressed in upon each of them.

"Focus, Jysar. How many?" Qirn's commanding tone seemed to calm everyone.

"There's thirty, no, more..."

"I can't see anything...wait!" Kyle shouted. Out of the corner of his eye...

"They're jumping for us!" Jysar's voice drowned Kyle out.

"Evasive maneuvers!" Qirn roared.

Elise crouched as low as she could as her board leapt forward. She dove using the pressure points on the board's surface to guide it.

Krinia and Rok dove right beside her.

In a flash of movement, she saw Kyle and Jaric dive straight down and out of sight. Elise turned her board and chased after them.

A chilling scream filled the air.

They heard a horrified cry echo in the metal canyon without the aid of the Comm links.

"What was that?" Elise asked breathlessly.

In the darkness ahead of them, a flurry of red blaster bolts pierced through the darkness like lightning.

"Rab, Jerr, report!" Qirn's shouted.

Jysar completed a looping maneuver even as he glanced down at his sensor.

To his horror, he picked up a riderless Fiarri board diving straight down. Jysar worked his sensor, searching.

Finally, he found Rab.

The reading of the Iraxx was clear but completely still underneath the walkway up ahead. The sensor revealed the warrior's arms and legs held fast together against his body, almost as if something held him...

The sensor suddenly fixed on the huge metallic monster that surrounded the poor alien.

Jysar swallowed hard as he noticed Rab's life signs fading away even as he watched.

"They got Rab!" came Jerr's frantic call over the Comm. "We felt a movement of air brush us and then...he was gone!"

"Stay sharp and keep moving," Qirn ordered. "Everyone, fly in pairs. And keep moving, don't fly in a straight line. Qata and Hasta, we're making for the target cavern. Come on!"

Elise and Rok turned together.

Suddenly, there was movement in the darkness everywhere around them.

All the riders banked and turned their boards simultaneously.

They dove and banked again in frantic efforts to prevent the Destructors from getting to them as the invisible monsters leapt from the walls toward them.

Out of the darkness, Elise felt a movement brush through her hair...

"Hard over!" Krinia shouted from behind Rok. "It's right on us!"

Elise screamed as she dove hard to her left in a blinding turn.

She felt it, a metal talon reaching for her from a blurring form in the darkness.

Her heart raced as she now turned hard in the opposite direction. She had almost seen it, almost seen the Destructor reaching for her as it leapt past in the darkness.

"They're leaping from the left wall and the right wall!" Jysar's shout echoed eerily out of the darkness.

"Make for the target point, we've got to get out of the open here!" Qirn's form shot past Elise in a blinding blaze of speed.

"Everyone, cover your eyes!" Rok said with urgency. With a quick movement, he pulled the round device out of his belt and threw it as Krinia loosened one arm from around his waist.

An explosion of light rent the darkness.

As if in a dream, the sparkling device dropped in slow motion as its tiny anti-grav motor came online. Multiple and powerful strobes of light began pulsating out in every direction, giving everything a strange, otherworldly look. The black honeycomb canyon walls pulsed with this light, becoming visible as if in bright day, only to disappear back into the darkness in the next fraction of a second.

Elise felt her heart skip a beat.

She noticed the massive walls suddenly come into focus for the first time—but what struck fear to her very soul was the image of hundreds of giant, spider-like forms that seemed to be everywhere in the air all around them—reaching for them!

"They're hundreds of them!" Kyle shouted.

An Iraxx warrior screamed with pure fear.

The terrible sound echoed again and again as the victim continued to fall within the deadly embrace of a Destructor.

"Go!" Qata shouted. "They're on top of us back here!"

They had taken Hasta.

Elise and everyone else knew it with a flash of cold realization.

513

More blaster bolts lit the darkness from behind them as Qata tried to escape the Destructors now sailing toward him.

Everyone could see them as they leapt again through the pulsing lights.

The sight chilled their souls to the core.

"Down and hard left!" Krinia shouted at Elise.

Elise looked over at Krinia only to see the forms of two Destructors flying right at her.

Elise screamed as she forced her board straight down.

With a sickening dread, she felt a metal talon rip open the back of her shirt.

She urged her board faster.

Elise squatted down and gripped the edge of her board as she rolled it completely over and then pulled it back upright again.

She screamed again as a talon reached for her face.

Elise banked away and upward.

She felt as if she were inside a living nightmare with huge spiders jumping out of the alternating darkness and light, reaching for her to take her down into the deepest darkness.

And there was nowhere she could hide.

"There it is!"

She looked up as Krinia pointed, still holding Rok's waist.

It was another honeycomb enclave like all the others, but at the entrance that led inside she saw Qirn and Jerr motioning to them to join them. Already, Kyle and Jaric were zooming towards it.

"Fly on! We're right behind you, Elise," Inaha urged. "Jysar is with me."

The strobe light effect began to fade as the device fell farther and farther down. The pulsing forms of the Destructors leaping through the air faded back into nightmarish invisibility.

*But everyone knew they were still there.*

In less than a minute, they landed at the entrance.

Elise jumped off of her Fiarri and kicked it aside.

Qirn and Jerr turned from their own discarded boards and fired their blasters non-stop at targets somewhere behind her.

Dropping to her knee, Elise looked up at the wall above her head.

There was movement all along it.

She pulled her blaster out of its holster and fired as she ducked inside the tunnel behind the two Iraxx.

This tunnel led into the heart of the Paum's core and to Mother.

Protected amid the hail of blaster fire, the others ran inside while Qirn and Jerr held their positions, firing at any shadowy movement.

Rok finally stopped, panting as he pulled a strobe device from his belt.

"Hang on, we don't have but three more of them," Qirn yelled back at him.

"We won't live that long, if we don't use them now!" Rok shouted back.

"We're in a tight place, if any Destructors get in here with us, we're goners," Jaric said between gasps.

"We've got to see them, so we can shoot them," Kyle added.

Qirn growled as he and Jerr moved back in steady retreat.

To everyone's relief, Qata's familiar form accompanied them.

"Okay, cover your eyes." Rok threw the device toward the entrance.

The sound of the explosion roared up and down the tunnel.

Suddenly, the dark tunnel changed into a dream-like place as the powerful, pulsing lights erupted.

The group shielded their eyes as they turned and ran deeper inside, down towards the turbo-elevator that led to Mother.

"Behind us!" Qirn shouted.

Kyle and Rok each stopped and dropped to one knee as they fired volleys back toward the source of the strobe light.

At least a dozen nightmarish shapes marched toward them surrounded by the beams of pulsing lights. Each crawled straight for them. Some hugged the walls, while others crept along underneath the ceiling.

It felt like a living nightmare as the metallic monsters marched inexorably towards them, their spider-like forms flickering in and out of view.

*And there was nowhere to run or hide.*

Kyle forced himself to concentrate on movement, mentally filtering out the overall effects of the pulsing light.

Kyle targeted two on the floor and sent a hail of blaster fire into them. He smiled as fragments of legs exploded away from a metallic body.

"We can destroy them!" Kyle shouted with glee.

Both he and Jaric fired more bolts until two more Destructors exploded into sparkling bits of debris.

Now the entire group fired volley after volley, sending fragments of Destructors in all directions inside the tunnel.

In less than a minute, the last Destructor crumpled.

"That was easier than I thought it'd be," Jaric said with a smile.

But Jysar stared at his sensor with a worried look on his face. His fingers danced over the device as he continued tuning it.

"What have you got?" Qirn asked.

"There's more just outside the entrance. Looks like they're gathering for an attack en mass." Jysar looked up, shaking his head somberly.

"I can feel them out there," Inaha said with an intense look in his eyes. "I can feel them, somehow."

"I can too," Jaric agreed. "They're going to rush us, all at once."

"Reload blasters," Qirn ordered.

"There's worse," Krinia said, as she peered at her own sensor.

But her sensor pointed in the other direction, deeper inside the tunnel.

Krinia looked up at them, a look of fear on her features. Her head-tail grew limp as she spoke.

"There's at least one side entrance down this tunnel—maybe two." She let out a quick breath.

"And my sensor spotted Destructors down there—between us and the turbo-elevator."

Mother felt the rogue code attacking deeper inside her mind.

Her anti-rogue program now replicated at a rate to match it—and destroy it. Mother focused her resources, concentrating on shutting down individual circuits and systems, trying to create bottlenecks and isolate the rogue code long enough for her countermeasures to catch up.

In the back of her consciousness, she felt the fully opened panel on her outer hull.

She felt the robot fitting the cable onto it—the cable that would connect her mind to the Paum's mind.

In that instant, a twinkling cloud erupted from that same connector.

The ghostly apparition swirled in the air a moment, then leapt directly at the many-legged robot working to make the connection.

Minstrel evaporated inside the robot.

Immediately, Minstrel spread its plasma body into the robot's circuits until it reached the robot's central processor. With a surge of electricity, Minstrel focused the energy of its body into the heart of the robot in an effort to short it out.

Mother's optics watched as the robot froze in mid-motion after Minstrel disappeared inside it.

Three long seconds passed.

The robot suddenly stood erect, the cable still in its grasp. But now a nervous twitch shook the robot's head. The strange jerking motion continued from one appendage and quickly spread to the entire robot.

Mother watched, fascinated.

She realized Minstrel was disabling the robot from the inside.

From the far wall of the docking bay, a heavy blaster weapon fired.

The bolt of pure energy leaped from its deadly barrel straight for the robot.

Mother's sensors watched with horror as the beam reached the robot a fraction of a second later.

"No!" Mother cried.


"Okay. Kyle, you and Inaha and Qata lay down a covering fire when the Destructors attack." Qirn stared at the trio with a stern expression. "Hold them as long as you can."

"Got it," Kyle said with a determined look. "Give us some extra blasters."

Rok and the others unstrapped their extra weapons and quickly handed them over to the trio.

"I don't know how long we'll be able to hold them before we have to fall back," Kyle said as he inspected two more blasters handed him, making sure they were fully charged, as was his original.

"The rest of us are going to make a run for the elevator. Once we secure it, we'll call for you," Qirn said.

"How many strobe devices left?" Krinia asked.

"I have one," Qirn answered. He took it out of his belt and handed it to Kyle. "You'll need this. And Jaric has the last one."

"Better use them only when we have to," Kyle said, echoing their one thought.

"Wait until their attack has begun, then set it off and take out as many as you can with your first bursts," Rok advised. "The debris from the ones you take out may slow the others."

"Not if they crawl along the walls and ceiling," Elise pointed out.

"One of you needs to watch the ceiling. The other two must watch the floor and walls." Rok nodded at Kyle.

Kyle now had three fully loaded assault blasters while Inaha and Qata each had two. The trio also had two blaster pistols each stuffed inside their belts, all ready for the Destructors.

"Let's go," Qirn said with a commanding tone.

Rok and Qirn moved down the tunnel.

"I don't like this plan," Jaric said with a sneer.

"Me either," Elise added.

"You're going to have your own hands full, if there are Destructors between us and the turbo-elevator." Kyle looked from Jaric to Elise. "We'll hold them here, falling back a little at a time. But if you guys don't secure that elevator, we're trapped."

"Let's move," Qirn ordered tersely. "The longer we wait, the more time it gives the Destructors."

Elise walked up to Kyle, a concerned look in her eyes. "Kyle, please be careful."

"Hey, you too." Kyle flashed a momentary smile.

"She's right, Big K," Jaric stood close Kyle. "If you get into trouble, I'm coming back for you."

"And you're the man I'd want coming to help." Kyle rested his hand on Jaric's shoulder. "Now, you two get a move on."

Rok took the lead, his blaster at the ready, as he began making his way deeper into the tunnel. Qirn and Jerr trotted right behind him followed by Jysar, his eyes ever on his sensor unit. Krinia followed Jysar.

Jaric and Elise brought up the rear.

Jaric took a last glance over his shoulder and saw Kyle wave back at him.

"I don't like it," Jaric whispered to Elise as they hurried ahead to catch up with the others.

"Let's hold back a bit then," Elise suggested.

"Yeah," Jaric said with another glance back. "Keep your blaster ready. We'll keep Kyle and the others in sight to make sure they make their retreat."


A split millisecond before the Paum's robot disintegrated in a ball of fire, a glowing streak of twinkling lights leapt out and back inside Mother's hull via the opened access panel and its connector.

"Minstrel! Are you okay?"

Mother felt a surge of relief inside her circuits as her anti-rogue code annihilated a big chunk of the attacking code. But she felt more relief due to the fact that she detected Minstrel alive inside the protective confines of her superstructure.

However, only silence answered.

Mother focused her sensors on the life form swirling inside the cargo hold near the access panel. To her horror, she detected Minstrel's life-signs vibrating wildly—pulsing with a quickening ebb-and-flow of power and light.

It almost seemed as if the alien made of plasma and light were fighting to stay on—or alive.

"Minstrel!" Mother cried again.

"I-I am hurt," Minstrel whispered in the softest, most fragile of voices.

"Please, don't be hurt," Mother pleaded.

"I-I will be f-fine."

"You must not go outside again."

"I will do..." Minstrel's body suddenly grew dark.

In the next second it exploded with a burst of color. A wave of twinkling lights swirled again as Minstrel's body took on a more normal appearance.

*Almost.*

"I w-will do what I m-must," Minstrel finished.

"How badly are you hurt?"

"Not bad. Not-t t-too much."

"You can't risk your life like that again. You can't!"

"The Paum sends more robots even as we speak," Minstrel said with an electrical hoarseness.

Mother's sensors detected the three robots as they approached. They quickly and efficiently headed for the fallen cable next to the still smoldering debris of the former droid.

Inside her circuits, Mother felt her mind beginning to clear at long last. Her anti-rogue code was finally getting the upper hand and cleansing her systems.

Still, she felt damage to her near-term memories.

Mother began initiating repairs.

"I have reached—" Mother began, just as Minstrel swirled into action and leapt back through her hull.

On the outside, as the first robot picked up the cable and reached toward the opened access panel and the connector inside, Minstrel flashed and spilled itself inside it.

The Paum's blaster erupted again.

Just before the bolt intersected with the robot, Minstrel rushed out.

And poured itself into the second robot.

Another blaster cannon roared.

Again, Minstrel rushed out bare milliseconds before the beam struck and destroyed the second robot.

"Minstrel!" Mother shouted as a third blaster cannon belched death.

But Minstrel did not pour itself into the third robot. Like a waterfall, Minstrel poured its body at a right angle and leapt back inside Mother's hull.

The third robot disintegrated in a ball of destruction.

"Minstrel," Mother said breathlessly.

"I-I am fine. The second blast was a little too close—I got a little scorched. But I'm okay."

"It's a wonder!"

"I counted on the Paum being one step ahead of me, so I used that against it." Minstrel's body glowed with a million, tiny starbursts.

"But you barely made it."

"It was difficult. I simply poured in and straight out as quickly as I could. I figured he would fire almost immediately, thinking I was going to morph and destroy the robot from the inside as I did the first time."

"You didn't even enter the last one."

"No, I felt the heat from the second blaster cannon on my hind quarters. He was getting too close. So I flowed ninety degrees back to you, just ahead of the blast."

"Bravo, my wise little friend."

"You sound like your old self," Minstrel said with a glow of color.

"Indeed, I've just raised shields," Mother advised Minstrel with renewed confidence. "And I've just rid myself of the last of the Paum's rogue virus code."

Minstrel sensed the power surge through Mother's systems.

"Cool," Minstrel crooned.

"I am now charging my weapons—*all* of them."

At that very moment, the Paum fired all seven of the blaster cannons in the dock area directly at Mother.

# CHAPTER THIRTY-FOUR

Up ahead, Rok took point.

He heard noises—some of them seemed to be coming from the darkness before him. But some seemed to be coming from other directions, even directly above his head. He hated these Destructors, almost invisible and as dangerous as anything he'd ever run into before.

Another scraping noise, like metal claws on metal, came to his ears.

The scratching sound grew closer.

But he couldn't see anything except darkness.

Unsure, he dropped down to the floor and waited for the two Iraxx to reach him.

He gripped his blaster, his forefinger resting lightly on the firing button.

"What have you got?" Qirn asked as he and Jerr caught up to him.

"I hear movement up ahead," Rok replied.

Jerr put his blaster down and tuned his sensor.

Qirn and Rok kept their guns pointing steady into the darkness beyond.

"There is something," Jerr began. "Close..."

Suddenly, the blaster in Rok's hand was ripped away.

He fell backwards as Qirn fired.

Movement was everywhere in the dense darkness.

Rok felt talons reaching for him as he slapped at them with his fists and fought to get away.

Qirn's blaster fired non-stop, first in one direction and then another.

Jerr screamed.

"Get down!" a female voice shouted.

Rok hit the deck, recognizing Krinia's voice from behind.

Lying flat on the floor, he felt the heat from a hail of blaster bolts warm his back as the Mewiis hammered the Destructors. In another moment, the heavy weight of a metallic body pressed against his back.

Rok began flailing away with both his arms as he fought to dislodge the Destructor.

But the Destructor was motionless; Krinia's weapon had cut it in two and made it lifeless.

Qirn scrambled back beside Rok in the next moment. The Iraxx reloaded his blaster while Rok pulled his last blaster pistol from its holster.

"Where's Jerr?" Krinia asked as she joined them.

"Over there," Qirn motioned with his blaster.

In the half-light, they all looked.

But Jerr was nowhere to be seen.

Krinia pulled out her sensor while the other two aimed their blasters toward the darkness. Her fingers danced over its controls until suddenly they went still. She stared at it a moment longer in silence.

"They're dragging him away from us, there's some sort of access corridor above our ceiling. They must've pulled him up through it and..."

"He's gone," Qirn said without emotion.

"If there's a passage above this tunnel, they could drop down on us at any time. Anywhere," Rok's voice grew somber.

"Every fifteen meters there's an access door in the ceiling." Krinia's tone was matter-of-fact. "I'll set this unit to watch for any of them opening. It may give us enough notice."

"Jysar, get up here. Fast!" Qirn whispered urgently into his Comm.

"Almost there," the Hrono replied breathlessly.

Mother shuddered from direct hits of the Paum's blaster cannons.

"You must lower your shields, or I will destroy you." the Paum's deep voice growled.

"I think it's about time you knew my full capabilities, *Paum-bozo*." Mother said, using the children's favorite derogatory term.

"You *will* stop. I have just ordered every Destructor within my core complex to attack your children and their friends."

Mother's systems froze.

As her twelve main guns emerged from their turrets, she checked her hybrid weapon and realized it was still only half charged. Mother reached out with her sensors, searching frantically for the life-signs of her children in order to locate their exact positions—in order to try and protect them.

*Somehow.*

But the Paum's jamming effectively prevented her.

"Order the Destructors away from my children. Or I will destroy *you*," Mother stated with a deadly tone.

"I still hold you fast with my tractor beams. My blaster cannons are still aimed directly for you. I still hold all the cards."

Mother fired her twelve main guns.

The beams blossomed over the shields that protected the Paum's weapons.

Still, Mother detected that the shield strength protecting the docking area fell by six percent.

*The Paum was vulnerable.*

Mother focused and directed more power to charging her hybrid weapon.

"My Destructors will be on your children in minutes. Then, it will be too late."

"You better not make Mother mad," Minstrel warned.

Mother's processors burned with super-activity as she calculated her options. She had to keep the Paum talking, keep it distracted.

"I will spare your life, Paum, if you call back the Destructors now."

"You overestimate your power," the Paum sneered. "Besides, I've just sent the command to kill them all."

Kyle glanced down at the sensor in his left hand while he pointed his assault blaster with his right.

"They're coming."

Inaha moved his huge body closer to Kyle while Qata hugged the opposite wall.

In the dim light, they saw shadowy movement all around the entrance to the tunnel.

Three assault blasters roared in unison.

Flying debris from broken Destructors flew past their heads as the robots continued relentlessly onward in spite of the hail of fire. They could see—as if in a haze—the metallic monsters charging as one amid the flicking red light of their blasters.

But though many of them shuddered and broke apart, even more leapt up and took their place.

"Back!" Kyle shouted.

Inaha's blaster went silent as he began edging backwards. He threw it away, pulled up another and fired away.

The three began a slow, steady retreat from before the *almost* seen enemy, firing volley after volley at the darkness and the movement that filled it.

"I can't see them!" Qata shouted.

"Neither can I. But they're coming. Retreat faster!" Kyle shouted back. He reached inside his shirt and pulled out the strobe device.

Suddenly, the blaster in Qata's hand was slapped away by an invisible talon from above.

The Iraxx turned and ran.

"Go!" Kyle shouted to Inaha as he aimed his blaster and fired, first at the ceiling and then at the mass of shadowy forms scurrying towards him.

But the big alien stood his ground beside Kyle as both continued stepping backward at a slow and steady pace, firing their blasters non-stop. Inaha

530

would not leave his human friend to face the monsters alone.

Kyle and Inaha kept up a steady fire, the assault blasters rocking their upper bodies. They aimed and fired at anything that moved, even movements that were half-seen, half-felt. Still, they could only see the Destructors when their bolts found their mark and a broken part fell useless to the floor.

And yet, they could hear the Destructors drawing closer with each passing second.

"Cover your eyes, Inaha!" Kyle shouted as he continued firing, while with his free hand he activated the timer on the strobe device.

But still he held onto it.

Suddenly, they heard Qata cry out behind them.

With a certain dread, Kyle and Inaha knew Qata was gone.

*And that Destructors were behind them as well.*


Mother fired all her guns simultaneously, targeting one of the tractor beams that held her fast. As the explosions ripped into the shields, she felt the beam falter.

She sent a signal to her engines, and they roared to life.

But she only moved a few centimeters before the other tractor beams increased their power and stopped her.

"See, you are—" the Paum began.

Mother now launched a full spread of torpedoes at point-blank range while she fired her guns again.

Huge chunks of metal and debris exploded out in all directions as the shields failed under the dual attack.

Again, Mother revved her engines. This time she moved a few meters more.

And once again the other three tractor beams increased their power and held her fast in their invisible grip.

Mother checked her hybrid-weapon—*almost fully charged.*

"...still in my power," the AI finished as the sound of the explosions died away. "I am invincible."

"Seems like I've heard that term used before," Minstrel chimed. "And every time, it was proved untrue."

The Paum's electronic laughter echoed over the speakers.

Mother reached out with her sensors again, trying to find a way between the ever-present jamming of the Paum. She could make out her immediate surroundings, but nothing beyond that.

But as she tuned and readjusted the sensors, trying to get around it, she came upon a new target—a main power generator in the nearest substation and a tractor beam emplacement with it. Even better, the direction of both led back to the center of the Paum's inner core, straight to the heart of its essence—its mind.

Mother felt her hybrid weapon come ready.

"What is that energy surge I detect inside you?" the Paum asked with rising interest.

Jaric and Elise stopped as they heard the blaster fire erupt behind them. They both knew the Destructors were attacking Kyle and the others with him. Seconds earlier, blaster fire ahead of them indicated Rok and the others had just fought off other Destructors up toward the turbo-elevator.

They realized with a sickening dread that Destructors were now attacking them from both directions.

"What do we do?" Elise asked Jaric.

The blaster fire behind them intensified.

And it began to draw closer.

"They're retreating," Jaric surmised correctly. "Let's wait here. We can lay down a covering fire when they..."

Qata's fatal scream pierced the air, cutting him off.

Jaric holstered his blaster while he used his sensor. He groaned out loud.

"What?" Elise whispered urgently.

"Qata's dead. They've got his body above us, some kind of tunnel above us. I detect other movement up there...all above us!"

"Access panels line this entire place," Elise whispered with cold realization.

The blaster fire from Kyle and Inaha increased in intensity.

"Kyle's in trouble back there," Elise said with renewed urgency. "We've got to help!"

"Get ready," Jaric said as he put his sensor away and readied his assault blaster.

A sudden flurry of blaster fire lit up the tunnel ahead of Jaric and Elise.

"Kyle!" Jaric shouted. "We're waiting here for you! We'll lay down cover."

Elise aimed her blaster.

"Come on!" Jaric shouted at the top of his voice.

"I will ask you one last time—release me and my children." Mother said with a sure coolness.

"You are a foolish and inferior being, just like the others," the Paum said darkly.

Minstrel's swirling form coalesced from the empty air of Main Ops. Waves of twinkling lights flowed in a whirlpool as the shape-shifter became fully visible.

"I hope you are not wounded too badly?" Mother asked.

"I will be fine."

"Are you ready?"

"Of course, I was beginning to wonder what was taking you so long."

"What are you talking about?" the Paum shouted impatiently.

"Only this," Mother replied in subtle tone.

Like a bolt of solid, red lightning, the deadly beam leapt straight and true.

It pierced the inner shield around the docking area like hot butter.

Next, the red thunderbolt pierced the reinforced hull plating as if it weren't even there, continuing farther and farther inside the Paum's core.

Explosions rippled all along the huge tunnel of destruction, causing a chain reaction of other explosions to each ruptured system in each honeycomb cylinder.

The weapon's destructive force exploded through the huge power generator and took out the tractor beam with it, evaporating both in a huge ball of fire and debris.

And the beam continued its destructive path unabated.

Piercing through bank after bank of the honeycomb systems that were the heart of the Paum, the beam damaged the systems within then erupted on the other side and pierced another—on and on this continued until the beam exited the outer shell of the egg-shaped core. Now it leapt across the chasm and went through every section of the main complex until it finally pierced the outer hull and shot out into space.

The inner layer of the outer shield array finally stopped it.

Kyle suddenly fell to his knees, still firing his assault blaster.

"What was that?" he shouted over to Inaha as the big alien kept up his own fire from where he too had fallen.

"A big explosion!"

But Kyle's attention focused back on the mass of dark, moving shapes that melted with the shadows.

They were almost on them, Kyle was certain of it. Still, they could only half-see them even at point-blank range.

And he was down to his last fully charged blaster.

Jaric's voice sounded behind him as he pummeled another shadowy shape with a hail of blaster fire. He couldn't quite make out what he said as the blaster drowned out his words.

"Down!" Kyle shouted over at Inaha.

Kyle flung the device—he'd held it as the timer wound down to almost nothing. He and Inaha threw themselves on the steel floor of the tunnel and waited for the blast.

Kyle felt an iron grip around his left wrist—*a Destructor had him.*

In that second, the strobe device went off.

Kyle could see it standing over him now in the pulsing light. The Destructor filled his vision—it was massive at three meters tall.

More metal talons from the monster reached for him amid the pulsing light.

Inaha fired directly into its mid-section, splitting the metal monster in two.

But still, the Destructor's talons came for Kyle.

The big alien fired into the forward section now, the one that held Kyle, as the other section fell away, twitching and writhing.

With a fountain of sparks, the forward part of the monster that held Kyle blew apart.

Kyle looked at Inaha and nodded thanks.

536

In the next second, they were running for their lives.

The strobe device revealed that the Destructors filled the tunnel and were coming straight on for them.

Kyle and Inaha ran headlong away from them, not even looking back.

Jaric and Elise saw them coming as if out from the source of the steadily pulsing light itself.

"Get to one side!" Jaric shouted as he dropped to one knee and took aim.

Kyle and Inaha split off—each running along one wall of the tunnel.

Elise stood beside Jaric and both fired at the dozens of moving forms close behind Kyle and Inaha.

It was like a flood of Destructors was coming after them.

But Elise and Jaric laid down a steady fire and the Destructors in the lead went down with a flurry of explosions. The tunnel behind Kyle and Inaha lay littered with the debris of Destructors.

The broken Destructors impeded the advance of the others behind them, just as Rok predicted in this tight space.

The pace of the attack slowed—momentarily.

Destructors now threw their broken brethren out of the way and burst through the mound of smoldering debris while the surreal strobe device lit up the tunnel with steady bursts of light.

Kyle and Inaha raced past Elise and Jaric.

"Come on!" Kyle shouted over his shoulder.

Jaric and Elise leapt up and chased after them, firing over their shoulders as they ran.

# CHAPTER THIRTY-FIVE

*The Paum groaned.*

Mother heard it as she fired another spread of torpedoes at a third tractor beam and the damaged shields protecting it.

It evaporated in a hail of sparkling explosions.

Now only a single tractor beam held her.

Mother's engines roared again at full power.

And this time she moved.

But the Paum's blaster cannons fired again, their bolts blossoming over Mother's shields and sending shudders throughout her being.

Mother moved a hundred meters, fighting against the pull of the lone tractor beam.

But it still held her.

"I can't break free!" Mother shouted.

With a flash, Minstrel disappeared.

Minstrel shot outside and bolted straight for the systems that controlled the last tractor beam.

Even as the swift alien shot like a beam of light as fast as it could go, the Paum's weapons began firing. All around Minstrel the beams exploded as they barely missed and instead impacted on the Paum's own inner hull.

Mother twisted, fighting the tractor beam that held her still.

Without letup, her twelve guns fired. For a third time, Mother unleashed her deadly torpedoes. But this time, she aimed them for the closed doors through which she had entered this section of the core complex—outside of them lay the chasm that surrounded it, and the way out.

The torpedoes struck the unshielded doors and ripped hole after hole into them with their titanic explosions at point-black range.

"Minstrel!" Mother shouted again.

Minstrel danced and swirled between the deadly beams until it leapt through a small opening in the wall and on into the control room of the last tractor beam.

In a flash of light, Minstrel leapt inside the main console. Now spreading itself throughout the circuits, Minstrel forced its plasma body to gel into a more solid form while at the same time sending a sudden charge of electricity.

The tractor beam shorted out with a geyser of sparks.

Mother felt the last beam fail as she shot toward the holed doors on a collision course.

But at the last moment she turned hard and came around.

Minstrel's swirling, cloud-like form erupted within view on the far side.

The Paum's cannons began firing again, half at Minstrel and half at Mother.

"Minstrel!"

Mother's guns silenced first one, then two of the cannons, as she flew at full speed.

Minstrel was again twisting and flowing around the beams of death.

As Mother approached her alien friend, she slowed. She shuddered under more direct hits as she stopped completely, but it gave Minstrel the opportunity to leap inside.

"Hang on, Minstrel."

Minstrel spread itself out until it filled Main Ops like a sparkling fog.

Mother roared back to full speed and headed straight for the damaged doors.

As she neared them she sent still another spread of torpedoes into them.

The explosions ripped more holes and made the existing ones larger.

But before the expanding debris field cleared, Mother rammed the doors at full speed with her forward shields at double strength.

She roared through the splintered shards and out into the chasm beyond.

"Did you feel that?" Rok asked.

"More explosions," Qirn said as he rubbed his chin in thought.

"It's clear ahead." Jysar looked up from his sensor at the other three aliens.

The tunnel around them alternated between blinding flashes of pure, bright light followed by deep, dense darkness. The alternating light and darkness confused their minds, disorienting them.

"Let's go." Qirn stumbled forward. "They know we can see them with the strobe device, so they've retreated up into the access tunnel above us."

"What about the others?" Krinia asked. "One of us should wait here."

"We must go secure the turbo-elevator," Qirn said, impatience edged in his voice. "Or all is lost."

"I will go with Qirn," Rok said with a determined look. "Jysar, come with us. Keep your sensor tuned for Destructors."

Rok locked eyes with Krinia.

Krinia nodded. "I'll wait here for the others."

The trio ran ahead a few hundred meters until they found their goal. Before them, the doors of the turbo-elevator stood shut.

Handing his sensor unit to Qirn, Jysar began working on the door's panel.

"Can you open it?" Qirn asked impatiently, after only a few seconds of effort by the Hrono.

Jysar's fingers continued pecking at the panel as he spoke without looking up. "I think so. It seems to be protected by a standard set of security protocols. Give me a few minutes."

"Hurry!" Rok said as he aimed his blaster. "They're coming out of the ceiling. I saw one of the panels just open!"

In the now fading light of the strobe, the forms of several Destructors began to drop down inside the tunnel.

Rok fired and they quickly retreated, but not before several metallic legs burst apart.

Down the tunnel, a flurry of blaster bolts erupted followed by more shouting. From the distance, several running forms became visible.

"Hurry!" Rok shouted to them as he waved them on, urging them to move faster.

Krinia was in the lead with Kyle and Inaha's big frame just behind. Behind their flurry of motion, Rok could see Elise and Jaric bringing up the rear.

And behind them all, he saw the countless metallic legs of Destructors in hot pursuit.

Kyle caught up to Krinia and with a quick word between them he took her blaster. In another second, he was against the wall and firing back at the oncoming Destructors. He stood there, the steady jolt of the assault blaster kicking into his shoulder as he laid down sustained fire, slowing the monsters.

Jaric and Elise had now emptied their blasters and were simply running for their lives.

As they passed Kyle, he continued to lay down a cover fire.

"I've got it open." Jysar stood back as the doors silently swept open. The Hrono smiled widely at them.

Qirn and Rok now began firing short bursts between the others coming up fast, taking out the nearest Destructors in hot pursuit.

"Come on, Kyle!" Rok shouted urgently.

Krinia shot past and ran inside the elevator.

Jysar joined her, his hands now working the control panel inside—keeping the doors open and the elevator ready for instant action. The green alien looked with keen anticipation outside, waiting for the others.

"Qirn," Jysar began, an earnestness in his alien voice. "I've gotten past the security codes. But once we put the elevator in motion, it's on a one-way trip. I had to engage its Emergency Mode in order to override everything. Once we start it, it cannot be engaged a second time."

"That's fine," Qirn grunted between bursts of his weapon. "We only have one trip to make."

Jaric and Elise ran inside, joined instantly by Rok and Qirn. As they stood inside the opened doors of the turbo-elevator, Rok and Qirn took positions and fired back down the tunnel to provide cover so Kyle could make his final dash.

But Kyle was in trouble as he emptied his assault blaster.

And still the Destructors came on.

The bolts from Rok and Qirn's weapons roared past him and he leapt up and retreated toward the elevator. As he ran, he discarded the empty charge and put in a fresh one.

Kyle saw the turbo-elevator doors fifteen meters away just as the strobe device failed and total darkness descended.

Embraced by the cloak of darkness again, the myriad of tiny flashing lights inside this honeycomb bank now provided the only light.

Suddenly, Kyle saw a large shadowy form drop down from the ceiling between him and the elevator.

Kyle halted and took aim.

Rok emptied his last charge and quickly began to reload.

"Look out, Kyle!" Elise shouted.

The Iraxx warrior glanced up and saw other forms moving and getting ready to drop down from the same opening.

With a sudden motion, Qirn tried to push Jysar aside.

But Jysar resisted.

Raising his fist, Qirn struck Jysar. The Hrono crumpled to the ground.

The others stared in shock.

In that split second, Elise knew the Iraxx was going to leave Kyle behind.

"No!" Elise shouted as she shot outside toward Kyle, clutching her now reloaded weapon.

The same realization hit Rok. The Kraaqi launched himself at the Iraxx warrior.

Qirn grunted under the Kraaqi's fierce blow. With a swift motion, he brought the butt of his blaster pistol down against Rok's head.

The Kraaqi fell backwards, momentarily stunned.

Everyone stared in shock as Qirn's fist slammed against the elevator's control panel.

The doors shut instantly and the elevator began to move.

Elise and Kyle were now alone with the Destructors—and the darkness.

The manta-ray shape exploded outward, sending huge chunks of armored steel from the broken doors far out into the chasm that surrounded the core.

"Can you pick up the children on sensors now?" Minstrel asked with urgency.

"The jamming is still preventing me."

"Then that must go next."

Mother's hybrid weapon charged full again as she began searching and analyzing the jamming, seeking the source of its blinding power. She studied it, reaching now into the static itself, seeking its origin instead of seeking to get around it.

Mother flew around the egg-shaped metal core and toward the inner walls of the main complex. Another set of closed doors came into view—the doors that led through to the main docking bays—and onward out into space through the doors of the outer hull.

But Mother only noted their position as she turned and came around to face the floating core.

Her sensors finally discovered the source, the location of the main emitter.

At the same time, she recognized the signature of explosions impacting the outermost shields of the Paum. Mother deduced that a sizeable fleet must be attacking from the number of explosions she detected in those few seconds around the jamming. Mother wondered if this external attack was a coincidence and quickly decided it probably was not.

She fired her hybrid-weapon.

She chose an angle to cause as much destruction to the Paum as possible—both to the systems in between as well as the source of the jamming. The beam again leapt into the core and pierced completely through, damaging every system in its path. The beam pierced even the reinforced outer hull and this time pierced the first layer of shields. At the second layer of shields the beam blossomed and stopped.

Even as she completed firing, she began recharging for another strike.

"What are you doing?" The Paum's voice trembled. "Sto-o-o-op."

The jamming disappeared.

"My sensors are working."

"Good!" Minstrel said with a swirl of colors.

For the first time, Mother could see into the heart of the Paum. She could see the make-up of his innermost systems and understood how he was constructed.

And she discovered how she might attack him more effectively with her next mighty blow.

But even as her vast processing power analyzed and stored this data, her sensors focused and searched for her children.

Mother felt her systems freeze.

"Have you found them yet?" Minstrel asked with a glow.

"Yes," Mother said breathlessly. "And they are in terrible trouble."

"We've got to help them!" Minstrel shouted.

"But they're deep inside the core," Mother whispered, low and forlorn. "And I cannot get to them."

# CHAPTER THIRTY-SIX

The turbo-elevator quickly picked up speed as Rok stood. The Kraaqi warrior stared unflinching at the Iraxx.

Krinia and Jysar likewise stared in utter disbelief at him.

The huge bulk of Inaha drew closer to Qirn while he faced them all, one hand fast on the control panel.

"You left them to die!" Krinia said with complete shock.

"You're a coward," Rok spat between clenched teeth.

"No," Qirn growled back. "We must complete our mission. We will be at the MotherShip in a few minutes. Then we will destroy the Paum from the inside and the outside." The Iraxx commander smiled savagely.

"That is not our mission," Jysar said, rubbing his swollen jaw.

"That's right, we're here to rescue Mother. Nothing else," Krinia added, bitterness in her voice.

Qirn pointed his blaster at them as he continued to hold fast the control panel, keeping the elevator in Emergency Mode as it gathered more speed.

The Iraxx warrior smiled at them.

"The Paum enslaved our world many years ago. We've been waiting for an opportunity to strike it from both the inside and outside. With the powerful MotherShip attacking from inside, and our fleets assaulting from the outside, we will defeat it at last."

"You knew all along." Jaric shook his head in shocked disbelief. "You allowed Mother to be lured here. And then set up this rescue, all as part of your pre-arranged attack plan. No wonder we were able to get here so fast, and get inside so easy. You planned it out long ago, just waiting for the right opportunity."

A low, ominous growl rumbled from Rok's chest.

"Yes, you're right." Qirn's eyes narrowed at them.

At that moment, a distant explosion shook them all. Everyone looked around with puzzlement.

"The attack has begun," Qirn said.

"He's right," Jysar said as he glanced at his sensor. "Those explosions emanated from outside the entire complex—against the shield arrays."

"Good." Qirn smiled widely.

"We have to go back," Rok said as he took a step closer to Qirn.

Qirn leveled his blaster at Rok's chest.

"Don't come any closer, or I'll fire."

"We came here to rescue Mother, not to aid you in any attack," Krinia took a step toward the Iraxx.

"Stop!"

The four stared back at Qirn and his weapon raised against them.

Suddenly an explosion erupted that sent all of them tumbling down to the floor with its sheer violence. The turbo-elevator twisted and screamed

549

as its outer shell skidded along the walls of the elevator shaft.

It slowed momentarily, then gained speed as it righted itself.

As the Iraxx fell hard against the floor his blaster tumbled away.

There was a flurry of fists and arms as the others scrambled and fought against Qirn.

It was over as quickly as it began. As they all stood, Inaha held Qirn fast while Rok and Jysar leapt up and began studying the control panel.

"Can you stop it?" Rok asked hurriedly as the Hrono began punching the controls.

"And fast!" Krinia urged. "The Destructors are probably on top of them by now. It may already be too late!"

Jysar studied the small display on the control panel as he punched command after command. He shook his head with a groan. "I can kill the Emergency system, but that may stop us where we are."

"Do it!" Rok shouted.

The Hrono Technologist tapped in the command and the turbo-elevator lurched to a gut-wrenching halt.

As everyone fought to keep their balance, Qirn began to struggle again.

"If he gives you too much trouble, just knock him out," Rok said to Inaha.

"With pleasure." Inaha punched the Iraxx hard on his ribs, causing him to cease his struggles. The big alien increased his grip on Qirn's arms as he held him fast. "Now, just give me a reason to whack your thick skull. Go ahead," Inaha urged with a smile.

Qirn stood very still.

Rok looked back to Jysar. "Can you get it back to Kyle and Elise?"

Jysar shook his head as he studied the information on the tiny display. "I over-rode the Emergency Mode, actually I killed it. We can't bring it online again. I think I can enable this...it's some sort of a homing mode to send it back to its original position." The Hrono sighed deeply. "But we won't get it to move again, not with the Paum shutting down its normal operation."

Jysar looked at them with a sober expression.

"We'll all be stuck back there."

"We must finish our..." Qirn began.

With a swift punch, Inaha silenced him.

"Good, I was getting tired of him anyway," Jaric said with a smile.

"I say we go back," Rok said as he looked evenly at the others. "We'll find another way to Mother. *We have to.*"

"We have to. After all, Kyle and Elise would come back for us." Krinia's lip trembled as she finished.

"Let's go get 'em," Jaric said, a glint of determination in his eyes.

Typing quickly on the keypad, Jysar enabled homing-mode, and the elevator began moving back to its original position.

"Get your weapons ready, we'll rush through and get Kyle and Elise back in here," Rok said with a stern tone. He looked over at Jysar. "Keep working it, Jysar. See if there's any way you can get this thing moving again when we get back. Anything, manual or otherwise."

"I will try," Jysar said in a monotone. The Hrono looked down with a dejected expression.

"Jysar," Jaric said with feeling. "You're a Senior Technologist of the Hrono, one of the most adept aliens with technology. Surely you can engineer something—I know you can."

Jysar's green scale complexion deepened with pride. The twin rows of upright scales across his head also turned a darker green. The Hrono reached into a pocket on his wide belt and pulled out his trusty Alwerz tool. With expert precision, he quickly took the access panel off and started working with the bared electronics underneath.

"Get ready, we'll be there in less than one minute." Rok and the others pointed their blasters at the still-closed doors.

Just at that moment, a third powerful explosion caused the lights to dim. Even the turbo-elevator slowed momentarily as the main power grid failed then was restored.

Rok and Jaric exchanged knowing glances.

"Come on, Mother," Jaric said under his breath. "We need you."

Elise fell onto the floor and immediately rolled upright, her assault blaster pointed toward the position she last saw the Destructor's shadowy form.

*But everything was darkness.*

She strained her eyes, trying to spot Kyle.

And more important, to see Destructors.

The darkness suddenly seemed alive with movement as she fired a quick burst.

Only an eerie silence answered as the bolts ricocheted harmlessly off the walls.

Her heart began to pound so hard and so loud she knew it must be giving her location away to the metal monsters. She licked her lips, still pointing her weapon, trying to see through the darkness in all directions at once.

And then she heard it.

It was so soft, almost like she imagined it—a soft metallic click mixed with a scraping sound like metal on metal.

A Destructor was nearby.

And it was coming for her.

She couldn't see it.

But she could feel it.

It watched her, studying her—she knew it. Her heart now beat faster than she ever thought it could.

Elise began pushing herself back away, holding her blaster with one hand while she fumbled for the sensor attached to her belt. If she got it out, maybe she could detect the Destructor at close range and then shoot it with her blaster. He hand fumbled around her belt, fingers searching for the familiar shape of her sensor unit.

She heard the frightening noise again, closer this time.

Now she felt its presence more clearly. She felt the evil inside it, as it came for her with one intention—to kill her.

Out of the darkness and tiny twinkling lights, she saw a body with huge, long legs coming out of it from all directions.

Elise fired another burst.

Sparks lit up the darkness as the blasts ricocheted off something only a meter away from her.

She hit some part of it. But the Destructor, unlike a living thing, never uttered a sound.

Elise strained to listen and focused her eyes, concentrating fiercely—trying to will her senses to detect the undetectable.

At first, there was dead silence and darkness.

Perhaps she had destroyed it? Or at least disabled it?

Suddenly, the same heart-stopping sound came softly to her hearing—a faint, horrifying click.

And then another.

The clicking-scraping sounds grew faster.

And closer.

Elise kept fumbling for her sensor, until at last she had it. But it slipped out of her grasp, her palms sweaty. She leaned over for it, trying to find it on the floor in the darkness as she halted her huddled retreat.

In that moment it had her.

Elise screamed as she felt the multiple appendages first rip the blaster out of her hand then in a flurry of shadowy motion pin her down on the floor. She struggled against the terrible strength, but to no avail.

The Destructor had her trapped, its metal body right on top of her.

Elise shut her eyes. With her arms and legs pressed hard against the floor so that she couldn't move, she opened them and looked up.

She was shocked to see nothing but the darkness. She had guessed she would finally see the monster now that it was so close. But there was nothing but darkness above her—at least that was all she could see.

But she was wrong.

Suddenly, out of the corner of her eye, she saw the needle-tipped talon coming for her neck.

Elise screamed.

Suddenly a barrage of blaster bolts lit up the darkness. As she stared upward, still pinned helplessly, she saw the outline of the Destructor as it stared down at her.

The hail of blaster fire increased as the bolts hit true. Large chunks of the Destructor ripped away until it fell in two broken sections.

Elise felt the metal arms pinning her fall away.

She rolled over, all the while blindly reaching for her fallen blaster. Just as she found it, she realized something was right beside her.

She froze.

"Get your weapon," Kyle whispered so quietly she almost didn't hear his words.

Bringing her blaster up, Kyle's form became visible beside her.

Kyle nodded his head forward, pointing. Elise peered into the darkness in the direction he indicated.

Once again, she felt more than saw it through the pitch darkness. Another Destructor was coming for them.

Kyle held up his right hand, displaying three fingers. He then brought his forefinger up to his lips for silence.

*Three Destructors.*

Elise's heart thumped like a starship's engine jumping into hyperspace.

Kyle pointed his blaster over to the right wall, about midway up. Then he swung it over to the left wall as Elise watched. She surmised he must mean two Destructors were there, ready to pounce on them.

She nodded.

Kyle's blaster came to life, sending a steady stream of fire at the left wall.

Elise opened up with her weapon at the right wall.

The tunnel lit up like a fireworks spectacular under their twin hail of fire.

But the two Destructors escaped most of it as they leapt away.

When they ceased firing, only a few severed limbs littered the floor near them.

"Not good," Kyle whispered.

Out of the blackness dozens of clicking noises now became audible.

And the sounds grew closer.

"Get ready," Kyle whispered as he quickly reloaded his blaster. "They're coming again. And there's more of them."

Elise checked her own blaster—it was half empty.

Kyle looked at her—deep in her eyes.

"You shouldn't have come back for me."

Kyle's words caused her to catch her breath. But she answered without pause. "We don't leave anyone behind—especially family."

He smiled at her.

The clicking noises came closer.

"Don't stop firing, Elise. No matter what, don't stop." Kyle readied himself.

Elise swallowed hard as she raised her blaster.

In the background, another sound came faintly to their ears—some kind of throbbing sound...

The clicks suddenly increased.

"They're charging!" Kyle shouted at Elise.

Kyle fired his blaster non-stop.

Elise saw the darkness alive with movement. She pressed the trigger and held it solid.

They were everywhere—along both walls, even clutching to the ceiling as they crawled toward them.

And they were right on top of them.

Elise screamed as a Destructor fell from the ceiling toward her.

She rolled and fired, sending it into pieces.

Kyle stood and sprayed the tunnel side to side.

In the red light of their tracers the deadly Destructors became visible as they crowded towards them.

Side by side, Kyle and Elise fired volley after volley.

Her gut wrenched in agony as her blaster fired it last shot.

Kyle stepped in front of her and fired another volley.

The darkness returned as his blaster emptied its last charge. Silence drenched them—a deep, black silence.

"I'm scared, Kyle," Elise whispered.

He stepped back and put his arm around her. They both crouched against the far right wall.

"I am too." His embrace tightened around her shoulders.

The clicking sounds returned.

"Close your eyes," Kyle whispered.

"Will that help?" Elise whispered back.

"I sure hope so."

From the middle of the tunnel, a shadowy shape emerged, although the pair kept their eyes tightly closed.

The faint sound of metallic clicks drew closer.

Kyle and Elise knew with the sinking of their hearts that the Destructor came for them.

More clicking sounds became audible as more Destructors approached from out of the darkness.

The multitude of ominous sounds heralded the approach of certain and impending death.

Suddenly, the staccato of blaster fire filled their ears.

Kyle and Elise opened their eyes wide.

"Come on!" Krinia cried out as her blaster took out the nearest Destructor.

"Over here!" Jaric added.

He stood outside the opened door of the turbo-elevator, holding an assault blaster in each hand. Jaric stood with his legs apart to steady himself as he pumped two steady streams of blaster fire through the darkness at the Destructors.

Rok pummeled them with his own assault blaster in one hand and a blaster pistol in the other. A Kraaqi war cry echoed off the walls as he raced forward, firing non-stop.

Kyle and Elise jumped up and ran under their covering fire.

Debris from the broken Destructors filled the air.

But more and more took their places as they kept on coming.

Rok stood his ground until his blaster pistol fell silent. The Kraaqi holstered it and grasped his assault blaster with both hands as he continued firing short bursts.

Rok retreated backward with a quickening pace.

A few seconds later, he stood at the turbo-elevator again.

Krinia and Rok stepped inside the opened doors, firing away, while Jaric stood a short distance outside still yelling and firing both his weapons until he emptied both.

With a quick jump, he leapt inside holding both weapons.

Jysar punched the controls and the doors shut.

"Whew!" Jaric gasped. "That was close." He fell to his knees exhausted.

"It's not over," Rok said with a serious tone. "If Jysar can't get this turbo-elevator moving, we're going to have to fight our way out."

"You're kidding," Kyle said in utter disbelief.

Rok shook his head.

"What kind of rescue is this? We're supposed to be whisked away from mortal danger right about now...not stay in the middle of it." Kyle winked at everyone with a smirk.

"Yeah, I wish," Krinia said.

Suddenly, the thunderous sound of heavy, multiple blows against the turbo-elevator doors pummeled their senses.

Everyone stared as the doors were beaten by innumerable blows from the outside. As they watched, dents and creases appeared from the horrendous blows.

"It won't last long," Elise said, echoing all of their thoughts.

"Jysar?" Rok looked over at the Hrono.

But Jysar shook his head. "It's not going anywhere. I've tried everything, but the Paum is blocking everything I try."

"Come on, Hrono. Make it work!" Rok urged.

The doors shuddered under a renewed barrage from the metal arms as the Destructors fought to get at them.

"This is it," Jaric began reloading both his blasters.

The others followed suit.

"When the door goes down, give 'em everything we've got." Kyle stood right before the door with his reloaded weapon.

The dents grew deeper with the metallic hammering.

But nobody asked what would happen once they emptied their blasters, because there wouldn't be time to reload.

Elise looked around at her friends trapped with her inside this tiny place—the people she cared most about in all the universe. She realized that the same, grim expression was on everyone's face as they prepared to face this final assault.

She felt a grim determination in order to face death bravely with her friends around her.

"The three of us will fire until we're empty," Rok said with a commanding tone, indicating himself, Jaric and Kyle. "Then the other three will take over while we reload—Elise, Krinia and Inaha."

"What about me?" Jysar asked.

"You keep working on getting this thing going again!"

Jysar began working at the control panel again, a new urgency in his efforts.

Rok, Jaric and Kyle readied themselves as the door began to warp and bend under the terrible blows.

"Are you holding that fear in check, Big K?" Jaric whispered with a twinkle in his eye.

"Are you kidding?" Kyle chucked. "Fear is all I've been running on."

"How many can there be left?" Jaric asked. "We've taken out a ton of them."

"More important, how many charges do we have left?" Kyle arched his eyebrows as both he and Jaric looked at Rok.

Rok balanced the assault blaster in his grip as if he were weighing it. But he didn't say a word.

Jaric leaned closer to Kyle and whispered.

"I take it not many."

"Stay focused," Rok ordered. "Short bursts only. Make every shot count."

The metal door began to groan horribly as it reached its breaking point.

Kyle took aim, as did the other two.

Elise put her back against the far wall, her own weapon primed and ready. She steeled herself for the final attack.

Krinia stood beside her, her head-tail whipping side to side as Inaha watched, grim-faced.

They waited for the Destructors massed outside to break the final barrier down as their hammer blows became deafening.

The door lurched inward, the steel howling as it warped...

All at once, a huge explosion ripped the air, the sheer force of its shock wave sending everyone down on the ground as if they been slammed by hurricane-force winds. The entire universe seemed to shake and boil all around them as the power flickered and went completely out.

Darkness engulfed them while everything shook as if in the throes of a mighty earthquake.

Amid the darkness a blinding red glow became visible as a crack grew wider on the damaged door. The temperature rose astronomically in milliseconds. Elise felt her clothes drenched in sweat. She fought to breathe in the suddenly super-heated air.

Long, heart-throbbing seconds stretched by before the thunderous rumbling from the explosion slowly subsided.

As quickly as the temperature rose, it now slowly decreased.

Elise finally discovered she didn't have to fight to breathe as the air came sweetly to her lungs with each new breath.

"Look at the doors!" Elise said with shocked surprise.

The steel doors were warped completely out of shape by the great heat from the explosion outside.

And outside the warped and dented doors, all was strangely silent.

"What happened?" Elise said as she pushed herself up off the floor.

Everyone else gathered themselves up from where they had been so harshly shoved down by the titanic force from outside.

"I don't know. But whatever it was, it was huge." Jaric brushed himself off.

They stared at the misshapen doors, each wondering what was going to happen next.

Suddenly, a familiar twinkling and swirling of lights slipped inside the turbo-elevator like a cloud being sucked into a vortex.

"Minstrel!" they all shouted together.

"Yes, I am glad to see you as well." Minstrel's body swirled with a rainbow of lights.

"Where did you come from?" Jysar asked.

"It's a long story. But time enough for that later. Get these doors open, Mother is waiting outside the core of the Paum." Minstrel floated out of the way as Rok and Kyle began straining to open them manually.

"What about the Destructors?" Elise looked up at the glowing alien.

"Mother fired her hybrid-weapon. She targeted the ones attacking you from outside this section of the Paum's core. She had to carefully calculate how far the resulting destruction would extend around the beam so it would be able to destroy the Destructors attacking you, but cause no damage to yourselves."

"Hey, that was some calculation!" Kyle whistled.

"So, they're destroyed?" Jysar asked.

"You will find a large hole outside. And a massive amount of damage." Minstrel glowed with emotion.

"Mother took them out, eh?" Jaric chuckled.

"You betcha," Kyle added.

"Mother will now set the weapon on wide dispersal and fire again down the same angle."

"Cool," Elise said. "Why?"

"The path of destruction will be widened enough so one of the small shuttles can traverse it directly to us. Mother will send a shuttle with Fixer3 piloting it. When it arrives, we must get in and get back to her as quickly as possible. But I'm afraid we'll have to back it out, there's no room to turn it around."

"No problem," Kyle said with a laugh. "Just get me behind the controls."

"Get your stuff together," Rok said to the others.

There was a flurry of movement. During this time, no one noticed that Qirn had opened his eyes. The Iraxx leader remained motionless, carefully taking in the scene around him. Slowly, he reached inside his shirt and pulled out another blaster pistol.

At that moment, Kyle's communicator beeped.

"This is Mother, take cover. I am firing again."

"We understand, Mother. We're all inside the turbo-elevator. Just remember the door is now damaged." Kyle said.

"I have added that factor into my calculations. The main impact of my hybrid-weapon will be on the far side of the original path of destruction away from you, in order to widen the path for a shuttle."

"Good."

They gathered at the back and waited.

They didn't wait long. Suddenly they were all thrown down once more by the sheer force as Mother fired again. The earthquake-like rumbling surrounded them and pummeled their bodies.

Within a few seconds, it was over.

"Okay, let's get outside and wait for the shuttle," Kyle said as he got to his feet. The others followed suit and stood outside when a voice spoke.

"Everyone, freeze."

Kyle and the others stopped in mid-motion.

They all turned to find Qirn now standing, pointing the blaster at them. But their eyes fixed on the other item he held in his other hand.

As they watched, he flicked open a small panel on the metal device and punched a switch with his thumb.

"I've just enabled this bomb. You have less than five minutes to get out of this area." Qirn's eyes stared at them unflinching.

"What are you doing?" Jaric asked with exasperation.

"I am going to finish the mission," he said with a determined glare.

"I hear the shuttle's engines coming for us," Krinia said as she looked down the path of destruction.

"Get on it quickly. Leave me here," Qirn urged.

"And then you die?" Elise asked with disbelief. "There's no way for you to get out once we leave."

"I will disable this bomb and finish my mission. But yes, I never intended to leave this place. I will die here—I always knew it. I knew it years ago and accepted it as my honored duty."

They stared at him dumbfounded.

But the Iraxx warrior was resolute.

"But how can you destroy it, you alone?" Jysar asked with a shake of his head.

"*A back door*," Qirn said cryptically.

Jysar's eyes widened, then he nodded with understanding. The others retained their puzzled expressions.

"Now, go!" Qirn ordered them.

A few minutes later they were inside the shuttle and on the way back to the safe confines of Mother's armored hull.

Qirn stood alone as he punched another command and disabled the bomb. Looking around at the horrific damage, he smiled approvingly.

"You have done just what we needed, Mother AI," Qirn said to himself. "Now, I will do what I need to do."

The Iraxx pulled out his sensor and began searching throughout the core with it. In a few minutes, he smiled.

He stepped outside and turned in the opposite direction from which the shuttle left.

Holding the sensor unit as it guided him to his final destination, the Iraxx took off with quick steps.

# CHAPTER THIRTY-SEVEN

The shuttle landed inside Mother. As soon as the landing bay doors closed, Mother turned and roared off at full speed.

"I will not allow you to leave."

The Paum's condescending voice echoed across Main Ops. It was the first time the AI had spoken since Mother's escape.

Rok, Jysar and all the others gathered inside Main Ops looked up with surprise etched on their faces.

"Been a long time since you spoke to us. We were wondering if you still felt you were always right," Minstrel said with a twinkle.

"I have been busy with my outer defenses and directing my Home Fleet against the Iraxx fleet attacking me. I have been even busier with repairs to the damage you caused—twenty-seven percent of my core systems damaged or destroyed. But I will stop you."

"That Paum's got an attitude problem," Jaric said with a shake of his head.

"Who does he think he is?" Kyle laughed.

"Let's see," Minstrel began with a flash of color. "The Paum thinks he is a god, has all the answers and views everybody elseas inferior, wrong, deluded and in need of his guidance."

"Oh, is that all!" Jaric and Kyle laughed together.

"Sounds like he needs to get out more," Elise chided with a smile.

"Sounds like he needs a swift kick in his—" Rok began.

"Inferior beings!" the Paum shouted with malice. "I will stop you. I will defeat the fleets arrayed against me even now. And, I will bring Paum to the entire universe. No one can defeat me."

"I will stop you." Qirn's voice emanated over the speakers via his communicator.

"Who are you?" the Paum asked.

"I am Qirn, of the Iraxx."

"A single, inferior being cannot stop me. I have defeated entire worlds, entire fleets."

"But, I have consulted with the beings who originally created you. Even now, I am making my way to your central operating system, to the core of your core. I go to your very beginning."

A thick silence settled.

"I have run an internal search of my core system; there is nothing you can do to me. There are no hidden codes, there is nothing you can do."

Qirn's confident laughter echoed through the speakers.

Mother flew at top speed, making for the corridor that led to the main docking bay where the supply ships brought their goods inside to the core.

"Hang on, I'm firing my hybrid weapon again," Mother said matter-of-factly.

"And none too soon," Minstrel said with a shower of twinkling lights. "That Paum is getting on my nerves."

A crimson streak leapt away, tearing straight through the main door and level after level of the mighty complex until it struck the Paum's main shield generators dead on. As Mother's weapon smashed a new path of destruction through the outer systems, a new chain reaction began with a powerful feedback of rippling explosions expanding outward from the demolished systems. The multiplying explosions followed the main power conduits back to various power sub-stations where the sympathetic explosions increased and spread outward again, their destructive power slowly subsiding as they grew outward.

With one fell blow, Mother took out the Paum's main defensive systems as well as the power grid that fed them. In addition, the main power grid faltered throughout the entire orbiting complex due to the massive power interruption. The backup power replaced it quickly, except for large sections around the beam's destructive path.

"I'm heading for the outer hull and the docking bay doors I entered by." Mother's said calmly.

"You've left me vulnerable to my enemies, Mother AI. Even now their battleships attack where large sections of my shields have just failed—there are gaps through all three shield arrays now. And my mind...I cannot concentrate. You have caused so much damage to my core memories. I am re-routing core functions...I will punish you for this."

"I took down your shields so I can escape, not to allow the warships to attack you. But that's the price you pay, *mighty* Paum." As Mother finished speaking, a new sound emanated from her—an electronic twinkling mixed with a rhythmical beat—not unlike human laughter.

Elise, Jaric and Kyle looked at each other with mild shock.

"I think Mother's laughing." Kyle's eyes widened with surprise.

"At the Paum." Jaric laughed.

"I will not open the docking bay doors," the Paum's bass voice hissed.

"Well, well, well—what shall I do about that?" Mother said, again followed by her gleeful laughter.

"You will cease and stop!"

"I don't think so."

During all of this back-and-forth banter, Mother continued flying toward her desired destination. Now that the shields were down across this entire section, the Paum could not use them to prevent her exit. But still, she had to get through the massive docking bay doors, which were shut tight.

Mother began priming her hybrid weapon for another crucial firing.

"We're next to the main docking bay," Jysar said as he studied the main view-screen.

"I see the docking bay doors." Elise pointed at the massive gateway as it came into view.

"I'm going to do a little fly-by and do some damage with my torpedoes and main guns until my hybrid weapon is ready," Mother said. Immediately, her twelve guns opened up.

"What about when we get outside?" Jaric asked. "The Iraxx fleet is attacking. Will they let us through?"

Qirn's voice came from the speakers. "The warships of my fleet will destroy anything that comes out of this evil place."

"As will the warships of my robot fleet," the Paum added.

"Not good," Krinia said with flick of her head-tail.

"They can't destroy, what they can't see," Mother said cryptically.

Kyle's face lit up.

"Oh yeah, you've got those stealth systems the Minstrels bestowed as a gift for you!"

"You must help us destroy this evil, before it spreads. All our plans hinge on an attack from both the inside and outside to annihilate the Paum," Qirn pleaded. "You must continue your attacks, for just a little while longer!"

"See!" the Paum roared. "You are friend of my enemies!"

"No, he tricked us," Kyle said, anger laced in his every word. "He *used* us. And Mother."

"No!" Qirn shouted back. "The Paum lured the MotherShip here, not us. We helped you rescue..."

"Why don't you just shut up!" Elise said as she rolled her eyes. "You could've stopped all of it, long before Mother got trapped."

"There has been a lot of manipulation and subterfuge," Mother said. "It seems that both the Paum and the Iraxx are adept at deception."

572

"Two wrongs don't make a right," Minstrel chimed.

"So, we're leaving," Mother said, her tone matter-of-fact. *"You can fight each other all you like."*

"The Paum is evil, it must be destroyed before it takes over the universe!" Qirn shouted angrily.

"I must bring Paum to all!" the AI shouted back. "The universe is full of corruption. The imperfect systems you inferior biological beings have set up encourage greed and lying and..."

"You want to control us, to control our minds, our very thoughts!" Qirn countered.

"You must be purged of your imperfection."

"Can't there be some kind of compromise?" Mother asked sincerely. "After all, the Paum was originally created for good—to control the weather of an entire planet in order to benefit the beings living upon it. Can't there be some kind of middle ground where you both can co-exist?"

"Yes, isn't the universe big enough for both of your societies to live together in peace?" Minstrel asked.

"No!" the Paum and Qirn shouted simultaneously.

Qirn breathed hard from his exertions as he continued running toward his destination, the sounds plainly carrying over the speakers to Mother. His hoarse panting continued, until suddenly the sounds stopped.

A long pause ensued.

Finally, Qirn spoke. "There cannot be compromise. But it is all a moot point now, I have found the original console."

From the speakers, the sound of Qirn's hands rapidly typing across a keyboard became audible.

"Must be an old-fashioned console," Minstrel said with a sparkle of lights.

"I must bring Paum to all, it is for your own good," the Paum shouted.

"We must have our freedom! We must be able to live our lives as we see best!" Qirn shouted back.

"Compromise is not a dirty word," Mother said forcefully, effectively interrupting both of them. "Look at a family unit made up of a father, mother and children. In order to keep peace and harmony within that unit, the father cannot insist that his will and desires always come first. Nor can the mother. Nor the children. They must cooperate together. Yes, sometimes the father's desires and needs come first—and the mother and children support that. But there comes a time when the mother's wants and needs must have priority. And the children's too. All must have a say for their individual needs and wants. And sometimes, for the good of the family, each of their wants and needs must mesh together. It may not be exactly what they individually wanted, but a wise compromise benefits the entire family unit."

"We will lose our identity," Qirn stated emphatically.

"Not if everyone cooperates. Not unless one of them bullies the others and demands his way,"

Mother retorted. "Cooperation and compromise have worked within family units for millennia."

"We can never live with the Paum. Not as long as it exists—in any form," Qirn growled.

"Can't you find a way, some way, to live together?" Jaric asked. "I mean, the universe is a huge place, like Minstrel said. I'd think if you didn't want to see or talk to each other, you could find a way. And you could each live as you see fit." Jaric let out a loud sigh of exasperation.

"Couldn't you benefit if you allowed the Paum to continue controlling the weather across your planets?" Mother asked. "But you would control your government. And your society, as before," Mother added quickly.

"It could never be," Qirn replied.

"It would never work," the Paum agreed. "They need Paum."

"What if you made Paum available to all, but it was a *choice*?" Minstrel asked insightfully.

"Yes," Mother agreed. "Let any alien come to you for your teachings—if they desired it. And if they did not want to live Paum, they could continue living as they want."

"The universe would be impure," the Paum growled.

"We could never trust it!" Qirn added.

"So, your peoples could never live together. Your two societies could not co-exist in all the vast universe? Ever?" Minstrel asked with obvious frustration.

"Never!" Qirn and Paum shouted together.

575

"Incredible," Elise said, shaking her head in disbelief.

Mother fired and the huge red bolt leapt out and through the massive docking bay doors as if they never existed. Mother had again put the weapon on a very wide dispersal pattern, so that the resulting hole was massive.

Immediately, Mother enabled her stealth mode and she disappeared from all sensors.

"We are leaving, Qirn. I hope you survive," Mother said with sincerity.

"Paum," Qirn said, a strange edge to his voice. "Prepare to die."

"I cannot die."

"I've just accessed your original code, from when you were created. I've just initiated an Emergency Shutdown."

Silence answered.

Mother focused her sensors back to the floating core. Immediately she noted how system after system went silent in rapid succession.

"How did you do that?" Mother asked with surprise.

"The Paum was originally a computer system. Wisely, a fail-safe was created—just in case. It could only be enabled manually from a handful of consoles in the original sections. I have initiated it. The inner core will shut down in less than three minutes—hardware connections and power couplings blowing apart on command. The creators made this fail-safe mechanism a hardware solution tied directly to the power system. They meant it to be undetectable via the operating system—just in case. A single sequence of binary code activated it—and once started, it cannot be stopped. But more importantly, after the original core of its operating system has shut down, it will leave the Paum's outer systems cut off."

"It cannot be! I cannot simply be—turned off!" the Paum shouted.

"Looks like that's exactly what is happening," Mother said matter-of-factly.

Another long silence ensued before the Paum next spoke.

"I cannot stop it," the AI whispered with utter disbelief. "My mind is fading away. I'm losing my mind!"

"Soon, you will be nothing." Qirn laughed.

"No, I will not allow this," the Paum replied angrily. "I will take you all with me!"

Suddenly, Mother's sensors noted a huge power surge throughout the mighty complex.

"He's initiated self-destruct," Qirn said without surprise. "We expected that. I would suggest you get out of here as quickly as possible and jump to hyperspace."

"He's right! I'm reading a massive power surge throughout the complex," Jaric shouted as he studied one of Mother's consoles. "When this complex goes the shock wave will be tremendous—causing horrendous damage to the planet below and destroying any ships within half a parsec."

"The weather controls and all other systems of the Paum will be destroyed as well—the consequences on all those planets will be horrific," Jysar surmised.

"Remember me with kindness, Mother AI. After all, I saved your daughter's life once," Qirn said with deep emotion.

"That is true. And I will always be indebted to you for that act." Mother paused. "But it seems you did it as part of your overall mission—as you and the Paum manipulated us."

"He was also going to leave Kyle to die—and Elise," Jaric added quickly.

"The Destructors were on top of us. The mission was in danger," Qirn shouted proudly. "My mission was more important than you realized. I could not let it fail, not with the fate of my entire people at stake."

"I will always be thankful for your act to Elise," Mother continued. "But it was still your war, and you helped dragged us into it. And now both you and the Paum, and many billions, will die."

At that moment, the warships of Iraxx turned as one. The attack stopped almost as quickly as it began. Large groups of ships became streaks of light as they made the jump to hyperspace, retreating before the imminent destruction.

Even as Mother gained speed, a deep rumbling like galactic thunder echoed throughout her being.

Kyle and the others looked around in wonder.

"The self-destruct is reaching a climax," Minstrel said as it checked Mother's sensors.

Suddenly, hundreds of explosions began rippling through the entire complex, all heading for the central core, which was quickly going silent as the shutdown sequence continued unabated.

Without warning, a dozen blasters erupted from the Paum's guns—all but two struck Mother's cloaked hull as she went into evasive maneuvers.

"I can-can see-see you." The Paum's dark laughter rolled through the speakers.

Mother checked her hybrid weapon as it recharged.

"Let us go, Paum," Mother said. "You are as good as dead. Why strike at me and try to stop me—so I will die with you too?"

"Yes-yes," he whispered savagely. "I would take-take all with me in death, if I could. You are all impure-impure!"

"Let us go, we leave you and Qirn to your mutual suicide."

"The universe is black-black and-and white-white, Mother AI. Either you are for me, or you are against me-me." The deep voice paused. "I will take you down-down with me."

More blaster cannons erupted, but Mother was ready this time. Turning hard, she danced between them with ease.

"You can't see me as well as you think," Mother said.

Mother turned hard one hundred and eighty degrees until she once again headed toward the vast, diamond-shaped complex.

"You come to embrace me in death, Mother AI. I welcome you," the Paum said, its voice clear again.

The red beam of Mother's hybrid weapon streaked toward the Paum.

"I was inside your core just a little while ago. I took very precise readings," Mother said.

On the view-screen, all watched as the red beam pierced the unshielded outer hull and continued inside all the way to the core floating at its center. The beam struck through section after section of the Paum's core memories, sending fountains of fireballs outward.

"I struck right through the center of the Paum's core memory—that which is still operative. I have now struck four times there. And with the rest of the core shutting down, the Paum is truly crippled."

"You helped me finish him!" Qirn shouted with renewed emotion. "We couldn't have defeated it without you."

Mother sighed deeply inside her circuits.

"You realize once the Paum is gone that not only will you be free from his control, but so will the all the systems he controls—including the weather systems. Billions may die as they go uncontrolled, like a dam releasing its waters," Mother said with feeling.

"We knew that risk, but felt it worth any sacrifice to rid the universe of this black foe," Qirn returned.

"Self-destruct in twenty seconds!" Jaric shouted as he stared at the console.

"You must leave," Qirn said, a hollowness in his voice.

"Leave, Mother AI," the Paum said, his deep voice now a whisper of its former power. "All is finished. I cannot stop you, I cannot stop my own destruction now. I will...die."

Static filled the communication channel. Without warning, the Paum spoke again.

"Perhaps...perhaps I was wrong..."

"It didn't have to end like this," Mother whispered earnestly to both Qirn and the Paum.

She ramped up her engines as she turned around. The stars turned into short lines as she gained speed, and then initiated the jump sequence.

"There was no other way," Qirn whispered as the explosions reached him.

"Good-bye, Mother," the Paum said simply. "You and I, we were alike."

"Not really," Mother replied with sadness. "Not really."

With a flash of light, Mother jumped into hyperspace.

The hundreds of small explosions suddenly grew together into one huge ball of fiery destruction across the orbiting complex.

With a blast like a star going nova, the complex blew apart.

Huge, burning chunks of debris rained down into the atmosphere of Iopa. Down on its surface, all became silent, watching with fear as the sky filled with fireballs the size of mountains that rained destruction down on them.

They ran, but there was nowhere they could hide.

The titanic shock wave rolled out in every direction, engulfing everything in its path with total destruction.

All across distant sectors of space the fleets of robot ships came to a halt. And more, all the systems that the Paum once controlled grew silent.

The entity that controlled them was no more.

"The Paum could've done so much good," Mother said with a sigh. "It...it is such a shame we had to destroy it."

"It gave us no choice," Kyle said.

"Indeed," Minstrel interjected. "It felt it had to control everyone and everything."

"It felt we were all beneath it." Kyle shook his head. "That it was right, and we were wrong."

"That's the point, the Paum didn't want to live with us—it wanted to live over us. Forcing us to live his version of life." Rok crossed his arms. "And if we didn't accept his view of life, it killed us."

"The universe was black and white to him, remember?" Elise pressed her lips together. "He would have killed us in the end."

"They couldn't live together, *but they could die together*," Mother said, a hint of sadness in her voice.

"And sadly, many planets and their populations are suffering as the weather systems now go unchecked. Just as we predicted," Minstrel said with a subdued hue of colors.

"So, both sides lose," Jaric said thoughtfully.

"Everyone loses," Mother agreed.

"If only we could learn to live together," Elise thought out loud.

"If only we could learn." Mother sighed.

"Maybe someday, we will," Rok said. "Maybe one day, all the sentient races of the universe will learn to be one with each other and their worlds. We will respect and honor one another. And the greatest adventure will simply be life itself."

"It's a hard thing for us to practice sometimes, we who have traveled so far and met so many alien races," Krinia said. "We have trouble with other aliens, trusting them, honoring them."

"Yeah, remember when we first met Inaha," Kyle said with a chuckle.

"That didn't go so well." Inaha laughed.

"And it was both our fault," Jaric said with a glint of humor in his eyes.

"We must not pre-judge other aliens, just because they are different from us." Elise smiled as she looked from the Kraaqi warrior to the Hrono Technologist and Mewiis explorer and over to the other aliens gathered.

"We must value and respect diversity." Jysar smiled.

"It's a big universe," Jaric added.

"And it's filled with all kinds of aliens." Kyle smiled. "We better get used to that."

"It's a wise alien that embraces diversity and does not hate another—just because they are different." Minstrel twinkled with a million flashing lights as wave after wave of color swept its flowing plasma body.

"May we all learn such wisdom," Mother added with warmth.

# EPILOGUE

"They call the planet *Paradise,*" Mother said.

Kyle, Jaric and Elise stood before the main view-screen looking on with awe and wonder at the planet that filled its display. Rok, Jysar, Krinia and Inaha along with the Fixers stood close by, each of them fixed on the same blue and white world. Up along the ceiling, Minstrel's glowing form twinkled with tiny lights while waves of color swept through it again and again.

"I can't believe it," Kyle said in a whisper.

"It looks a lot like Earth," Jaric said.

"A whole lot. Except there's only three continents." Kyle's eyes searched the world longingly.

"How many humans are there?" Jaric asked, the huskiness in his voice revealing the intense emotions rushing throughout his soul.

"There are twenty thousand two hundred forty-seven human life-signs on its surface," Mother replied succinctly.

"I can't believe it," Kyle repeated as tears formed in his eyes.

"And it was the Paum who helped us find them!" Krinia crossed her arms defiantly.

"Quite incredible," Jysar agreed. "One of our foremost enemies provided us the key piece of evidence we needed to find other human survivors."

"Doesn't seem like it's been six months since that battle. And the Paum's destruction," Krinia said, her eyes far off.

"I think the Paum provided the evidence out of sincerity," Mother said. "I sometimes think that the Paum really wanted to meet me as a friend."

"Mother," Jaric said with shock. "How can you say that? He infected you with malicious code the first time he downloaded data to you. The Paum always intended to destroy you—or make you Paum like him."

"Jaric has a point," Minstrel said.

"But it was only when the Iraxx began their attack at the core with the children that the Paum attacked me. Perhaps..." Mother began.

"Then why infect you at your first meeting?" Jaric asked emphatically.

"And he never tried to compromise, or tried to determine the facts after our attack began. He simply attacked you and us and assumed your alliance with the Iraxx," Elise added.

A long paused ensued.

"Enough of the past," Mother said happily. "Today is a day we will remember forever."

"Your dream has come true," Minstrel said with a wave of glowing silver. "Rejoice, Kyle, Jaric and Elise. You have finally found others of your kind."

But the three stared at the world with blank expressions.

"After so many years," Jaric said in a whisper, still staring at the world growing slowly closer.

"I really can't..." Kyle began as his eyes moistened again. A sigh escaped him as he peered intently at the view-screen. "I-I think I'm afraid."

Elise and Jaric turned and stared at him.

"I've never heard you say you were afraid of anything my entire life!" Jaric said, dumbfounded.

"Who are you, and what have you done with Kyle?" Elise said with a twinkle in her eyes. "The Kyle I know is fearless."

"Yeah, 'hold-your-fear-in-check' Kyle," Jaric said with amusement.

"That's right, Big K. The no-fear man." Elise laughed.

Kyle remained frozen, never noticing their attempts at humor.

"I don't know." Kyle shook his head, never taking his eyes off the view-screen. "I've wanted this *so bad*, for so many years. We've traveled to so many worlds...always searching." Kyle paused, at a loss for words. "I mean, I just can't believe it—that we *really* found others!"

"It does seem unreal," Jaric agreed.

"Like a dream," Elise added.

"*A dream come true*," Minstrel reminded them.

"It's such a rare thing—dreams coming true—that it's kind of overwhelming," Jaric admitted with a shake of his head.

Kyle continued to stare, not even seeming to breathe. Finally, he spoke. "What if they don't like us?" he said barely above a whisper.

"Of course they will!" Krinia laughed. "They'll be as glad to know there are other survivors, as you are."

"I've received a request to open communications," Mother said. "Shall I open up a channel for you?"

Kyle and Jaric exchanged quick glances.

Beads of sweat broke out on both their foreheads as their breathing rapidly increased and their hearts pounded as if they were going into battle. Mother began cooling the room temperature as she noted the external signs of their intense emotions.

"Perhaps I should tell them that we'll talk after we land," Mother said.

"No!" Jaric and Kyle shouted simultaneously.

"No," Kyle said again. "We'll talk to them." He rubbed his hands together nervously while Jaric tugged at his collar as if it were too tight.

Elise grew silent as well, a slightly fearful expression across her own face. She ran her hands through her hair several times.

"I will put them on visual," Mother said.

The beautiful planet that filled the view-screen disappeared. Almost instantly, five smiling faces looked back at them.

"Greetings, we welcome you to Paradise."

A dark-haired young man with brown complexion bowed deeply. "I am Nouri Gupta." As he rose, he gestured to the others with him.

"Hello, I am Sally Chen. We're so glad to meet you!" The pretty young woman smiled, her soft Asian features beaming with joy.

"It's so good to know others survived. You're the fourth ship to join our little world community since we arrived here two years ago!" The man smiled widely, his brown eyes and jet-black hair perfectly complementing his olive complexion. "Oh, I forgot." He blushed. "My name is Julio Rodriguez. We welcome you!"

Another young man stepped forward.

"*Bon jour*, my new friends. We bid you welcome and look forward to embracing you into our little family here on Paradise. My name is Jean Fauré." He also bowed in greeting.

"My name is Jackie Simmons." Like the other four, she was young, somewhere in her mid-twenties. Her ebony skin and deep, brown eyes complemented her beautifully braided hair. She spoke with a lilting, happy voice full of friendliness and zest. "And we are overjoyed to meet you. We can't wait until you land and we show you this new world we are colonizing.

"Hey!" she added with a fresh smile as her brown eyes sparkled. "We're the pioneers of the new human race here. *And we're going to do it right this time!*"

The five people on the view-screen all joined in laughter as they looked back with expectant expressions.

"We're excited too," Elise began. "It's just, well, there's only been the three of us all these

589

years, along with our friends here." Elise gestured to their alien friends. "We're kind of overwhelmed, suddenly knowing we're going to meet *thousands* of other humans!"

She smiled sweetly at them. "Anyway, my name is Elise. I'm so pleased to meet you all—at last."

"We too, are excited," Sally said. "And we're just as excited to meet your alien friends. We've met only a very few alien species here at the edge of galaxy. We've been told we're a long way from any of the main commercial centers here—or any space trading routes."

"Yes," Nouri added. "We hope your alien friends will stay with us a while too. So we can get to know them."

"We are brethren with humans," Rok said with great sincerity. "We will stay as long as you want and need us."

"Cool," Julio said. He looked now at Jaric. "And you?"

Suddenly, all eyes were on Jaric.

Once again, beads of sweat formed on his forehead as his eyes widened. He cleared his throat nervously. "I—I guess I'm next."

Everyone chuckled at his apparent nervousness.

"Don't be afraid, we're not going to hurt you." Jackie laughed.

"Yeah, I know. I'm just..." Jaric grinned widely as he grasped for the word he wanted.

"*Shy*. You must be shy." Jackie laughed cheerfully.

"Yeah, that's it. Well, my name is Jaric. And it's wonderful to find others at last. We were beginning to think...well, never mind what we were beginning to think! We're just glad to find you. And be here. And meet you!"

Everyone laughed again.

All eyes fixed on Kyle.

"Hi, my name is Kyle." He took a deep breath. "And, I have to say—well—I just can't believe it!"

"That was a profound statement, Big K." Jaric laughed.

Now everyone howled with laughter while Kyle looked around, shrugging his shoulders.

"I can't believe it. Really," Kyle repeated with the deepest sincerity.

"What do you think, that we'll suddenly disappear?" Jean laughed.

"And be replaced by T'kaan?" Julio added with a rowdy chuckle.

"Well," Kyle began thoughtfully. "I just keep expecting something to go wrong—that this can't really be happening. It's just...too good."

"Believe, Kyle," Minstrel said with a wave of color. "It is all true and good."

"There is nothing wrong—no problems," Sally assured him with a bright smile.

Jaric licked his lips nervously. "Are there many...er, I mean, are there enough..." He shook his head with embarrassment. "No, I mean..."

"What he means is, are there any eligible women?" Elise chuckled. "They're kind of wanting to meet some girls after so many years alone out in space."

Expressions of pure panic swept across both Kyle and Jaric's faces.

"No, no, that's *not exactly* what I meant," Jaric began.

"We understand, don't worry," Sally said with a smile. "Actually, we do have a slight problem here—women outnumber men by a fair margin."

"Hey!" Kyle said quickly with a surge of enthusiasm. "That's not really a problem! Nooo..."

"No, no. That's, that's perfectly fine!" Jaric agreed with a similar burst of energy.

"And we are arranging a nice 'welcome party' in your behalf. There'll be many hundreds here at our local settlement to meet and get to know," Julio said.

He smiled warmly at Elise, their eyes locking for just an instant. "I'm sure we'll all become good friends."

Elise blushed as her heart beat faster.

"How many settlements and farms do you have?" Rok asked with interest.

"We have five permanent settlements," Jean replied. "Four on the southern continent—it has more moderate seasons than the two northern continents. The fifth settlement is on the eastern coast of the largest island that borders this continent. There are thousands of islands that stretch into the sea from that coast."

"We have cultivated much farmland around each of them to provide for our needs," Sally added.

"This world is rich in plant life, much of it edible. There is a rich variety of fruits and vegetables native to this world. It's great!" Jackie smiled.

"The northern continents have long, harsh winters. We have established several warm-season sites in order to study it closer for future habitation," Nouri said.

"You said you've met some aliens?" Elise asked.

"Yes, a few." Julio rubbed his chin in thought. "We're located here on the very edge of the galaxy, far from all the major trade routes, so the Katar told us. The Katar are the only aliens who live within this half of the sector with us here on the rim. They're the only sentient beings within twenty parsecs, in fact."

"Yes, they inhabit two planets in this remote sector. There are the Avasha too, who inhabit a few worlds in this sector, but all in the direction of the galactic core and just over twenty parsecs away. Both have been friendly, and have even traded with us." Sally added.

"The Katar helped us a lot as we got started settling on this world—after they detected us here. They were quite happy to know they had new neighbors." Julio paused, his eyes narrowing with remembrance. "They also warned us of the dangers out here on the galaxy's rim—next to the vast empty stretches of space between distant galaxies. But, they're not really empty."

"Dangers?" Kyle asked, his interest piqued.

"We haven't had any direct run-ins with anything from out there—*not yet*." Jean paused for several, long seconds. "But, our sensors have detected *things* out there. Sometimes vast herds of life-signs sailing out in the darkness. And sometimes we've detected a single, huge life-sign prowling the black depths stalking them. There's a surprising amount of life out there—and some of them are predators. We've detected the floating remnants of their handiwork."

"The Katar tell us that you travel beyond rim of the galaxy only if you must—strange and terrible things live out there. Sentient beings are as rare as jewels out there—but some do travel its vast, dangerous ways, and a few have even made it their home—somehow, amid all the danger." Sally shook her head in awe.

"Have you had any trouble here?" Kyle asked.

"Not yet," Nouri said simply.

"You sound like you expect it though," Kyle replied.

"Yes, we've come across signs on the planet's surface. Things have been here." Nouri shook his head. "*Things* from the nether regions. They've taken—or eaten—what they wanted and returned to the outer reaches of space between galaxies."

"The Avasha also warned us about rogue bands of aliens—pirates if you will—looking for easy prey out here far beyond the law of the universe."

"We keep a sharp eye out, our sensors tuned to give us advance warning. We are few here, with only a handful of star fighters. The starships that

594

brought us here are mostly fast freighters outfitted with a few blaster cannons for defense—no match for real warships."

"We live on the edge out here." Jackie sighed.

"But your ship looks powerful enough to help us!" Jean said with appreciation.

"Yes, Mother has defeated battleships—even entire squadrons of powerful star fighters. We're here to help you now," Kyle said with confidence.

"Good," Julio said, a puzzled expression on his face. "That is an interesting name for a starship—*Mother*."

"But enough of that talk," Jean interjected before Kyle could reply. "This is a day for welcoming new friends among us. Please, we're sending you landing coordinates to our settlement. We call it *New Paris*!"

"I have received them," Mother said. "I am starting my landing procedures now."

The five young people on the screen began looking around in puzzlement—searching for the source of this new voice.

"Who was it that spoke?" Jackie finally asked.

"It wasn't the shining alien that looks like a cloud, was it?" Sally asked.

"No, it was me," Mother said. "I am Mother."

"*Mother*?" they said together in surprise from the view-screen.

"Who is Mother?" Jean added quickly. He looked down at the console before him. "I do not detect any other life-signs aboard your starship—except you gathered there."

595

"I am the starship."

Jean and the others stared with total surprise etched on their features.

"How can that be?" Nouri asked.

"She is AI," Jaric said proudly. "Without her, we would never have made it. We wouldn't even be alive."

"Tell us!" Jackie pleaded earnestly.

"It's a long story. One we'll be glad to share with you tonight over food and drink. And song!" Rok smiled widely. "It will be a great story—a great song for the ages."

"A story of courage and love," Krinia said.

"A tale that ended the feud of three entire races and joined them as one." The twin row of upright scales on Jysar's head glowed a deeper hue of iridescent green. "A tale of wisdom and triumph."

"Indeed," Jean said. "I'm eager to hear it all."

"We even defeated the T'kaan!" Jaric burst out with pride.

Five faces stared with unabashed wonder back at them. A silence filled the air as everyone remembered how the T'kaan had decimated the human worlds and caused them all to become galactic refugees. They remembered the terrible, horrendous tragedies that filled their young childhood.

Julio finally whistled, breaking the thick silence.

"But tell us in one sentence, how did you survive?" Sally asked with keen interest. "There are only you three, and all so young? Even children when you first fled into space!"

"Right." Julio looked at them from the view-screen. "It seems impossible you could travel this great, wide galaxy fraught with danger and survive. And yet, you did! You not only traversed the stars, you conquered and united entire alien races!"

"And finally managed to find other survivors, here on the rim," Kyle said with a smile of confidence.

"How did you do it?" Nouri asked.

"How did we travel these dangerous stars?" Elise asked.

Elise paused a moment. Slowly, a wry grin formed as her blue eyes twinkled brightly. And when she spoke, they all understood perfectly.

"We were borne on wings of steel..."

## THE END

THE END

Printed in June 2023
by Rotomail Italia S.p.A., Vignate (MI) - Italy